SPINDLE CITY
BLUES

William Daubney

William Daubney (signature)

America Star Books
Frederick, Maryland

Hardcover 9781634484237
Softcover 9781633824317
eBook 9781634484213
PUBLISHED BY AMERICA STAR BOOKS, LLLP
www.americastarbooks.com

Dedicated to the memory of Joseph "Art" Charland

And

Charles "Chuck" Diotte,

Good husbands

Good fathers

Good men

A writer never does it alone. Many thanks to my brother, Paul, for coming up with the perfect title, along with a veritable treasure trove of ideas, characters and scenarios. I owe you, Paul.

In 1866, workers in Cohoes, New York, were constructing Harmony Mill number three, a huge, sprawling textile mill close by the magnificent, breathtaking Cohoes Falls, located on the Mohawk River. During excavation for the project, the skeletal remains of a mastodon were discovered.

Stunned and thrilled by the rare find, amateur, as well as professional archeologists, scoured the surrounding area for years, hoping to find yet another example of the extinct behemoth.

Disappointed, every one of them came up empty, their efforts all for naught...until July of 1959, that is.

CHAPTER 1

June 19th, 1959, turned out to be a wonderfully warm, balmy day. It was also Rodney Hobb's birthday. At twenty-one years old, he should have been enjoying himself on this special Saturday, basking in the glow of his family's good cheer, along with his gorgeous girlfriend's undivided attention. Dee Dee LeBarron was crazy about him and he was crazy about her. Yeah, Rod should have been happy today, but he wasn't. He just sat there morosely, his hand under his chin, propping his head up, deep in thought, bringing to mind the statue of the *Thinker*, the one that that teenager on TV, *Dobie Gillis*, sat next to, during the opening of his show.

Rod's Dad, Francis Xavier Hobbs, better known as *Duke* to his pals, had retired from the Cohoes Police Department six months earlier. Rod's uncle, Harry Finnegan, was still on the job, however, looking at another five years on the beat before he too could call it quits. *Put in your twenty years and then walk away, the pension immediately kicking in while you're still a reasonably young man. That*, according to Duke and Harry, was the only good thing about being a cop nowadays.

Between his Dad's and his uncle's considerable influence in the police department, Rod had been hoping they'd be able to grease the skids for him, help to snag him a job on the force. In his opinion, Rod was convinced that he'd make a great cop. He was smart, well spoken, and most importantly, to his way of thinking, anyway, he could be a real badass tough guy when the situation called for it. *Yeah, "Hot Rod" Hobbs would be a force to reckon with,* he told himself.

Today was supposed to represent more than just simply another birthday. A guy had to be at least twenty-one to get on the force. Naturally, Rod had been waiting impatiently for this day to get here. His application had been promptly submitted yesterday. His uncle and father called in some favors, squeezing a few people for an assist, doing what they could to move things along. Then, early this morning, his uncle informed him that things weren't looking so hot. The department, as it turned out, now insisted that candidates had to have a high school diploma.

Rod was crushed by the bad news. He'd dropped out of high school in his junior year, chomping at the bit to earn enough money to buy some flashy wheels and lots of cool threads. His parents had raised holy hell with him, but to no avail. He'd long been a lousy student and was facing a full five years in High school before he'd ever earn a diploma. The family battle raged on for days, his parents eventually throwing up their hands in defeat, finally relenting. Rod had been working his butt off ever since, putting in forty hours at Hull's Chrysler-Plymouth dealership as a grease monkey, and another ten or so hours as a member of the city's auxiliary police force. He wore a pretty snazzy uniform, yet the job rarely amounted to anything more than directing traffic on Sundays...ensuring the safety of little old ladies as they crossed the street from St. Agnes' church.

"What's the matter with you today, Rod? I would've thought you'd be all smiles this morning. Instead, you're acting like someone just stole your car or something!" Dee Dee complained, her lips pursed together in a tight line. "You've hardly said a word to me since I got here!"

She wasn't one who took kindly to being ignored.

Rod took a deep breath, letting it out slowly. They'd been sitting together on his front stoop at sixty-six Vliet Street for about an hour now, soaking up the rays. He knew Dee Dee was right. Here she was with gifts up the wazoo for him...everything from gabardine slacks from Seymour's Men's shop, ones that she herself had already pegged, to a form-fitting Banlon shirt and a new pair of gleaming low ducks, along with a slick Zippo lighter and yes, even a carton of Luckies. Yeah, he'd been acting like a jerk and he knew it.

He suddenly turned and kissed her on the cheek. She smiled. If it had been night time, there would have been no need for streetlights. Dee Dee's dazzling smile would've put out more than enough wattage to light the whole damn street up.

Sometimes he'd temporarily forget just how nuts he was about her.

At five foot-two and *stacked*, as they say, in the parlance of the day, she was a genuine knockout. In Rod's eyes, anyway, Dee Dee LeBarron bore a striking resemblance to Susan Pleshette, the sexy Hollywood starlet. Her full lips, spellbinding hazel eyes, perfectly sculpted nose and dark, lustrous hair, along with her patented swivel-hip walk, had captured Rod's immediate and everlasting attention. They'd met at the Saint Agnes' Canteen four years earlier. The Canteen had been created some years before, to provide a place for teens to dance, enjoy a good time and hopefully, stay out of trouble. Generally speaking, it'd worked out pretty well. Of course, that all depended upon one's definition of the word *trouble*.

Rod had caught her eye just as she walked through the door. She'd never been there before. Of that, he was certain. He never would have forgotten that face...or body. Immediately and successfully outmaneuvering the competition for her favor, Rod proceeded to stick to her like white on snow. The infatuation turned out to be quite mutual and so, that was that. A romance had blossomed that evening, and had been in full bloom ever since.

"So what was the sulky mood all about?" she inquired coyly. "Did you finally wake up to the fact that I even exist?"

Rod's face flushed a bit, eyes downcast, looking more like a ten year-old who'd just walked out of the confessional booth, than an aspiring police officer.

"Guilty as charged. I'm sorry, Baby. It's just that the bad news about the job kind of floored me," he confessed, shaking his head in disbelief. "Yeah, it was sort of like being on the receiving end of an unexpected punch in the nose."

"Now *that*'s something you've definitely already had enough of," she said playfully, tweaking his nose gently between her thumb and forefinger.

Rod always been a kid who could take care of himself. He'd never lost a single schoolyard fight and as he grew older, his reputation as a brawler to be avoided at all costs, took hold in the various bars and poolrooms throughout Cohoes and Troy. Unfortunately, Rod himself bought into it all, reading too many of his own press clippings in a sense, believing he was capable of whipping anyone, anywhere, anytime.

At sixteen he signed on to become an amateur boxer. After sufficient training, or so he thought anyway, Rod stepped into the ring for his first match. He won, but his nose got kind of mashed up. We've all heard of boxers who suffered from what's termed a *glass jaw*. Well, Hot-Rod took it a step further, eventually being credited locally for the genesis of the term—*glass nose*.

His only loss came at the hands of a Troy kid, a big bruiser named Andy Vincent. Technically as well as physically, Vincent's skill level was light years beyond anything Rod had ever before encountered. To be charitable, let's just say it wasn't a pretty sight and let it go at that. At the conclusion of the mismatch, Dee Dee and Rod's Mom plaintively urged him to throw in the towel on his boxing career, as if he needed their urging. He'd pretty much made up his mind to ditch his career one minute into the second round. Talk about being outclassed! Determined to break free of the flattened nose syndrome, Hot Rod Hobbs stopped his car on the way home that night, at the intersection of Columbia and Main Streets, getting out just long enough to toss his tied-together gloves up in the air. They caught on the power lines on his very first try. In time, virtually everyone in the city knew whose gloves those were. After a year or so had passed, the laces finally rotted away, the gloves falling to the road. Word on the street was that a little kid named Kenny Busta snatched them right up, quickly running home before some bigger kid could jump him and swipe the gloves for himself.

"Yeah, you're right about that, Dee Dee. This nose of mine has already been through enough wars."

She giggled as she gave his nose one final tweak.

"Maybe it's good that your nose got messed up a bit. Otherwise, you'd be downright perfect-looking, leaving me to spend all my time shooing away the other girls."

"Yeah, sure."

She probably wasn't all that far off the mark with her scenario. At six foot-one and two hundred pounds, Rod caught the attention of many a fawning girl. What with his piercing green eyes, smoothly barbered, glossy black hair, high cheekbones and dimpled chin, it was no wonder that many of the local chicks thought he bore quite a resemblance to Fabian, the latest of Dick Clark's endless discoveries. All that aside, I doubt that any of those teen idols ever carried themselves in the fashion that Hot Rod Hobbs did. He wore his physicality the way a flashy lawyer wore an ultra expensive suit... with cock-sure, supreme confidence and just a hint of haughty arrogance. That's not to say that Hobbs had a big head. No, Rod simply believed in himself.

CHAPTER 2

Later that evening they stopped at Stewart's on Remsen Street. Rod had a craving for a *Make-your-own-sundae*. It took a full five minutes to create the god awful mish-mash that he carried over to the table.

"How can you eat that?" Dee Dee asked. "I mean, come on, will you? First, your Mom made you your favorite meal of meatloaf and mashed potatoes with all the trimmings. Then we went up to Guptill's where you spent more time feeding your face with popcorn, Super Crisp Potato chips and Bilinski's Hot Dogs than you did skating. What's with that, anyway? If I didn't know better, I'd swear you must be pregnant!" she exclaimed.

Rod had just shoveled a huge spoonful of glop into his mouth and was now busy spitting it back out into a napkin, his shoulders quaking with mirth.

"Don't me make laugh when I'm eating, will you? You know how I am. One of these days you're going to be the cause of my choking to death," he warned.

The clerk, a stout, matronly woman dressed in white from head to toe, suddenly rushed over, clearly concerned.

"Excuse me, sir, but are you all right?"

"I'm fine, thank you. It just went down the wrong pipe, I guess."

Evidently satisfied, the clerk shuffled back to the counter.

Dee Dee smirked from ear to ear.

"If it were *me* choking, she probably wouldn't even have left the counter. You, however, being the guy with the movie star looks and all, she of course waddles right on over, hoping you'd require some mouth to mouth action."

"Cut it out."

She laughed, reaching across the table to squeeze his hand.

"Come on, Rod. Snap out of it. You've been operating in only two modes today—eating and sulking. After all, it isn't every guy who's got a gorgeous babe like me for a girlfriend. You ought to be jumping for joy, just to be in my company."

A slow smile worked its way across his face.

"You got me there. Yeah, I'm definitely one lucky cat."

He then leaned forward, taking yet another shot at a monstrous spoonful of peanut-laden mush. He may have just admitted that he was indeed a very fortunate lad, but his face certainly didn't reflect any joy over it.

She picked up on his thoughts like a gypsy mind reader.

"Now you're regretting your decision to quit school, aren't you?"

He put his spoon down and reached for a napkin.

"I suppose. Yeah, maybe I am," he admitted rather reluctantly. "How did you know that, anyway?"

She gave him a smug look.

"Hot Rod, my love, let me tell you something, and please, listen very closely."

"I'm all ears."

"Women examine these kinds of things on a level that guys like you could never, ever even begin to comprehend."

"Is that a fact? Hey, what do you say we run over To Danny's and pick up a pizza. We'll take it back to your house and watch some TV," he suggested, purposely changing the subject while glancing at his wristwatch. "If we hurry, we ought to be able to make it home in time to watch *The Honeymooners*."

Dee Dee sighed, edging ever closer to the end of her patience, bringing to mind a frustrated teacher, one faced with a thick-headed student, a pupil who just didn't, or couldn't, grasp a simple concept that the teacher was trying to convey.

"Did you even hear a word I said?"

"Not really. I was just waiting for you to finish."

"Rod, that's enough. You're just beating around the bush, avoiding what you know we have to talk about. If we're going to get married, like we're planning on doing, you have to learn to come clean with me when something's bugging you. So, with that in mind, I expect you to give me the scoop on what's going on inside that thick noggin of yours...starting right now."

He knew when he was beat.

"Okay, but let's go over to your house. I'd rather talk about it there."

Rod's 1957 Chevy Belair ragtop was his pride and joy. Two-toned in tropical turquoise and ivory, and festooned with chrome *Laker* exhaust pipes and teardrop skirts, it rarely ever went a day without being carefully washed, dried and buffed to a mirror shine. Occasionally, he took some heat from fellow employees and management about his driving a Chevy, while working at a Plymouth dealership. Rod never let it bother him, though. He wasn't planning on staying there anyway. As much as he loved working on his own car, he derived no pleasure or satisfaction whatsoever, from working on other people's autos. Besides, his goal was to be a cop, not a career grease-monkey.

As he pulled up in front of Dee Dee's place, a gray, clapboard, three-story building on Lincoln Avenue, she suddenly leaned over and kissed him.

"Okay, Hot Shot, grab the pizza from the back seat and let's make like a banana and split!"

"Corny...very, very corny."

She poked him in the ribs.

"Who are you kidding? You love it, jug head!"

Once comfortably seated upon the sofa, Rod made short work of the small pizza.

"Gee, maybe you should've ordered a large one, you know? I mean, what with you being a growing boy and all."

"Give me a break, will you?" he whined, cutting her short. "I was hungry. What was I supposed to do, deny myself pleasure on my own birthday?"

She gave him a look. He gave her a look. They both burst out laughing.

"Keep it down out there, you two," came a voice from a nearby bedroom. "We're trying to sleep, you know. We got to get up early, so pipe down!"

Dee Dee's mother and father were in the bedroom directly across from where Rod and his girl were sitting. You couldn't blame them for complaining about the laughter. After all, it wasn't like they could close the door to their room, effectively drowning out any sound. There was no door, just a floral chintz curtain that hung down over the entrance.

"What's with your mom? She's usually a night owl," Rod asked, his voice low.

Stifling a giggle, Dee Dee whispered, "After eight o'clock mass at St. Rita's, she and her cronies from the Rosary Society are hopping on a chartered bus up to the Saratoga Harness Track, right after Father Riley blesses the bus, of course. Mom's all excited about going, especially because the good Father himself is joining them. No doubt they'll railroad him into calling out the Bingo numbers that are picked from the cage, all the way up and back."

"Bingo? How in the hell are they going to play bingo on a bus, of all places?"

"Easy. Mrs. Nocello convinced her husband, Joey, to cut some plywood into strips, the width of two bus seats, cover them with green felt and uh, excuse the pun...*bingo*, instant game boards!"

"Come on, you're pulling my leg."

"Nope, it's the truth. Think we ought to submit it to *Ripley's Believe it or not*?"

Rod shook his head in disbelief.

"Come on, let's go out on the back porch," she suggested.

It was a beautiful summer evening, warm, yet not at all uncomfortable. The moon was full and bright, the stars were out in force, and the crickets were merrily chirping away.

"You know, Dee Dee, you got some nice comfortable chairs out here and it's a great night and all, but I got to tell you that sitting on this porch makes me a tad nervous. One of these days, the whole damned thing is going to snap off and drop a good hundred feet to the yard below."

She giggled, leaning over to rest her hand on his forearm.

"Well, let's hope it's unoccupied, if and when that ever happens."

The house was easily a hundred years old, each floor a separate flat with its own back porch. The porches on the first two floors were in decent shape, but *Dee Dee's?* Being precariously perched upon her porch, produced a sensation similar to that which one felt while careening headlong down the terrifyingly sheer slope of Atlantic City's roller coaster.

"Okay, big boy, quit worrying. It's not going to plummet to earth tonight, so let's get this show on the road."

"And what show would that be?"

"You *show* me what's going on inside that thick head of yours, and then I'll *tell* you what you can, or can't do about it. We got a deal?"

He sighed, defeated.

"We got a deal."

"Well, all right then. First off, what's with the day-long blues? So you can't get the job you want because you dropped out of school. So what? It's not the end of the world. You already got a good job *and* a decent part-time one, as well."

"Yeah, thanks a bunch for pointing that out," he replied glumly. "Two dead end jobs and *what?* You expect me to jump through Hula Hoops with joy?"

She eyed him reproachfully.

"You know, I'm just saying... just saying now, keep in mind, but this has got to be said—Sometimes you're your own worst enemy. You know that?"

Rod's eyes rolled toward the dark sky.

"Cut me some slack, will you? You know how badly I wanted to nail that job down!"

"So go to night school. Get the credits you need to earn a diploma and then you'll be all set."

"Why, I must be developing a hearing defect. Tell me I didn't hear you just say those two dirty words—*Night School!*" he spat, embittered by the very idea of such an outrageous suggestion. "Oh, sure. Can't you just see me walking into the high school principal's office and asking her how I go about getting into night school? I can just see it now, her getting up from her command post desk, smirking and strutting over to me, bosom puffed out like a rooster getting ready to do battle, a fight she knows she already won. I can just hear her now: '*Well, well, if it isn't Mr. Hobbs, the cocky young man who claimed he didn't need an education. The same boy, who I warned that if you think getting a diploma's too much work, wait until you're forty and still cashing a minimum wage check. The same one who I asked—You think education is a lot of trouble? Wait until you try ignorance on for size, Buster! And so, here you are today, standing before me, four years later. What's the matter, Mr. Smarty Pants? Finding out that living on Easy Street isn't so easy after all?*'"

"Calm down, Rod," Dee Dee said soothingly. "You don't have to ask her about it. My cousin, April Kennedy, works at the Board of Education. I'll ask her how you should go about it."

Rod threw up his hands in disgust.

"Screw that! I'm not about to go to any damn rinky-dink night school and that's the end of it!"

Dee Dee sighed heavily. Frustrated, she shook her head. *Trying to get through to him is like trying to explain nuclear fission to a chimp!* She fumed.

"Well, no matter how you feel about it at the moment, you may still want to give it some thought over the next few days."

"Not going to happen," he insisted rather heatedly.

"You never listen."

"Yes I do. I just don't agree with you this time."

"Well, if we're going to be married, you'll have to learn how to agree with me...on most things, anyway," she warned, barely suppressing a smile.

"Truthfully, I don't really know if that's within the range of my abilities."

No sooner were the words out of his mouth, before he instantly found himself regretting them.

Dee Dee punched him hard.

"Ow! My shoulder! Damn, I'm sorry. I didn't mean that. It's just that—" he stumbled, his words tapering off. He pretty much knew what he wanted to say, but just didn't know how to say them.

"You better be sorry, *Mister!*"

"Okay, okay. Relax, will you? I was only kidding around. Hey, get me something to drink, would you? Getting smacked around always did make me thirsty."

"You *better* have been kidding around," she replied, cocking her arm, threatening to let loose with a follow-up punch. "Don't you ever forget who the boss is around here, buddy."

"Yeah, right. Sorry, I don't what came over me. I must have had a memory lapse, *Boss!*"

"Well, don't let it happen again, *Mr. Hot Rod Hobbs.* Speaking of being the boss, you know the good thing about it is, my high rank automatically comes with privileges, don't you know?" she remarked in a sultry tone, suddenly rising, making her way over to Rod's wicker chair, where she proceeded to make a big production out of lowering herself down onto his lap.

"Now then, about that drink. We got water, Dudek's chocolate milk or grape Kool Aid. So, what'll it be?" She inquired coyly as she cuddled up against him, her arms slipping around his neck.

"Mmm, what drink? Did I ask for a drink? Skip the drink. You're not going anywhere, Baby."

CHAPTER 3

"What's bugging you tonight?" his pal asked.

Rod shrugged listlessly, his face creased with the woebegone look of a man whose world had just caved in.

"Come on, bozo. Tell your ol' buddy Butch what's eating you. Lord knows everybody else tells me their troubles. Of course, I guess that just comes with the job."

Butch O'Brien, one of the bartenders at Bourkie's Wonder Bar, or as the regulars referred to it, the *Blunder Bar*, had been pals with Rod since first grade. Short and stocky, Butch had a beet-red complexion set off by a nose the size of a small Idaho potato. Greased-up red hair combed straight back into a Duck's ass, and a mouthful of jagged, crooked teeth that resembled a busted picket fence, completed a face that Butch liked to describe as being a work in progress. Problem was, there never seemed to be any progress.

Butch was a great guy to have as a friend, however. Loyal as a good dog, he could always be counted on to help a pal out in any way that he could. And just like that same good, loyal dog, he could also sense when the people he cared for, were down in the dumps.

"Want me to crack you open a cold Schaefer's?"

"Nah, I'm good," Rod replied sullenly.

"What? *You're good?* You've been sitting here for two hours nursing that same warm bottle of suds. You *must* be in a bad way, Hot Rod. You're about half a keg behind your usual intake. Come on, open up. Spill the beans. What's bugging you?"

Rod sighed as he reached for a pack of Luckie's from the cuff of his rolled-up, short sleeved shirt. Butch always wondered what with the bulging biceps and all, how in the hell Rod ever managed to fit the pack of butts into the skintight sleeve in the first place.

"I got it," Butch offered, lighting Rod's cigarette with a beat up Zippo.

"I got turned down by the cops."

"Want to run that by me again? Sounds as if you offered to be arrested, but they said *no*."

"Funny."

"I thought so," Butch replied drolly. "So, you're saying you didn't get the job? I figured you were in, no question, what with all the pull your family has."

"Yeah, me too. Unfortunately, though, you've got to have a diploma nowadays," Rod explained glumly.

Butch was at a loss to come up with anything comforting to say, so he simply made light of it all.

"You want, you could always sign up for one of those matchbook cover—*Become a Private Detective correspondence courses*. That would kind of make you like a cop. Well, sort of, anyway."

Rod gave him a sharp look.

"You're a lot of help, you are. A private detective! That job comes with about as much legal authority as a milkman's."

"Yeah, maybe it isn't such a hot idea after all," Butch admitted. "You become a private detective and then everybody would probably refer to you as a *dick*."

"That too."

"So what's plan B?" Butch inquired, sticking a toothpick into a corner of his mouth.

Rod snuffed his smoke out in the glass ashtray.

"Wish I knew," he groaned, gently running his hands over his pomaded hair, careful not to muss it up.

"Bourkie's been talking about adding another bartender to the payroll. I know you're sick of the grease monkey stuff, so why not give tending bar a shot? You want, I'll even put a word in for you with him."

Rod glanced around, taking in the *seen better days* décor. One appraising look at the drab green walls, last painted when FDR was president, the metal stools with their torn, red vinyl cushions, the *Wurlitzer* juke box that only worked about half the time, same as the TV and the *Fitzgerald's Beer* wall clock did, and he'd seen enough.

"I appreciate it, Butch, but no thanks. I'd rather take a job following the *Freihofer Bakery* wagon around, scooping up horse manure at each stop, than work in here."

His well-meaning pal seemed mildly offended.

"Why? It's an honest living, isn't it? Besides, you'd even get to play the part of a cop every once in a while," he added, reaching under the bar and producing a big ol' dinged-up nightstick.

"Jesse Fonda gave it to Bourkie years ago, for those times that the cops maybe couldn't get here quickly enough," he explained, softly slapping the nasty looking club against the palm of his other hand.

Rod shook his head.

"I'll pass."

Butch sighed, unable to comprehend how anyone could look askance at such a great job.

"Tips are pretty decent here and you wouldn't even have to pay income tax on most of it! Hell, I've been putting my tips away for a year now, saving up to maybe buy a new Edsel or one of them Nash Metropolitans."

Rod tossed him a skeptical look.

"How's that working out for you?"

"Well...uh, not so hot, actually, but I'm getting there, little by little."

Suddenly a loud voice from further down the bar called out, "I heard that, Butch. Who you kidding? By the time you got enough cash to buy one of them cars, they'll probably have been discontinued."

The guy was young, just eighteen. Sporting the ever popular Flattop haircut, his dark hair glistened with Vaseline or some other kind of goop.

Butch smirked.

"Who asked you, Tommy? I want an opinion, I'll ask an adult. You, I'll ask if I got a question about tricycles or scooters."

The kid laughed.

"I'm just sounding on you, Butch. Don't get all bent out of shape."

Butch tapped the Billy Club against the palm of his hand.

"Never mind worrying about me, Carter. You need to worry about maybe getting this stick jammed up your patoot. That's what *you* ought to be concerned about," Butch cautioned good-naturedly.

"Yeah, right. Hey, how about another beer for me and Burnsie, and while you're at it, change the channel, too, will you? Ed Sullivan's going to have Brenda lee and Fabian on tonight."

Butch dutifully poured two Dobler draughts, setting them down in front of the young guys.

"Yeah, I'll change the channel for you, Tommy. We can't be missing Fabian, you know," he said, smirking a bit. "Every time he's on TV, all the local girls start swooning, half of them remarking about how much a certain guy named Hobbs resembles him, the lucky dog."

Rod's face flushed a bit, just as it always did when the conversation turned to the subject of his uncanny resemblance to Fabian, the rock and roll teen idol.

He stood up and stretched.

"How about a game of darts? Anybody up for it?" he asked, hoping to change the subject.

"That depends," said a husky voice from behind. "They get any new darts lately? The old ones got about as many feathers in them as a plucked chicken."

Rod spun around to face a guy at one of the back tables. He was playing Solitaire with a grimy, dog-eared deck of cards that had seen better days.

"I don't which is in worse shape—these cards or those crummy darts," the guy mused, scratching his head.

The man's name was Lenny Fishowski. Naturally, from the time he was a small boy, everyone simply referred to him as *Fish,* a gross misnomer if there ever was one. As it turned out, Lenny had early on developed a keen interest in gambling. By age ten he was already accomplished at cleaning out his little pals' pockets. Whether it was pitching pennies, playing poker in West End Park, or betting on the outcome of little league games, Fish invariably came out ahead. As he grew older, the venues, along with the stakes, had risen significantly, but the results rarely varied—Fish won.

By age sixteen, many a loser had suggested that Fish's name ought to be changed to *Shark*. Of course, no one had ever had the nerve to personally suggest it to him, and for good reason. Fish was a big, ill-tempered guy with a pronounced penchant for violence.

"Nothing wrong with those darts," Butch grumbled.

Fish snickered.

"Yeah, nothing a good fire wouldn't cure. So what do you say, Hobbs? You want to shoot or not?"

Rod nodded, making his way over to the beat-up Toohey dart board. As Fish stood up to join him, Rod ventured a glance at the big man. A shade over six-four, the twenty-eight old man was bull shouldered with a torso like a beer keg, rotund, yet as hard as a sheet of Alleghany Ludlum steel. Prematurely balding, he combed his remaining greasy black strands forward, ala Julius Caesar. Big, oversized ears, ones that brought to mind the image of a Lincoln Continental with both front doors swung wide open, framed a face cratered with acne scars, a smushed oft-broken nose, and a cruel, crooked mouth.

It was the eyes, however, that one tended to remember most. Deep set and dark, like glimmering black mirrors of glass, his penetrating gaze seemed to bore right through a guy, forcing most to quickly look away. Rod, however, wasn't one of them. He knew enough to give Fish a wide berth, yet he had absolutely no fear of him. Fish was well aware of this, and grudgingly respected him all the more for it.

"You know, that punk at the bar makes a good point, Mr. *Hot Rod*. If you wanted, you could be playing hot and heavy spin-the-bottle with half the single babes in Cohoes tonight. Instead, you're shooting darts with a guy whose face resembles a dented pizza pan. What do you think that says about you? Me? I got to wonder about you a little." Fish ventured, his words dripping with sarcasm.

Rod threw his first practice dart, a Bull's eye.

"I'd say my personal life isn't any of your business." he replied calmly, nailing yet another bull's eye.

"And as such, you should consider the subject now permanently closed," Rod added, shutting the big bruiser out as effectively as a bolt on a door.

Fish chuckled as he made a big show of raising his hands, palms outward.

"Now don't go getting all ticked off at me. I was just saying, you know...just saying."

Rod handed him the darts.

Fish tossed them onto a nearby table.

"Hey, Butch, before I really get into this game, throw me together a Singapore Sling, will ya?" he asked. "I'm in the mood for something exotic. A guy can only drink just so much beer."

Butch looked away from the TV and blinked.

"A *what*? A *Sing-Song-Sing*? What the hell is that?"

Fish shot him a scornful glare.

"Never mind, dimwit. Just pour me another beer. Apparently, I had a little memory lapse, forgetting that you couldn't make a snowball without first consulting a diagram."

Rod made no attempt to disguise his annoyance.

"Hey, this ain't exactly the Hendrick Hudson Hotel bar in here, you know. The last time somebody ordered a drink like that in this place, Eisenhower was probably in diapers, so lay off of Butch."

Suddenly all went dead still, the conversations at the bar abruptly snuffed out; the only sound that of Brenda Lee belting out "I'm sorry."

Fish pinched the bridge of his nose, shaking his head in a condescending, tut-tutting manner.

"It's lucky for you that I happen to like you, sonny boy. Otherwise we'd be going at it right now."

Rod's jaw tightened, his face a mask of defiance.

Just as he was about fire back, Butch came out from behind the bar, throwing his arm around Rod's shoulder.

"Hey, did I ever tell you guys about the time I was on the *Freddie Freihofer* Kiddies' Show?"

Both men stared at Butch, as if he'd just claimed to have been aboard the Russian satellite, *Sputnik*.

"No? Well, let me tell you about it right now, then. I was the oldest kid to ever appear on it—in the entire history of the show. Yep, I was eleven. Of course they had an age limit of eight but Mom wanted me to be on it so badly, she went and lied about my age. She told the producer that I was eight, but kind of husky for my age."

Fish sighed in annoyance, shifting his weight from one foot to the other.

"Go back behind the bar," he thundered, his face tight with tension. "While you still can," he added threateningly.

Butch blanched, but forged ahead anyway.

"Let me just finish. The kicker was...I was on television before we even *owned* a television! Now, ain't that something?"

Fish threw him a glacially cold glare.

"Consider this your last chance to go back behind the bar, numb nuts," the huge man warned, flexing his massive forearms, the tendons bulging like steel cables.

Rod shot him a hard look, while at the same time giving Butch a gentle shove toward the bar.

"Get out of here. Go back where you belong, Butch. I'll be up there in a minute."

Butch's eyes darted from one man to the other. He looked as if he wanted to stay put, maybe take one more stab at putting out this small fire, before it blazed into a three alarm inferno. Either that, or be there to lend his best pal a hand, if it came that. He sincerely hoped that it wouldn't.

Rod suddenly took Butch by the arm and led him over to the bar. He then turned and headed back toward the dartboard.

He nodded to Fish.

"You go first," he said, icicles dripping from every word. Fish's acne-pitted face softened just a touch, a humorless smile beginning to form at the corner of his mouth.

"You got guts, Hobbs. I'll give you that."

CHAPTER 4

The Sunday afternoon dance at the Cohoes Elk's club always drew a big crowd. Invariably, it was packed with teenagers, along with a handful of slightly older couples. On this particular Sunday, Rod and Dee Dee opted to stop by, along with Butch and his girlfriend, Linda Davis.

Well, to be frank, the guys didn't exactly *opt* to go, so much as they were coerced into going. The new dance, the *Twist*, was all the rage, and today, a contest would be held to determine just *who* precisely, were the finest twisters in Cohoes.

Butch spied an unoccupied table toward the back of the hall and the guys instantly made a beeline for it.

The girls showed up a minute later, not looking any too happy about the table's location.

"What's with guys, anyway? Whether it's in a classroom, on a bus, in church, or in a place like this, you all automatically gravitate to the area furthest from the action. What's up with that?" Dee Dee asked, clearly puzzled and annoyed.

"Because by sitting back here, we can see the whole room," Butch explained. "Besides, we guys like to have our backs to the wall, regardless of where we are."

The girls exchanged knowing looks.

"Uh-huh, right. You never know when *Zorro* might try to sneak up from behind and shish-ka-bob the two of you on his sword," Linda, a pretty blond girl, wisecracked.

Butch was unfazed by the barb.

"Hey, a man's got to do what a man's got to do. Come on now. Sit down and enjoy the music, ladies."

The girls sighed as they grabbed a seat.

The event was being hosted by a local celebrity, a Deejay known as Boom-Boom Branigan. He was a household name around the area, and convincing him to sign on to emcee this contest was considered quite the coup.

Branigan was about forty, average height, a tad chunky, with a rather florid complexion that suggested he probably liked his booze...a lot. Then there was the hair. Thick, black, and wavy, the Elvis hairdo was daily shaped, combed, sculpted, and then subjected to enough shiny, gooey pomade to withstand gale force winds.

Today, he donned a hot pink knit tie and a shiny black suit, one of those glow-in-the-dark numbers made from some kind of indeterminable fabric.

All that aside, he was a pretty nice guy, however. Being loud, bombastic and bold sort of came with the job description and couldn't be held against him. *Branigan's Shenanigans*, as he himself referred to his shtick, may have occasionally gotten on the older crowd's nerves, but one thing was for certain. Anyone who hired Boom-Boom for a day always got their money's worth. A born showman, today, as usual, he had the young folks eating out of the palm of his hand, like hungry pigeons flocking to a peanut vendor.

Of course there was always the exception.

"Hey, *Daddy—O!* Mr. Stanton, the undertaker, just called. He said he wants his black suit back!" some kid taunted from the floor.

The music was loud, but no one for a minute doubted that Branigan heard the barb. He was used to kids sounding on him. As the youngster, a well known fourteen year old with the nickname of *Stick,* kept applying the verbal needle, Branigan simply smirked, looking like a cat that had just cornered a mouse.

Motioning over an Auxiliary cop by the name of Thibodeau, Boom-Boom discreetly pointed out the offending party. A few brief words were then exchanged between the two men. Moments later the kid was escorted out the door.

Butch tapped Rod on the arm.

"Security?"

Rod shrugged.

"Guess so."

"You wouldn't think they'd have a need for a weekend warrior at a Sunday dance."

"Well, then you'd be wrong, as witnessed by what you just saw and heard."

"You're an auxiliary cop. You mean you could have requested this duty, too?"

Rod yawned and stretched his arms.

"I suppose, but no thanks. I already did my Sunday duty, protecting old ladies from getting run over by cars as they leave church. Besides, I wouldn't want to clash with Thibodeau over the job. I like the guy, and I know how much he digs this kind of thing."

Chubby Checker's "Twist Again" suddenly reverberated against the walls, near deafening in its' intensity.

Dee Dee stood up, swaying to the beat.

"Come on, Hot Rod. Let's get to it," she said, her come-hither smile illuminating the room the way few smiles ever could, like sunshine on a mirror.

He grinned at her.

"How come it's plain old *Rod* most of the time, but when you want me to do something you know I don't feel like doing, suddenly it's *Hot Rod*?"

Her eyes twinkled with amusement.

"I'll tell you while we're twisting," she replied, pulling on his arm. "Up...get up!"

Reluctantly, Rod complied, their friends trailing right behind him.

He may have resisted, but once he was up on the dance floor, Rod cut loose with abandon. They were *so* good, so accomplished at this new *Twist* dance, that virtually all eyes were upon them.

The four of them danced to three more tunes before heading back to the table.

Once seated, Dee Dee turned and gave Rod a hard, appraising look.

"What?" he asked, puzzled.

"The redhead in the tight poodle skirt dancing next to us, that's what. The tart who's cruising for a bruising!" she snapped, her eyes blazing with anger.

Rod spread his hands, palms up, a perplexed look in his eyes.

"*What redhead*? I didn't notice any redhead up there. What are you talking about?"

She snickered.

"The one who kept making eyes at you. The one who, in a word, as you guys like to say—is *stacked!*"

Rod's eyes rolled upward as he exhaled loudly.

"You're dreaming. She never even looked at me."

Dee Dee zeroed right in on him now. Leaning back, her fingers laced together upon her crossed knees, a smug, humorless smile bloomed upon her face.

Rod looked away, unable to hold her gaze. He'd stepped in it and he knew it. *If only the redhead hadn't had a body built for commandment-breaking! Then I wouldn't even have noticed her,* he lamented.

"If as you say, you didn't notice *her*, then how would you know that she never looked at *you*?" Dee Dee inquired, her words stinging, like an unexpected slap in the kisser.

Try talking your way getting out of that.

He cleared his throat, stalling for time to come up with some sort of lame reply. Fortunately for him, rescue came in the form of a most unlikely source.

"What's going on, kids?"

The voice belonged to a man of about sixty-eight. Tall and gaunt, the skin so taut across his face, it looked as if his cheekbones might just pop right through. Washed-out, dull blue eyes bored into Rod.

Rod nodded to the man, an Elk in good standing.

"How are you, Sal?"

"Good. I just came from a committee meeting upstairs. Mind If I join you for a minute? Got something I want to bounce off you," he said, pulling over a chair from an adjoining table.

Both girls rolled their eyes.

"Time for us to visit the powder room," Dee Dee called out over her shoulder, as they rushed off.

"I'm going to go grab another Coke. Be right back," Butch said, as he too quickly vacated the table.

The man with the receding hairline grunted and shrugged, shoving an unlit cigar into the corner of his mouth. His pitiful comb-over looked as if it had been painted on with a hairbrush that had been missing half its' bristles.

"Like I always say, Rod—it's a good thing I'm thick skinned," the man remarked dryly. "Otherwise, I might just get offended by people running off whenever I show up."

Rod shrugged, unable to come up with a suitable reply.

Salvatore Coccalido owned a very successful construction company. He never wanted for work, mostly because he had the right kind of connections, both political and strong arm. It was long rumored that his competition was coerced into either bidding excessively high on many a potential contract, effectively ensuring non-acceptance of their bids, or they simply skipped bidding certain jobs all together. Occasionally, one of his competitors might get stubborn and refuse to toe the line, but that was rare and easily rectified. One visit from a couple of Sal's Neanderthals, a pair of Schenectady brothers named Guido and Nick Trentine usually did the trick. If for some reason the initial warning wasn't taken to heart, the second visit, one that introduced an impressive array of *Louisville Sluggers* into the conversation, never failed to produce the desired results.

"What can I do for you, Sal?" Rod asked.

The man took the unlit cigar out of his mouth and tossed it on the table.

"Come on outside for a minute. This noise they call music is giving me a splitting headache."

"Yeah, okay," Rod reluctantly agreed, rising from his chair.

Once outside, Sal made a big production out of lighting a fresh cigar, puffing hard on the fat stogie until they were both enveloped in a cloud of thick smoke. Rod stepped back, waving the smoke away.

"Jesus, Sal, you ever give any thought to switching over to cigarettes? It only takes a second to light one, and the smoke it gives off is next to nothing."

"Nah, I'll leave the cigarettes to you. Me, I like my cigars."

Obviously, Rod thought to himself. *At everyone else's expense.*

Sal's breath could blow windows right out of a building. Between the effects of smoking twelve cigars daily and a mouthful of badly decaying teeth, one whiff of Sal's breath and dogs started crying and baying at the moon.

"Cuban, they are, the best money can buy," Sal insisted. "Well, for the moment, anyway. If however, this punk over there, the one with the beard, has his way, we can kiss the importation of Cuban cigars goodbye."

Getting impatient now, Rod shifted his weight from one foot to the other.

"Yeah, that's good to know, but what is it that you wanted to talk to me about, Sal?"

"Damn, it's hot out here, isn't it?" Sal remarked as he brushed away ashes from his lapel.

Dressed in an ill-fitting navy blue, dandruff-flecked suit, one that hung loosely from his spare frame, Sal was never get going an offer to pose for *Esquire* magazine. A garish magenta tie flying at half-mast, fell short of his belt buckle by a good five inches. The matching magenta suspenders didn't do much for him either.

"Why don't you ditch the coat and tie? There's nobody to impress out here." Rod suggested reasonably.

Sal waved off the suggestion.

"Don't worry about it. Look, over the years, back when I operated a book, a little numbers racket, and a few tables upstairs over Oscar's place, you ran quite a few errands for me, and to tell you the truth, you impressed the hell out of me, kid. Most of the other street punks that I used for odd jobs, occasionally tried to make a little *personal withdrawal* from the bags, figuring I'd never notice," Sal grumbled. "Good luck with that."

Rod glanced over toward the club's entrance.

"I got to back in there or she'll be having a fit, Sal."

"Hold your horses, kid," Sal cautioned, starting to get a little irritated. "This ain't going to take but another minute or so. Damn, trying to have a conversation with you is like wrestling with a porcupine!"

Rod lit a cigarette.

"Okay, you were saying?"

"Yeah, like I was saying, some of those little street monkeys from time to time tried to dip their hands into the cookie jar. Then I'd catch them at it, and threaten to feed their nuts to the squirrels. That always took care of the problem. But *you*? You were as trustworthy as they came, never once trying to nick me for a buck here, or a buck there. That impressed me."

Rod began to feel intensely uncomfortable. It was starting to sound like an awards ceremony, all the nice words and compliments. The only thing missing was a plaque.

"So now, I find that I have a problem, an internal problem. Seems that I've had some valuable equipment regularly up and disappear off a construction site. My instincts, which by the way are never wrong, tell me that an employee or employees are making off with the stuff. I could post a night watchman, one of my own guys, but then, which one can I trust?" he wondered aloud. "The answer is— none of them!" he snapped, his tone as sharp as a blade. "It'd be like hiring a fox to guard the henhouse. I can't trust a damned one of them!"

"Sorry to hear that, but what's it got to do with me?"

Sal scratched the gray stubble on his chin, fixing Rod with a hard gaze.

"I want you to come to work for me, son."

The young man's jaw dropped. Taken completely by surprise as he was, Rod's face brought to mind someone caught unexpectedly in the flash of a camera.

"Me?" he asked, incredulous.

Sal nodded, a rare smile flickering at the corner of his mouth.

"You see me talking to anyone else?"

"Uh...well, no, but why me?"

"I already told you—because I can trust you, that's why."

"But I already got two jobs."

Sal blew some smoke rings.

"Yeah, lubing cars and directing traffic on Sunday mornings. Hell of a future, that is. I also know you're pretty disappointed about not getting the cop job, so this is an opportunity for you to get over it. You can make some decent money for a change."

Rod just stood there, stunned.

"What are you taking home, anyway?" Sal asked. "Seventy, seventy-five a week? Chump change! I'll double it, just for starters."

"I...uh," Rod faltered, his words trailing off.

Sal drapped an arm around his shoulder, a fatherly gesture.

"Finger the sons-a-bitches that are robbing me blind and I'll throw you a three hundred dollar bonus, to boot. So what do you say to that, son? Not exactly chicken feed, is it?"

Before Rod could muster a reply, Butch suddenly appeared in the doorway.

"Excuse me, but if you don't get back in here, she's going to have your scalp, Hobbsie. The contest is about to begin, and I wouldn't want to be you, if she has to sit it out."

"Yeah, yeah, be right there."

Butch nodded, turned, and went back in.

"I got one question, Sal," Rod said, nervously running a hand over his hair. "What happens after the thief or thieves get caught, *if* I can catch them, that is? What then? I mean, once it's over with, what else do you have for me to do?"

Sal shook his head, a hint of disappointment on his face, as if Rod had almost failed an audition.

Spreading his arms wide, he asked: "You think I'd ask you to quit your paltry little jobs, come to work for me, and then turn around later and tell you to take a hike? For chrissakes, I'll have enough different jobs for you to do; you'll be kept busy for the next twenty years, kid!"

Rod stared down at his feet, unsure as to what to say or do.

Sal squeezed Rod's forearm.

"Tell you what. Take a few days to mull it over. Then drop by the office, or give me a call, okay?"

Rod nodded numbly as Sal shoved a business card into his shirt pocket.

"There you go. Phone number's right on there. *Cedar 7-6666.* I'm giving you a few days to think it over, but absolutely no longer than a week. Got that?" Sal cautioned.

"Yeah, I'll definitely get back to you," Rod promised as he turned away, making for the entrance. Suddenly, he pulled up short. "One question, though. Why now? Why today, of all days?"

Sal smirked.

"Actually, that's two questions, but to be frank, I've been chewing it over for a few days now, thinking about how you'd be a real good fit. Once I saw you sitting in there, I made my decision on the spot."

Rod still appeared puzzled by it all.

Sal forced an indulgent smile.

"Look at this way. People always want what they're never going get—a lot more money in their paychecks. But *you*? Well, it's your lucky day, Rod."

"Now then, you better get back in there before your girl fits you for some cement boots."

Kidding though he was, the mere mention of *cement boots* sent a slight chill down Rod's spine. Sal had lived the role of a dangerous man for so long now, it fit him tighter than his Fruit-of-the-Looms. *Hmm, I don't know about this*, Rod fretted to himself.

"Consider yourself lucky if I don't serve you a knuckle sandwich for dinner, Buster!" Dee Dee ranted. "Better yet, maybe I'll just bounce some cans of tuna fish off your thick noggin!"

Yeah, she was fuming. Rod had only *just* made it back in time to dance in the Twist contest, he and Dee Dee coming in second to a couple by the name of Paul "Chick" Daubney and Mary Ellen Ward. In honor of the winner, the next record that Boom-Boom played was Annette Funicello's "Tall Paul."

First place was good for ten free games of bowling at the Cohoes Lanes, along with an album of Chubby Checker's greatest hits. Unfortunately, a second place finish only merited a couple of Hula Hoops and a small case of Star-Kist tuna.

They were sitting now at the Van Schaick Country Club bar, alongside Butch and Linda. It was a pretty classy place and Butch's cousin, Stanley Jakowski, familiarly known as *Stosh* to friends and family, was bartending tonight.

"Hey, Stosh, give us all another round, would you?" Butch asked his cousin.

"What, did you just come into an inheritance or something?" Linda probed, her tone tinged with suspicion. "This place charges a pretty stiff price for their booze."

Butch grinned as he chewed on the end of his swizzle stick.

"No problem. It just goes on my tab and of course...I never pay it."

Both girls stared at him, incredulous.

"What are you two looking at me like that for?" he asked, clueless.

"How on earth can you run a tab, yet never pay it off?" Dee Dee demanded to know.

"Easy. I just don't do it. Hell, to me, anyway, that's the whole point of running up a tab."

Rod gestured for the girls to lean in close.

"His cousin puts the drinks on some well-to-do member's tab. The member then pays it off at the end of the month, never bothering to question any of the charges. The guy's a big spender, buying drinks for the whole bar on a regular basis, so it's not like he'd ever notice anything suspicious going on," he explained, his voice low.

Dee Dee's eyes popped open wide in disbelief.

"But that's being dishonest, Butch!" she protested in a hushed tone.

Butch shrugged his shoulders.

"More like being opportunistic, if you ask me," he replied evenly.

"But you could get Stosh fired, you idiot!" Linda chimed in, her pretty face turning crimson.

Stosh looked up from the drink he was mixing, shooting the group a dirty look.

Butch got the message, quickly raising a finger to his lips.

"Keep it down, Linda!" he whispered.

Rod had enough on his mind without having to listen this. He glanced at his watch.

"Come on. It's six o' clock. Drink up and we'll go get a bite to eat."

"Good idea," Butch concurred, lifting his lo-ball tumbler of Chivas Regal to his lips and draining it. " Okay, I'm ready to roll."

"We're not going eat here, in the dining room, are we?" Linda inquired nervously. "It's way too expensive, and you are *not* going to play games with a dinner check, Butch!"

Rod made a calming gesture with his hands.

"No, don't worry about that. We're going to take a ride over to Thornie's Diner in Troy. Besides, they'd never allow Butch into the club's dining room. Not with that ill-advised outfit on."

Butch's jaw dropped.

"What? What's wrong with what I'm wearing?"

"Nothing. Nothing that is, that a good bonfire and a bit of sartorial intervention wouldn't cure. I mean, come on, will you? The black Chinos are fine, but what's the deal with wearing white socks with brown dress shoes and a purple and orange Hawaiian shirt? I can understand wearing your shirt outside your pants to hide the paunch and love handles, but those *colors*? What'd you do? Get dressed in the dark?"

Butch grumbled while the girls giggled.

"Some pal you are, picking on your best friend's clothes," he complained, chewing on some ice cubes.

"Hey, only your friend would tell you. Strangers? They'd be too busy rolling on the floor with laughter," Rod assured him, shaking his head in wonder. "It's definitely not an outfit for the scrapbook."

"Gee, thanks. Oh well. Let's hit the road. Yeah, Thornie's sounds good to me. It's more my fiscal speed, anyway," Butch admitted as he and Rod each tossed a buck tip on the bar.

"You okay to drive, Rod?" Linda asked, a cocked eye appraising his face.

"Do I look like I'm three sheets to the wind?"

"Well...no, but I just wanted to be certain," she replied, still a bit unsure about him.

Rod grinned, slapping a hand against his thigh.

"I got a hollow leg."

Nobody said a word until Rod had driven a good mile or so. Then Linda picked right up where she'd left off.

"That bar bill must have been around twenty bucks! If I'd known what you two were up to, I never would have agreed to go there!"

"Me either," Dee Dee piped in, clearly annoyed.

"Well, at least you left a tip and didn't stick the member with that, too," Linda conceded, albeit only begrudgingly.

Butch shook his head.

"Actually, that's not true. A fifteen percent tip is automatically applied to the tab, so technically speaking, Stosh got tipped twice," he said matter-of-factly.

"That's terrible!" Linda exclaimed, elbowing him hard in the ribs.

"Ouch! All right—all ready, so you're right, okay? I mean, now that I think of it, there really *was* no need for us to leave him an extra two bucks, at all."

Linda shook her head in frustration.

"That's *not* what I meant, Butch! Oh, sometimes you are such a—" she sputtered, leaving her sentence unfinished as she turned away huffily.

Rod sighed noisily.

"Okay, so we won't bring you two there again, okay? Now then, why don't we just change the subject?"

Dee Dee gave him a curious look.

"Good idea. How about you tell us what kept you outside for so long? It couldn't have been the company you were keeping. Sal, the human insect repellant, drives away every mosquito within fifty yards, so what gives?"

Rod shifted uncomfortably in his seat.

"Wait until we get inside," he mumbled, pulling up in front of the big diner.

Thornie's, an attractive, modern looking eatery, had only been open a short while, and thus, was still gleaming. The exterior, as well as the interior fairly sparkled. Most of the other diners in the area tended to fit the classic image of a greasy spoon and so, people flocked to Thornie's in droves. Tonight was no exception. The place was packed, yet after a short five minute wait, the foursome was ushered to a big, red, plush vinyl booth in the rear of the building.

Somebody dropped some coins in the jukebox. Clyde McPhatter— "A Lover's Question."

A pretty young waitress garbed in a pink uniform with white trim on the collar and sleeves waited on us. Rod glanced at the nameplate pinned to her uniform.

"Hello, Yvette. How about starting us off with two large Cokes and two coffees?"

The cute blond smiled, nodded, and then walked off toward the counter.

Rod lit a cigarette, drawing the smoke in deeply.

Butch leaned back in the booth, his arm around Linda's shoulder.

"So, you two are going to be on vacation all next week. What've you got planned?" Linda inquired casually.

"We're going to have fun, that's what," Dee Dee replied, her eyes twinkling with anticipation. "Lake George, Kaydeross Park, a clam steam at Lanthier's Grove, roller skating at Guptill's, Crooked Lake, some dancing and oh, yeah...the stupid bus trip to Yankee Stadium."

Butch laughed.

"Why do I get the impression that you'd rather skip that trip?"

She grimaced.

"Because I *would* rather skip it, that's why. I hate baseball in general, and I hate bus trips to ball games even more. It's just an excuse for guys to get a load on and act like idiots."

"Well, why are you even going then?" Linda asked reasonably.

Dee Dee sighed, her eyes rolling upward.

"Because a certain Mr. Hobbs insists upon it. He vows that this is the year he's finally going to get Mickey Mantle's autograph," she complained. "As if *that's* going to happen!"

Rod was about to fire back when Yvette suddenly showed up with their beverages. She then promptly took their orders for burgers and fries.

After she'd ambled off to the kitchen, Butch leaned over and poked Rod's shoulder.

"Sounds like a great week you got planned. An expensive one, though."

Rod sucked hard on his cigarette, blowing smoke rings toward the ceiling.

"Yeah, well, I put aside all of the overtime money that I earned this year."

"I just hope that *my* job is still there when my vacation is over," Dee Dee interjected, frowning.

"What do you mean by that?" Linda inquired, curious.

"Well, two years ago, after graduating from Keveny, I went to work in the office at Swanknit. If you remember, it burned down while I was on vacation. Then I went to work in the office at the Super Crisp Potato Chip factory. I took a short vacation that summer and while away, it too burned itself out of business. Let's just hope the Star Woolen Company doesn't have a fire while I'm off!"

"Nah, don't worry about that. It'll never happen," Linda remarked encouragingly.

Butch nodded his agreement before going on to ask the burning question, one that had been nagging at him for hours now.

"Okay, so what gives with you and Sal?"

Rod took another deep drag on the Lucky.

"He offered me a job," he replied, his face expressionless.

His three companions blinked, clearly stunned by the news.

Dee Dee, in particular, stared at him as if he were a complete stranger.

"Want to run that by me again, Hot Rod? My hearing must be a bit off tonight."

Rod's face went grim. Snuffing out his cigarette, he took a deep breath, bracing himself in preparation for the coming storm.

"He offered me a job—at twice the salary I'm making now!"

"No!" Dee Dee exclaimed, not so much contradiction, as simple disbelief.

Butch used a finger to make a twirling gesture at the side of his head, indicating that a certain someone must be going cuckoo.

"Have you been hanging out at the Troy Beatnik coffeehouse, sharing some reefer with the poets? I mean, are you out of your mind? *Work for Sal?*" Butch cried, incredulous. "If his breath doesn't kill you first, one of his countless enemies surely will!"

"Are you crazy?" Dee Dee snapped, patrons at the surrounding tables glancing over now, curious about the outburst.

Rod gestured with his hands, indicating that she needed to lower her voice.

She drew in a breath, exhaling it loudly. She then stared at him, fuming.

"You know, I used to think you were one sharp cookie, a regular vault of common sense. Now, however, it looks as though I'm going to have to revise my opinion downward. Evidently I'm not the shrewd judge of intelligence that I thought I was."

If sharp words could draw blood, Rod would've been down a couple of quarts in record time.

He steepled his hands, as if in prayer, tapping the ends of his fingers together.

"Look, Dee Dee, it's the chance of a lifetime for me. He's going to double what I earn now from working two jobs. Where else am I ever going get a shot at making *that* kind of money?"

"I think maybe you're underestimating your abilities."

He lit another Lucky, blowing a plume of smoke into the air.

"I think maybe you're overestimating them."

She gave him a hard, appraising look, making a face that was a warm-up prior to pitching him a rip-snorting zinger, right down the ol' pike.

"Yeah, maybe you're right. Maybe I am," she claimed, shaking her head, trying to convey to him the seriousness of the situation. "I thought you were a smart man. Guess I was wrong about that. Obviously, you're still just a naïve kid."

Rod stared down at the table as the jukebox played Frankie Avalon's "Venus."

"One question," Butch said. "If you're planning on spending a lot of time around Sal, how

you planning on surviving his breath?" he asked. "Walk around with cotton balls jammed up your nostrils? Surely you haven't forgotten that, Sal, is to the City of Cohoes, what bad smells are to a zoo. Maybe you just never got a good whiff of him. Next time you see him, sidle up close to him, and then you'll know what I'm talking about."

Why is that when someone or something, smells bad, people want everyone else to take a whiff, too? Rod mused. *Another one of life's great mysteries.*

Two hours later Rod dropped Butch and Linda off at the Van Schaick Country Club's parking lot. As Butch was about to open the door to his beat-up, 1950 red Buick Roadmaster, a car that didn't look as if it had long to live, he hesitated for a moment, unwrapping a stick of Blackjack gum, popping it into his mouth.

Rod's Chevy was parked next to him, the engine idling. He always waited around to make certain that Butch's jalopy started up okay. Sometimes it did. Sometimes it didn't.

"What are you waiting for?" Rod asked. "The Buick to magically transform itself into a new Edsel?"

Butch turned and leaned down, one hand on the Chevy's door.

"Nah, but now that you mention it, if and when I ever do have enough cash, I'm leaning toward buying one of those new compact cars Chevrolet's bringing out next year. I think they're going to call it

Corbair, Corpair, or something like that. I read about it in *Mechanix Illustrated*. The engine's mounted in the rear, so it ought to be great in snow. It's a pretty good-looking car, too, even if it is a little runt. I'm thinking maybe a black one with a red interior. Oh, and hey, they're supposed to be great on gas too!"

Rod stared at him.

"Butch?"

"Huh? What?"

"*Corvair*. It's called a *Corvair*. Now then, quit beating around the bush. I know you got something to say, so just spit it out."

Butch took a deep, quick breath, expelling it in a loud whoosh.

"It's uh...just that I think you really ought to listen to Dee Dee. I mean, taking a job working for Sal can only end badly for you. Hell, you'd be the only sane guy on his payroll! Look at who he employs—a bunch of psychics like Fish!"

Even Dee Dee lifted herself from her funk long enough to giggle madly.

"Psychics?" she exclaimed. "You think that just *maybe*, you meant to say *Psychos?*"

Butch's pale cheeks turned crimson.

"Yeah, that's it," he replied sheepishly. "Okay, so Cape Canaveral ain't ever going be knocking on my door, begging me to be America's first man in space. So shoot me."

"I heard they got an opening for a monkey in a rocket, though." Linda quipped. "You ought to be able to snag that spot."

"Some girlfriend you are," he groaned.

Linda leaned over and kissed him on the cheek.

"She's only kidding you," Rod reminded him.

"Hey, I never claimed to be the next Einstein, but you got to admit, I do make one helluva best friend, now don't I?"

Rod smiled broadly.

"Well, don't I?" Butch prodded him.

"That you do, Butch. That you most certainly do."

CHAPTER 5

The following evening Rod and Dee Dee grabbed a bite to eat at Earl Gradoni's Pizza Parlor and then headed for the Latham Drive-in. The main feature was *The Blob,* a low-budget film that revolved around a gooey, amoeba-like alien from outer space that for two hours, tangles nonstop with actor Steve McQueen. To put it charitably, neither the film nor the actor were ever mentioned in the same sentence with the words—*Academy Ward*.

Rod hoped that by going to catch a couple of movies, she'd be forced into remaining silent—something he dearly wished for. She'd been hammering away at him all afternoon. Normally, he'd be thrilled to death to be on a week-long vacation. Under the current circumstances, however, it just meant that Dee Dee would have even more time than usual to pound away at him.

Ten minutes into the film and they were both bored out of their gourds. She slapped at her forearm, effectively reducing the mosquito population by one. A moment later she smashed another one into her forehead.

"Want me to put the top up?" he asked.

She swatted at yet another, this one feasting on her knee.

"I don't think it's an option anymore. Either that, or we get eaten alive."

They both got out of the car and began raising the top, one of them on either side. Once they were back inside, he levered the clamps that locked the top securely in place.

She sighed wearily, smushing yet another bug against the dashboard.

"Darn, we forgot to roll up the rear windows," she groaned as she slithered over the seat back and went to work rolling them up.

"I could've gotten them," Rod said.

"No big deal," she replied as she made herself comfortable again.

"Maybe we should've gone to the Saratoga Drive-in instead. At least they spray the area with bug killer before they open the gates. These people never do," she complained.

"They'd do everybody a big favor if they came over here right now and sprayed the movie screen, too," she went on. "This has got to be the crappiest motion picture since *The Creature from the Black Lagoon* hit the theaters in fifty-five."

"Sorry, I thought you might like it. Butch and Linda saw it two nights ago and loved it."

Dee shot him a skeptical look.

Rod shrugged.

"Well...at least Butch loved it, anyway."

She snickered.

"That's not saying much. Lord knows I love Butch to pieces, but his concept of great drama usually involves *Roy Rogers, Will Rogers or Buck Rogers,* with maybe some *Hopalong Cassidy* thrown in the mix."

Rod grinned.

"What about Ginger Rogers?" he inquired playfully.

"Only if she's dancing with Roy Rogers."

Rod threw back his head and laughed until his sides began to ache.

"Oh God, you're killing me, girl!"

She jabbed him in the ribs with her thumb.

"Don't joke about that. It could actually happen, you know. You're on pretty thin ice as it is, buster!"

"Yeah, I've kind of noticed," he replied, his laughter trailing off. "Hey, reach behind the seat and grab us a couple of cold ones, would you, Honey?"

Dee Dee dutifully complied, handing Rod his ice-cold can of Schaefer's, while also snagging one for herself.

"Now let me have the church key, will you?"

She gave him a blank look.

"I don't have one. That's your department. I figured you brought one."

"Oh, that's just great! Six cans of beer and nothing to open them with," he moaned, exasperated to no end.

"Take it easy, will you? There's probably one in the glove compartment," she suggested reasonably. "Let me check it out."

After a minute or so spent noisily rummaging around in the glove box, sure enough...she came up with a slightly bent, yet perfectly serviceable church key, the words—*Ballantine's Beer* etched into either side of it.

"Ah, that tastes great!" Rod exclaimed, downing half of the can's contents in one long swig. "By the way, how did you know the church key would be in there?"

She laughed.

"Because that's where I put it the last time we came here, genius. You need to get yourself about a dozen of them and distribute them throughout the car—a couple in the trunk, maybe one taped to the back of the battery; a few under the seats, a few more under the mats, and then you'll be all set."

"Funny. Fun–nee."

"Glad you think so," she shot back playfully.

"So what's the name of the next movie, again?" he asked.

"*Gidget*. It's one of those dumb surfing movies with Sandra Dee and James Darren."

"She must dig the sound of that name. After all, she's married to Bobby *Darin*."

"Big thrill. Who cares? She's a *has-been,* just waiting to happen," she declared. "Annette Funicello's got it all over her, and let me tell you, this Patty Duke kid is a real comer, too."

"You don't sound too enthused about watching it. Want to take off? Maybe check out what's playing at the Saratoga across the Road? There's still time to catch the second movie, if it looks good."

Dee Dee gave him a long, drawn-out sultry look.

"What?" he asked.

"I'm going to cut you some slack tonight, Hot Rod, but only if you promise to reconsider your decision to take that job."

He sighed, his eyes rolling upward, about to respond to her wholly unreasonable request when she suddenly raised a finger to his lips, effectively scuttling his intended reply.

"Just think about it some more before you jump into the fire, okay? That's all I ask. Just give it some more thought."

Rod slowly and reluctantly nodded his agreement.

"Promise?" she asked.

He raised a couple of fingers in the air.

"Scout's Honor."

An impish smile bloomed across her beautiful face.

"Cross your heart and hope to die?"

"Yep, that too."

"How do I know you're not lying, just trying to get on my good side tonight?"

"Do you see my nose growing?"

"Well, no, but then I don't see it shrinking either, Pinocchio. Besides, as Milton Berle would say—*I can always tell when you're lying.*"

Rod arched his eyebrows.

"Oh, really? How?"

Dee Dee never skipped a beat.

"You're lips are moving."

He laughed.

"Then you'll just have to take my word for it."

Suddenly she leaned across the seat, wrapping her arms tightly around his neck.

"Oh, and about that idea of yours? Leaving here and heading over to the Saratoga? Forget about it," she murmured in a husky tone. "After all, one passion pit is just as good as the next."

CHAPTER 6

Rod could not have wished for a better day to take a ride up to Lake George, a major resort area about fifty miles north of Cohoes. The sun was shining brightly and the temperature was in the mid eighties, a balmy breeze helping to make the heat more tolerable.

He had an hour to kill before he was due to pick up Dee Dee. As he sat on his stoop, a million things ran through his mind. First and foremost, he'd promised to call Sal within a few days to give him his answer.

No sense in putting it off, he thought to himself as he leaned over to click off his Philco transistor radio, the plaintive lament of Paul Anka's "Lonely Boy" abruptly drifting off into silence.

As he lit a Lucky, the smoke curling into the air, his eyes wandered off to the left. There on the corner of Mangam and Vliet, stood a classic Mom and Pop grocery store. Just below, and off to the side of the hanging purple and yellow *Wagner's Ice Cream* sign, was a smaller one, a navy blue, Bell Telephone Company payphone sign.

Both of his parents were home, and with just the one phone sitting on a table in the living room, he knew that any hope for privacy was futile.

He stood up, his white tee stretched tight across his deep, muscular chest. As he began to make his way over to the store, a red Freihofer Bakery wagon slowly angled off the road, the driver guiding the weary old chestnut mare to a stop in front of the store.

As Rod climbed the steps to the entrance, the door suddenly swung open. The owner of the store, a broad-shouldered, fit man in his late thirties stood there, an apple in each hand.

"Good morning, Rod."

"How are you, John?"

The blonde-haired grocer grinned broadly.

"No complaints, my boy. No complaints at all."

Rod stepped aside so John could make his way over to the horse.

"Hey, Fred," john called out to the deliveryman.

"I got to tell you, John—this old gal kicks it up a notch whenever we get within a block of your place. She's never going to win any race, but I swear she always steps on the ol' gas from Garner Street on down. You've spoiled her rotten with this daily dose of apples," the older man claimed as he stacked his basket tray high with fresh bread, cakes and donuts.

"I'm thinking about changing her name from Kitty to *lightning*," the short, heavyset deliveryman quipped as he made his way up the steps. He'd been waging a war over the same fifty pounds gained, lost, and regained for over a decade now.

Rod followed right on his heels.

He walked over to the cooler, slid the top back and grabbed a bottle of Royal Palm orange soda. Reaching for the opener mounted on the front of the cooler, he popped the cap off and took a long swallow.

"Good morning, Rod."

"Good morning, Virginia," he replied, digging in his jeans pocket for some change. Fishing out fifteen cents, he set it down on the counter in front of the pretty woman.

"Thanks, Rod. What's going on? No work today?"

"I'm on vacation, Virginia."

"Well, good for you! Anything special planned for the day?" she asked, her warm brown eyes shining brightly.

Prior to settling down and raising a family, Virginia had been a moderately successful nightclub singer in Manhattan. Fortunately, the ensuing years had been very kind to her. Despite the inevitable wear and tear that comes with bearing, and then raising five kids, she'd nevertheless managed to retain her good looks and sparkling personality. Rod liked her a great deal.

"We're going up to Lake George, right after I make this call," he told her, heading for the payphone.

Dropping a dime into the slot, Rod suddenly felt something rubbing his against his leg.

"Hey there, Horse," he said, leaning down to pet the big black and white cat, one with a most unlikely name.

"Only here could you find a cat named *Horse* and a horse named *Kitty*," the Freihofer man remarked as he stocked the red metal rack with his goods.

Rod laughed.

"Never thought about it that way, but you're right, Fred," he agreed, as he dialed Sal's number. "It is pretty unusual."

"Coccalido Construction Company."

"Yes, could I please speak to Sal?"

The woman hesitated for a moment before answering.

"May I ask who's calling? He's very busy at the moment."

"Rod Hobbs. He's expecting my call. It's very important."

The woman seemed altogether unimpressed.

"As I said, he's very busy at the moment. I strongly suggest that you try again later in the afternoon," she replied rather haughtily.

Crap! I want to get this over with before I lose my resolve, he thought to himself.

He took a deep breath.

"Well, I strongly suggest that you tell him I'm on the line. Like I said, he's expecting the call and knowing Sal, he won't be happy to learn that you gave me the runaround, lady."

An almost palpable, icy silence filled the line as she considered her options.

"I certainly don't appreciate your rude insistence, *sir*," the woman said in a frosty tone, pausing for one frigid moment before adding, "Although it goes against my better judgment, I will, however, transfer you now to his office."

"Gee, thanks," he replied sarcastically. "That's really swell of you, lady."

"I'm transferring you now," she hissed, her words dripping with disdain.

Sal picked up on the fourth ring.

"Sal here! Hey, what'd you say to my sister, Angie? She's fit to be tied," he said in a raspy voice.

Rod gulped. *Sister!*

"I uh...figured you'd want to hear from me as soon as possible, so I had to kind of twist her arm a bit to, uh...you know, get her to put me through to you," he explained nervously.

Sal coughed, the sound of it like sandpaper on copper.

"So what's it going to be, kid? Are you coming aboard or not?" Sal growled.

Rod scratched the back of his head, nervous.

"Well, what do you think my answer is?" he replied, immediately regretting his choice of words.

Dead silence.

"Uh...Sal? Are you still there?"

"If I already knew your answer, we wouldn't be having this conversation in the first place, now would we, kid?"

Rod went a little pale around the gills.

"Sorry about that, Sal. That was stupid of me."

"Yeah, it was."

More silence.

"So what's it going be?"

Rod took a deep breath, letting it out slowly.

"I'm ready to come to work for you, Sal."

Rod could hear him puffing on his cigar.

"Good. How soon can you start?"

"Well, I'm on vacation this week. How about if I go to Hull's next Monday and give them a week's notice?" he suggested reasonably. "And then I'll do the same with the Auxiliary Cops," he added hastily.

"*Notice?*" Sal sneered. "Just forget about that notice crap. You think either of them would give you a week's notice before canning you? Never happen. Just call them both and tell them that you're moving on to bigger and better things."

"I uh...well, to be truthful, Sal, I don't know if I'd feel right about doing it that way. I think I at least owe them—"

"You don't owe them diddly-squat!" Sal snapped, cutting him off. "That stuff the church peddles about how the meek will inherit the earth?" he asked, pausing for emphasis. "Ain't ever going to happen, so just call and tell them you quit, *period*!"

"Okay," Rod replied quietly.

"Atta boy. That's what I want to hear. Okay, so finish up your vacation and then meet me around ten on Monday morning."

"At the office?"

Rod could hear him puffing away as he considered the question.

"Nah. Tell you what. Meet me at that hot dog joint in troy."

"*Hot Dog Charlie's?*"

"No, the other place. I can't think of the name of it, off the top of my head. The one on Congress Street. You know, the one with the Greek guy in the window, running a mustard ladle over the hot dogs laid out along his hairy arm, like a gorilla playing a violin."

"*Famous Lunch?*"

"Yeah, that's it. See that? You're already earning your pay! Anyway, I got to take a look at a possible job in Troy, so it's as good a place as any to meet."

"Okay, I'll see you there, then."

"Hold on there for a second. Just some words of caution—in the future, when you call here, if Angie tells you I'm busy, do yourself a favor and take her word for it."

Rod rubbed the back of his neck.

"Got it."

"Good, because I really was busy. IRS is on my back and I got my accountant in here going over some important things with me."

"Got it," Rod repeated.

"Oh, and another thing, and trust me on this—you don't want to get on Angie's bad side. Annoy her once, she might let it slide. Annoy her twice and she'll take a lead pipe to your erogenous zone. So unless you're aspiring to audition for a soprano role on the *Firestone Opera Hour*, I suggest you tread lightly around my sister. We clear on that?"

Rod felt his breath catch in his throat.

"Oh, yeah. Absolutely."

Sal snickered.

"Thought you might," he replied with a chuckle, the line suddenly going dead.

Rod removed the receiver from his ear and stared at it intently, as if somehow the receiver contained the answer to the question that was now plaguing him. *What on earth have I just done?*

From behind the burnished oak counter, Virginia glanced over at him, genuine concern on her sweet face.

"Is everything okay, Rod?"

Lost in thought, her words startled him.

"What? Oh, no, everything's fine, Virginia. I was just, uh...thinking about something, that's all."

She looked relieved.

"Well, okay then. I was just wondering. You looked kind of spooked there for a moment."

"House phone not working?" her husband John inquired, looking up from the beer cooler he was now stocking.

"No, I just wanted a little privacy with that phone call, that's all."

John's eyes took on a hint of mischief.

"You're not two-timing Dee Dee, now are you?" he teased.

A bit of red somehow managed to creep into Rod's deeply tanned cheeks.

"Aw, come on. You know better than that, John."

The grocer's face broke into a wide grin.

Virginia swatted him on the shoulder with a rolled up *Troy Record* newspaper.

"*John Daubney*—now you cut that out right this minute!"

John laughed.

"Simmer down there, Honey Bunch. He knows I'm just kidding him, now don't you, Rod?"

Rod smiled sheepishly.

"Yeah, I know, John. Well, take care, folks. I got to go pick her up now," he said, heading for the door.

"Hey, Hot Rod. Catch!"

Rod spun around just in time to snatch a shiny red Mackintosh from the air.

Grinning, he proceeded to take a big bite out of it.

John winked at him, a devilish smile playing across his face.

"Remember, an apple a day might just help keep the other girls away."

Virginia hauled off and swatted him again.

Lake George's *Million Dollar Beach* was blazing hot.

Dee Dee lowered the volume on her pink, *Admiral* transistor radio, the sound of Bobby Rydell's "Kissin' Time," barely audible now.

"I can't take any more of this," she complained as she stood up, shaking the sand from her beach towel. "Between the scorching heat and these screaming little kids, I'm ready to head over to *The Garrison* right now."

Rod removed his Foster-Grants, rubbing the red indentations on the bridge of his nose.

"I can definitely dig that," he agreed, as he too stood up. "You won't get any argument from me."

As they gathered their stuff together Dee Dee noticed a couple of sixteen year-old *wanabee* studs admiring her figure. Actually, she didn't mind, not even a bit, just so long as they observed the unwritten rule, and didn't get carried away or worse yet—get caught staring at her with their tongues hanging out by a certain Hot Rod Hobbs.

And of course, they did just that.

Rod flexed his impressive biceps as he squinted at them, narrowing his eyes like a sniper sighting down a high-powered rifle barrel.

"You boys looking for trouble?" he wanted to know, his voice menacing, his words hitting them like hurled rocks.

As one, the pimple-polka dot complexioned boys blanched, their eyes as wide as saucers.

"Uh...who, us? Oh, no, sir! We're just uh, uh—" one of them replied shakily, at a loss to find the words that just *might* extricate them from this touchy situation.

"What's that, Kid? Speak up. I can't hear you!" Rod demanded sharply, his eyes boring into them.

The other one, a skinny, acne-festooned boy, attempted to reply, but nothing came out, his mouth opening and closing like a beached fish.

Rod strained to maintain his stony glare, but just couldn't hold it any longer. A big grin suddenly broke through.

"Relax, guys. You're going to get live for another day, after all," he informed the immensely relieved boys, "A word of advice, though— you took your training wheels off too soon. You need to work on your sneak-a-peek skills, maybe go to summer school and take a course in advanced slyness, or something."

The Garrison, the popular bar on the main drag, was packed to capacity. Rod did, however, manage to snag two stools, down at the end of the long Mahogany bar.

"That was downright cruel," Dee Dee insisted as she sipped her Tom Collins.

Rod snickered, reaching for his cigarettes.

"Hey, maybe I just saved them from catching a beating somewhere down the line. Hell, I did them a favor," he replied with cock-sure certainty.

She shook her head in wonder.

"Some favor."

Now back into her street clothes, she looking like a million bucks in her pink pedal pushers and white cotton blouse, her gold hoop earrings glinting brightly against her deeply tanned cheeks.

"First time I ever saw two sunburned kids go all pale in the face," Rod quipped as blew a stream of smoke into the air.

Dee Dee put her drink down and began digging in her purse. A moment later she was applying a touchup of pink polish to her perfectly manicured nails.

"You took the job, didn't you?" she inquired softly, her eyes focused on the task at hand, her mind fixed on something else entirely.

Rod took a hard pull on his smoke, his face tightening a bit.

"How did you know?" he asked, baffled.

"I know you better than you know yourself, that's how," she replied without looking up.

He took a big swig of his Schaefer's, gently placing the empty glass back down on the coaster.

"You mad at me?"

"Mad? No. Disappointed? Yes."

"Well, I hope you'll be able to get over it," he said as he motioned for the bartender to set him up with a fresh one. "Because arguing about it, certainly won't solve anything."

"Neither will *not* arguing about it. Besides, arguing is more fun," she replied, delivering a poke to his shoulder.

"You want another one?" he asked.

She glanced at her glass, her face expressionless.

"No, I'm good."

"With more money coming in, now we'll be able to move up the wedding date, you know," he cheerfully informed her, a futile bid to alter the dynamics of the conversation.

"Hmm."

"*Hmm?* That's it? That's all?"

She put the bottle of polish down on the bar and began to gently blow on her nails, speeding up the drying process.

"Well, no. At least now, Father Ashline will get to perform the ceremony before he dies of old age."

His brow wrinkled in confusion, Rod said, "But he's not all that old."

"Exactly."

He scratched his head, clueless.

"I'm afraid you lost me."

"Just another wrong turn on the Monopoly Board of life, lover boy," she explained, patting him on the back of his wrist. "I imagine it won't be your last wrong turn, either."

"Huh?"

She leaned over and planted a juicy kiss on his lips.

"Oh, never mind, Rod. Go throw some money in the Juke box—some Patsy Cline slow stuff. I suddenly feel like dancing to some sad songs."

He rubbed his chin, more confused than ever. *Women!*

CHAPTER 7

"So you really went and did it, huh?" Butch asked, cracking open a fresh bottle of Schaeffer's for Rod.

"Yep, I really did, my friend. I really did," Rod replied, pouring his beer into a pilsner glass.

It was early Wednesday evening, just about at the midpoint of Rod's vacation. Dee Dee was getting her hair cut down at Alice's Salon on Cayuga Street, and so, Rod decided to pay his pal a visit.

"Well, good luck to you," Butch offered. "You're going to need it."

Rod gave him a dirty look.

Butch threw his hands up in surrender.

"Hey, just kidding. I was just saying, you know?"

Rod grumbled a bit before raising his glass to his lips.

"I suppose you could be worse off—like having to serve in the army, for example," Butch mused. "If not for your flat feet, and my bad knee, we'd both probably be sloshing through knee-deep mud somewhere in east bejesus, eating *Kennel-Ration* for breakfast, lunch and dinner."

Rod laughed.

"I believe it's called K–rations. *Kennel-Ration* is dog food, Butch."

"Precisely my point," Butch replied, deadpan. "And now with this nutcase, Castro, governing Cuba, how long do you think it'll be before the marines are sent over there to run that wacko commie out of there? It's going to happen, Rod. Mark my words. It's going to happen!"

Rod fired up a Lucky.

"Maybe," he replied, inhaling deeply.

"Aw, you don't believe me, I can tell. But just you watch. I might have the IQ of a Golden Crust jelly donut, but when it comes to stuff like this, I got a sick sense, and can figure out in advance what's going to go down."

Rod's eyes rolled upward.

"*Sixth*."

Butch squinted at him, puzzled.

"*Sixth* what?"

"*Sixth* sense...as opposed to *sick* sense."

"Oh, is that what they call it? Really? I didn't know," he admitted, scratching the top of his head.

"Yep."

Butch silently began wiping down the bar, embarrassed.

"I better go see if anyone else needs a drink."

An hour later Rod Picked up Dee Dee at the hairdresser's shop.

"Well?" she asked as she got into the car, her hair freshly trimmed and styled.

Rod leaned across the seat and kissed her.

"*Well?*" she repeated.

He glanced over at her as he pulled away from the curb.

"Well, *what*?" he asked, mystified.

She punched his shoulder lightly.

"My hair! You're supposed to tell me how nice it looks, dum-dum."

"Oh—*that!*" he said, assuming a look of injured innocence. "Yeah, sure, it looks great, Baby—*really, really* great, and I mean it!" And he did, her long tresses framing a fashion model's cheekbones.

"You better," she warned.

He laughed.

"Oh, I know the drill, believe me," he assured her as he pulled away from the curb. "I just seemed to have forgotten it for a moment. By the way, who was that girl you were chatting with on the way out the door?"

"The pretty one with the light brown hair? Oh, that's Laurel Fort. I went to grade school with her at St. Agnes'; A real nice kid. Anyway, she was telling me how she usually goes to the Hollywood Salon on Remsen, but decided it was time to give Alice's place a shot."

Rod made a stab at appearing interested.

"No kidding? So was she happy with the haircut that Alice gave her?"

Dee Dee raised her hand and wiggled it a bit, a so-so gesture.

"Laurel said she's probably going to give Donna Julian's salon a whirl next time, unless of course, her boyfriend, Art Charland, *really* likes how Alice did her hair today. Laurel is crazy about Art, and if he says her hair looks great, then, knowing her as well as I do, she'll be Alice's best customer."

"True love," Rod quipped.

She readily agreed as she leaned forward and switched on the radio, the soft tones of Perry Como suddenly coming through the speakers.

"*Hot Diggity-Dog Ziggity-Boom!—What you do to me-Boom!— What you do to me,*" Dee Dee sang along, effectively drowning out Mr. Como's vastly superior offering.

"You know, I got to get you one of those sweaters that he always wears on his TV show. They're even marketing them now under the name "*Perry Como Sweaters*," she informed him, just as the song mercifully ended.

Rod took a long pull on his Lucky as he turned onto Remsen Street, the small city's main drag.

"Not my style. I mean, thanks and all, but I'd never wear one."

She arched her eyebrows.

"Oh, really? And why *not*, may I ask?"

Little Richard's "Long tall Sally," started playing. Beating her to the punch, Rod leaned over and turned the radio off, unwilling to be subjected to Dee Dee's off key sing-a-long version of the hit classic.

"What'd you do that for?" she asked, clearly peeved.

He rubbed his forehead.

"Got a little headache. The music only makes it worse."

She glanced at his face, suspicious.

"Oh, really?"

"Yeah, it started a few minutes ago."

"Well, we'll just have to get you some aspirin then."

"Uh-huh."

"Pull over here. I'll run into Marra's and grab you some."

Rod dutifully glided into a spot in front of the big drug store.

As he waited for her to return, he switched the radio back on.

Tommy Edwards' velvet-smooth "All in the Game" came through the speakers.

I'm either going to have to keep some ear plugs handy, or she's going to have to take some serious singing lessons, he thought to himself.

A few moments later Dee Dee exited the store, motioning for Rod to roll down the window.

"I'm going to walk down to Walsh's Newsroom and get you something to wash these down with."

Rod nodded as she walked off, Walsh's just down a few buildings.

She was back inside the car within three minutes, her hands full. Two bottles of orange-flavored *Sun Spot* soda.

"Here," she said, handing him one. "They don't sell *Royal Palm*, so this'll have to do."

"This is fine. Thanks."

She shook two pills out of the bottle and handed them to him.

"Take these and you'll be as good as new in no time," she assured him. "You can't be riding the Tilt-a-Whirl at Hoffman's while a headache's pounding away at you."

Rod swallowed the aspirin, following it up with a deep swig of soda.

"Okay, time to rock and roll," she exclaimed, slapping her hand against the dashboard.

That said, Rod pulled out into traffic, turning onto Columbia Street, heading for Hoffman's Amusement Park in Latham.

Hoffman's offerings consisted primarily of Kiddie rides, yet they also featured a somewhat formidable Ferris wheel, along with a few other rides that promised to be memorable, if not downright stomach-churning.

"How's the headache?"

"What?" Oh, that. It's uh...gone now. Thanks to you," he quickly added.

She gave him a funny look.

"Well, okay, if you say so. Come on, I got to get you in shape before the big-time carnivals come to town," she insisted, leading him by the hand toward the Tilt-A-Whirl.

The *O.C. Buck Carnival*, along with the *Strate Shows*, were two mammoth traveling carnivals, ones that annually came to the nearby sleepy village of Menands, just a month or so apart. For two weeks each and every summer, the quiet little village roared to life, eleven acres of flat land along the Hudson River suddenly ablaze in dazzling neon glitter and glitz. If you couldn't find anything there to get your juices flowing, then you were probably dead, and just didn't know it yet.

Between the plentiful gut-wrenching rides, the incredibly greasy, yet sinfully delicious food, the abundant games of chance, the creepy fortune tellers, the freak sideshows, or the stripper tent and animal acts, they offered something for everyone.

Ahem! Just to clarify for the reader—please note that the stripper tent and animal acts were in no way connected.

At any rate, these were the carnivals that Dee Dee had just referred to, as they got in line for a jolt on the Tilt-A-Whirl.

"So, did you tell your parents yet about your new career choice?" she inquired coyly.

Rod ground out his cigarette under his heel, his eyes downcast.

"Not yet. Maybe tomorrow."

"Coward," she chided.

He sighed loudly.

"Give me a break, will you?"

She playfully poked his ribs.

"I was just saying, that's all."

Looking to lighten things up a bit, she then smoothly changed the subject.

"So, you claim that a Perry Como sweater wouldn't fit your style. Well, tell me then, *Mr. Hot Rod Hobbs*, you handsome hunk of man, you...just precisely *what,* do you perceive your style to be?" she teased, a smirk beginning to form across her perfectly shaped mouth.

The Tilt-A-Whirl came to a stop, the passengers about to extricate themselves from the tight pods.

Rod fidgeted a bit before rising to the bait, clearly a bit flustered.

"You know, sort of more along the lines of how Brando, or James Dean dress," he replied a bit sheepishly.

She gave him an appraising look as the people filed past her.

"What, no Tab Hunter or Troy Donahue look?"

Rod sneered.

"Pretty boys."

"Hmm, well I'll have to think about all this while we're spinning around. Come on, *Marlon*—all aboard!"

CHAPTER 8

Rod had no sooner walked in the door when his Dad was instantly in his face.

"Sal Coccalido called earlier. Now why would that contemptible lowlife want to talk to *you*?" he demanded to know.

His father and mother had been sitting in the parlor, the TV on, tuned in to Jack Paar, when Rod had suddenly strolled through the door. His Dad was out of his chair like a shot, pausing only to lower the volume on the Emerson TV.

Rod considered his choices, quickly concluding that he had but only one, and that was to cut to the chase. Come clean and fess up.

"I uh...took a job with him," he replied hesitantly.

His Dad was a big man, tall and thick-shouldered. His graying hair, trimmed close to the scalp, contrasted sharply with the tide of crimson now flaming across his rugged, angry face.

"You did *what*?" he roared, incensed now, twin infernos flaming in his eyes.

Rod's mom jumped up and turned off the TV.

"Take it easy now, Frank. Let's just calm down and listen to what he has to say about all this. Maybe there's more to it than meets the eye," she suggested reasonably, not for a minute, however, believing a word of it.

Frank stood there, his face beet-red, hands clenching and unclenching at his side, wide chest heaving uncontrollably, the very image of a heart attack just waiting to happen.

Rod's mom gently took her husband by the arm, slowly leading him to the sofa.

"There now," she said soothingly, as they sat down together on the plastic slip-covered floral sofa.

Gazing over at her handsome son, her bright brown eyes fixed him with a hard, no-nonsense, reproving glare, the kind of look that sons the world over immediately recognize, instantly fear and invariably wilt under.

"All right, son. Let's get on with it. Spill the beans," the aging brunette beauty said evenly, her hands tightly clasped together on her lap. At forty-four and still slender, Elinor Hobbs had been a professional stage dancer in her youth, and still looked as though she could probably wow an audience.

Rod sat down heavily in his mother's chair, his elbow dislodging a lace doily from an arm. Bending down, he picked it up and placed it back on the chair, smoothing it out with the palm of his hand.

"You know, Mom, I never have understood why you put doilies on something that's already protected by plastic."

His mother shot him a wintry glare.

"You're stalling, Rod. Quit it."

"Yeah, I suppose I was," he admitted weakly. "Well, okay, here's the deal: Sal offered me a forty hour job at twice the salary that I make now, putting in fifty hours. How could I *not* take him up on his offer?"

Rod's father was seething, his son's words, like a glass of ice water in the face.

"Easy—you just say no!" he bellowed, rage and frustration emanating from him, like heat from a radiator.

"I can't!" Rod snapped, his own temper now beginning to flare.

His Mom quickly raised her hands, palms outward.

"Stop yelling—both of you!" she commanded. "There's no need for either of you to be screaming like lunatics. What are the neighbors going to think?"

"Who the hell cares what they think?" Frank groused, yet in a noticeably lower voice. "Bunch of old busy-bodies."

Rod nervously lit a Lucky, blowing the smoke out the side of his mouth.

"Look, Dad, me and Dee Dee want to get married, right? Well, at the rate I've been going, I'm not going to be able to afford to get married until I'm thirty. It's so hard to save anything on the measly salary I make!"

Frank sighed deeply, willing himself to take his anger down a notch.

"You got a good shot at becoming a full-fledged mechanic before the year is out. Old man Hull told me that himself," Frank countered reasonably. "You'll be making another two bucks an hour. What's wrong with that?"

"I don't want to be a mechanic, that's what's wrong with it!" he fired back, his own anger rising to the surface.

His dad waved his objection off, as if it were just so much empty talk.

"You don't want to be a mechanic? Ha! During the depression, when I was a kid, a man would kill to get a job as a mechanic!" he spat, truly disappointed in his son. "So instead of aspiring to earn an honest day's wages as a mechanic, you're going to work for that crooked scoundrel, Coccalido? What the hell's the matter with you?" he growled, his voice rising once more.

"What exactly is it that you're going to be doing for him?" Elinor interrupted, her brow wrinkled in worry.

"Security work, mostly," Rod replied, grateful for his mom's question. Anything to get his father off his back, even if only for a moment, was more than welcome.

"Mostly?" his father echoed. "For God's sakes—" he erupted, his wife rapidly cutting him off.

"Frank! Will you *please* calm down?"

The big man grimaced as he stood and pointed an accusing finger at Rod.

"Here I am a retired cop and what does my only son want to do? Why, Mr. Big Shot wanabee goes to work for a crook, a guy with mob connections that go back forty years! That's a helluva thing, that is!" he snarled, heading for his bedroom. "I wash my hands of you!"

Frank slammed the bedroom door shut behind him, the Hummel collection in Elinor's curio cabinet violently quaking and shaking, threatening to crash through the fragile glass door at any moment.

Elinor jumped up and ran toward the cabinet, gently grasping either side of it, holding it steady until the little figurines ceased their perilous rocking motion.

"If even just *one* of these were damaged, I'd kill him," she mumbled under her breath.

Rod stood and stretched.

"I'm going to bed now, Mom," he told her, barely stifling a yawn.

She let go of the cabinet, satisfied that her precious knickknacks had survived the assault, still intact. Turning to face her son, she somehow managed to smile.

"Your father will get over it, provided you stay on the straight and narrow, and not get involved in anything more than this so-called *security* work," Elinor said unconvincingly as she kissed her son softly on the cheek. "Just promise me that if this Sal character tries to involve you in anything illegal, that you'll hit the door running. Can you promise your mother that?"

"Yes, Mom, I promise," he vowed, hugging her gently.

Stepping back, she gave her son a thoughtful, appraising look.

"If only you could carry a tune. With your looks, Dick Clark would snap you up in a Philadelphia minute," she mused, "Maybe you ought to write him a letter, with some photos included. What the heck, you're a dead ringer for that Fabian kid and let's face it— Truth be told, he can't really sing a lick either!"

Rod called Sal the following morning. His father, still seriously miffed, had been reading the morning paper in the living room which ruled out any possibility of using the home phone, so he headed for the corner store payphone across the street.

After exchanging quick pleasantries with Virginia, he slipped a dime into the slot and dialed Sal's number. It was busy. He waited a minute and then redialed. It was still busy. Sighing impatiently, he hung the receiver back on the hook.

"No answer?" Virginia inquired, a warm smile on her face.

"No. I'll give it a minute and then try again. Want to give me a pack of *Sen-Sen,* please?" he asked as he reached into the soda cooler, extracting a bottle of orange flavored *Royal Palm.*

"Let me have one of those tins of *Between-the-acts,* too, if you don't mind, Virginia. Your son, Chick, tells me they're pretty good, so I'm going to give them a try," he said with a smile.

Virginia wrinkled her nose in distaste.

"My son, Paul, or as you kids refer to him—*Chick,* is going to be in hot water if I catch him smoking these little cigars," she warned ominously. "Sixteen is too young to be smoking anything!"

Rod's grin foundered. *Great, now you got the kid in trouble, Big Mouth,* Rod thought to himself.

"Well, actually I can't honestly recall who it was that told me about them. It may have been Chick, but then again, I probably heard it from someone else—Roger Trudell, most likely. My memory isn't all that hot, Virginia," he lied as he put sixty cents down on the counter.

She gave him a dubious look.

"Your memory isn't very good? At twenty-one years old? Ha! Tell me another one."

Rod gave her an "aw, shucks" look, his face reddening a bit. Desperate to change the subject, he asked Virginia how her oldest son, Bob, a professional bowler, was faring these days.

"Oh, Bob is doing just great! He's bowling in a tournament in St. Louis right now!" she boasted, her face beaming with pride.

"Really? Wow, that's wonderful," he replied, leaning down to pet the cat, the feline with the wholly unlikely name of *Horse.*

"Excuse me, Virginia. I'm going to give that number another try now," he said, walking over to the phone, the big cat trailing just behind.

This time he got through. Sal's sister, Angie, answered the phone.

"Uh...could I please speak to Sal?" Rod asked softly, his tone as polite as he could possibly muster.

"Who's calling?"She barked.

Rod gulped.

"It's uh...Rod Hobbs."

Dead silence, her boiling contempt for Rod, the only thing coming through, soundlessly transmitting itself over the line, like scalding hot water through a copper pipe.

"Oh, it's *you*," she eventually acknowledged, her words dripping with acid.

"Uh...yes. Could I um...please speak to Sal now?" he asked hesitantly. "If you don't mind, that is," he quickly added.

More silence.

"Hold on. I'll see if he wants to take your call," she said icily.

"Thank you," he answered softly.

"Sal here!"

"Yeah, Sal, it's Rod. I understand you called the house looking for me."

"That's right. I did. Your old man didn't sound too happy about it, either," Sal grumbled.

Rod sighed.

"Sorry about that."

"I'd like to know what the hell I ever did to him."

"I don't know, Sal," Rod replied, pausing to take a deep breath. "Don't pay any attention to him. He's just gotten kind of grouchy since he retired. Sorry if you feel as though he insulted you."

"I couldn't ever be insulted by your old man's attitude. In order to feel insulted, I'd have to first value his opinion and I certainly *don't*!" he spat, his tone as sharp as a razor.

"Anyway, the reason I called your house was because I need to move up your starting date to tomorrow," he explained, his voice calmer now.

"Tomorrow? But I'm not supposed to start until Monday, remember?"

"Yeah, well, things change quickly in my business. You may as well get used to it now, Rod. Anyway, about tomorrow—come down to the office at nine."

"With uh...all due respect, Sal, I think you forgot that I'm on vacation and already have plans for tomorrow," he reminded him.

"Tomorrow at nine! Be here," Sal growled just before the line went dead.

What have I gotten myself into?

CHAPTER 9

They had planned on spending the day at Crooked Lake. Those plans, however, went right out the window after Rod's conversation with Sal. To say that Dee Dee was disappointed at hearing the news, would be like referring to the Cohoes mastodon as just another elephant. She went up one side of Rod and right down the other.

"I can't believe this!" she exploded over the phone. "You're supposed to be on vacation until Monday!"

And so it went. He let her vent, never once interrupting the flow of her wrath. Once she'd run out of gas, her displeasure trickling off into a pool of icy silence, Rod sheepishly admitted that he didn't blame her a bit, *yet what could he do?* He'd already begun scaling a slippery slope the day he agreed to sign on with Sal, and there was definitely no going back now, he explained. His hands were tied, for despite Sal's words to the contrary, Rod had gone ahead and given notice at both jobs.

Rather than offer a few words of sympathetic understanding, which was what Rod was hoping for, Dee Dee hung up on him. *So much for understanding.*

Rod showed up at nine sharp. The construction company was located in a dilapidated building off of Cataract Street, in an area known colloquially as the *Orchard*. The rambling two-story frame structure had seen better days. Green asbestos shingles were peeling off the exterior in sheets, most of the windows had hairline cracks in the glass, and the roof was sagging inward. *Certainly not much of an advertisement for a construction company*, Rod mused.

The doorway was ringed with strands of filthy Christmas lights, lights that obviously never came down. He attempted to open the door, but to no avail. Badly warped, the door wouldn't budge. Giving it another try, he grasped the doorknob firmly, turned it, and then pushed forward with all of his weight behind it. With a God awful, hellacious screech, the old oak door suddenly sprung open, Rod's forward motion propelling him straight into the receptionist's metal desk. Bracing himself as best he could for the inevitable impact, his hands took the brunt of it, his palms slamming into the steel edge of the big gray desk.

Embarrassed and more than a little shaken, Rod slowly raised his eyes, his face scant inches from a female countenance that putting it charitably, could stop London's Big Ben clock in mid-tick. *This must be Angie*, Rod thought to himself. *Great—as if she didn't already hate me!*

If, as the old adage goes, looks could kill, then Rod would have bought the farm right then and there. The razor-sharp, deadly daggers that her eyes were hurling at him would have put a tiger out of business.

"Let me guess. You must be that Hobbs guy, the one who goes out of his way to irritate me," she hissed. "Most people who come in here usually just open the door, like any normal person would, but you? You come flying through like a bull looking to skewer a matador! What the hell's the matter with you anyway?" the seething woman snarled. "You ever hear of manners, or are you seriously underdeveloped in that department, too?"

Rod didn't even attempt a reply. He correctly sensed that a battle of verbal volleyball with the witch would only end badly for him. He'd already gotten off on the wrong foot with her, and now he'd only made things worse.

"Hey, I asked you a question, sonny boy. Are you deaf, too, on top of having a room temperature IQ?"

"I'm sorry," he replied softly. "The door was stuck and just wouldn't move."

"No one else ever seems to have a problem with it sticking," she retorted as she attempted to readjust her hairdo.

Rod guessed her to be about sixty-five years old. At five feet tall and of a corresponding width, Angie was built along the lines of a short, stubby Sumo wrestler. Round-faced with a head like a cannonball, her pinched puss featured a hooked, hawk-like nose, set off by a faint, yet noticeable moustache and dark, deep-set eyes that at the moment, glowed like burning embers. Her thick, bushy, caterpillar-like eyebrows were long overdue for a good mowing, and her downturned mouth suggested the look of the perpetually disappointed, a look that probably fit her to a tee. *Cohoes' answer to the "The Bride of Frankenstein?"* he thought to himself.

It was her hair, however, that held Rod transfixed with amazement. Blue-rinsed, it was piled high into a tall B*ouffant*, all fluffy and poufy, wide at the base and narrowing at the top, bringing to mind an upside down cone. Soaring high, like a billowy cloud of blue-white cotton candy, Rod stared as the woman attempted to right the cone, much as a sea captain would try to right his listing ship. Try as she might, however, Angie couldn't seem to prevent the ever-increasing sideways tilt from toppling right over.

Cursing up a storm, she yanked open a desk drawer and pulled out a can of *Aqua-net* hair spray. While supporting the perilously teetering spire with one hand, she vigorously sprayed up one side of the cone, then reversing hands, attacked the other side.

Her gravity-defying efforts almost went for naught, however. Convinced that her *Leaning Tower of Pisa* hairdo was no longer in danger of toppling sideways to the ground, Angie attempted to remove her hand from the side of her head. Unfortunately, the sticky, heavy-duty hair spray had pretty much bonded her pudgy hand to her hair. Cursing like a sailor, she gingerly worked to free her hand, her goal realized only after a few long, tense moments had passed.

"See how much trouble you've caused me, crashing through the door and into my desk like a runaway freight train?" she spat. "Sal needs his head examined, hiring a lamebrain like you!"

Unbeknownst to her, Sal was standing right behind her, at the entrance to his office, taking it all in. He didn't look particularly happy.

"What's all the damn commotion out here?" he growled, his eyes puffy, his face as pasty and gray as week-old pizza dough.

What had been a frosty atmosphere to begin with, the temperature in the cramped room now plummeted from merely cold to sub-zero and icy, all in a Cohoes minute.

Rod fidgeted, nervously shifting his weight from one foot to the other.

"Sorry, it was my fault, Sal," he admitted, a hangdog expression on his face.

"Yeah, well, sorry don't cut it," Angie interjected hotly. "If you expect to last around here, then you better shape up, buster!"

Sal glared at her, flashing the side of his gnarled hand across his throat, a universal gesture, one that more than suggested she needed to zip her mouth shut.

Tougher than a week-old steak though she may have been, Angie nevertheless clammed right up, her lips pursed together tightly. From Rod's viewpoint, Sal may as well have just issued a command to his dog, a surly family member, one well acquainted with the consequences that come with defying its cruel master.

"Come on in, Rod," Sal barked.

I wouldn't be surprised to learn that she files down her teeth into fangs, either, he mused, as he followed Sal into the grungy looking office.

Everything was coated with a thick layer of dust, or more to the point—good ol' crud. From the creaky, cracked tile floor to the beat-up desk and sagging file cabinets, not a square inch was spared a veneer of greasy grime. Even the drab, mustard colored walls, probably last painted a bright yellow around the turn of the century, were generously streaked with some indefinable and indeterminable form of rank, darkly ominous mold. Like a shiver on the prowl, looking for a fresh, unsuspecting spine to run up, the room seemed to take on a life of its own, silently transmitting an eerie, inherently evil warning to all who dared to walk into it. '*A word to the wise—enter at your own risk,*' it seemed to caution.

Suddenly Rod shook his head vigorously, as if by doing so, he could rid himself of his far-fetched and totally absurd thoughts.

Sal gave him a curious look.

"You got a headache or something?" he asked, firing up one of his stinking cigars.

"Nah, I was just uh...aah, forget it. It was nothing."

Sal studied Rod as he leaned back in his rickety old wooden chair, a wreath of cigar smoke nearly obscuring his face.

"Why do I get the impression you don't exactly approve of my surroundings?" he asked, his voice raspy, his words tinged with displeasure.

Rod didn't really know what to say, so he opted to just wise-guy it. *Not at all a good choice.*

"Well, it's just that it looks like it would make a perfect setting for that Boris Karloff TV show, that creepy one called '*Thriller.*' Add some cobwebs and it might even work for an episode of the *Twilight Zone,*" he deadpanned, all the while holding his breath. *I must have a death wish!*

"You must not be married, Sal," he unwisely continued. "Either that, or your wife has never once come here to visit," he remarked matter-of-factly, a hint of a smirk beginning to form at the corner of his mouth.

Sal puffed hard on his Cuban stogie, taking it out of his mouth just long enough to send a thick stream of pungent smoke straight into Rod's face.

"No wife. Never had one and never will, not that it's any of your business, mind you," he replied, pausing to take another hit from his cigar. "I'll tell you what. Put a cork in the nickel and dime, wiseass comments and I won't fire you the first day on the job. Think you can handle that, *Hot Rod*?" he asked, heavy on the sarcasm.

"As for your cutesy comments regarding the décor in here, let's just say that I like it just the way it is," he continued. "To my way of thinking, this place has real character, and was I, say, in a rash moment, to suddenly decide to clean it up, slap some paint on the walls, etc...well, then it just wouldn't ever be the same. The place would lose its *Mojo*, if you follow what I'm saying here."

"*Mojo?*"

"That's right—*Mojo.*"

"Well, okay then. Now that we got that out of the way, you want to tell me what you expect of me today?"

"First things first. You need to run back home and change into some work duds. What's with the snazzy outfit? You look like you're going to the "Love Letters in the Sand" Sunday afternoon dance at St. Augustine's, or something," Sal groused.

He was right, though. Rod had foolishly decked himself out in a black and white paisley shirt, black, pegged gabardine slacks and a pair of *Pat Boone style* white bucks.

"You can't wear clothes like that around a construction site. What the hell were you thinking anyway, coming here dressed like that?"

Embarrassed, Rod mumbled something unintelligible in reply.

"Here's five bucks," Sal said, flipping the bill across the desk. "Swing by the White Eagle Bakery on your way back and pick up three dozen assorted donuts. Be back here in forty minutes."

Rod shoved the greasy bill into his pocket as he stood up.

"Another thing—you got to lift up on the door as you turn the handle. Got that?"

"Got it," Rod replied sheepishly as he pulled Sal's door shut behind him.

Angie was busy writing notes on a legal pad. She looked up and glared at him, her face, one that only a snapping turtle could love—round, pugnacious and severely wrinkled.

As he strode toward the old warped door, he said a little prayer, asking for some divine intervention, should it be required.

Fortunately, none was needed. As instructed, he carefully lifted up on the stubborn door while simultaneously turning the knob. The old girl popped right open with nary a hitch. But for a loud squeak emanating from the dry hinges, Angie may not have even noticed him.

"Make sure you get at least two of the custard-filled ones!" she snapped, without ever once looking up.

Rod didn't bother to reply. Five minutes later he was home. Fortunately, his parents had already left to go shopping at *Monkey Ward's*. That was fine with him. He wasn't in the mood for another go-around with his Dad. Changing his clothes quickly, he was back out the door in no time flat.

He needed gas, so Rod stopped at Rivet's Amoco station on Columbia Street. After forking over four bucks and change to the attendant, young Jim Vore, one helluva great kid, he then headed for the bakery. The delectable aromas emanating from the *White Eagle* could be detected from a block away. Fortunate to have snagged a parking spot right in front of the popular bakery, he was in and out within five minutes.

The good news was that this time, Sal's front door cooperated. The bad news? Somehow or other, Rod had managed to drop the box of donuts onto the floor.

"When it comes to clumsiness, it looks like you have unlimited potential. Let me guess—your favorite candy bar must be *Butterfingers*," Angie remarked drolly. "My donuts better not have been smushed, donkey-boy."

Fortunately, all of the donuts had survived the collision with the floor. Dipping her meaty paws into the box, Angie lifted each of her donuts into the air, inspecting them from a variety of angles, searching for imperfections. Grudgingly satisfied, she made short work of them.

Sal stood in the doorway, his old brown fedora in hand.

"Grab that box and let's go."

"Here's your change, Sal," Rod said as they walked over to Sal's 1959 Cadillac Eldorado.

"Keep it," he replied, sliding in behind the wheel of the dusty black behemoth.

"But it's a couple of bucks."

"Forget about it," he scoffed, waving off the money. "Now then, I'm going to take you over to the site, introduce you around, and then I'll fill you in on your job duties."

Rod nodded as he pushed the power button for the window on the passenger side. Sal had just lit up another stogie, instantly filling the land yacht with thick, gray smoke. The interior of the car stunk to high hell.

Sal snickered.

"Yeah, it probably does smell a little ripe in here. Better get used to it, kid."

"No problem, Sal," he lied. *A little ripe? That's like saying Noah's Ark only stunk a little*, he mused.

Three minutes later Sal turned left off of Mohawk Street, guiding the big Caddy through a set of open gates and down a temporary access road. The deep ruts in the dirt road caused the car to sway and fishtail, jolting Rod and sending Sal's cigar ashes onto his lap.

As Sal parked in front of a pair of construction trailers, Rod asked: "I'm surprised you bring this car down here. It's got to be murder on the suspension and the exhaust system. Don't you have a pickup you could use?"

Sal got out of the car, ignoring Rod's question.

As they walked over to one of the trailers, Sal stopped to stub out his cigar.

"Yeah, I got plenty of pickups, but they ain't my style. I'm a Caddy guy, through and through," he explained as he yanked the flimsy trailer door open. "If this one goes belly-up from being bounced around construction sites, then I'll just go get me a new one. *That's* the beauty of being a rich guy, kid," Sal boasted, smirking.

The interior of the construction trailer was about what you'd expect. The furnishings consisted of a scarred-up old desk, a few wobbly chairs, and a dented metal file cabinet along with a folding table that was home to a large bundle of blueprints. A two year old *Dzembo's Dairy* calendar complemented the décor perfectly.

Sal tossed his keys onto the desk.

"Grab the donuts out of the back seat," he ordered, glancing at his watch. "It's break time, feeding time at the zoo."

Rod responded dutifully, making his way out the door just as a guy the size of a gorilla brushed past him, stopping just long enough to give Rod a hard, appraising glance. Sneering, the big ape then continued on his way, two more behemoths hard on his heels.

Back inside now, the box of donuts in his hands, Rod got a closer look at the three men. The one who'd given him the wiseguy sneer was about thirty, maybe six foot-four and an easy three hundred, not an ounce of which appeared to be anything other than pure muscle. His biceps stood out like twin cantaloupes, his broad shoulders supporting a tree stump of a neck and a head like a basketball. *Must be related to Angie*, he thought to himself.

He had a butch-waxed crew cut, the jowls of a Saint Bernard, an Adam's apple the size of a tennis ball, a smashed in nose, mean pig-like eyes, and a mouthful of bad teeth. The gap between the two front ones was wide enough to accommodate a couple of pencils. *Yeah, definitely related to Angie.*

The other two were cut from the same cloth—triplets, would be Rod's guess. A trio of goons that God must have assembled from a box of spare, mismatched parts. All three had pronounced harelips and possessed that flat, vacant, emotionless look in their eyes, a look usually associated with the genetically defective, guys a few notches down on the evolution chart, sandwiched somewhere between the Cro-Magnons and Tarzan's furry friend, *Cheetah,* the chimp.

Suspicious though they were of this stranger in their midst, their gluttonous appetites quickly overrode any further thoughts about Rod.

As the three made short work of the donuts, Sal leaned back in his chair, puffing on his stogie, a canopy of thick smoke settling in under the low ceiling.

"Let me introduce you guys to each other. Rod, these are my nephews, Angie's triplets, *Sleepy, Dopey and Happy*. The one with white powdered sugar all over his mouth is Dominic or as I like to call him—*Dopey*."

"The one with the droopy eyes? That's Angelo, better known as *Sleepy.* Then there's Tony, the one with the piece of bloody tissue stuck to his chin. I nicknamed him *Happy* because the last time he smiled, was when he punched out a nun in fifth grade."

"Saint Agnes'. It was Sister Pascal and she had it coming, let me tell you," Happy elaborated between bites of his jelly donut. "It made my day," he boasted, pumping his arm in the air. Happy looked as if you could strike a match across his teeth and he wouldn't flinch.

"Yeah, subtlety never was Happy's strong point. Taken as a group, their combined IQ is about the same as the city speed limit, but when it comes to loyalty, they'll put a trio of German Shepherds to shame every time," he crowed with cocksure finality.

"Boys, this is Rod Hobbs, or as he likes to be called—*Hot Rod* Hobbs. He's the kid I was telling you about. Rod's an all right guy."

Happy stopped eating abruptly, his small, dark eyes boring into Rod, calculating, as though measuring him for a coffin.

"Is that right? Are you *really* an all right guy?" he probed, squinting, as though he were lining Rod up in a telescopic sight.

"That's what they tell me," Rod replied without the slightest hesitation.

The big man smiled, exposing a line-up of the largest teeth Rod had ever seen, bringing to mind a row of weather-worn, decaying tombstones.

"We'll see," Happy grumbled as he offered Rod his meaty mitt.

Rod took the proffered hand in his, knowing full well what to expect next. Sure enough, Happy immediately attempted to crush Rod's hand in his vise-like grip, squeezing the bones together for all he was worth, certain that he'd bring the new man to his knees where he'd tearfully beg Happy to let go.

He'd figured wrong, however. Although the border-line psycho was exerting incredible pressure on his hand, the torque as unrelenting as a toothache, Rod wasn't about to cave in. With his facial expression blank, Rod gave as good as he got. The big ape glowered as it slowly dawned on him that this wasn't working out the way it normally did.

"You ought to smile once in a while, Happy. It's good for your face," Rod quipped.

His words hung in the silence, like an unexpected slap to the chops.

Rod's comment from out of the blue threw the dimwit into a stew of confusion, bringing to mind the old 'Can't chew gum and walk at the same time' adage, for no sooner were the words uttered when Happy suddenly released his grip on Rod's hand. Evidently ol' Happy couldn't squeeze a man's hand and think at the same time.

Believing that he'd somehow been tricked and made a fool of, he reacted the only way he knew how—with anger.

"Don't ever call me Happy again. Only my uncle gets away with calling me that. You call me Tony, or better yet—don't talk to me at all," he warned, his jowls quivering as he fixed a menacing scowl upon his craggy face.

"Take it easy now," Sal interceded soothingly. "I don't want you guys getting off on the wrong foot," although clearly, that train had already left the station. Rod correctly sensed that he'd just made an enemy for life.

As if to further drive that point home, the jumbo-sized galoot suddenly made a big show out of forming a fist, his knuckles badly scarred, no doubt from innumerable collisions with other people's teeth.

"All right, that's enough!" Sal snapped, losing his patience, a quality he was never known for in the first place.

"The three of you—back to work!"

As the trio of cavemen began lumbering dutifully out the door, each of them hesitated just long enough to shoot Rod a threatening glare, a look normally associated with a rabid wolf.

Sal threw his feet up on the desk, the smoke from his cigar curling up and over his nicotine-stained fingers.

"The three blind mice, screwed from the moment they were born. I probably ought to get them fitted for Mouseketteer hats. You know, most men aspire to be more than they are. As you can see, my nephews aspire to be less. Not a one of them could rub two thoughts together on their best day. Collectively, they got the brains of a pound of pork chops, but what can I do?" he whined plaintively. "They're family. Besides, if I didn't give them a job, then who in the hell would?" he wondered aloud, clearly exasperated by the burden he'd been saddled with.

Rod correctly sensed that Sal's question hadn't necessarily been posed to him, but rather to the world at large and as such, Rod didn't feel a need to reply.

Sal rubbed at his eyes.

"You're going to *have* to learn to get along with them," he warned.

"Don't worry. I can handle them," rod replied confidently.

"Yeah, if I were you, I'd *really* work on learning how to handle them," Sal suggested, his tone as sharp as his barber, Bernie Heroux's razor.

The significance of his pointed words wasn't lost on Rod. *How am I going get along with three guys who are running about two quarts low on brain oil?*

"So there you have it, Rod. They're the only men I can completely trust, yet they're incapable of ever getting the goods on whomever it is, that's robbing me blind. *Incapable?* Hmm, did I say that? Yeah, that about fits them to a tee," he mused." They're about as capable of being aware of what's going on around them, as three corpses in Fitzgerald's funeral parlor."

Rod didn't quite know how to respond to Sal's display of frustration so once again, he wisely opted to remain silent.

Seemingly lost in thought, Sal rubbed his thumb over the top of his huge diamond ring, a ring big enough to serve as an anchor for Lake George's paddlewheel boat—the *Minne—Ha-Ha.*

"Okay, enough of this. Come on, I'll show you around the job site. Grab a hardhat off the top of that file cabinet and follow me."

Once outside in the blinding sunlight, Sal pointed in the direction of a group of workers that were milling around a stainless steel-sided *roach coach*, sipping coffee from disposable cups.

Sal placed two fingers in his mouth, letting loose with a shrill whistle.

"Break's over, boys. Get back to work."

As the men began to wander off, Rod recognized a face he hadn't expected to see there. It was Lenny Fishowski, the part time gambler and full time bully who'd attempted to humiliate Butch, and intimidate Rod a few weeks back at Bourkie's Blunder Bar.

"I didn't know Fish worked for you, Sal."

"He's my foreman. You two know each other?"

"Yeah, but somehow I never thought of Fish as being a fan of regular work."

Sal stopped dead in his tracks, his eyes taking on a sharper intensity as he considered the implication in Rod's statement.

"You'd never know it. He's worked for me for three years, never missing a damn day. Why'd you say that about him, anyway? You know something that I don't?" he asked suspiciously, his face taut, the skin as tight as the fabric on a lampshade.

Rod cleared his throat. "Nope. It was just an idle observation, that's all."

Sal nodded, evidently satisfied with Rod's explanation. They moved on, heading down the recently bulldozed road, toward the river. Huge earthmovers of every description were clanking and clattering away, the air acrid with diesel fumes.

Sal came to a stop mere inches from the lip of a gigantic pit. Front end loaders, dump trucks, bulldozers, you name it, and it was down there.

"What exactly is it that you're going to construct here?" Rod inquired.

"I'm building an auxiliary hydroelectric plant. You see those waterfalls over there?" he asked, pointing in the direction of the breathtaking sight. At a height of ninety feet and over a thousand feet in width, the sight of the Cohoes Falls churning and roaring at full blast, was indeed enough to take a person's breath away. It was that impressive.

"Well, a brain trust of top notch state engineers recently concluded that there's a heap more power in them there falls, just begging to be harnessed. Consequently, they decided to have an additional plant built and I'm the one who's building it."

"But I'll be damned if I'm going to let anyone steal equipment off of this site!" he stormed, his face hardening, his eyes colder than February ice.

"What's been stolen? I mean, what kind of equipment has disappeared, and how did the thieves get in here?"

"They used a bolt cutter or something to snap the padlocks in half. Three padlocks! Two weeks ago, it was a portable generator. Then last week another one was stolen, along with a number of expensive power tools. The list of stolen stuff goes on and on! What really bugs me, though, is that all of it was swiped while my nephews were supposedly keeping an eye on things at night!" he spat, his dark anger churning like boiling tar. "My sister should have had herself spayed, neutralized or sterilized! Three *Howdy-Doodies* with the IQ's of a bag of horseshoes!"

"Did you file a report with the cops?"

"The cops? Yeah, as if they'd ever lift a finger to even try to catch the thieves!"

Rod backed away a step, not out of any fear, but rather to avoid yet another blast of Sal's fetid breath. *The man needs to gargle with Clorox!*

Sal puffed hard on his stogie in an attempt to calm himself down.

"Anyway, that's why I put them back on the site as helpers. Strong backs—weak minds. That's where you come in. For the time being, until we catch whoever these clowns are, you'll be working nights, Monday through Friday. Somebody else will cover the weekends."

"Nights?"

"Yes, nights! That's when cockroaches operate—when it's dark. Nobody's going to swipe anything in the daylight!"

"Okay, but just one question—what am I supposed to if indeed I do catch him, or *them*? Make like a citizen's arrest or something, and if so, with what? I can't exactly point my finger at them, making believe it's a gun."

"I got a throwaway piece for you, a thirty-eight with the serial numbers filed off."

Rod thought he must be joking, but he wasn't.

"You'll start Monday night. I'll give it to you then, along with a twelve gauge that you'll patrol the site with."

Rod did a double-take, not quite believing his ears.

"Uh, excuse me, but don't I need a permit to carry a pistol?"

Sal waved Rod's concern off.

"Don't worry about it. You're covered. Take my word for it. Besides, it's only intended to serve as a backup and you don't need a permit to carry a shotgun on the site," he assured Rod.

Truth be told, Rod didn't feel at all assured.

"I don't know about this," he admitted, clearly uneasy now. "I didn't think I'd be carrying weapons."

Sal pulled a cigar from his pocket and slowly removed the wrapper, his fingers rolling the cellophane into a tight little ball. He then jammed the stogie into his mouth as he hunted around in his shirt pocket for a match. After lighting it, he yanked the stinking cigar out of his mouth and shook it in Rod's face.

"Did I say anything about shooting anybody? The guns are just intended to hold these two-bit thieves until I get here."

Rod was puzzled.

"You mean, until the cops get here?"

Sal squinted speculatively at him, his mind processing Rod's words, considering how best to respond. Suddenly he smiled a humorless smile, his cold eyes glinting, his yellowed teeth barred, bringing to mind the image of a demented baboon. Pointing a finger at Rod, he then cocked his thumb, as though aiming a pistol, and made a popping sound with his tongue.

"Sometimes life presents certain people with a bill, and then demands immediate payment. You know what I mean? Guys just begging to get their tickets punched?"

Rod felt as though his blood had suddenly turned to ice water.

"I don't think I'd ever want to have you for an enemy, Sal," Rod replied, wondering if perhaps Sal wasn't a few arrows short in the ol' quiver.

He shot Rod a glacial glare. "No, you most definitely wouldn't. All of my enemies are in the graveyard."

"We'll discuss some other things in detail later on, son," he went on. "All you need to know, right now, is that a man is the sum total of what he owns, and the loss of even *one* possession diminishes his self worth," he snarled, his tone as cold and biting as January wind. "People that have stolen from me usually find themselves wishing that they hadn't."

A ripple of uneasiness ran down Rod's spine.

The balance of the day was spent learning his way around the site, filling out employment forms, and being introduced to key personnel, men such as Lenny Fishhowski. Rod would've gladly skipped over that aspect of the day.

Fish eyed him coldly from the get-go.

"Well, what do you know? If it ain't *Hot Rod* himself, in the flesh!" Fish sneered as he lit a Chesterfield.

"What do you say, Fish?" Rod mumbled in a low-effort attempt at cordiality.

"This is a surprise—you working for Sal," the big man replied, uncharacteristically edgy, like a guard dog that senses something dangerous approaching.

"Yeah, well, good paying jobs are hard to come by these days, so I consider myself fortunate that Sal decided to hire me."

Wrapped in a thick blanket of smugness, Fish replied cryptically: "True enough. Even a blind squirrel occasionally trips over a juicy acorn."

Rod glared at him.

"Funny."

Sal threw up his hands, his face tightening with irritation.

"Okay, enough with the verbal wrestling. You two may be working together from time to time, so I strongly suggest that you lose the attitude, boys," Sal warned them as he tossed Rod a set of keys.

"They're for that green Chevy *Apache* pickup, the one parked next to the trailer. You can use it for now, so you don't have to worry about destroying the undercarriage of your car. Bring somebody down to the office later to drive your car home," Sal suggested.

"Oh, and don't forget that today's Friday, so no eating meat," he cautioned, a rare attempt at humor. "Not even one bite. No such thing as a *semi-sin*, you know."

"I won't," Rod lied as he envisioned the thick, juicy meatball torpedo he had his heart set on eating tonight at Gradoni's.

"And don't forget to say Grace before you eat your seafood," Fish chimed in sarcastically.

"Oh, I won't," he replied over his shoulder as he walked toward the pickup. "I just wish that fish didn't stink so much."

Fish's pock-marked face turned crimson, his hands balling into fists at his side.

"Say again?" he yelled as Rod climbed behind the wheel of the truck.

Rod put the pickup in gear and rolled forward, braking as he pulled alongside the two men. Leaning out the window, his face mere inches from Fishowski's, he casually repeated his last comment.

Fish tugged at his bottom lip, considering his options, as if capable of thought.

"Well, I've decided to let it slide this time and not take that wisecrack personally, *Hot Rod*."

Rod grinned from ear to ear.

"Oh, but I wish you would," he cheerfully replied, stomping down on the accelerator, leaving Fish to choke on a cloud of dust. *No doubt about it—the best moments in life are when you manage to get the last word in!*

Rod never did get to Gradoni's for that *Atomic* meatball Torpedo, opting instead for a mouth watering serving of prime rib at Toma's, an Italian restaurant run by Mike, Carmen, and Freddie Toma, three of the nicest guys you'd ever want to meet.

"Shame on you, eating meat on Friday," Dee Dee tsk-tsk'd, a look of mock disgust on her pretty face. "Now you'll have to go to confession tomorrow."

Rod wiped his mouth with a napkin.

"Can't. You forget, tomorrow's the Saturday bus trip to Yankee Stadium," he reminded her. "Besides, I wouldn't go to confession anyway. I need to commit a few more sins before going. I like to make it worth my while, get my money's worth, you know?" he replied with a suggestive wink.

"Got any particular sins in mind?" she asked in a sultry tone, her eyes twinkling with unrestrained amusement.

Dee Dee, as usual, looked stunning in a pink and white print sundress, a gold chain with a tiny crucifix hanging from it, around her slender neck. Her hair was thick and lustrous, the overhead lights dappling it with tones of gold.

"The night is young," he replied, a playful leer firmly in place. "Maybe, just maybe, after you finish your salmon casserole and we go pick up my car, perhaps I can think of something pleasurable for us to do."

She smiled devilishly.

"Ooohhh, Hot Rod, I'll bet you most certainly will," she replied softly, reaching across the table to squeeze his hand.

CHAPTER 10

Seventy-two people, mostly teens, milled around impatiently in front of City Hall. The bus was five minutes late and everyone was getting antsy.

"You think maybe the bus company forgot about us?" Kevin Burns asked, apprehensive. He was only twelve years old and clearly worried that he might miss out on his first Yankee game.

"Nah, don't worry about it. The bus will be here any minute now," his older brother, Larry, assured him.

As if on cue, the big *Trailways* charter bus suddenly lumbered around the corner, spewing a cloud of black diesel fumes in its wake.

Seventeen year-old Katy Bolton, a born organizer if there ever was one, let loose with an ear-numbing, shrill whistle.

"Listen up, everyone! Here's the seating arrangement and let me remind you, as earlier discussed, there'll be no exceptions," she warned. "And furthermore, there'll be no boozing on the bus, either. Got that?"

No one replied. They were all too busy laughing.

"I mean it! Everyone better behave!" the cute, bespectacled brunette bellowed, mostly for the benefit of the driver, who had just clambered down the steps of the bus. "We clear on that, people?" she growled.

"Yeah, yeah, we gotcha. Don't have kittens over it, Katy. I'll keep an eye on everybody for you," Martin 'Porky' Stanton volunteered, smirking.

Katy's eyes rolled heavenward.

"Yeah, right. In your dreams, Porky! That'd be like appointing a fox to guard the henhouse," she replied, clearly not amused. "Its' guys like you that I'm worried about."

"No sweat, Katy. I got it covered," Porky's older brother, Squeaky Stanton, vowed.

"Great, Squeaks. That'll bring it to *two* foxes in the henhouse. Come on now, seriously, I expect everyone to behave themselves," she lectured, turning to face the bus driver. "What's your name, sir?"

"Anthony Killian," the tall, good-looking driver replied cheerfully.

"Well, Anthony, do yourself *and* me a big favor and read these people the riot act, would you?"

Anthony grinned knowingly.

"Are you expecting them to get out of line?"

"I don't know. If I did, we wouldn't be having this conversation in the first place," she admitted.

"Well, I don't know if I *want* to be having this conversation, but yeah, sure, Katy, I'll lay down the law to them," he replied good-naturedly.

"Okay, kids, I want you all to have a good time today, but remember—no drinking for minors, no cursing from anyone, and no running around on the bus, or being late for departure. Got that?" he cautioned.

A big cheer went up. Just precisely what fueled it was anyone's guess, but the possibilities were endless, none of them good. Most of these kids were determined to lock and load and raise holy hell before, during, and after the game.

"Okay, troops, prepare to board," Katy ordered. "On the left side of the aisle, from the rear forward—Grogan and Gilligan—Porky and Squeaky Stanton—Kevin and Larry Burns—Tommy Carter and Chick Daubney—Steve Koval and Russ Goncharuk—Don and John Derico—Gil Ethier and Boo Mannix—Chink and Wimper Harpis—Gary and Jic-Jac Oliver—Jimmy Lacy and Donnie Holbrook—Ringer and Piwnica—Steve Walsh and Champy—Willie and Muck—DeCicco and DeCicco—Dean Martin and Ron O'Connor—Cecucci and Siggy—Madigan and Madigan—Buchanan and Buchanan." And on it went,

Katy calling out seat assignments for the right side of the bus as well.

"But I don't want to sit next to my brother!" Porky complained. "His freaking breath could lift the tiles off a roof!"

"I ain't sitting next to my brother, either," Pete DeCicco insisted. "He passes more natural gas than Niagara Mohawk ever dreamed of doing!"

"Shut up and sit the hell down!" Katy fired back, her tone gruff and uncompromising, a voice that would've done a Marine drill instructor proud.

Rod, Dee Dee and their pals, Butch and Linda, took their seats in the sixth and seventh rows. As they made themselves comfortable, Dee Dee began to giggle.

"What's so funny?" Rod asked.

"Oh, I was just thinking, that's all."

"Thinking *what*?" he asked, clearly puzzled.

"I was thinking what our old High School principal would say if she were here today, viewing this motley crew," she explained, as she unsuccessfully attempted to stifle her laughter.

"What the hell are you two talking about?" Butch asked from behind.

"Miss Hickey would take one look and say: *Yet another collective exercise in sheer stupidity, probably memorable only for its' advancing of said stupidity to even greater heights today,*" Dee Dee said with a giggle.

"Yeah, that'd be about right," Linda concurred, shaking her head.

"Maybe they'll surprise you and actually behave themselves," Butch ventured half-heartedly.

That unlikely comment drew even more chuckles.

"When elephants fly," Dee Dee quipped, the bus pulling away from the curb and into traffic.

As it headed for the New York State Thruway, Katy got up from her seat and stood in the aisle, a commanding presence if there ever was one.

"Listen up. One final reminder—anybody gets out of line, gives me any lip or starts a fight, either coming or going, you can expect to be tossed off the bus and I don't care if it's in Saugerties, the Bronx, or East Podunk. Once you've earned a boot off this bus, you're a permanent goner! Anybody got any questions?"

"Yeah, you want to ask Anthony if the first aid kit contains any ear plugs?" Donnie Holbrook asked with a straight face. "I don't know about anyone else, but your General Patton routine sort of wears on the ol' eardrums, if you catch my drift," he wise-cracked, grinning. "I'm just saying, you know?"

Even Katy couldn't help but join in the laughter.

"Keep it up, Holbrook, and you won't make it to Selkirk," she half-heartedly warned him.

Once everyone got settled back down, Katy took her seat directly behind the driver and alongside a pleasant, young deaf fellow by the name of Iggy Nolan. The pairing of the two wasn't an accident.

As the bus lumbered through the toll booth, a number of guys broke out their narrow, felt-covered, folding game boards, boards that fit snugly across the armrests. Engineered to bring a smile to many a traveling Blackjack and poker player's face, the boards worked like a charm. The rhythmic sound of cards being shuffled and dealt filled the air.

Shortly thereafter, Jimmy Lacy walked to the rear of the bus and set up shop, switching on his GE transistor radio to the sounds of Dodie Steven's "Pink Shoe Laces," throwing open the lids of his two coolers, hawking bottles of Piel's, Schaefer's, Dobler's, Fitzie's, Ballantine's and Utica Club beer at forty cents per bottle.

"Just be damned certain none of them bottles end up in the hands of any of these under-aged kids, Lacy," Katy cautioned him from the front of the bus.

"Oh, don't worry about us, Katy," Young Jimmy Buchanan assured her. "I'm not going to drink any of that stuff," he vowed as he craftily transferred a thin flask of Old Crow bourbon from the inside pocket of his *Yankee* windbreaker to a spot just beneath his thigh. *Buker* may have only been fourteen, but it was a hard fourteen. The kid was tough as nails.

Ten minutes later, the seat assignments went pretty much out the window. Katy threatened, growled, cajoled and snarled, but in the end, the guys had their way.

Midway to the stadium, Anthony, the bus driver, announced that their only stop would be at the Harriman "Big Apple" Plaza. He went on to advise that it would only be a fifteen minute stop. *So much for that!*

Twenty minutes later the bus pulled into a parking space at the sprawling Harriman rest stop. As the passengers stepped down from the bus, a seriously overweight kid of thirteen kept turning around, staring at a girl who'd been sitting up toward the front of the bus.

"What are you looking at?"Jerry *'Jic-Jac* 'Oliver inquired of his pal, Chucky "Chubbs" Ziwicki.

"Huh? Oh, that girl, the one who was sitting up front. I kind of, uh, got eyes for her, you know what I mean?"

Jic-Jac took a gander at her, shrugging. "She ain't all that pretty, you ask me."

The stocky kid grinned smugly. "Actually, that's good. I won't have much competition then."

"Aw, shut up, Chucky. You ain't got too many smarts, you know that? Besides, it ain't polite to call a girl ugly."

"I didn't say she was ugly!" the kid protested. "Besides, you're the one who said she isn't pretty!"

"So?"

"What do you mean *so?*"

By now, they were almost to the door of the main building.

Jic-Jac sighed wearily, as though he were toting an unbearable weight upon his shoulders.

"What's your point, Chubbs?"

The kid's face went blank.

"*My point?* Well, my point is that you—" he began, but then inexplicably lost the thread of his thoughts. "Oh crap! Now I went and forgot my point!"

Jic-Jac gave him a gentle poke to the ribs.

"You're only thirteen and already you're losing your memory? I guess for guys like you, getting old really sucks, huh?"

Twenty minutes later Anthony turned around in his seat and told Katy she needed to send out a search party for the missing passenger.

Katy nodded as she scanned her fellow passenger's faces, looking for volunteers not already half in the bag.

"Hobbs and O'Brien—come on with me. We got to go find Chubbs."

Rod and Butch dutifully complied.

"I'm going kick this kid's behind," Katy fumed.

"Take it easy, Katy. Maybe he's in the bathroom, finishing up, you know?" Rod suggested reasonably.

She shot him a dirty look.

"Okay, in that case, Rod, you take the men's room while we check out the rest of the building for the pain in the neck."

No sooner was Rod through the door of the men's room when he heard the plaintive cry of a young lad in distress.

"It won't unlock, I tell you! Somebody go get a janitor or somebody, to get me outta here!" the kid pleaded with his would-be rescuers. A group of three men milled around the door to the stall, taking turns at trying to yank it open.

"Hey, Chucky, it's me—Rod Hobbs. Forget the door—just get down and slide out under it. Come on, the bus is ready to leave."

"No way! I already tried that, and got pinned there for three minutes. And don't ask me to climb over the door, either. There ain't no way that's ever going happen!" he cried, frustration oozing from every pore.

"Crap!" Rod exclaimed as he pulled his Yankee tee shirt over his head and off, handing it to Butch, who'd just walked in. "I'll slide under the door, and if I can't get it to unlock, then I'll boost him over the top."

Butch did a double-take. "That's hernia territory, you ask me. Want me to run over to the gift shop and see if they sell trusses?"

"Park the humor, will you?" Rod replied, exasperated. "Chucky, I want you to stand on top of the john now. I need room to slide in there."

A moment later Rod was inside, having snaked his way under the door and into the stall. He jiggled, shook, twisted and cursed the lock, but it was all for naught. It flat-out wouldn't budge.

Resigned to the task at hand, he motioned for Chucky to step off the toilet lid and onto Rod's waiting palms.

Rod grunted as the kid complied, putting a strain on Rod's back, the likes of which would have had Charles Atlas himself sweating bullets. Then, just as the boy's pudgy fingers grasped the top of the door, it suddenly swung open, the lock snapping off, the door groaning under the weight of its unlikely burden. A screw popped loose from the top hinge, pinging onto the tile floor.

"Let go, Chucky, before the whole damn door falls off!" Butch yelled.

The kid dropped like a lead balloon, right onto his rear end.

"Okay, come on. Get up. We got to get out of here before we get billed for a broken door," Rod warned, yanked the boy to his feet.

"How's your back?" Dee Dee asked Rod for the umpteenth time.

The game was midway through the sixth inning and Rod's back was admittedly, more than a bit sore. Of course, dead-lifting a two hundred and fifty pound kid by the palms of one's hands would do that to a guy.

"It's not bad," he lied. "I'll live."

She leaned over and kissed him. He turned toward her, checking her out, thinking that her looks were the stuff of Hollywood central casting. He was a lucky guy.

"Another fifty or so kisses, and I'll probably be as good as new," he predicted with a wink.

"Too bad we got here after batting practice was over. Maybe you really could've had a shot at asking Mickey Mantle for an autograph," she said wistfully.

"No big deal. Besides, the best chance for an autograph is when they're walking into the stadium, long before the game starts. Either that or when they're leaving, heading for their cars, and by then our bus will have been long gone," he said matter-of-factly. "It doesn't really matter, anyway."

She poked his shoulder playfully.

"That's all right. I'll give you *my* autograph later tonight. I'll write it across your chest in lipstick," she promised, her eyes twinkling with mischief.

A big grin lit up Rod's handsome features.

"Is that a promise or merely a threat?"

She gave him her patented, sultry *Lolita* look.

"Neither. It's a fact, Lover Boy."

Rod winked at her again, taking her hand in his.

"What's the matter, Hot-Rod? Cat got your tongue?"

"Baby, you really know how to jumpstart a fella's motor, revving it right up."

She leaned over and whispered in his ear, "You don't know the half of it, big boy."

The Yankees won, outscoring the Indians ten to two, so the Cohoes troop was happy. Of course the definition of the word *happy* was all relative. Some were *so* giddy, as a result of imbibing copious quantities of *liquid happiness*, that they had to be, to put it charitably, *assisted* from the stadium and onto the bus. At least no one got lost or left behind—this time, anyway.

It had been a rare loss for Cleveland's Bob Lemon but a big day for Mantle, having connected twice off of Lemon, his second *Ballantine blast* traveling over 460 feet. Life was good if you were a Yankee fan and the Cohoes bus was full of them.

Chucky had been terribly embarrassed by his run-in with the toilet door and as such, he was very, very quiet during the long ride home, content to simply sit there, staring down at the floor morosely. His case of the blues didn't go unnoticed. Rod decided to take a shot at trying to cheer the kid up.

He stood and worked his way down the narrow aisle, passing a considerable number of snoring young men and boys along the way. For the most part, the younger boys had been denied any chance at a swig of booze. The older ones...well, that had been a whole different ballgame. Enough said.

"Hey, you think the bus could drop us off in front of Boyer's Bar?" Squeaky Stanton asked of no one in particular. "The night is still young, you know."

"Nah. Good idea, but the driver will never go for it," Terry Richards replied. "Besides, I'm barred from there—for a while anyway. Something to do with fighting."

Rod could see that the kid sitting next to Chucky, Jic-Jac Oliver, was dead to the world. Propping his elbow across the top of the seat, he leaned down and gently poked the despondent kid's arm. Startled, the boy jumped. Once he saw who'd poked him, however, he relaxed.

"Hey, Rod," he said sheepishly, "I'm uh...real sorry about what happened in the bathroom this morning."

Rod reached down and good-naturedly tousled the kid's blond hair.

"Aah, don't worry about it. It could've happened to anybody. No big deal," he said consolingly.

The soothing words seemed to have had the desired effect. The boy smiled as he nodded his reluctant agreement.

"Yeah, I suppose, but thanks again, just the same."

Rod patted his shoulder.

"No sweat," he replied reassuringly, turning to head back to his seat.

"Wait! Oh geez, I almost forgot!" Chucky cried.

Rod stopped in his tracks

"Forgot *what*? What are you talking about?"

"I uh...I got you something, something I know you...uh, uh... always wanted," the kid stammered. "I know because I heard you talking about it with your girlfriend."

Rod was perplexed. *What in the hell is he talking about?*

"You've lost me, kid. You want to run that by me again?"

"Here, this is yours now," Chucky said as he reached up and took off his brand-spanking new, woolen Yankee cap and offered it to Rod.

"What are talking about? I don't want your hat," Rod replied, incredulous.

"Sure you do, and it ought to fit you just fine, too. I got a big head and so do you."

Baffled, Rod took a deep breath, blowing it out wearily.

"Why, on God's earth, would I want your hat?"

A huge, rather smug smile blossomed across Chucky's pudgy face.

"Because I got it for you," he announced proudly.

Ever more bewildered, Rod's eyes rolled to the roof of the bus, as if searching it for an extra ration of daily patience.

"Are you saying that you got me that hat, the same one you were wearing, when we departed from Cohoes this morning? If so, then you've managed to confuse me to no end, kiddo."

Chucky's grin grew wider.

"Yeah, I guess I haven't made myself clearly understood. Sorry about that. But here, just take the cap and flip it over," he instructed. "Then read what's written on the underside of the bill. You're going to like it. I guarantee it!" the kid crowed with cocksure finality.

On second thought, maybe I should've left this nutty kid locked up in the Thruway can while I had the chance, Rod mused speculatively.

He sighed. Reluctantly, he took the cap from Chucky's outstretched hand and flipped it over. Naturally, the bus's interior light was quite dim and so Rod fished in his pocket for his Zippo. Pulling it out, he flicked the wheel against the flint. A bright flame bloomed, illuminating the underside of the baseball cap. Rod could see that something had been written, or rather had been scrawled, across the white underside of the navy blue cap's bill. He strained his eyes, trying to make out what appeared to be a signature of some sort. Shrugging his shoulders, ever more mystified, he turned to hand the cap back to Chucky, when it suddenly dawned on him—like a bolt out of the blue, *navy blue* no less! That was Mickey Mantle's signature! Rod had memorized it years ago, as a kid, dreaming of the day he just *might* be able to get close enough to wrangle, beg, or plead an autograph out of *The Mick*!

This was incredible, he marveled to himself.

"When did you get this autograph, Chucky?" Rod demanded to know. "Did you get it while at another game?" When did he sign this?"

Chucky grinned from ear to ear as he held up his palms.

"Whoa. Slow down with the questions, will you?"

Rod stared at him quizzically, as if seeing him for the very first time.

"In the top of the third inning, with two outs, I left my seat and made my way down toward the ritzy section, the one right by the field, near the dugouts," Chucky explained. "I got as far as the steps leading down to the big-buck seats overlooking the Yankee dugout. The usher, some nasty dipshit who looked like *Woody Woodpecker* in a red uniform, told me get my duff back up there in the nosebleed section where I belonged. He wasn't about to let me go down there in the high-rent section. No sir, he surely wasn't!"

Rod could scarcely believe what he was hearing, yet the kid's far-fetched tale held him spellbound.

"So then I just sort of milled around the general area, waiting for Cleveland to make their third out. Finally, Larry Doby pops out to shallow center field, Mickey Mantle, of course, making the catch," Chucky recounted, casually taking a sip from his bottle of *Ma's Root Beer*.

"So what are you saying here, exactly? You telling me that you walked up to Mantle during a game and scored his autograph? Get outta here!" Rod cried scornfully.

"Hey, dial down the volume, will ya, Hot Rod?" Katy complained. "We got drunks...I mean *people* trying to sleep, sleep it off, or whatever. Anyway, tone it down a bit."

Rod paid her no attention whatsoever.

"Okay, Chucky," Rod probed calmly, the whole story starting to smell fishy now. "So what's the punch line to your little joke? Shame on you, kid! After all the trouble I went to, all the sore muscles you caused me, *me*—the human can opener, and this is how you show your gratitude?"

A look of alarm flashed across Chucky's pudgy face.

"No, wait. You're wrong, Rod. Just hear me out, *please!*"

"So talk!" Rod barked gruffly. "I can hardly wait."

Chucky ran his hand across his forehead, wiping away a thin film of perspiration.

"Anyway, like I was saying, the Yankees start trotting in from the field, ready to go to bat. I start figuring how long it'll be, how many more seconds before Mantle will reach the lip of the dugout. My mind starts racing. Next thing I know, I'm barrelassing down the aisle of the pricey rows, heading for the corner seats next to the dugout. As I'm forcing my way into the aisle, stepping on lots of toes, getting cursed at, I can hear *Woody Woodpecker* closing in on me, yelling for me to stop, no doubt embarrassed by the fact that a short, tubby kid has outraced him. Then, just as Mantle and the others are about to enter the dugout, I start screaming '*Dad! Hey, Dad! It's me—your son, Mickey Junior!*"

Rod couldn't believe his ears!

"Well, needless to say, I definitely got Mickey's, Yogi's and Moose Skowron's attention. At first, Mickey looks at me as if I was just another nutcase, but then he shakes his head and grins, as if to say—*I thought I've seen it all, but this one takes the cake!*"

"At this point I know I gotta make my case quick, because the Woodpecker's only about twelve steps away from nabbing me."

"*Hey, Dad!*" I called out again to Mantle. "*What's the matter, Dad, you don't recognize your own son? Come on, Mom sent me down to ask you to autograph this hat for Milt, our milkman. She promised him you'd do it. Tomorrow's Milt's birthday and you're going on the road to Chicago tonight, after the game! She wants to stick it in the milk box for him!*"

"By now, Woody's got me by the back of the shirt collar, struggling to drag me away, but what with me being as heavy as I am, and him built like a scarecrow, the quiff can't budge me. Then I feel the arm of yet another usher on me. Now I know I've about had it, so I go all out, giving it my best shot, trying for a home run!"

"Hey, Dad! C'mon, tell these mugs to lay off me, will ya? After all, I'm your son, Mickey Junior, for God's sake! What kind of father are you, anyway? "

"Just as I'm thinking my goose is cooked, here's Yogi, Skowron and Mantle peering up and over the dugout roof, watching and listening to the live action. Yogi's busting on Mantle something fierce, playfully nudging him, making him laugh. Now, I know Mantle's got four guys ahead of him, before he'll be up, so if it was ever going happen, this was the time. Meanwhile, the Nazis in red were just about pulling my arms of the sockets."

"The last thing I see is Casey Stengel's wrinkled old puss staring over at me. The goons are finally having their way with me, dragging me out of the aisle, when suddenly I hear *'Let him go, fellas. That's my boy."*

"The ushers were dumbstruck, glued to the spot, their mouths hanging open in disbelief. Mantle then waved me forward with a big flourish. The ushers released their hold on me and I quickly waddled over to the side of the dugout, stepping on a bunch of feet as I went. Mantle stood there laughing, one leg up on the dugout step, ballpoint pen in hand. *'Let's have it, son,'* he said with a big grin, reaching for the hat in my hand. *'Lord knows you've earned it,"*

Rod was struck speechless.

Chucky shrugged his shoulders. "Well, that's my story, and now that's *your* hat, Hot Rod."

"But you need to keep this for yourself, Chucky." Rod insisted. "Think about everything you went through to get it."

The boy grinned broadly.

"Nope, it's yours. I owe you for busting me outta the can, pal. Besides, look at what else I got," he boasted as he dug around in his shirt pocket, eventually producing a folded square of white paper. "Here, read it," he said excitedly, thrusting the paper into Rod's hand.

Rod slowly unfolded the square and held it in his left hand, his lighter hovering over the words contained within.

'*Son, remind Mom that it's high time we put you on a diet.*'
Your Dad, Mickey Mantle.

CHAPTER 11

"It feels good not to have to put on the Auxiliary Cop uniform today, for a change. To tell you the truth, directing traffic on Sundays outside of St. Agnes' church was beginning to wear on me. Some of the old folks think my hand signal to stop, is actually a signal to floor it. Two weeks ago, Old man Thibeault almost punched my ticket, narrowly missing me by inches as he flew past me in his old Buick."

"I hear you," Dee Dee sympathized, her arm on Rod's shoulder. "Well, let's enjoy this Sunday off, then. Besides, it's our last day of vacation. What do you feel like doing today?"

They were sitting together on Rod's stoop, Dee Dee's pink Zenith transistor radio pumping out "There goes my baby," by the Drifters. They'd just returned from ten o'clock mass where Father Ashline had mercifully delivered the shortest sermon of his career. Chalk one up for the good Father. The heat inside the church had been downright stifling, the big altar fans whirring away impotently.

"What time is it now?" he asked.

Dee Dee glanced at her *Lady Bulova*. "Eleven twenty."

"What do you say we catch a matinee downtown? They're showing *Some like it Hot* and *North by Northwest*. Sound good?"

"It floats my boat. We got time to grab some lunch?"

"Doesn't start until two, so yeah, we got plenty of time. Where do you want to eat?"

"You pick."

"I picked last time," Rod said, unwrapping a stick of Beeman's, popping it into his mouth.

"Yeah, and you did a real good job of it, so do it again."

"Ha-ha. You're a real card, you are, a regular Lucille Ball."
She laughed.

"I'll take that as a compliment, but meanwhile, pick a place to eat. Nothing fancy."

"Hmm, too bad Kresge's is closed on Sundays. I could really go for one OF those *mystery meat* Sloppy Joe sandwiches and a cold mug of Richardson's Root Beer. I'll tell you what," he said, fishing in his pocket, pulling out a quarter and handing it to her. "Here, you flip. Heads—we drive over to Ted's in Watervliet and grab a quick fish fry; tails—we swing by Charlie's and feast on some hot dogs. Deal?"

"Deal," she agreed, flipping the coin in the air. "Heads. Charlie's, here we come!"

"That really hit the spot," Rod said, smacking his lips together as he pulled out into traffic. "I don't know exactly what's in that secret meat sauce they use, but it's incredibly tasty, whatever it is."

"Meat."

"What?"

"They put *meat* in the sauce."

Rod made a fist, leaning over and sticking it just under her chin, ala Ralph Kramden of the *Honeymooners.*

"Oh, you're asking for it, Alice. You're *really* asking for it now," he threatened, his imitation of Jackie Gleason's bus driver character leaving much to be desired.

"Now, Ralph. Just calm down now, Ralph, before you have a coronary," Dee Dee replied in a spot-on, perfect duplication of Audrey Meadow's voice.

Rod stared over at her, truly impressed.

"How IN the hell did you ever learn to do that?"

"Easy. I'm a woman, and as everyone except *men* knows, women are great listeners," she fired back, a smug smile lighting up her extraordinarily lovely features.

"Keep it up, wisenheimer, and you'll be paying your own way into the movies," he threatened playfully.

She chuckled, removing her sunglasses, giving him a look.

"Keep it up, *daddy-o* and you'll be singing 'Lonely Boy,' after I cut you off," she countered, her coy smile widening.

Rod momentarily took his hands off the wheel, his arms raised in surrender. "You win. Actually, you had me at—*After I cut you off.*"

Dee Dee snickered. "Yeah, I figured as much," she quipped, leaning forward, turning on the radio. Bobby Darin's "Mack the Knife" came through loud and clear as she began snapping her fingers, swaying to the music.

Please, please don't sing along, he almost said aloud, but then thought better of it. *What's a little suffering, now and then?*

"What did you think of the movies?" Rod asked as he cruised down Remsen Street.

"Loved them both, especially, '*Some like it hot*'. Tony Curtis and Jack Lemmon in drag!"

"Marilyn Monroe certainly didn't look too shabby, either," He offered.

"You would say that."

"So what now? It's only six-thirty. Seeing as how this is our last vacation day, we ought to finish it off in style," Rod suggested.

"You have anything in mind?"

"Actually, I do. The Menands Speedway is putting on one of their *Wreckum Derbies* tonight. It starts in about a half hour. You up for it?"

"It's Sunday night. Not a lot of choices, so yeah, why not? Watching cars slam into each other always makes my day."

"It's either that or bowling."

"Hmm, how's the vacation money holding up?"

"I got about ten bucks left. It's enough."

"On second thought, maybe we ought to just call it a night," she suggested reasonably. "I forgot that I have to get up early for work tomorrow."

Rod chewed that over in his mind. "Maybe you're right. Tell you what. Let's swing by Danny's, pick up a pizza and then head over to your house. We'll watch a little television; catch the *Gisele MacKenzie show, Candid Camera,* and your favorite of all—Ed Sullivan. Then I'll beat a path for home."

"Sounds good. Let's do it, but only if you let me pay for the pizza."

Rod laughed. "In that case, let's get a large one with all the trimmings."

"Hey, go for it," she replied, leaning forward to turn on the radio, the sound of Lloyd Price's "Stagger Lee" pouring through the speakers.

Unfortunately, she began singing along with Lloyd.

Maybe, in time, I'll get used to it, he tried to convince himself. *Yeah, sure, around the same time Nikita Khrushchev signs on with the Jesuits.*

CHAPTER 12

Sal told Rod to show up at the site at eight, just before sundown. Right on time, he met Sal inside the trailer.

When he entered the rusting white trailer, the air was layered with smoke, the fading sunlight streaming through the small, filthy windows. Sal sat at his desk, his feet propped up, his eyes latched onto Rod's, his thoughts, whatever they were, impossible to decipher. That was something that bothered Rod. Sal's flat, dull eyes never seemed to contain, or reveal any definable emotion. You never knew what he was thinking.

"Have a seat."

Rod plopped himself down on a metal folding chair.

Sal was dressed in yet another of his rumpled, black pinstriped suits, complemented by bright red suspenders and a coffee-stained, yellow and red floral bow tie. He looked like a cross between a funeral director and Dagwood Bumstead. It would be a dangerous mistake, however, to take Sal anything less than seriously.

"So how was your weekend?" he inquired of Rod...as if he really cared. If Sal had any genuine interest in anyone outside of his own frame of reference, he rarely showed any sign of it, his barely concealed contempt for others, a lifelong trait. Sal was only interested in talking about what he owned and what he planned on owning, totally uninterested in anything that wasn't directly related to him.

Rod shrugged. "It was okay."

Sal nodded. "Okay, here's the deal," he said, raising himself from the creaking swivel chair and walking over to a battered metal cabinet, flinging the double doors open. "Put this on," he directed as he handed Rod a well-worn leather shoulder rig, followed by a high mileage, snub-nosed thirty two caliber revolver. It looked as if it had seen plenty of action, the walnut grips scarred and pitted, the barrel nicked up pretty bad.

"You're going to carry this, too," he said, laying a gleaming Ithaca twelve gauge, pump shotgun across the desk. "I removed the sportsman's plug, so that it'll hold five slugs. You're a hunter, so I assume you know what I'm talking about. Am I right?"

Rod suddenly felt as though he was sitting atop the business edge of a razor blade.

"Yeah, I'm familiar with it," he replied softly.

Sal sat back in his chair and fished around in his jacket pocket, eventually producing a pipe. He began scrapping out the bowl of the Briar pipe with a jackknife, then wiped the blade clean with a handkerchief, folded the knife, and casually flipped it onto the desk. He clenched the pipe between his yellowed, rotting teeth and lit it, drawing loudly on it, his full concentration seemingly on this simple act, yet all the while his gaze had remaining locked onto Rod's face, his cold, expressionless eyes seemingly capable of reading Rod's thoughts.

"We already went through all of this, but seeing as how you look kind of edgy about the whole thing. I'll go over it again," he offered, like a teacher faced with a reluctant student.

"You catch him or *them* red-handed, you point that shotgun at their faces and tell them to lie down on the ground, face first, and then hook them up with these, hands behind their backs," he instructed, reaching into a drawer, producing two sets of steel handcuffs.

Rod could feel a cold sweat forming across his body.

Sal's gaze intensified as he sucked on the pipe, a thick plume of woodsy-smelling smoke rising into the air.

"If you want, take the cuffs home with you and practice with them, maybe dreaming up a game or two with your girlfriend along the way. You know what I'm saying? You could even make believe you're a cop on that TV show—*Naked City,*" he suggested, a lascivious leer on his face. "Or a new dating show, like *Hot-to-trot Hookup,* or something of that nature."

Rod felt his blood begin to boil, a flush of color creeping up his cheeks.

Sal held up a placating hand. "Just kidding. Don't get your BVD'S all bunched up. I was just joking around, trying to get you to lighten up, that's all. I never figured you for a puritanical, goody-two-shoes, but hey, that's your business."

Rod didn't care for Sal's remarks, but knew he had no choice but to let them slide.

"No problem."

"Good. Fortunately, an appreciation of my sense of humor isn't a job requirement. Nabbing whoever's been making off with my property, however, *is* something that I'll be expecting you to do."

"I'll do my best, Sal, but what makes you think the thief or *thieves* will be back to steal more?"

Sal snorted dismissively.

"Vultures always return to the location of their last meal, hoping to get lucky again. Whoever made off with my equipment will be back for more. Count on it, the scumbags!" he snapped, stoking the seething cauldron of anger that boiled within him day and night, looking forward to getting his hands on the thief, wrapping up his fury into a neat little package, then tying it up with a nice thick ribbon of revenge.

He got up from his chair and leaned across the desk, his face mere inches from Rod's, his rancid breath strong enough to knock the shoes off a horse.

"Like I said, first you catch them. Then you cuff their hands behind their back," he reminded Rod once more. Then you march them in here, make them lie face down on the floor, and then you call me. Got that?" he barked, jabbing his nicotine-stained index finger in Rod's direction. "I don't care what time of the night it is, either. Just pick up the phone and call me!"

Rod pressed the bridge of his nose with his thumb and forefinger, as though trying to pinch away his mounting worries.

"Say I get lucky and actually nab the thieves. Then I call you. What then? What are you going to do with them?"

Sal clenched his jaw, sighing. "That's the kind of question that, believe me, kid—you really don't want to know the answer to it," he warned, the skin on his face drawn tight against the skull, his rotting teeth bared, his eyes burning with stark malevolence.

Rod sucked in his breath, letting it out slowly, steeling himself against the growing pressure in his forehead. He suspected he'd be eating a lot of Bayer Aspirin in the months ahead.

As it turned out, however, the first night passed without incident. Rod figured his biggest concern shouldn't be about catching some bad guys, but rather how to combat the boredom that came with patrolling a construction site for eight hours. Every time he thought about it, though, he'd remind himself of the big paycheck he was going get every week. Suddenly, he'd find himself smiling contentedly.

The first week on the job went by without a hitch. Gratefully, no bad guys showed up and now it was Saturday night and he was free to relax. Dee Dee was busy attending a friend's bridal shower and so he was a free man for the evening. The bride-to-be, Kathie Haney, better known as *Honky Tonk Haney* to her friends, was a good kid but a real piece of work, as well. Rod hoped her future husband knew what he was getting himself into. Get her Irish up and a man could end up paying dearly for it. Two years earlier, her boyfriend of the moment had really irked her over something or other. He paid the price. She grabbed a rope and tied him up, leaving him to spend the night on her front lawn, stewing over the error of his ways. Another well-intentioned kid, a guy named Artie Johnson, volunteered to teach her how to drive. Big mistake on his part! No sooner was she behind the wheel of his Ford Fairlane convertible and he began to lose patience, yelling at her every couple of minutes or so. Never a big fan of perceived verbal abuse, she flipped him the finger, told him to shove his driving lessons someplace where the sun don't shine, and then proceeded to exit the car, just as it was beginning its' steep descent down Younglove Avenue.

Word on the street was, poor Artie's hair started turning prematurely white that very day.

Yet another time, she found herself in a rather sticky predicament while enjoying a few cocktails at Boyer's Bar. Totally forgetting that she had agreed to a date for the night with boy #1, who should walk in but the lad himself! A minute later, boy #2, another guy she had a date set up with, shows up, also. Talk about your nerve wracking situations!

Ever resourceful, *Honky Tonk* determined that the answer to her dilemma lie in the confines of the Ladies' room, or to be more precise, the *window* of the Ladies' room. Unfortunately for her, the proprietor correctly suspected that Kathie was up to something. Halfway out the small window, she was nabbed. A week later, bars were installed across both bathroom windows. Yeah, no doubt about it—the girl was a living legend throughout the city, and deservedly so.

Rod was feeling pretty good about himself tonight, what with having gotten his first paycheck yesterday, and what a paycheck it was! Sure, he had plenty of valid reservations about working for Sal, but one look at his check and those doubts floated right off into space, at least for the moment, anyway.

Perched comfortably atop one of Bourkie's well-worn barstools, Rod was enjoying a cold Schaefer's and a hot roast beef sandwich while waiting for his pal, Butch, to get a free moment to chat. It was Saturday night and the place was jam-packed, the Wurlitzer jukebox churning out The Platter's "Smoke gets in your eyes." It was a most appropriate tune, as the air was rife with layers of smoke, and fumes of draft beer and whiskey.

Rod was passing the time listening to an old-timer named Pat Shea, *Pops* to the locals, run on and on about his deceased wife.

"She could outspend the Saudi Arabians—with my hard earned money!" he ranted, just getting warmed up. "Everybody assumed that I'd miss her after she bought the farm. Well, it's been six years now since the old bag croaked and take my word for it—I miss her about as much as I'd miss a kitchen cockroach! Who'd miss fifty years of guerilla warfare?" he spat, a whistling sound emanating from his loose false teeth. "Some people might think that sounds cold, but if she had her way, I would have keeled over the day after my pension kicked in. The miserable witch only wanted me to live long enough to collect the pension that *she'd* end up with, but not a day longer than that, and I'm supposed to miss her?"

A young woman sitting a few stools down overheard his scathing rant and took exception to it. "That's terrible—talking about your deceased wife that way!"

"Just giving the devil her due, Toots," he replied bitterly.

Pops was on a roll now, his eyes already taking on an alcoholic luster. He had to be derailed early on, for once he got up a head of steam there was no stopping him. A professional cynic, in the neighborhood of seventy years old, give or take a decade, the weathered lines in his face had been etched one beer and a shot at a time. He wore black plastic eyeglasses, the frames taped together in the center with white adhesive tape. With a receding hairline of wispy white hair, he had a florid, drinker's complexion, not at all unusual for a man who spent his days welded to a barstool. Appropriately enough, his torso bore more than a passing resemblance to a Piel's beer keg. Short and stout though he was, his stomach protruding like a sack of sand over his belt, Pops rigorously compensated for his physical shortcomings by never doing anything in moderation, or ever giving an inch in an argument.

He nudged Rod.

"Hey, you know, despite the fact she doesn't know enough to mind her own business, that's a pretty good looking dame," he remarked admiringly. "Hmm, come to think of it, I could really go for her. What the hell, lately I been thinking about getting remarried, anyway, signing on for my next installment of misery, so why not do it with a young broad?" he mused, leering in her direction. Fortunately, neither the woman nor her big, broad-shouldered companion heard the remark.

"Hey, Pops, keep it down, will you?" Rod cautioned. "Besides, if you're looking for a woman, why don't you look for one your own age?"

"Who the hell wants a woman my age? Christ on a crutch! You ever take a good look at most women my age? Hell's bells! It's enough to give a man terminal constipation!"

"You two ready for a refill?" Butch asked as he emptied their ashtray.

Rod nodded while Pops made a big production out of *supposedly* giving serious consideration to ordering yet another shot of Four Roses with a beer back.

"Aah, what the hell! Yeah, go ahead—one more shot and another Fitzie's can't hurt. I'm already three sheets to the wind. One for the ditch won't make any difference now," he rationalized, once again glancing over at the attractive young woman.

"On second thought, I think I'm going to forget about her. Way too young for me, anyway," he admitted in a rare moment of moral clarity. "It'd probably be a sin or something. I'll tell you, though—the guy with her? Did you get a good look at his mug? That man's got a serious case of the ugglies. His parents should've looked into birth control. What in the hell does she see in a jamoke like him, anyway? Screw him and the horse he rode in on!"

"Shh! Lower your voice, Pops!" Rod hissed.

Each and every evening, seven nights a week, Pops vowed that he was going to limit himself to three rounds of drinks, and then go home early for a change. Unfortunately, by the time he'd consumed his self-imposed limit of three rounds, his resolve to put a cork in it, went right out the window, along with his resolve to go home early. I doubt that he would have *ever* gone home if not for his dog *Lucky*. Pops knew he had to feed Lucky and then take him for a nightly walk. Well, the dog walked, anyway. Pops, he just more or less staggered along behind it.

How he'd ever arrived at the name *Lucky* for his pet mongrel puzzled everyone. The poor dog was three-legged and borderline blind. Pops loved him anyway.

"Where was I? Damn, getting old sucks! I can't remember a thing lately. What the hell were we talking about, anyway?" he muttered, as Butch set the drinks down in front of them.

"Your dear departed wife, probably," Butch guessed. "The script rarely changes."

The cantankerous old man flipped Butch the bird. "There goes your tip, Bluto."

"It's *Butch*, and gee, I'm really going to miss that dime," Butch quipped as he walked off. "Now I may never get that new Corvair."

"My wife!" Pops grumbled as he turned to face Rod. "Your pal, numb nuts, behind the bar, thinks he's quite the comic, but speaking of the ball and chain I married, did you know that Monsignor Mulqueen came to visit me, a week after the funeral at St. Bernard's?"

Rod shook his head no.

"We go way back, the Monsignor and me. I've known him for at least forty years. He wanted to know how I was holding up."

"That was nice of him to come to your house."

"My house? Nah, he didn't come to my house. My goody-two-shoes, misguided sister, Aggie, ran into him in Timpane's, telling him I was drowning my sorrows down at Matty Grestini's joint, and could he maybe pay me a visit, console me, hear my confession or something? Turns out the good Father took a ride over there for nothing. I'd already left and was now downing a few cold ones at Mario Sbrega's gin mill on Willow St. Anyway, somebody At Matty's told the Monsignor where I'd gone and the next thing you know, in he walks. So we take a table in the back corner, for a little privacy, you know? He starts off by asking me if I'd been pleased with the funeral services. I admitted that I'd been drunk for approximately the whole time, from the wake, to the mass, to the cemetery, so any recollections I had of the whole shebang were rather vague and cloudy," Pops explained matter-of-factly. "For some reason, my answer seemed to cause the good Father a bit of discomfort, so I offered to buy him a drink. That suggestion seemed to cause him even more discomfort, so I told him: '*Come on, Monsignor, everybody knows you like your Johnny Walker Black. Have one on me."*

"How'd that go over?" Rod asked, clearly amused.

"About what you'd expect from any priest sitting in a saloon. He made the sign of the cross, but then took me up on my offer."

Rod laughed.

"So then he starts talking about how drowning my sorrow in booze isn't going to ease my grief. Only prayer can do that, he insists," Pops continued. "I explain to him that I don't have any grief, just *relief*. He tells me that a good Catholic husband shouldn't harbor such blatant animosity towards his dearly departed wife. I tell him there wasn't anything dear about her and furthermore, how dare he suggest that I'm not a good Catholic!" he spat huffily. "I admitted that granted, like a lot of old-school Irishmen, the Celtic pagan was still alive and well within the darker compartments of my mind, but that *never* prevented me from being a pretty damn good Catholic! I then felt further compelled to remind the Monsignor that considering how much I'd thrown in the ol' collection basket every Sunday for a pile of years, to cover the pew rent, I believed I was as good a Catholic as they come and *nobody*, not him, begging his pardon, or my devout cousin Dobber Walsh, or even Pope Pius the twelfth himself, would ever convince me otherwise!"

Rod was genuinely intrigued now. "Oh, boy. That must have gone over like a lead balloon."

The old man grinned broadly, his top denture slipping a bit.

"Nope. He just leaned back on his chair, fired up a stogie, puffed on it and smiled as he said," *'If indeed the meek shall inherit the earth, I wouldn't plan on getting any of it, Patrick, if I were you.'*

CHAPTER 13

Rod had been on Sal's payroll for three weeks now. The money was great, but the boredom was getting to him. Initially, he'd fervently prayed that the thieves would never return, sparing him from becoming involved in what could potentially, prove to be one very dangerous, messy situation. After three weeks of patrolling the site with a flashlight and shotgun, however, Rod was eager for a break from the monotony. Desperate for some company, *any* company, at this point, he would've even welcomed an appearance by the bad guys. At least he'd have someone to talk to. *'Lie down on the ground face-first, hands behind your back, or I'll ventilate your skulls with this here shotgun!'*

Not exactly casual small talk, but then he wasn't exactly in a position to be choosey. *At least it'd be somebody to talk to. Better than nothing,* he told himself.

The day had been a typical July scorcher, the humidity so thick, you could just about bite into it. By nightfall it had cooled off considerably, but that wasn't saying much. The heat and humidity were still downright stifling.

As Rod strode past a huge Caterpillar grader, he reached into his oversized work shirt pocket, pulling out his *Philco* blue and gold transistor radio, clicking it on. At least he had radio station *WABY –BABY* to keep him company. After adjusting the volume lower, he gently shoved the radio back into his pocket, the sound of Richie Valens' "La Bamba" somewhat muffled by the fabric, yet still audible. Humming along with the music, he fired up a Lucky Strike before resuming his patrol of the grounds.

A nearby copse of chestnut trees glowed with clouds of fireflies. The evening sky was awash in brilliant moonlight, the stars studding the heavens with a twinkling glow, the moonlight reflecting softly upon the shimmering surface of the river. The legendary, local TV weatherman, Howard Tupper, had gotten it right for a change when he claimed it was to be a dry night, with nary a rain cloud in sight.

Well, in Rod's opinion, at least for the moment anyway, Tupper's credibility was a sight better than that of NBC Newscaster, John Cameron Swayze. For years, Swayze had moonlighted, doing *Timex* "Torture Test" commercials, everything from strapping a watch onto Rin-Tin-Tin's rear leg for a week, or driving a Hudson Hornet's wheel directly over a *Timex*, to having athletes like Rocky Colavito hit batting practice home runs with a *Timex* taped to the handle of the bat, or better yet, pugilist Sonny Liston wearing one while pounding the living crap out of George 'The Bleeder' Chuvalo. *"The watch that even Chuvalo's head couldn't stop,"* Swayze crowed proudly. *"Just like George, it takes a beating and keeps on ticking!"*

Yeah, right, all except for the one I own, Rod grumbled to himself, taking it off his wrist and vigorously shaking it for the tenth time that day. Holding it to his ear, he cursed under his breath.

They toss one into the Grand Canyon and then rush down to discover that it's still ticking. Me? I drop mine onto Mom's thick, plush carpet and it kicks the bucket—a week after the one year warranty expires, no less. I got rooked out of seven bucks! I'd love to personally tell Swayze where he can stick his Torture Tests!

Grateful for the unusually luminous moon, Rod could now clearly make out the sight of the majestic Cohoes Waterfalls. At ninety feet high and a thousand feet across, it was indeed a magnificent sight to behold. Completely unfettered and unrestrained, the falls were running at max power now, massive quantities of surging water crashing violently onto the jagged rocks below, billowing white foam churning the river's surface.

From time to time, depending upon demand and circumstance, the power authority officials regulated the flow as they saw fit.

Evidently, this wasn't one of those times. Totally unrestricted and roaring away in all its glory, it brought to mind the image of a certain beautiful woman, his girlfriend, Dee Dee, in a romantic setting, letting her hair down, just going with the flow, allowing the warm current of romance to take her and Rod wherever it may.

He shook his head, trying to clear away the distracting thoughts. *No sense in getting myself all worked up now. Hmm, there's always later, though*, Rod mused as he walked off, resuming his duties.

Moments later he was standing on the edge of the cavernous pit, where, within a few weeks, the footings for the new, secondary power plant would be poured. Shining his oversized flashlight down into the pit, he methodically scoured the area with the bright beam. Satisfied that there was nothing down there but dirt, he switched the flashlight off, jamming it into his back pocket as the sound of the *Flamingo's* "I only have eyes for you," emanated from his shirt pocket.

He was in the process of putting his Zippo's flame to a fresh Lucky when he felt the first drop of rain land on his ear. Looking up into the sky, he was rewarded with a big, juicy raindrop directly into his left eye. *You ask me, it looks like Howard Tupper's due for a new career. No rain, he promised. Yeah, right. I think it's time for Howard to step down, maybe take over the hosting bit on 'Teenage Barn' or the 'Freddie Freihofer Show.' A man needs to know his limitations.*

Rod tossed his smoke into the pit, the rain coming down harder now. Turning to head for the office trailer, he suddenly stopped dead in his tracks, convinced that he'd just heard a highly disturbing sound originating from the pit, an unearthly sound, if there ever was one, one that a frightened animal might make, a very large frightened animal.

The rain was coming down in buckets now, the black clouds groaning and crackling with thunder. Already soaked to the bone though he was, Rod nevertheless felt eerily compelled to take the flashlight out of his back pocket and shine it back down into the pit. Crouching down, he leaned out over the rim just a bit, playing the beam here and there, but finding nothing but mud.

Lightening pulsed across the sky, momentarily illuminating the pit even further. Rod knew he should hightail it for the trailer before he got barbequed by a bolt, yet he stubbornly gave it one more shot, absolutely certain now that he had indeed heard something, a faint, plaintive cry of distress, followed by a surreal moan of some sort. *Damn, only three weeks on the job and already I'm losing my mind*, he murmured to himself. *Hearing voices, no less.*

Inching out yet a little further over the rim, his transistor radio suddenly slipped free of his shirt pocket, tumbling down into the muck below, Dave Brubeck's "Take Five" fading as it fell.

Idiot! I'm an Idiot! If I had half a brain, I would've taken five, myself, at the first raindrop, he fumed.

Suddenly the storm intensified, ratcheting itself up yet another notch. *As if that were possible!* Rod groaned inwardly. *How much worse can it get?*

He was about to find out.

As he stood up, his shirtfront plastered against his chest, he got his answer.

The rain now fell in solid sheets, chestnut tree branches thrashing and twisting as the wind gusted, lightning bolts sizzling, spitting and crackling overhead, the black shale cliffs illuminated, the falls itself, faintly iridescent.

He ran as fast as he possibly could through the deepening muck. By the time he made it into the trailer, a three minute dash, he'd been roundly battered, beaten, buffeted and bewildered. His clothes clung to his body like a second skin, a clammy feeling if there ever was one. His head was pounding as the torrents of rain clattered against the aluminum roof.

First things first, he reminded himself. That radio was a gift from Dee Dee. If he lost it, or if it were rendered useless by the rain and mud, he'd never hear the end of it.

Spying a black, rubber raincoat hanging from a hook, he quickly donned it before grabbing Sal's umbrella and heading back out into the storm.

The instant he stepped out the door, he knew the umbrella was a waste of time. There was no way it would hold up, the wind threatening to rip it to shreds within moments. Reopening the metal door, he quickly tossed the umbrella back inside the trailer. As it was, Sal's twelve foot-wide, canvas company banner was rippling and popping in the wind, swelling and tugging against the knotted ropes that held it. The umbrella wouldn't have stood a chance.

As he slogged his way through the mud, his flashlight barely penetrating the intense curtain of rain, the wind swirled inside the trees, blistering the bark, the overhead branches creaking, cracking, snapping off and falling to the ground.

Bone-rattling thunderbolts of raw electricity rippled across the black sky, illuminating the pit as a shaft of lightening savaged a stately old chestnut tree, splitting it from stem to stern within milliseconds, the ensuing flames and smoke immediately snuffed out by the torrential downpour.

I should be in that damn trailer, Rod chastised himself. *At least it's grounded by those rubber tires...I think, anyway. Out here, I'm just begging to get zapped! All this for a stupid radio! I could go buy another one just like it at National Auto tomorrow, but no, stupid, stubborn me has to go find that particular radio because it has sentimental value. Idiot!*

Amazingly enough, the wind suddenly began to die down, the rain letting up considerably as he trudged along, supremely grateful for the break in the storm. Fog now began to roll across the river, the silhouette of the falls faintly visible through the mounting mist.

As he gingerly made his way down the slippery, muddy ramp into the pit, rain sluiced through a hundred ruts and channels, the streams quickly forming into vast puddles at the bottom. He knew his chances of recovering the radio were getting slimmer by the moment.

Fortunately, just as he reached the foot of the earthen ramp, the rain tapered off even further, settling in as a mild drizzle. He carefully made his way over to the east wall where he'd been crouching, when the radio had plummeted into the pit. His thoroughly soaked boots made loud sucking sounds as he plodded through the mire of mud, silently cursing his misfortune as he went.

Upon reaching his destination he directed the beam of light up the side of the east wall in an effort to establish just exactly where he was, when the radio took the plunge. A few moments later, convinced that he now had a pretty accurate inkling as to just where the radio probably landed, Rod began to slowly walk forward, hugging the wall as he went, the powerful beam of light illuminating the immediate area.

After a fruitless thirty minute search, he was about to throw in the towel when suddenly the beam picked up a slight glint of gold against a glimpse of baby blue background. *Eureka!*

Bending down, he reached into the muck and lifted the radio free. Incredibly enough, considering that the speaker grille was clogged near-solid with mud, the heart of the little radio was still beating, albeit faintly, but nevertheless stubbornly pumping out The Diamond's "Little Darlin'," for all it was worth.

He smiled inwardly. *Take that, John Cameron Swayze! Bet your Timex couldn't hold a candle to this little baby!*

Relieved, as well as tickled by the fact that his Mighty Mouse of a radio had weathered a hundred foot drop, followed by one hell of a torrential drenching, not to mention the ensuing mud bath, Rod stood up and began making his way over to the ramp.

That was when fate intervened. He'd no sooner taken two steps when he tripped over what he assumed to be nothing more than a thick tree branch, a victim of the hellacious storm, no doubt. Catching himself just as he began to topple over, Rod glanced down at the offending branch, the beam of his flashlight playing across its surface. It was long and thick, coming to a point at the end.

Hmmm, it doesn't look like any kind of branch that I've ever seen before, he thought to himself, leaning down to touch it, shining the light directly onto its surface. Severely checked and hairline-cracked throughout, the *thing*, whatever it was, had Rod puzzled. *Petrified wood, maybe?* He'd seen a few examples of it somewhere, in the state museum in Albany, more than likely.

Putting the heel of his boot to work, he began excavating along one side of it, little by little exposing more and more of whatever the hell it was. After he'd managed to dig a five inch trough on either side of the mysterious object, he squatted down alongside of it, holding the flashlight scant inches from the *thing*. Again, he was struck by the nagging thought that he'd seen something similar to this, somewhere, sometime in his past. The more he ran his hand over it, the further convinced he became that it definitely wasn't a length of petrified wood, but rather some kind of...*some kind of what?* He asked himself, racking his memory for a clue as to where he'd seen something just like this, once before.

He gave up five minutes later. While heading off for the ramp, however, he suddenly and inexplicably stopped dead in his tracks, turning to stare one more time at the strange object.

If someone had ever asked Rod for a clear explanation of just *why* he'd gone back and shrouded the odd thing with a thick layer of good old Cohoes mud, he'd have been hard pressed to provide them with a precise, logical answer. Hell, Hot Rod Hobbs is seventy-six years old now and to this day, he still doesn't know just *what* exactly moved him to shield the mysterious find from view.

As the years passed, Dee Dee eventually convinced him to just chalk it up to good ol' intuition and leave it at that.

Yeah, over time, Rod pretty much bought into her take on the whole thing. Well, mostly anyway. Sure, as far she knew, he'd accepted her advice and put the whole thing to bed, sort of.

Still, he never completely stopped puzzling over this rarest of rare discoveries, one that inarguably represented a defining moment in his life, a mile marker along the trek if there ever was one, and just think—it all occurred right here in Cohoes, on a stormy summer evening in July of 1959.

CHAPTER 14

Rod didn't sleep well, a truly rare occurrence. Normally you could fire a Howitzer cannon across the bow of his bed and he wouldn't have woken up, but not today. Weird dreams paraded through his mind. Images of a huge, unidentifiable animal, accompanied by panic-stricken, eerie cries relentlessly interrupted his sleep. Finally, around noontime, he gave up the ghost and rolled out of bed, the sunlight streaming through the window, momentarily blinding him. As was his daily habit, he called Dee Dee even before he'd had his first cup of coffee.

An hour later, showered and shaved, he fired up the Chevy and headed off downtown. Spying a spot in front of Breslaw's furniture store, he pulled in, shut off the engine and crossed the street.

Dee Dee was waiting for him at Kresge's lunch counter. She had company. Pops, the feisty curmudgeon from Bourkie's Blunder Bar was sitting alongside her, pounding his gnarled fist against the counter, insisting upon something or other.

"What's with the big ruckus, Pops?" Rod asked, sitting down alongside Dee Dee, giving her quick squeeze and an even quicker kiss.

Pops looked exasperated.

"Rena Trimm, here, self-appointed queen of the counter, doesn't believe that my grandfather, Francis Xavier Shea, is one of the men in this old newspaper photo," he explained huffily.

The matronly woman behind the counter rolled her eyes, sighing.

"I didn't say I didn't believe you, Pat. I simply said your claim would be a hell of lot more plausible if his *name* was printed there, under the photo."

"Yeah well, that could apply to that yellow mystery meat you serve here, too. Nobody knows what the hell it is, but you and Kresge insist that its ground beef. Tell old Man Kresge to print new menus up, and this time, come clean and put the actual name of the mystery meat under the picture of the so-called *Sloppy Joe* thing you pass off as a ground beef sandwich!" he complained gruffly. "Next thing you know, you'll be serving yellow *Spam* in here!"

Rod laughed as he leaned over and gently patted Pops' shoulder.

"Take it easy, Pops. Mrs. Trimm only works here. She just does her job, and, I might add, a real fine job at that."

Mrs. Trimm looked up from the grill and preened, tossing Rod a grateful smile as she adjusted her black hair net. She was a nice woman, albeit one that sported a faint moustache and chin whiskers. A lot of kids made fun of the unwanted growth, but not these three. They all thought the world of her and wouldn't have cared if she'd grown a full beard. They loved her.

"Why, thank you, Rod. I do believe you just earned yourself a free Richardson Root Beer."

Rod beamed.

"I accept. While you're at it, you mind fixing me and Dee Dee up a couple of those delicious sandwiches, just like the ones Pops is moaning and groaning about?"

Pops looked at him as if were a Martian, just recently arrived from the galaxies.

"So you're going to bust my chops, too?"

"Nah, we really like them, Pops, yellow meat and all," he admitted. "Hey, let me see that photo, will you? You got my curiosity up."

Pops eyes lit up, eager for an opportunity to convert an innocent into a true believer.

"You bet. Here you go," he said eagerly, carefully placing the yellowed newspaper clipping in front of Rod and Dee Dee.

"Look at the date at the top—September, 1866," he said excitedly. "Now look below. That there's a photo of my grandfather, may he rest in peace, along with the other two Micks who discovered the remains of the Cohoes Mastodon, while excavating the site for

Harmony Mill number three," he boasted proudly. "This newspaper clipping and two more just like it have been in the family for ninety-three years, yet Mrs. Trimm, or should I say *Prim*, flat-out refuses to believe that one of those men was my grandfather!" he huffed indignantly.

Rena heard every word of his tirade yet remained totally unruffled, content to sing along with the song emanating from the GE portable radio atop the root beer keg, Joe Jones' "You talk too much," while pointedly directing her gaze in Pops' direction.

"What are you staring at me for?" he asked her, clueless.

Rod nudged him. "This is the one that's on display at the state museum, right?" he inquired, his interest growing.

Pops gave him a condescending look. "Well, yeah...duh. How many other mastodons have they found lately? It isn't like finding the bones of a cat or a cow, you know! It'll probably be another five hundred years, or maybe longer, before they even have a prayer of ever finding another one in Cohoes, or anywhere else, for that matter."

Dee Dee leaned over to snatch a glimpse of the old photo. "Wow, I really dig it, Pops! To think that your own Grandpa was in on the find! That's far out, man!"

Pops looked puzzled. "*You dig it?* What the hell does that mean? The only digging here was done by my grandfather."

Rena patiently filled Pops in on the vernacular of the day, as she set his sandwich down before him.

"That's the problem with young people today," he fumed. "This Rock and Roll junk is only serving to corrupt the English language. I equate this claptrap so-called music with the effect of communism on the youth of today! Why, Dave Garroway and Frank Lescoulie were talking about it just this morning on the *Today Show*!"

Rena suppressed a yawn as she placed the sandwiches in front of Rod and Dee Dee.

"How about the chimp, *J. Fred Muggs*? What'd he have to say about Rock and Roll and communism?" she teased. "Nah, on second thought, he was probably too busy scrounging around for a banana to offer an opinion."

"Humph! A regular Imogene Cocca you are." Pops groused.

"Gee whiz, that really means a lot, coming from you, Pat."

Rod heard none of it. Between bites of his sandwich, he was busy navigating the murky waters of his imagination, little by little successfully connecting the dots. His mind, like a slow-turning roulette wheel, was beginning to tell him that he just *might* be in line for one *very large* payday.

He reached back into his memory, clearly recalling the fully assembled skeleton of the Cohoes Mastodon on display at the state museum. The tusks, he'd been informed by a museum guide, were too heavy to be mounted directly onto the skeleton, so rather than risk compromising the structural integrity of the behemoth frame, lightweight, man-made tusks were attached to the head. The genuine tusks were then placed in a glass display case, situated directly in front of the assembled skeleton.

Rod recalled staring at the real-deal tusks, fascinated by their sheer size. Yellowed, checked and hairline-cracked by time and nature's elements, they were truly a sight to behold. *Yeah, and I do believe I may have beheld it once again, just last night, as a matter of fact*, he marveled to himself.

Yeah, once he realized what he'd discovered, it didn't come to him in a sudden flash of insight, but more like an avalanche, starting small, but growing inexorably until it swamped it everything.

His mind was racing now, bouncing around with pinball energy, setting off all the bells, caroming off the rails, intent on bagging a record score.

"Too bad Kresge's doesn't serve brew-skis here at the counter. A man can handle only just so much root beer, unless of course, old man Kresge decided to implement a bottomless refill policy," Pops remarked, his words interrupting Rod's thoughts, bringing him back to earth.

"Huh? What's that, Pops?"

"Pat was saying we ought to have a free refill policy on the soda," Rena explained. "It's never going happen, though, because people like him would abuse it mercilessly."

"Not listening to me, eh, Rod?" Pops asked peevishly. "Just for that, you can foot the bill for the ice cream sundae I'm planning on ordering. Let me have one of those balloons, Rena."

"Grab two more while you're at, please," Dee Dee chimed in.

The air above the back counter was generously festooned with inflated balloons. Anyone could order a sundae and rather than pay full price up front, they could opt for a balloon. Once deflated, courtesy of a pair of scissors, a tiny slip of paper inside would reveal the cost of the sundae. It ranged anywhere from a penny right on up to full price. Needless to say, the promotion went over quite well with the customers.

Rena got right to it.

"All right, Pat, yours is only going to be five cents," she announced as she grabbed two more balloons. "Let's see now, Rod," she said as she snipped off the ends of them. "Okay, one will cost you twenty cents and the other will only be seven cents. Not bad. You made out well, Rod."

"Great," he replied absently, his thoughts light years away from the cost of sundaes.

"You know, this reminds me of the temporary job I took after I got laid off from the Ford factory," Pops recalled. "I was driving a truck for the *Original Crispy Pizza Company*, getting paid under the table, so as to not screw up my unemployment benefits. Here I was delivering frozen pizzas to stores in the area when one icy January day I got myself into a helluva jam," he said. "Wait til you get a load of this story," he crowed. "It's one for the record books!"

As it was, no one was paying a bit of attention to him. Rena was busy preparing the sundaes while Dee Dee was intent on watching her do it, and Rod...well, as we already know, his mind was elsewhere.

"Jaysus, don't all clamor at once to hear my tale of woe! What, am I boring you or something?" Pops squawked, all put-out over their obvious lack of interest. "If Hot Rod spins a tale, *everybody* listens. If I tell a story, *nobody* listens!"

Rena found herself at a place she didn't often visit—the end of her patience. Glancing over her shoulder at him, she shot her old friend a withering glare.

"Still trying to develop that personality, I see. As you should've noticed, I'm rather busy at the moment, Pat, yet regardless of that, I actually was indeed listening. Now, why don't you just hold your horses for another minute or so while I finish up here, and then you can talk until you're blue in the face."

Pops grunted and groaned as he swiveled his stool toward Rod. "It's a good thing for Rena that I happen to like her."

"Is this going to be a story that we've already heard a few dozen times, Pops?" Dee Dee teased good-naturedly.

Pops grinned, despite himself. "They say that hope springs eternal," he wisecracked. "And I'm hoping you won't remember the story."

"Now there's a hopeless possibility," Rena piped in, setting a hot fudge sundae down in front of Dee Dee.

"Is this the story about the time you tried to move a bridge with a truck?" Dee Dee inquired, lifting a spoon to her mouth.

"Humph. So what if it's a rerun? You'll still be in for a treat. Hell, all of my true stories improve over time. You ought to know that by now. Don't be such a cynic, young lady."

"I'm not a cynic. I'm a skeptic," she quipped.

"And I'm realist. I know that you'll never rest until you put us to sleep with your story," Rena chipped in. "So go for it. After all, few things provide me with such joy, a sense of purpose, that your tired old tales give me, so knock yourself out while you're enjoying the sundae," she said, sighing wearily.

Pops dipped his spoon into the whipped cream topping. "Say what you will, but it's still a story for the ages," he insisted, wiping his lips with a napkin. "It was a frigid cold Saturday afternoon and the streets were slicker than a pickpocket's fingers. I turned off Saratoga Street and onto Bridge Avenue when suddenly the six-wheel box truck started slipping and sliding. I flat-out couldn't control it and the next thing I know, the truck climbs the curb and proceeds to go right over Carlson's ice rink wall, just barely missing a few skaters below. The truck drops right smack dab into the shallow end of the rink, sinking up to the door handles. Somehow, Iver Carlson and a few others managed to fish me out of the truck. Luckily, I didn't have a scratch on me, but *Iver*? He was having conniptions, yelling and fuming like Desi Arnez after somebody swiped his bongo drums!"

"It was a half hour before a guy from Berdar's showed up with a tow truck. He tried and tried to yank the truck out of there, but it just wouldn't budge. Meanwhile, the temperature's dropping even lower and because of that, the ice is beginning to re-form around the truck, locking it in tight. I called my boss to let him know about the unfortunate accident."

"How'd that go?" Dee Dee asked, although she already knew the answer.

"Well, let's just say it didn't bring any sunshine into his life."

"Anyway, he arranged for a guy in a truck with a winch on the back, to come over and give it a shot. All the while, Iver Carlson's face was getter redder by the minute, if such a thing was possible. He's ranting and raving, the veins in his forehead and neck pulsing and bulging like crazy—a heart attack waiting to happen. He calls my boss back and starts screaming, threatening a lawsuit, and how he's going to have to shut down and be forced to refund all of the skater's admission money."

"The boss, who's also the owner, offers to have me pull the inventory from the truck and if Carlson agrees to use his own ovens, everybody at the rink will get free pizza—all they want of it. That calmed him down a bit. Not much, but enough. Within an hour, the skaters were filling their frosty-cold faces with piping hot pizza. It was like a party to them. Hell, some of them were even posing for photos while perched on the fenders and hood of the truck. They acted real disappointed-like when they had to get off, so that the winch could haul the truck out of the ice, and indeed it did just that, on the first attempt, no less."

"You left out the part where you got fired," Rena reminded him. "That's the best part, sort of like the cherry atop the pizza."

"Funny. The Martha Raye of Cohoes, you are," Pops muttered under his breath. "Anybody ever tell you that you can be a royal pain in the ol' keyster?"

"All the time. At least three times a week, actually." she shot back without skipping a beat. "Maybe a bit less often, during leap years."

"Well, it all worked out okay," Dee Dee reminded him. "If I recall correctly, Ford called you back to work about a week after you'd personally orchestrated the Cohoes version of *Ice Capades on wheels.*"

"Yeah, that's about how it went," he replied, stifling a yawn. "Well, it's about time for me to head on over to the Legion Post for some liquid dessert, something with a nice head of foam on it."

"On top of a stomach load of ground beef, root beer and a hot fudge sundae?" Rena cried, incredulous.

"Sure, why the hell not?" he replied defiantly as he stood, arching the kinks out of his back. "Besides, my back only bothers me when I'm sober. To me, that's as good a reason as any to stay drunk."

Dee Dee was aghast.

"That's the craziest logic I've ever heard! Why don't you go down to the VA and have your back checked over? And give your liver a break for a change, while you're at it, why don't you? A little dose of sobriety might do you a world of good, Pops," she lectured, her heartfelt advice falling on deaf ears.

He smiled sadly, staring down at the creaky, old oak floor, as if seriously contemplating her well-intentioned advice.

"Nah. I know you mean well, Dee Dee, but that train has already left the station," he replied dismissively. "A long time ago, truth be told. Besides, sobriety's overrated. Why get sober in the afternoon, when all I'm going to do is get bombed all over again at night? It's like making the bed every day. *For what?* You're only going mess it up again later."

All three sighed in unison. "What are we going to do with you, Pat?" Dee Dee asked, shaking her head, frustrated.

"I don't know, kiddo, but I know exactly what *I'm* going to do with me. I'm going to walk outside now and head on over to the Post, lighting up a *Raleigh* along the way, spicing up the fresh air with some good ol' Brown and Williamson tobacco smoke."

Later that afternoon Rod and Dee Dee took a spin down to Ginny's Soft Ice Cream stand on the Cohoes Road. Dee Dee opted for a Coke, content to watch and marvel at her boyfriend's seemingly bottomless capacity and appetite for ice cream.

"You had a hot fudge sundae two hours ago. Now you're doing battle with the tallest cone I've ever seen. What's next—A Banana Split?"

"Hey, now there's an idea! After all, I'm still a growing boy. I need my calcium," he insisted, ice cream dripping down upon his fingers.

"Well, growing boy, after you finish the leaning tower of ice cream, we better head back to my house. As it is, I'll only have about an hour to get ready to go to the Avon party at Kitchie Hayden's mother's house," she moaned, sighing. "Nothing against Kitchie—lord knows I love the girl, but I'd rather spend the time with you, before you have to go to work."

"Yeah, I really wish you could, too," he lied. Truth be told, he was chomping at the bit, impatient to get over to Bourkie's and tell Butch about what he'd stumbled across last night, or rather, what he *thought* he may have come across.

For some reason, unknown even to him, he hadn't yet said a word about it to Dee Dee.

"I was looking forward to curling up on the couch together, watching *Peter Gunn* and *Naked City* with you," she said.

"Me too," he again lied, leaning over to kiss her.

After dropping her off at home, he immediately sped over to Bourkie's. The bar was fairly busy, working men fresh from their jobs lining the brass rail.

"What's up?" Butch asked, setting a Schaefer down in front of Rod.

"I got to talk to you about something. Actually, I may need your help with something later tonight, after you close up."

"Sure, but with what? We don't shut down until three, you know."

"Yeah, I know. Look, lean in closer and I'll tell you what's on my mind."

Butch listened intently as Rod began to fill him in, his eyes growing ever wider as the tale unfolded.

"You got to be pulling my chain!" he exclaimed. "No way!"

Rod hurriedly raised a finger to his lips.

"Shh! Keep it down."

"Sorry. Listen, I'll be right back. I'm dying to hear the rest, but first I got to take care of some of these guys."

The lighting in the bar was pretty dim, but Rod could clearly make out the large, shadowy figure of Lenny Fishowski as he shot darts with a big, tall kid named Pookie Schmeer and another local, Frannie Kelly.

A moment later, Fish threw his darts and then walked over to a nearby table, picking up his empty beer glass, heading to the bar for a refill. He sidled up alongside Rod's stool.

"Hey, Hot Rod. Catch those thieves yet?" he asked with a sneer, his breath foul, strong enough to peel paint off a car.

Rod turned slightly, taking in the man's wide, lumpy, pitted face. Fish was smiling a humorless smile, his big teeth crooked and rotting, reminiscent of a picket fence in need of some serious repairs.

"Nice haircut," Rod remarked offhandedly, commenting on the receding black hair which had been recently mowed down to the nub, resulting in a five o'clock shadow atop the head, matching the one on his face.

"Yeah, well, it gets pretty hot, wearing a hard hat all day. It won't be long and you'll be wearing one too...that is, after you nab the bad guys that have been stealing from Sal," he replied, pausing to fire up a Chesterfield. "A couple of thoughts on that—What if they don't come back to swipe more stuff? What if your presence there scares them off? Better yet, what if they flat-out don't plan on *ever* coming back for more? Ever considered that?"

"Sal is convinced they'll be back for more, one of these nights," Rod answered. "Just like greedy cockroaches that like to operate in the dark."

"*Cockroaches?* Ha! That's a good one! Yeah, and if he gets his hands on them, he'll likely take a sledgehammer to them cockroaches. That's Sal's style. Me, I prefer to be more subtle. Hell, I could probably beat a tiger to death with a feather."

"Yeah, I can just picture it now."

Fish shot him a curious look as Butch set a fresh *Utica Club* down in front of him.

"You don't like me much, do you?"

Rod shrugged.

"Frankly, I don't have any opinion of you one way or the other," he replied unconvincingly.

Fish chugged his beer, draining the pilsner glass dry. From behind, his pal, Pookie, was calling to him, reminding Fish that it was his turn to shoot. He ignored him.

"Frankly, I think that's a piss-poor answer," he growled ominously, dropping, and then crushing his cigarette beneath the heel of his heavy engineer's boot.

"Think what you want."

Fish leaned in closer, his breath fetid, his eyes cold and hard, like black glass.

"I always do," he said, pausing to light another smoke. "Funny thing is, most people end up liking me, or at least making believe they do."

"Just before I was dishonorably discharged, an army shrink told me that in his opinion, I was charismatic," he went on. *Charismatically psychotic*, I think he called it. Now ain't that a laugh?" he asked, his face mere inches from Rod's "So, what do you think of that diagnosis?"

"I think you need to get out of my face. That's what I think," Rod snapped, his patience at an end.

"Poison Ivy," by the Coasters began play on the jukebox.

"What's the matter, Hot Rod, or should I say *Hot Shot*? Afraid you might catch something from being too close to me? I don't have poison ivy, you know" he sneered, assuming an air of wounded dignity.

Rod stared straight ahead, his blood pressure climbing.

"Go shoot your darts and quit bugging me."

Fish flinched, as if slapped, a menacing scowl taking up residence on his ugly, cratered face.

"You know, actually, I never did care for you, Hobbs, but some reason it bugs me to think that you don't *like me!*" he spat angrily. "I wonder what that army headhunter would make of that!"

Rod turned, forcing out an indulgent smile, like a shrink trying to deal with a hopeless patient.

"Why don't you drop *Dear Abby* a line? She could probably give you an answer, Fish. If not, then try asking Rod Serling. You'd be right up his *Twilight Zone* alley, I'm sure."

"Hey, Fish! Are going to shoot darts or not?" Frannie Kelley yelled across the barroom.

"Be right there," the big man replied in a surprisingly even tone. "I'm just finishing up something here."

Deadlocked in an intense duel of icy glares, Fish blinked first.

"Let me leave you with this thought, Hobbs—how would you like to be my first homicide victim?" he hissed, his face crimson, the thick veins in his forehead wriggling and pulsating like angry snakes.

"What was that all about?" Butch asked. "Fish looked as if he was ready to spit bullets."

Rod brought his friend up to speed.

"Damn, if I didn't know better I'd think you must have done the Rip Van Winkle thing and went to sleep for the last ten years! Have you got a death wish or something? I heard Fish almost killed his drill sergeant a few years back, beating the poor guy to a pulp, and then you tell him to go get bent? Jumping Jesus! Talk about playing in heavy traffic! "

Rod huffed impatiently.

"Did I ask you for your opinion?"

"Geez, I was just saying, you know?" Butch replied, his arms raised placatingly. "Just saying, that's all."

"Yeah, yeah," Rod replied dismissively. "Listen, I got to tell you the rest of my story, but first, go make a run down the bar. Make sure everyone's set and then come right back. Oh, and crack me open another cold one while you're at it."

Rod lit a Lucky Strike, tapping his feet against the brass rail to the beat of Presley's "A Big Hunk O' Love."

Butch returned moments later.

"The three of them have been staring daggers at your back, ever since Fish filled his pals in on your conversation," Butch informed Rod in a near whisper.

"Like I really care what *Kukla, Fran and Ollie* are saying about me," Rod replied sarcastically, blowing it off. "Forget about them. I'm about to lay something on you, something that's going to knock your socks off. Just remember, this is for your ears only. You don't share what I'm about to tell with *anyone*, not even Linda. Got that?"

Butch puffed out his chest proudly while raising his hand. "I swear, on Bishop Fulton J. Sheen's head that Elliot Ness himself couldn't get me talk about it—whatever *it* is."

Throughout the next four minutes, Rod gave Butch the scoop on what he believed to be the find of the century.

Just as Rod finished recounting his tale, Butch let loose with a long, low whistle.

"You gotta be pulling my leg!" he cried, shaking his head in disbelief. "How do you know it wasn't just some plastic thingamajig, some phony-baloney tusk, planted there by Allen Funt, setting up another one of his *Candid Camera* stunts?"

Rod sighed deeply, the sound like a tire deflating.

"Sometimes I think the screw-up fairy, instead of the stork, delivered you to your mother—and then decided to stay, to make sure you skipped right over *dumb* and proceeded directly to *stupid*," Rod speculated, clearly frustrated by his pal's cerebral limitations.

"What? Okay, so maybe that's a little farfetched, but hey, no need to insult me over it," Butch complained, justifiably more than a bit miffed.

"Sorry. You're right," Rod admitted, genuinely apologetic now. "I was out of line. It's just that I'm all hepped up over this. Man, If we can dig this thing up tonight, then get it out of there and stow it securely hidden away, I got to believe there'll be a big payday in the near future for us, my friend," he gushed enthusiastically.

"We? What'd you need me for?" Butch asked, clearly puzzled.

Rod looked at him as if he'd just stepped off a Martian spaceship.

"Are you kidding me? You know how big those animals were? Even if it's all right there, in one spot, and not scattered around piecemeal, it'll still take God knows how long to dig it all up and get it the hell off the site! I sure can't do it alone. Besides, if my hunch is correct and it really is what I think it is, the tusks and skull are going be heavier than hell. You got to help me, Butch!"

"Okay, okay! But remember, I don't get out of here until after we close, at three."

"I need you to come down with a sudden fever tonight, around ten o'clock. Bourkie will be working the back room as always, keeping an eye on the poker game, so he can take over the bar for you. Go home, throw on some old clothes, call your grandfather and ask if you can use his truck for a week or so, then go get it, and drive it down to the site. He'll let you use it. He never says no to you for anything. I'd use the company truck, but I can't risk somebody seeing me in it when I'm supposed to be down at the site. Oh, and also ask him if you can temporarily store some stuff in that old rickety barn of his up on Western Avenue.

"That should put you down at the site right around eleven, or eleven-fifteen," he went on. "Park the truck up the street and then walk down to the gates. I'll be waiting there for you."

"Got it. Want me to bring anything? Shovels? Grandpa's wheel barrow?"

"No, there's loads of those things right there. If you want to bring anything, bring bug repellant and a few six-packs of beer. It promises to be thirsty work."

"All right. I'll see you then. Thank God, tomorrow's my day off," Butch said, yawning. "Something tells me I'm going to want to sleep all day long."

"Hey, if this works out the way I'm hoping it will, you'll get that new Corvair in no time flat," Rod reminded him. "*And* an Edsel, to boot!"

Butch looked far from convinced.

"I guess."

Rod grinned as Sinatra's latest hit, "High Hopes" came through the jukebox speakers, loud and clear.

"Just listen to the man's lyrics, Butch. It about says it all, my friend."

CHAPTER 15

Fortunately for them, the late evening was clear and balmy, ideal conditions for trolling for mastodon remains, or so Rod thought anyway.

Butch's mouth dropped open upon viewing the ancient tusks up close.

"So what do you think of those babies?" Rod asked.

"I think we've just entered the *Twilight Zone*, is what I think! I don't know about this!"

Rod shot him an appraising glance.

"You're not going to bail on me, are you? I need your help, and you know that."

"Hell no, I'd never do that to you," he assured his friend. "It's just that I don't much care for work that comes with blisters."

By the time they got the first load of incredibly heavy bones loaded onto the truck they were ready for a beer.

Sitting on the lowered tailgate, Butch handed Rod a church key and a can of *Genny* Cream Ale.

"Why'd you bring this crap? I hate this stuff," he groused, rolling the icy cold can across his forehead, trying to cool himself off a bit. The muscles in his arms were knotted like rocks, his skin slick with sweat, his shirtfront plastered against his chest.

"I thought it'd be good for a change," Butch explained.

"Yeah, well, do me a favor and *don't* think, will you?"

"It's that bad?"

"Worse."

"Okay, next time I'll bring some Dobler's."

Rod grimaced.

"I'd sooner drink battery acid. I want *Schaeffer's*, Butch, nothing but Schaeffer's. Think you can remember that?"

Butch laughed.

"Come on. Where's your sense of humor, Hot Rod?"

"I parked it until we get these bones out of here. I'm not in the mood for humor at the moment."

As Butch opened his can of beer, a big fat juicy raindrop landed on his hand.

"Great. Now it's starting to rain," he groused dejectedly.

Rod chugged his beer down.

"Drink up. We got to get back down there while we still can. Bring the rope with you. We may have to hoist up some of the bigger ones."

They were lucky. The rain clouds moved on quickly. Struggling to unearth more of the huge skeleton, however, was anything but quick. They labored for five more hours, digging down into the muck, loading bones into wheelbarrows, pushing them as close as they could to the base of the ramp. From there they carried the bones up to the truck. The ones that proved too heavy and cumbersome to tote were tied with rope and then hoisted up to the lip of the pit.

"I'm whipped," Butch complained. "Not to mention that dawn is on the way. We need to get out of here."

Rod nodded wearily, his shovel dropping to the mud.

"Yeah, that's enough for one night."Glancing at his watch, he noted that it was almost 5:15.

"Come on. Let's just spread this mud around evenly, so that no one's the wiser. Just make sure that no bones are poking through it."

"What about our footprints all over the place?"

"We'll fill them in with mud, and level them off with our shovels. Then, as we walk up the ramp we'll drag the shovels behind us, smoothing it out as we go. That'll do it. Then tomorrow night, we'll get right back at it."

"How many more bones do you figure are still down here?"

Rod shrugged.

"The hell if I know."

"Well, we must have gotten at least a third of them, don't you think?"

Rod sighed in exasperation.

"How would I know?" he replied testily, finding himself at the limit of his patience. "Do I look like a museum curator to you? What I know about mastodon skeletons, you could fit inside a Cott's bottle cap. Now stop asking stupid questions!"

Butch's face fell faster than a busted elevator.

No sooner had the harsh words left his mouth and Rod instantly regretted them.

"Aw, I'm sorry, pal. I didn't mean that. I'm just tired and tense, that's all," he apologized, patting his best friend's shoulder.

Butch brightened right up.

"That's okay. I do ask a lot of stupid questions, but then as Miss Hickey, our principal, always claimed, my IQ is only marginally higher than a turtle's, but not by much. So what do you expect?" Butch said with a laugh.

"Never mind what that prison warden said. Your mind is just fine, buddy," Rod assured him. "Anyway, let's finish up and get out of here."

"Yeah, we still got to unload the bones and pack them away in the barn."

"That's right. Come on. Let's get moving. "

The old International Pickup chugged up Columbia Street, belching and wheezing asthmatically all the way. To make matters worse, whatever springs it might have had once upon a time, had long since gone to the big suspension shop in the sky.

"Think she's going to make it?" Rod asked, clearly concerned. "The tranny sounds as if it's got rocks rattling around in it."

"Yep. Don't worry. This old gal is just like Gypsy Rose Lee, a little droopy and worn around the edges; maybe even a helluva lot slower with the moves, but she can still bring a man where he wants to go."

Rod stared at him.

"You're comparing this truck to a retired stripper? Do her brakes wail like a banshee, too, sounding like a cat in a dryer?"

Butch laughed.

"And here I thought you were the kind of guy who looked for the inner beauty in a gal, even if she is a bit long in the tooth," Butch joked.

"Nope, that's not me. Donnie Holbrook, maybe, but not me. "

That drew an even bigger belly laugh.

"I don't know about that. Donnie's last girlfriend seemed pretty darn good-looking to me."

"Yeah, but then you were probably drunk at the time."

"Aw, come on. Donnie's a good friend of yours. Don't be like that," Butch countered. "And I'll have you know I wasn't drunk. Stone sober I was, and I tell you she was indeed good-looking," he insisted.

Rod was enjoying himself now, and wasn't ready to let it go just yet.

"Well, I suppose you could call her good-looking, just as long as there's no other girls around for the sake of comparison...that, and if the room is dark."

Butch giggled.

"Man, that's cold," he chided Rod kiddingly. "One thing, though, did you know Donnie went and had her name tattooed on his arm?"

"You're kidding!"

"Nope, and now he's stuck with it. I mean, what's a guy supposed to do after he goes and does that, and then she takes a hike on him?"

"Date someone else with the same name?" Rod offered.

"That kind of limits his options, don't you think?"

"Donnie will think of something. He always does. If not, he'll have to settle for always wearing long sleeved shirts on his future dates. He's a piece of work, that boy is."

"Donnie? Oh yeah. They threw the mold out after making him. He's one of a kind. I'm just not exactly sure what kind he is," Butch replied, laughing.

It was 6 am by the time they yanked off the tarp, unloaded the bones, dragged them into the ramshackle barn,and covered them up with some rotten, old, gray hay that'd probably been sitting in there since 1935. Fortunately, Butch's grandfather hadn't stepped foot in the old barn in many a year and wasn't about to do so, either, any time soon. The poor old fellow walked with a cane nowadays, an unfortunate victim of rheumatoid arthritis. That, combined with the fact that his home was, for him anyway, a good twenty minute walk from the barn, pretty much ensured that he wouldn't be poking around in there today, or any other day, for that matter. Rod doubted that anyone else would either, as the nearest neighbor was quite a ways off and the barn was set back a good three hundred feet from Western Avenue. Yeah, Rod was feeling pretty good about his choice of a hiding place.

And then it hit him—the worry bug.

What if someone discovers the bones, someone who maybe watched, as we unloaded our cargo? He fretted. *What If we return with another load tomorrow night, only to find that our first cache of bones has been stolen? What if this—what if that?*

Rod sighed. He'd just discovered that he didn't much like contemplating the strings of chance that held his dreams of wealth together.

CHAPTER 16

Unfortunately, Rod's parents were already up when he walked through the door. They each glanced up from the newspaper sections they were perusing, giving him a *look-what-the-cat-dragged-in* look. His Mom took it a step further, like she was shopping in Nasser's Market, looking over a suspect peach, wondering how it'd gotten so crummy looking so soon.

"Take those boots off. You aren't walking through the house wearing those filthy clodhoppers," she ordered.

As he bent down to untie the mud-encrusted boots, his father threw in his two cents, too.

"Well, Son, how's this high paying job of yours working out? You ask me, it looks like you've gone from a hero to a zero in a Cohoes minute. Even Mister Magoo would be able to see that. What's Sal got you doing, burying his enemies? You're wearing more mud than a World War one doughboy."

Rod sighed, his eyes lifting to the ceiling. Exhausted, he wasn't up for a verbal duel.

"Funny, Dad, real funny."

His father laughed a humorless laugh.

"Well, if this so-called job of yours doesn't work out, you can probably catch on with St. Agnes' Cemetery. They're always looking for some fresh gravediggers."

Taking full note of the insult beneath *so-called job*, Rod's face turned the glowing crimson of red-hot steel. Bone tired and cranky, he wasn't in the mood for this crap.

He sent his father a glacial look, acid enough to etch glass.

"You think that little of me? Thanks a lot, Dad," he spat, his voice laden with sarcasm.

His dad chuckled, like a man who'd just heard a good joke.

"Father Ashline's always reminding us that we reap what we've sown. Well, right about now I'm not too proud of what I reaped from all that sowing," he snapped, scoring a cut right to the bone.

"Frank!" Rod's mother cried, truly aghast at what she'd just heard. "How dare you talk that way to your own son!"

Frank threw the newspaper across the table and then angrily stormed out the back door, slamming it behind him. Miraculously, it didn't fly off the hinges, but it sure wasn't due to a lack of effort.

Rod's mother buried her face in her hands as she began to sob.

His own anger melted away as he walked over to his mother, gently placing his hands upon her quaking shoulders. He wanted to say something, something that would be calm her down, make her feel better, but the words wouldn't, or couldn't come. In the end he settled for kissing her on the forehead before heading for the bathroom.

Upon awakening eight hours later, his first thought was *damn, my aches have got aches!* A dull throbbing scoured his shoulders and the cords in his neck. Wincing as he sat up, it took a few moments for him to collect his thoughts. He'd slept fitfully, strange, eerie dreams filled with the most God-awful sounds of anguish and terror haunting his sleep. The screams, as near as he could recall, weren't like anything he'd ever heard in his life, at least not from a human being. Troubled by the nature and content of the dreams, a swift series of connect-the-dots thoughts followed as he tried unsuccessfully to pull the dreams back into his conscious mind, but they were long gone, like smoke up a chimney.

He stood and stretched his sore muscles. Even in the best of times Rod wasn't one to leap out of bed, ready to attack any challenge the day might bring. Today, if he had his druthers, he'd just as soon plop back in bed for a few more hours of shuteye, but it wasn't to be. He'd promised Dee Dee that he'd take her to Toma's for supper.

After he'd shaved, showered and dressed, it was time to go and pick her up. Rod hurriedly shoved his boots and clean work clothes into an Empire Market grocery bag and then headed for the door. He tried his best to avoid his mother, but it wasn't to be.

"What's your big hurry?" his mother asked. Standing over the stove, fussing over a pot of pea soup, she gave him the kind of look that as a little kid, never failed to make him feel guilty, even if he'd done nothing to warrant it. Evidently, he still had some of that little kid left in him because here he was, feeling guilty.

"Well, Ma, I got a few errands to run before I pick up Dee Dee."

"What kind of errands?"

"I got to go the Ukrainian shoemaker, the guy with the shop in his cellar over on Mangam Street. He put new heels on my high ducks. I got to pick them up."

"Where else do you have to go?"

"Uh, I don't know, Ma. I just got things to do, you know?" he replied, impatient as ever.

"Well, before you start taking care of the *things you got to do*, I need you to run down to the butcher shop and pick me a nice meaty ham bone to put in this soup. I called him an hour ago and told him to put one aside. He knows what I like. Now take the money off the counter, and make sure you hurry back."

Rod blew out his breath as he scooped up the two dimes and headed for the door.

"Hey, what's this—no kiss for your mother?"

Rod dutifully complied.

"Now that's more like it," she said, adding "And about this morning, forget what came out of your father's mouth. He didn't mean a word of it, believe me. He's just worried about you."

Rod didn't offer a reply. Some things were better left unsaid.

The butcher shop was just a short drive away. Rod got down there in about three minutes. The place was typical of butcher shops everywhere, a bit chilly inside, lots of sawdust on the floor, big, white refrigerated meat cases and a couple of guys in long white aprons, one of whom was the owner himself. The man had the kind of hands you'd expect a life-long meat cutter to have. In other words, he was missing a number of fingers. Two on his left hand, while on his right, his forefinger and little finger were nowhere to be found. Of course, seeing as how he liked to take a nip every now and then from the bottle of J & B that he kept discreetly tucked away, or so he thought anyway, under the cash register counter, it was no surprise that the butcher was running low on fingers. Even so, however, he nevertheless was a pretty cheerful guy. Just how much of that cheerfulness could be directly attributed to his daily intake of Scotch, no one could really say.

They exchanged a little small talk, along with twenty cents, and then Rod was on his way. Just as he was about to get into his car, however, he decided to cross the street to buy cigarettes. Sam Eacy's little corner store was jam-packed with merchandise and the diminutive fellow did a brisk business. Upon walking in, Rod saw two boys about eleven years old, each hand Sam a nickel. He in turn handed them each three Lucky Strikes.

Their transactions completed, the boys sauntered out the door, stopping but briefly to light up.

"Give me two packs of Luckies, will you, Sam?"

Little Sam smiled, reaching up to extract the two packs of smokes from the overhead rack.

"I see you're still doing the *three for a nickel* thing, Sam. Tell me, do you have a minimum requirement, say Kindergarten age, or can toddlers waddle up to the counter and make a buy?" Rod inquired playfully.

Sam grinned, shrugging his shoulders.

"If I don't sell them to the kids, somebody else will, so it may as well be me, right?"

"I guess. Anyway, take care, Sam."

His Mom carefully examined the ham bone, turning it this way and that as she scrutinized every inch of it.

"Humph. Not much meat on here, certainly not twenty cents worth, anyway. I'm going to have to have a talk with him."

"Okay, Ma. You got your bone. Now I got to go."

"Wait a minute. Are you coming back for dinner?"

"I'm going to Toma's with Dee Dee, remember?"

"Yes, but come back here before you go to work, young man. You hear me? You need to take some of this soup to work with you."

Rod's eyes rolled upward.

"Yeah, ok."

"And don't give me that look. You've got to eat, you know. Those are long hours you're working down there."

"I said *okay*, didn't I?" he said huffily.

If looks could kill, Rod would have been six feet under.

"Watch your tone of voice, young man! Must I remind you that this is your *mother* that you're talking to?"

"Yes, Ma, I know," he replied sheepishly. "Don't worry. I'll be back for the soup. I promise."

After picking up his shoes, he headed downtown, stopping briefly at Seymour's Men's and Boy's Shop to check out the popular merchant's latest arrivals. Nothing caught his eye. Rod, however, had certainly caught Seymour's eye. About forty, paunchy and prematurely balding, Seymour was an okay guy, generally speaking, except when he was staring at you through his Buddy Holly glasses, his accounts receivable alarm clanging away in his head.

"Hey, Hobbs, don't you still owe me $11.50?"

"No, I paid it off two weeks ago!" Rod reminded him tersely, a little hot under the collar now.

Seymour's expression turned pensive, the wheels turning. After a few moments, the clanging appeared to cease.

"Hmm, oh yes, I remember now. Sorry about that," he said, although not appearing to be in the least bit sorry.

Having adjusted to the changing breeze as adroitly as a politician might, Seymour launched into his trademark shtick, that being a routine that had virtually every young customer, if not believing, then at least considering, that the clothes Seymour recommended for them made them appear as handsome as Troy Donahue, Ed *Kookie* Byrnes, James Dean or at minimum, Wally Cleaver. Hell, a pink polka dot pig could have flown by with a White Owl cigar stuck in his teeth and Seymour would have crowed *'Have I got just the suit for you!'*

"Did you see this? It would look terrific on you!" Seymour gushed enthusiastically. Ever the consummate hustler, he continued on, holding the white Perry Como sweater up against Rod's chest. "Why, these are all the rage today! You need one of these, son, and the blue piping *really, really* brings out the blue in your eyes. Come on, try it on!"

Now Rod was beginning to regret having ever stopped here.

"No, I don't think so, Seymour. It really doesn't interest me."

The merchant appeared to be offended...but then he always did.

"What? It doesn't interest you?" Seymour put down the sweater and placed a fatherly, yet totally insincere hand upon Rod's broad shoulder. "Son, let me tell you, this is the *absolute* very latest in fashion. Why, just the other day that popular young singer, Fabian, was on the Dick Clark Show and what do you think he was wearing? I'll tell you what he was wearing. He was wearing an exact copy of this particular sweater, *that's* what he was wearing!"

"I don't know, Seymour. I still don't think it's for me," Rod replied half-heartedly. Seymour was working his usual magic, whittling down a potential customer's resolve, little by little, dollar by dollar.

The wily merchant stared at him, a finger raised to his lips, as if a sudden thought had just occurred to him.

"You know, come to think of it, you bear a striking resemblance to that Fabian boy, you know that?"

Rod's face may have been deeply tanned, yet he could feel his cheeks getting red hot. He certainly enjoyed being complimented about his uncanny resemblance to Fabian, but he hadn't yet learned how to gracefully accept the compliments without also getting embarrassed by them.

Bottom line, he walked out of Seymour's with a box that contained not one, but *two* Perry Como sweaters, and a wallet that was fourteen dollars lighter.

As the door closed behind him he could faintly hear *"And don't forget to stop by, come September, when I get the new shawl-collared sweaters in. They're going to be all the rage this winter and you can even pay for them over time!"*

While driving to Dee Dee's house, Rod was still trying to figure out why he'd given in and bought two sweaters that he really didn't want. Then, appropriately enough, the voice of Elvis Presley came over the radio singing—"A fool such as I". It didn't do a thing to improve his mood. He turned the radio off.

Dee Dee picked right up on his sour mood.

"What's with you? You look like you got the blues, Hot Rod. Job not agreeing with you?"

"Nah, it's this headache. I feel like somebody's chopping wood in my head."

"Well, lucky you, because I still have that bottle of aspirin in my purse."

Rod groaned.

"It'd be like shooting an elephant with a BB gun. I don't think anything will help."

"Once you eat, it'll probably go away. What'd you eat today, anyway?"

He had to think about it.

"Nothing."

"Duh. Well, there you go, Ace," she said, shaking her head in disbelief. "Fortunately, we're about to be served, so I imagine your headache is on the way out."

They were sitting in Toma's on White Street, their favorite neighborhood place. It was homey, everybody knew everybody, and Freddie Toma's food was downright delicious, as well as reasonably priced. Hell, Rod and Dee Dee's dinners even included a small bottle of wine.

The waitress placed the two spaghetti and meatballs dinners in front of them. They smelled great.

"There you go, *Hot* Rod," said the pretty waitress. "Think it's enough?" she kidded. The serving was huge. Her name was Louise Patregnani but most people simply called her Lulu, a lifelong nickname. She was as cute as the day was long, a fact that wasn't lost on Dee Dee. A bit on the tall side, Lulu's big, gorgeous brown eyes, lustrous dark hair and *knock-em dead* smile all combined to make Dee Dee more than a little wary of her. She had it in her mind that Lulu had some plans for Rod, and Dee Dee wasn't included in them. Of course, she felt that way about any pretty girl who so much as smiled at him. Sometimes she felt as though she'd be better off, had he *not* looked so much like Fabian. That aside, however, Dee Dee couldn't help but like Lulu. The girl was hilarious.

"I think this will tide me over just fine, Lulu. Just bring some more bread when you get a minute, would you?" Rod replied.

"*For you?* Oh, you betcha," she said with a wink.

Dee Dee laughed, marveling at her inability to get annoyed with the young waitress.

"You know, that little charmer's a real piece of work. No doubt she's going to go places in this world, make a name for herself."

Rod agreed with her.

"Make one helluva good lawyer, that's for sure."

CHAPTER 17

At least it wasn't raining tonight and the effects of the scorching hot day, had, if not totally, dried up the muck enough to have made it at least more navigable than it'd been the previous night. This, along with the bright full moon, Rod took to be good omens. Now if he could just get his pal to shut up for a while. When it came to Butch, freedom of expression was an overrated privilege.

"I had a hard time with Bourkie earlier tonight. I don't think he believed me about suddenly getting sick again. Come to think of it, I doubt that my customers did, either."

Rod decided to indulge him. After all, Butch was helping him out *and* risking the loss of his job, to boot.

"Who were the customers?"

"Well, it was a real slow evening. Actually, I was starting to think it must be Mormon night or something. By the time seven rolled around, I only had two customers at the bar—Fitzie and Dubble Bubble."

Rod stopped shoveling.

"Fitzie? You mean like Fitzgerald from the funeral home?"

"Naw, it's just a guy named Fitzie. You don't know him. He's an old guy who drops in from time to time."

"So what's his real name? Fitzgerald? Fitzsimmons?"

"I don't know. They just call him Fitzie."

"Well, maybe Fitzie is his last name."

"Nope. They just call him that because he drinks a lot of Fitzie's beer."

Rod shook his head.

"Now I've heard everything. So what was the other customer's name again—Bazooka?"

"Close. Dubble Bubble."

"Let me guess. They call him that because he's always chewing gum."

"Close again. We call him that because he's always blowing bubbles with his gum. Actually, him you may know."

"Maybe, if you tell me his real name."

"Don't know it. He's just Dubble Bubble, that's all."

"Don't know him."

"Didn't think you would."

Rod resumed digging.

"So let me get this straight—this guy chews gum, blow bubbles with it, *and* drinks, all at the same time?"

"Nah, when's he ready to take a swig of his beer, he tucks the big wad of gum up in his cheek, like a squirrel with an acorn," Butch went on. "Come to think of it, maybe that's why he's got a face like a hamster. I'll you, though, hamster-faced or not, the guy's got money. He lives in a big house up off of Manor Avenue, in one of those *leave-it-to-Beaver* neighborhoods."

Rod had had enough.

"Okay, what do you say we give the chatter a rest for a few minutes, huh? Come over here and give me a hand lifting this one. I think it's probably going to be the heaviest bone yet."

They dug down along the sides of it, effectively making room to pry it up and out—hopefully.

"Help me drag two of those big planks over here," Rod said. "We'll use them to lever it free."

After five minutes of struggling to free it from its muddy tomb, they finally managed to lift what could only have been, and indeed was, the skull of a Mastodon, out of the hole. Its huge, toothy jaws were wide open, suggesting that perhaps the last sound the poor animal ever made had been one of sheer desperation and terror.

Exhausted by the effort, they both plopped down on the ground, sweat pouring off them.

"You know, I was thinking earlier that what if..." Butch remarked, running a handkerchief over his brow.

"What if? What if *what*?" Rod interrupted, utterly distracted, his eyes riveted upon the skull that until tonight, had been buried beneath all this muck for thousands of years. He was genuinely awed by the sight of it.

"Well, what if it turns out to be something else? You know—a big, gargantuan, prehistoric hog or something."

"A hog?"

"Or something. I mean, all your hopes, all of my hopes, too—suppose it turns out *not* to be one of Dumbo's hairy ancestors? Then all this talk of scoring a big payday will be just be a lot of mumbo-jumbo."

Rod's gaze never wavered from the skull as he replied, "Don't call him *Dumbo*."

"Huh? What's the difference? I was only joking."

"It's being disrespectful to the dead."

"Yeah, okay, but how do you even know that it was a *him*? Did we find a bone that you identified as being his, uh...you know, his tally whacker?"

"I just know. But as for your second question, how the hell would I know one bone from another? " Rod asked rather testily.

"Yeah, I guess you wouldn't," Butch replied sheepishly.

"Forget it. We got to get this into the back of the truck."

"Uh, I hate to tell you, but I don't think the two of us can lift it up there. This sucker is heavy, real heavy."

"We're not going to lift it ourselves. We're going to tie some ropes around it and then I'll use the winch on the back of one of the company trucks to hoist it up and onto the truck bed."

Rod's plan worked, despite the skull coming down onto the truck bed a bit more heavily than he'd wished it had. Nothing broke free of the skull, however, probably because they had cushioned the cargo bed with four thick canvases.

"Whew, I'm guessing that was your first time using a winch?" Butch inquired, tongue in cheek.

"Yep. How'd you know?" Rod replied, grinning.

"Just a lucky guess. Hey, how about a brewski? I think we earned one, don't you? Besides, digging up mastodon bones always brings out my thirst for beer."

Rod yawned as he lifted his arms and stretched.

"Sounds good to me, as long as its Schaeffer's," Rod answered, sending a suspicious look in Butch's direction.

"Yep, that's what I brought with me, so don't worry," Butch assured him before adding, "Speaking of worry, you ever give any thought to Sal maybe stopping by while we're digging, loading the truck, or worse yet, on our way to the barn?"

"No, I don't allow myself to think about *any* of those things."

"You're kidding. I mean, how can you *not* consider those possibilities?" he asked, handing Rod a Schaeffer's.

"I just don't, that's all," Rod said firmly, punching open his can of beer.

"Yeah, well, here's another one to think about—suppose he stops by and you aren't even here?"

Rod shrugged.

"I don't worry about that either. I'd just tell him that I left something at home and drove back to get it."

"Using Grandpa's truck to get there?"

"Whatever. Don't worry about it."

Unconvinced, Butch kept right on worrying, mulling it all over as he worked on his can of suds.

"How about if while you're gone, he comes down and notices that even *more* of his equipment has been stolen and *you*, his star security guard, is nowhere to be found?"

Rod abruptly stopped chugging his beer.

"Congratulations. You finally came up with the one possibility that I do worry about," he admitted uneasily. "But then, what are the chances of that happening?"

"Better than the odds of finding the remains of a mastodon, I'd say."

While Rod chewed that over, Butch pressed on.

"Sorry to rain on your parade, but I got another one for you—suppose he found *me* here with you? What do you think he'd say to that?"

"I don't know. You tell me."

Butch scratched his head.

"I don't know either. That's why I asked you."

"Use your imagination."

Butch took a swig of beer, tilting his head, putting a finger to his lips, as if considering both the question, as well as some kind of answer. He came up empty.

"I guess don't have an imagination, but then I'm just a bartender. Refilling empty glasses doesn't require much in the way of imagination," he confessed. "But I'll tell you, you don't play games with guys like Sal without running up a tab. We better hope that none of these scenarios actually happen, or we'll both end up as food for earthworms."

Rod drained his can of beer, scrunched it up and tossed it in the truck bed. Cupping his hands to his mouth, he fired up a Lucky with his Zippo. He was getting jumpy now, looking around in every direction, especially toward the gates. Truth be told, he'd of preferred that none of Butch's questions had ever come up.

His pal picked up on this and attempted to down play it all.

"Aw, I was just saying, you know? I doubt that any of those things will really happen, so I wouldn't worry about. I was just saying, that's all—just saying, you know?"

"Yeah, well, let's get back to work," Rod muttered, an icy shiver running down his spine.

They had successfully unloaded their precious cargo and were now on their way back to the site. Worried about breaking the huge skull, they'd piled hay right up level with the tailgate, then rolled it off the truck, directly onto the hay. At least that went well. Once they'd finished unloading some other sizable bones, they locked up and jumped back in the truck.

Butch was still panting from all the exertion.

"I think I'm going to take the bull by the horns, go on a diet and give up smoking, too...any day now."

As Rod nervously hummed along with WPTR'S offering of Santo & Johnny's "Sleepwalk," Butch kept up a steady chatter, like a machine gun loaded with words.

"I don't know about you, but I was kind of worrying about, you know, what if we ever got stopped by the cops and they pulled those tarps back? How would we explain having Jumbo's skull in the truck with us? Tell them you're *Jungle Jim* and I'm *Gunga Din,* and that we always ride around with an elephant skull in the truck, just for good luck?"

"It doesn't matter, because we're not going to get stopped, so talk about something else, would you please?"

Butch went silent as the old truck grumbled and stumbled down Columbia Street. Well, silent for a few seconds, that is.

"Once we get all the bones up there, the entire skeleton, that is, are we going to lay it all out? You know, like you lay out all the parts for a model airplane, just to make sure they're all there?"

"Yes."

"I hope we get them all."

"Don't worry. We will."

"By the way, I never told you this before, but that old barn gives me the creeps."

"Why? It's just a barn."

"I don't know. It just does. Every time we go in there, I half expect what's-his-name, Norman Bates, that wacko from that new movie, *Psycho,* to show up."

"Butch, do me a favor?"

"Yeah, sure."

"Shut up."

"One last thing. I was just thinking that Father Flanigan is always saying that idle hands are the work of the devil, so yeah, let's be all Christian-like and get back to digging"

Rod gave up.

"Getting you to shut up once in a while? Cripes, it'd be easier to teach a Rhino how to play hockey."

Butch giggled like he was going to bust a gut.

"Or easier to find a politician that'll say an honest Act of Contrition?" he offered.

Rod reached across and patted Butch's shoulder.

"You know, conversations with you are a lot like going to see old man Blais, the dentist. The appointment always seems to last longer than it actually does."

They laughed together all the way back to the site. *There's nothing like having a good friend*, Rod thought to himself. *Even if does never shut up.*

CHAPTER 18

The following evening they were right back it. Butch had tonight, and the following evening off, so at least he wasn't in the position of having to lie about being sick. Rod had been worrying about that. He'd hate like hell to be the cause of his best pal losing his job. Evidently Butch himself wasn't worrying about it a bit, however, as his spirits and energy seemed quite high.

"What do you think? Another night and we're done, Hot Rod?"

"Yeah, I would think so," Rod replied, although not all that confidently. They'd taken out about sixty percent of the skeleton, or so he thought anyway, yet the remaining bones were proving to be increasingly more difficult to remove. Unlike the first two nights where the ground was soft and mucky, the further down they went, the more difficult it became to extricate the bones, the lower side of the ribcage, in particular. It was encased in rock-hard clay and the only way they'd pry it loose was to chip away at the clay, little by little. It was going to be a long night. At least it would be a reasonably bright one, though. A full moon hung in the sky and a million tiny stars filled the heavens, twinkling brightly, like little specks of diamond dust. The extra light was certainly appreciated.

"This is like trying to break concrete with a toothbrush," Butch grumbled, dropping his pick and lighting a Pall Mall. "Hey, lend me a few bucks, will you? I'm running low, what with not collecting any tips these last two nights."

"Yeah, sure. How much you want?"

"I don't know. Ten bucks, maybe?"

"How about five?"

"How about ten?"

"All right, but it'll clean me out. I don't get paid til Friday, and all this eating out with Dee Dee lately has been putting a dent in my wallet."

"I'll pay you back...if we don't get murdered by Sal first."

Rod tossed his pick aside, wiping the sweat from his forehead with the back of his hand.

"You're going to get an ulcer from this needless worrying," he warned his pal, forking over the ten spot.

Butch opened a couple of cold ones, handing one to Rod.

"Better to worry and not need to, then to need to and not worry."

Rod scratched his head, clearly befuddled.

"What'd you say?"

"It's an old saying. Ben Franklin used to say it...or, I don't know, maybe it was Mayor Roulier. It makes a lot of sense, though, doesn't it?"

"No."

"Well, in that case, let's change the subject. How about I ask you this—how is it that you're almost broke, considering the huge pay raise you just got?"

"I told you. We've been eating out a lot. Oh, and by the way, forget about paying back the ten bucks. Put it in the gas tank of grandpa's truck."

"Good idea. Hey, I know you don't want to hear this, but I got to ask you—is what we're doing considered illegal?"

Rod rubbed his chin, deep in thought.

"That's not a bad question, Butch. To tell you the truth, I haven't even thought about that possibility."

"Well, I have. After all, my training is in beer, not crime. I wouldn't want to get arrested by the *Untouchables*," he said with a laugh. "That Elliot Ness guy scares me."

"I don't think we have to worry about a TV cop nabbing us, but now that you mention it, if we did have a legal problem, it would be with the state because being this close to the river, this land belongs to them."

"How do you know?"

"Sal mentioned it in passing."

"Maybe we ought to check into that further, to see if by taking Jumbo out of here, and then selling him, would we be guilty of committing some kind of crime? We don't need any Broderick Crawford-type state cops breathing down our backs."

Rod tossed the stub of his cigarette on the ground, crushing it under his heel.

"That's not a bad idea. Yeah, I'll do that," he agreed, reaching for his pick, ready to resume digging. "Only thing is, in my book, its finders-keepers...or at least it ought to be, anyway. Perry Mason is always claiming on TV, that possession is nine tenths of the law, so I'd say we'll be in pretty good shape, if push comes to shove."

Butch wasn't buying what Rod was selling.

"Nine tenths, huh? Well, maybe that's so, but it's that last tenth that worries me."

Utterly exhausted and downright filthy, they made their way up Columbia Street, the fruits of their labor snugly under wraps. The bones jiggled around a bit in the truck bed, but by now the guys pretty much had bone-packing down to a science. Not a one of them had broken while in transport.

This venture was turning out to be a lot more work than Rod ever dreamed it would be. Every night after they loaded the truck, they had to fill in the hole, using the softest dirt available, tamping it down, but not too hard. After all, they were just going to have to remove it again the following evening. Rod had been leaving a big branch atop the dig as a location marker, but he didn't bother with that anymore. At this point he could have walked blindfolded to the spot.

Butch had been uncharacteristically quiet during the ride. Rod gave him a playful poke.

"I smell wood burning, Buddy. What are you thinking about now?" he asked, steering around a pothole.

"How are we going to find a buyer for Jumbo? Have you thought about that?"

Rod admitted that he hadn't.

"What's the going rate nowadays for mastodon skeletons, anyway? It's got to be priceless," Butch gushed, envisioning himself tooling down Remsen Street in a new black Corvair, all the girls waving to him.

"Everything is priceless until someone puts a price on it."

"Well, we got to figure out how we're going to market Jumbo. Maybe we'll have to use an agent, a fence. Cut him in on the profits. I know we ain't going to find a mastodon skeleton buyer in Ma Bell's yellow pages, that's for certain."

"I doubt that there's a local fence who deals in mastodon skeletons, but we'll see. I have to think on it."

Butch started laughing.

"Maybe he'll fetch a higher price if we pass him off as a female. We can call him *Jumbolina.* Dress him up in drag, maybe deck him out in a tent-sized, pink and black poodle skirt, along with a huge white hanky on his head, so that he'll look like a devout, female, Catholic mastodon, one that regularly attended mass at Saint Patrick's."

Rod stared at him, shaking his head in wonder.

"No good, eh?"

"No good," Rod assured him.

A moment later Butch started laughing again.

Rod asked him what was so funny now.

"It's just that when you said you have to think on it, an image of Madeline '*Mad dog*' Hickey, our old principal, came into my mind."

Perplexed, Rod asked, "What's she got to do with anything?"

"I was just remembering the day that she told you not to think too much, that thinking was a strain for you, because you had the IQ of a bag of horseshoes," Butch recalled, laughing so hard that his sides began to hurt. "Then she added, '*You may be over six feet tall, but only about an inch of it is brains, Mr. Hobbs!*'"

Rod wasn't amused.

"Come on, you got to admit that she had some pretty good lines," Butch insisted.

Rod wasn't buying. He recalled those embarrassing moments all too well. The memory of her tongue-lashing still stung.

"Suffice to say, she and I don't exchange Christmas cards," Rod huffed. "Let's talk about something else."

"Okay, how's this? My parents asked me what I'm doing with gramps' truck and so I told them I was helping you with a landscaping job, one that you're doing on the side for Sal."

"Did they buy it?"

"Yeah, no problem, although my Dad did suggest that you ought to get *a lot of gone* between you and Sal. Dad's known him for years, and says to tell you to watch out for Sal, especially if he starts patting you on the back."

"Why?"

"Because he'll be feeling for the best spot to stick the knife in, that's why."

Rod tried his best to not be spooked by what he'd just heard. Tried, but failed.

"If you're trying to scare the pudding out of me, Butch, it's working," he groaned.

They rode the rest of the way to the barn in silence.

CHAPTER 19

The following afternoon they met at Ralph's Bar & Grill, down on the island, for some chow and a few cold ones. After feeding their faces, they planned on shooting a few games of nine-ball over at Candyland, the local pool hall. Meanwhile, Dee Dee was at work, another four hours to go before quitting time. Rod would catch up with her later.

Ralph Signoracci's place was a popular one, in large part due to the delicious Italian food his wife, Anne Signoracci, prepared daily. Clean and relatively quiet, it was one of Rod's favorite haunts.

Walking in, he was greeted by the jukebox offering of Sinatra's "Fly me to the moon," the selection, a testament to the older crowd's taste in music. Although not Rod's kind of song, he could live with it. Hell, he could live with "Roll out the Barrel," just so long as it was accompanied by some of Anne Signoracci's cooking.

Spying Butch at the bar, Rod made his way over there. As it was, Butch was getting his ear bent by none other than Rod's favorite Cohoes character, "Pops" Shea.

Pops was in the middle of warning Butch of the dangers associated with any attempt at navigating the treacherous waters of his least favorite institution, that being marriage. This was nothing new. It may have been his least favorite institution, but it was also his favorite one to rattle on about.

Pops took a short break from wife-bashing, just long enough to yank his trousers up a bit, to about mid-ribcage height, cinch his belt tightly, and then shake Rod's hand. Once Rod was seated, Pops went right back at it. He was in his glory. After all, his audience had just been doubled.

"I was just telling Butch about last night. I was over at the Post and by ten o' clock I was drunk as a skunk, or at least I believed myself to be, even if there weren't any skunks around for comparison's sake. Hell's bells, I couldn't have been any stiffer if I'd been embalmed! Anyway, long story short, Clarence Buchanan asked me how the wife was doing. Obviously, he wasn't one to keep abreast of the local obituaries. I told him she died, croaked quite a while ago, actually. I went on to claim that an autopsy proved that the cause of death was attributed to chronic *Nagatitis*, or, to put it in layman terms, she kicked the bucket as a result of being a persistent nag, a dawn to dusk pain in the ol' fanny!"

"I thought we're not supposed to speak ill of the dead, Pops," Rod kiddingly remarked as he paid for his beer.

Pops gave him a curious look.

"Ill? I didn't say she was ill. I said she was dead."

Rod laughed, gently slapping the old fellow on the back.

"You hungry, Pops? Care to join Butch and me for lunch? I'll buy."

"Naw, I only just had breakfast about an hour ago—*Wheaties and Whiskey,* the all-American breakfast. Got up kind of late, you understand. Of course, that's what being three sheets to the wind, once you finally hit the sack, will do for a man. So, no, I don't have any appetite for Eyetalian food at the moment, but if you insist on spending money on me, I can always use another bottle of Fitzie's."

Rod motioned the bartender over and ordered a round of drinks, along with a pair of hot meatball sandwiches for him and Butch.

Pops took a moment to thank Rod for his generosity, before embarking upon a fresh trail of stories. Squinting back through the veil of time, albeit, by way of an alcohol-hazed filter, the elderly gent began to recall the days of his youth, a time when he was preoccupied with just one thing—romance.

"Back around 1910, a couple of years before I got hitched to the witch, I met this other woman. She had about eight years on me, which didn't mean diddly because after all, we were both still pretty damn young. French-Canadian girl she was, and pretty as a daisy, to boot. Dark hair, olive complexion, with a figure that got my blood flowing pretty doggone good, I'll tell you. I'll grant you that she had the beginnings of a faint mustache, but I was willing to overlook that because the rest of her was so downright mouth-watering!"

Rod could sense that Pops was looking back in time, recalling the image of the woman quite clearly, a dreamy look descending upon his craggy, leathery features. Despite his big gut and the dark, sagging pouches that lay under his eyes, a cataract beginning to cloud on one of them, there was more than a hint there, of the young lad who had once occupied this face.

"Sounds as if she was a real doll," Butch noted. "So what happened? You two hit it off pretty well, or what?"

The glimpse into a once-youthful Pops suddenly vanished, replaced by the more familiar face, one that was weary and worn.

He knotted his hands behind his head and leaned back on his stool, looking up at the ceiling.

Feeling a bit spooked by Pop's sudden shift in demeanor, Butch opted for a little levity.

"What are you doing, Pops? Looking for an answer from God?"

Pops lowered his eyes and fixed them upon Butch.

"Yeah, and he just told me to sacrifice *you*, preferably by way of a bonfire."

Rod didn't know what to make of all this. Fortunately, the arrival of the sandwiches could not have been better timed.

As he and Butch attacked the food, Pops seemingly recovered from his bout of wistfulness, settling back into the role of professional yarn spinner.

"She told me she was a widow. I didn't press her for the details of her husband's demise, either. To be honest, I didn't really care about how he died, just so long as he died. Hell, I was just happy to find out that she was unattached and available," he declared boozily, pausing to light up a Raleigh before continuing on.

"Anyway, we became quite the item, all her neighbors gossiping about us. Hot and heavy we were for each other, that's for sure. It got so that after about three months of playing house, I decided to ask her to marry me, so one night after a particularly exhilarating round of carnal delight, I popped the question," he recalled, sighing heavily. "I even suggested that we get married at Saint Marie's, what with her being French-Canadian and all. Besides, I thought it'd be pretty nifty, getting married in French."

Rod put his sandwich down and took a sip of beer, all the while staring at Pops.

"So what'd she say?"

Pops shook his head sadly.

"She said she'd love to marry me except her husband was due back in about a month."

Butch had just lifted his pilsner glass and was in mid-swallow when Pops dropped that bomb. Choking, his face turning crimson, Rod pounded Butch on the back a few times. Eventually, the choking and coughing subsided, the redness receding from his pal's face.

"Are you kidding me?" Butch asked, incredulous.

"Nope. Turns out that he was a merchant marine, out to sea half the time. She claimed that she despised him, and hoped he'd fall overboard and get eaten by sharks."

"Well, why'd she ever marry him, if she hated him so much?" Rod asked reasonably.

"She said it was a family thing, prearranged up in Quebec, that sort of thing."

"You mean, like they were cousins or something?" Butch inquired.

"Naw, nothing like that. It was just two old families doing things the old fashioned way."

Rod ordered another round of drinks, firing up another Lucky as he did.

"I can hardly imagine what your reaction must have been like, once she spilled the beans."

"I screamed bloody murder, that's what my reaction was. I kept yelling: *'But you told me you were a widow!"*

"What'd she say to that?" Butch asked, wide-eyed, intrigued by it all.

"She screamed right back at me, yelling: *'Well, I would be, if he'd just do me a big favor and drop dead!'* which by the way, would have really made my day, too."

"Geez, that really stinks, Pops," Butch commiserated. "I'm real sorry to hear all this. Your life could have turned out so differently."

Pops tried to form a smile, although his craggy features weren't conducive to expressing a happy look even under the best of circumstances, and this certainly wasn't one of them.

"Well, I'll tell you this much—The woman certainly could heat up my blood, if you get my drift, just like a glass of *Dago red* does."

Rod swiftly motioned to Pops, putting a finger to his lips, the universal *watch your mouth* signal. The proprietor was, after all, an Italian-American gentleman. Gratefully, no one but Rod and Butch seemed to have heard Pop's ill-timed comment, or if they did, no offense was taken by it.

Completely oblivious to it all, Pops continued to plow forward.

"I have to admit that I rather enjoyed that feeling of being in love, or half way in love, anyway." he sighed. "But then, the next f......bit of f......luck that I have with an f......dame will be the first," he spat, the old ornery Pops suddenly resurfacing. You have to understand that Pops regarded curse words the way a bad cook uses spices—on the theory that if a few were good and gratifying, then more were even better.

"Aah, you know, sometimes the f......juice just ain't worth the f......effort it takes to squeeze it out. And people wonder why I'm a confirmed pessimist? Buy me another beer, will you, Hot Rod?"

Rod happily complied. *Anything to get the old man into a better mood.*

"Hey, where'd you get the money for this?"Butch asked. "Last night you said you were giving me your last ten bucks, until payday."

"I forgot that I'd stashed thirty bucks away in my dresser drawer," said Rod.

"Well, in that case, I'll have another Schaeffer's—maybe another sandwich, too."

Rod picked Dee Dee up just as she was leaving work. As usual, she looked great. The sky blue sundress, generously sprinkled with bright yellow polka dots, fit her like a glove, that is to say, it definitely complemented her figure, to put it mildly.

As they headed in the direction of her home, Rod kept glancing at the recipient of his admiration and affection. She caught his eye.

"What?" she asked, her hazel sparkling mischievously. "Haven't you ever seen a pretty girl before?"

Rod grinned, his hand reaching for hers.

"Hey, haven't you heard? You're supposed to keep both hand on the wheel," she chided with a wink.

"Sometimes a guy just can't help himself, especially when the girl is you," he replied, squeezing her hand, as the voice of none other than the man himself, Fabian, emanated from the radio singing "Turn me loose," his latest big hit.

Dee Dee giggled.

"What's so funny?"

"I was just thinking about how you and Fabian have more in common than you might think."

"How's that?"

"Well, truth be known, he really can't sing a lick...and either can you."

"You should talk," Rod replied, her shrill, off-key singing a regular source of irritation for him.

"Oh, I don't know about that. Jack Prock once remarked that he thought I had a wonderful singing voice," she said proudly.

Rod's rolled his eyes upward.

"He was trying to steal you away from me. That's why he said it. If he thought that by telling you that Connie Stevens was a piker compared to you, he'd have said that, too, in a heartbeat," he insisted, a little hot under the collar now.

"Relax, big boy," she said, squeezing his hand tightly. "I was just kidding around, trying to get a rise out of you, that's all...but you got to admit that your singing does leave a lot to be desired," she added with a giggle.

"Hey, I'll have you know I was a member of St. Agnes' choir... for about a week, anyway," Rod shot back, his voice dripping with mock indignation.

She laughed.

"Yeah, until Mr. Volpe, the choir director, told you that as a singer, you had one heck of a good future as pothole filler for the city."

She'd nailed it. Rod couldn't help but laugh at himself.

"Tell you what, though," she went on. "With his voice, If Fabian wasn't the handsome guy that he is; he wouldn't have *ever* had a prayer of getting hooked up with Dick Clark. If not for those good looks, *he'd* probably be working for the city of Philadelphia as a pothole filler right now!"

That fairly accurate appraisal caused them both to break out in mirth.

Dee Dee's mother, the former Delores Delisle, had prepared a nice, traditional French-Canadian dinner, her husband Benny's favorite meal, and so, was justifiably a bit put out by the fact that Rod had eaten so sparingly. He tried to assure her that while the meal was absolutely delicious, his appetite, thanks to a late lunch at Ralph's, wasn't all that big. Truth be told, this *Coq au Vin* thing she'd cooked up might have had a fancy frenchy name, but to Rod it was just chicken, carrots and mushrooms, with *way too much* garlic added. Like housewives the world over, she felt insulted, convinced that he was lying about the late lunch. To her mind, he just flat-out didn't like the food she'd cooked. Saint Marie herself could have come down from heaven to assure her that Rod had told the truth, but it would've had no effect whatsoever...and to think, she was Rod's future mother-in-law.

Eager to escape the evil eye that Mrs. LeBarron continued to cast in his direction, Rod suggested that they go for a little ride. Dee Dee readily agreed that it was indeed a great idea.

After driving around Troy for a while Rod headed for Green Island, eventually ending up in what was known as "the prairie," an area of flat land that separated Green Island from Cohoes. Wide open with lots of winding dirt roads and nary a tree to be seen, it was where many a Cohoes kid had learned how to drive a car, but that was during the daytime. Come dark, it was a haven for romantically inclined teens, that is, until the patrol cops happened to drop by.

None of this, however, was on Rod's mind at the moment. His motivation for stopping here tonight had to do with one thing and one thing only –giving her the lowdown on Jumbo.

He had a feeling that this probably wasn't going to be his best evening ever. Nervous as hell, his knees were jiggling like they were plugged into an electrical outlet. She knew something was up. Dee Dee could read him like a street sign, one that said—*Bad news ahead*. He wondered just how much of his story she could handle. After mulling it over, he almost decided to not find out, but then, after about three minutes of mumbling and stumbling he finally spit it out. Her reaction was about what he'd expected it to be. In other words, she was furious with him.

"So what do you think?" he asked shakily.

"Let's hold off on what I think, long enough for me to ask: What are *you* thinking, believing that you can make money off a prehistoric skeleton? What are you going to do, sell it to somebody on the installment plan, offer them green stamps, to boot?"

Rod held his hands up, palms outward in surrender.

"I was thinking, and still am thinking that I could make a small fortune for us, that's what."

"Are you serious?" she asked, fixing him with a look that could break rocks.

"Serious as a funeral," he said sheepishly.

"Yeah, and it's probably going to be yours!"

Rod sat there, contemplating a suitable response, but came up dry, so he got out of the car and lowered the top, making as much noise as he possibly could, hoping to drown her out. He fell short of his goal. He could still hear her loud and clear.

Back inside now, he reached over to raise the radio volume on Guy Mitchell's "Heartaches by the number." Dee Dee leaned forward and turned it off.

"What are you doing?"

"Wrong question," she spat, her eyes aglow with anger. "A better question is what are *you* doing?"

"If you'll just let me explain..."

She cut him right off.

"And here I thought you had the makings of a smart cookie! How on earth could you come up with such a harebrained scheme? Did the Mastodon Fairy come to you in your sleep and whisper in your ear? As sure as God made little green apples, it couldn't possibly have been Butch's idea. I love the guy, but he's got the IQ of a moth and while he may not be the dumbest guy in Cohoes, he's probably running a close second! So, that only leaves *you* to be the architect behind this cockamamie brainstorm."

Rod fired up another Lucky, using the lit end of the butt he'd just smoked. His nerves were getting the best of him. Her words cut through him like a sword, his face reddening, as if she'd just slapped it. *No one could deflate a guy like his girlfriend could*, he thought.

"Cut me some slack here, will you?" he whined.

"The only cutting that'll be involved here is when Sal cuts your throat. For God's sakes, you're just a minnow swimming with sharks! Don't you get that?" she cried. "Why am I even surprised by this? You always have been one to do things first, and sort out the consequences later. Well, this time, if you go through with it, I'm liable to end up a widow before I even become a wife!" she cried, nervously puffing away on a Salem, the smoke billowing skyward.

"Dee Dee, you've got to trust me on this. It's all going to work out and we're going to end up loaded with cash," he insisted, trying hard to convince himself of it, as much as convince her of it. It wasn't an easy thing to do.

She shifted her body away from him, signaling that the conversation was over...for the moment, anyway.

CHAPTER 20

The night was as dark as the inside a coal bin, and nearly as quiet. But for the occasional forlorn whistle of nearby passing trains, there wasn't a sound to be heard.

"So I take it that she was less than thrilled with the news," Butch remarked drily.

Rod kept shoveling, never breaking rhythm.

"You'd be right."

He was still worked up over Dee Dee's inability to see the upside of his plan, along with the cold shoulder she'd given him for the rest of the evening. Hell, she even refused to kiss him good night! That was a first.

After dropping her off, he'd gone home hoping to catch a little shuteye before heading off for the graveyard shift. *Graveyard?* he thought to himself, clearly grasping the irony of the term.

So much for a nap, however. He couldn't sleep so he had to settle for tossing and turning, going a few rounds wrestling with the sheets. The sheets won. Giving up on it, he rolled out of bed and got dressed, sneaking out the back door so to avoid seeing his father. Rod wasn't in the mood for yet another argument.

"Well, can you blame her for worrying?" Butch asked as he dropped his shovel and lit a Pall Mall. "I imagine that from her point of view, she sees us heading down a one way street, one that might just lead to the land of six feet under...and she isn't the only one that worries about it," he freely admitted.

Rod lowered his pick to the ground and hunkered down beside it. He reached into his rolled up sleeve for the pack of Luckies, putting his Zippo to one. Glancing over at Butch, he noticed that the greasy crap that his pal had gooped into his red hair, was now running down the sides of his flushed face in rivulets.

"Your hair, Butch."

"What about it?"

"It looks like an oil well dripped on your head, that's what."

Butch self-consciously ran the back of his hand across his forehead. It came away coated in sticky gunk.

"That's from all the sweating and panting. I swear to God I'm going to give up beer and cigarettes...any day now."

Rod was intimately familiar with the vow. Butch made it at least twice a month.

"Well, until you do, why don't you wear a baseball cap when you come down here?" Rod suggested, knowing full well Butch wasn't about to give up his beer and smokes.

"Didn't think of that," Butch admitted, wiping his hand off with a hanky. "How about a brewski? I could really go for an icy cold one. Hell, if it was any muggier tonight, I'd probably be passing out."

He was right. Heat was one thing, but the oppressive humidity in the air tonight felt as though you could cut it with a knife.

They both went quiet as they sipped their beer. Looking up at the evening sky Rod noted that not only was it a sweltering night, but also the darkest one they'd had to toil under yet. There was but a slim sliver of moonlight to work under and not a star in the sky.

"I was just thinking about an educational TV show I saw once," Butch recalled. "It was about archeology. It showed these archeologists digging up some dinosaur bones. They were taking their sweet time about it, too, let me tell you. They were digging ultra-carefully with little trowels and scrapers, then stopping every minute or so to run a dry paintbrush across the bones."

Rod didn't seem very, if at all, impressed by the information.

"Yeah, so what's your point?"

"Well, here we are doing the same kind of job as they were doing... well, sort of, anyway, but we're using about as much finesse doing it, as the bouncer at Corky's uses when he gives a troublesome drunk the ol' heave-ho out the door."

"There's a big difference here. Those professionals have got however long it takes to do their job. We, on the other hand, have only had about a week to pry Jumbo out of here."

"True, but hey, we ought to be finished come night's end, right?"

Rod mulled it over a bit before replying.

"Yeah, I'd say so...and we *better* be finished with it, because the footings get poured tomorrow."

"Hope we don't leave any important bones behind. It might prove hard to sell only ninety percent of Jumbo to a serious collector."

"I expect we'll get it all," Rod assured him as he glanced over his shoulder, staring in the direction of the office trailer. "Hey, did you hear that?"

Butch quickly turned around.

"Hear what? I didn't hear anything except you talking. Why, what do you think you heard?" he asked, a nervous tremor in his voice.

Rod didn't immediately reply, his entire focus on the parking area, a hundred feet above them.

"Come on. We're going to take a walk up there," he said finally, a grim look on his face.

Butch looked a bit spooked.

"Just what exactly was it that you thought you heard?" he again asked, not at all certain that he really wanted to know.

"The sound that a branch makes when someone steps on it... snapping it in two."

"Come here." he continued. "Cover up those bones and then help me throw the tarp over the hole. I'll douse the lanterns once we're done."

Four minutes later they'd reached the lip of the hole, stopping there to look around.

"Where are the guns Sal gave you to carry?" Butch asked, a slight tremor in his voice.

"In the trailer. I don't need any damn guns," Rod replied, cocksure of his ability to handle anything with his fists.

Butch wasn't so sure about that.

"If you say so."

"I do. Okay, let's take a look around."

They made a beeline for the trailer.

The door was still locked. Rod inserted his key and then cautiously peered inside the trailer. Nothing seemed to have been disturbed. He stepped inside to check things out a bit more closely. Everything seemed fine. The shotgun was in the corner, leaning up against a wall, and the pistol was still where he'd left it, on the shelf inside his locker. He never carried it off-premises, of course, but then he'd yet to carry it on-premise, either. Had he known this, Sal wouldn't have been at all happy with Rod.

Butch had waited outside, pacing. He seemed relieved when Rod came back out. No surprise there.

"Everything okay in there?"

"Yep. Let's take a look-see around. Turn on your flashlight."

They walked around for half an hour, stopping here and there to play the beams over the more wooded areas. Nothing struck them as being suspicious, so they wandered over in the direction of the tool shed. Rod unlocked the big padlock and swung the door open. The hinges could've used a good lube job, as witnessed by the way Butch nearly jumped out of his skin.

"Damn, it sounds like a cat in a room full of rocking chairs!" he exclaimed, looking a little pale around the gills.

Rod stepped inside and ran the beam of light around. Seemingly satisfied that nothing was missing, he walked back out and locked up.

"Maybe I was just hearing things," he grudgingly admitted. "But I don't think so."

"Could have just been the wind," Butch suggested.

"I don't know how, seeing as there *is* no wind tonight."

Butch shrugged as they made their way back toward the pit.

They agreed that at least in their opinion, they'd managed to extricate every bit of Jumbo's remains. Exhausted, but feeling pretty darn proud of themselves, the two amigos eased themselves into the old truck and headed for the barn.

Rod turned on the radio. WABY was playing Henry Mancini's theme from the hit TV show, *Peter Gunn*.

"That *Peter Gunn* actor, Craig Stevens, is one cool cat, you know? If I had his looks, I'd have to fight the girls off," Butch insisted.

Rod couldn't help but smile.

"You haven't done so badly for yourself. Linda's a knockout."

"Yeah, that she is. Funny thing is, sometimes I still can't believe that a girl like her could fall for a guy like me. I mean, think about it for a minute. It's pretty much the equivalent of Ann Margaret going out with Maynard C. Creps, which of course would never happen."

Rod chuckled.

"You're too hard on yourself, buddy."

"Maybe so," Butch said as he reached under the seat, producing two boxes of Crackerjacks.

"Where'd they come from?" asked Rod.

"Under the seat."

Rod sighed.

"I know *that*! What I meant to say was—*why* are they under there in the first place?"

"A man's got to eat, doesn't he? You never know when the urge will hit you, so I stash snacks all over the place. Besides, it's four in the morning. What are we going to do, stop at Smith's restaurant for *surf & turf*?"

Rod opened the box Butch had handed him, steering the truck with his knees. The tiny, cellophane wrapped prize that came inside the box, was lying right near the top of the caramel flavored popcorn. Rod snorted when he saw what it was.

"What'd you get?" Butch asked.

"You won't believe it. Here, look for yourself."

Butch's broad smile lit up the night.

"You got a plastic elephant charm!" he exclaimed. "Seems only fitting, if you ask me."

CHAPTER 21

They met at the barn the following afternoon. The plan was to lay out the skeleton, checking to see if any pieces of the Jumbo puzzle were missing. It proved to be quite the project.

"This is a lot harder than I thought it would be," Rod admitted.

"Well, at least we got these old pictures, as something of a guide. If not for them, we'd be up the creek without a paddle."

Butch was referring to photographs of the famous Cohoes mastodon skeleton, the one that was discovered almost one hundred years ago. The photos were featured in an old book that Rod had borrowed from the city library. Butch was right. Without the photos to go by, they'd have been working in the dark. As it was, there was still of guesswork going on. They'd managed to loosely piece together about seventy percent of the skeleton on the barn floor. Just *how* accurately it had been laid out, remained to be seen.

"I got to leave here in about an hour," Butch reminded Rod. "That'll give me just enough time to shower and change before heading to work. Wouldn't it be something if we could finish this up before then?"

"Yeah, except I'd don't have a clue as to how the rest of these babies fit into the big picture."

"The one you're holding looks like this one," Butch said, pointing as he shoved the photo page in front of Rod's face. "It's one of the lower leg bones, I think."

Rod nodded slowly, his eyes moving back and forth from the skeleton to the photo, like a fan watching a tennis match.

"I think you're right," he said, laying the big, heavy bone down, right where Butch had suggested. Stepping back now, he had to agree that Butch had been right. "Good eye, buddy."

Butch beamed with pride. It wasn't often that he felt all that smart.

Rod left three hours later. He was feeling pretty good about things. They'd managed to piece together about ninety five percent of the bones, some of which still had bits of reddish-brown, bristly hair attached to them. As for the leftovers, he tried not to think about them. He'd leave those pieces of the puzzle to whoever ended up buying Jumbo. The tusks, checked and chipped though they were, were fully intact and Rod considered them to be the key components—*the key to someone's vault*. With that thought in mind, he slept soundly through the morning and afternoon.

Dee Dee had gone to a St. Rita's Rosary Society meeting with her mother, the thrust of which dealt with the upcoming Bazaar and rummage sale. Having some free time on his hands, Rod fired up the Chevy and headed over to Bourkie's.

The place was real busy, Mickey Labombard, having drawn a crowd around him at the dartboard. He was shooting from his knees, something he'd mastered long ago. Mickey, a helluva nice guy, was better at shooting darts from his knees, than any of his opponents were, while shooting upright. Mick put on quite the show.

Meanwhile, over at the bar, Butch was busting his hump trying to keep up with refills, the glitzy, colorful, old Wurlitzer churning out the Coaster's "Poison Ivy" in the background. *A most appropriate song*, Rod thought to himself as he spied Fish sitting at a table in the back, his arm around a local floozy, one who was well known for doing the horizontal Polka with any guy willing to ply her with free booze. In terms of the type of lowlifes that he attracted, Fish was the human equivalent of flypaper, and so, it was only fitting that she was glued to his arm.

Rod caught Fish's eye. One look was all it took to see that he was already half in the bag. Of course, that was to be expected, seeing as how it was payday Friday. Earlier in the afternoon Rod had run into him down at the job site, where he'd gone to collect his own paycheck. They'd literally almost bumped into each other. Rod opened the door to the trailer just as Fish was exiting it. Fish stopped dead in his tracks, his arm folded, shooting Rod a look of pure poison.

"You mind stepping aside, Fish, so I can get in there?" Rod asked, making a supreme attempt at nonchalance.

For a long moment Fish didn't reply, or move, his dark eyes full of undisguised malice. He casually rolled a matchstick across his teeth. Then, albeit only grudgingly, he took a step back into the trailer, clearing space for Rod to enter.

"How good to see you again," Fish said, his tone implying that there was really nothing good about it.

The odor emanating from him would have turned a skunk green with envy. Rod would've bet that his clothes hadn't been washed since Elvis was a virgin. Combine that with breath that could knock a moose out cold and you get the picture. His foul breath could give Sal's a run for the money any day of the week. Yeah, the makers of Listerine weren't making a cent off those two.

Rod took in Fish's face, one that had more pits and holes in it than Bourkie's dartboard did. It was cratered like the surface of the moon. The man also had a five o'clock shadow that kicked in at seven in the morning, an hour after he shaved. The crooked yellow teeth, the short, Brylcreamed comb-over, and the bit of bloody tissue stuck to his cheek, all pointed to the fact that Fish got the short end of the stick when his genetic dice were rolled. Heavily slope-shouldered with a Neanderthal's forehead and jaw, in Rod's estimation, after the million years it took for humans to learn how to walk upright, here was Fish, living proof that not all had evolved at the same rate. Some people were still better suited to life in the trees.

"Yeah, makes my day seeing you, too," Rod replied drily.

Anger flared in Fish's eyes, his hands flexing at his side, a clear indication of his desire to deck Rod, right then and there, the rule of the caveman kicking in—club first, ask questions later. *Going ape*, if you will.

Rod didn't bite. He knew that their day of reckoning was certain to come, but this wasn't the time, or the place. With that in mind, he patted Fish's shoulder as he walked past him and into the trailer. He could clearly feel the daggers directed toward his back.

He figured he'd just collect his pay from Sal and be on his way. It didn't quite work out that way.

Sal was sitting at his dusty desk, a big stogie stuck in the corner of his mouth. He was wearing a rumpled gray suit, a black clip-on bowtie and his trouser cuffs had inched up his legs, revealing shins as white as fish bellies. He didn't look happy, but then he never did. He glanced up at Rod, his eyes as cold and lifeless as black glass.

"Have a seat, kid. We need to talk."

This can't be good, Rod worried.

"What kind of raggedy-ass job are you doing?"

Rod was taken aback.

"What do you mean?" he asked, totally lost.

Sal picked up a pencil and began drumming it against the palm of his hand. His stare never wavered.

"You diligently patrolled the area last night, like you're supposed to?"

"Of course I did," Rod answered, trying hard not to gulp. "Why do you ask?"

Sal didn't immediately reply, the wheels in his mind busy at work.

Rod shook a Lucky from his pack and lit it, the click of his Zippo, the only sound in the cramped trailer.

Sal leaned toward him. It seemed casual enough, but when Sal leaned in your direction, it didn't feel casual, especially when his eyes were like two black thumbtacks threatening to pin you to the wall.

"Fish told me that when he went into the tool shed this morning, looking for one of the big power saws, it was nowhere to be found. Neither was its twin. They seemed to have disappeared, yet they were there when we locked up at five last night. I, myself saw them there. So, sometime between midnight and eight this morning, somebody made off with them," he said matter-of-factly. "With that being said, care to tell me how they could have been swiped, if you were doing your job the way you're *supposed* to be?"

There was a decided edge to the question—sharp and unforgiving.

Rod's thoughts were going a mile a minute, clanging into each other, threatening to go off their tracks as he strove to maintain his cool. It wasn't easy, but in the end, he prevailed, opting for a bluff, hoping it would fly.

"Sal, if someone stole those tools, it definitely didn't happen while I was on duty," he declared, projecting a healthy dose of conviction through his statement, at least outwardly. "I walked the area constantly, taking only a half hour to eat in here," he lied. "There's no way anybody could have gotten into that shed! Besides, they'd have needed a key or they would have had to bust the lock, and I would have heard them breaking it!" he insisted forcefully. "Was the lock busted?"

Sal exhaled, the smoke coming out of his nostrils at an upward angle, like a dragon breathing fire. He remained quiet for a long time as he chewed on Rod's words. When he did speak, his words came out slowly.

"No, it wasn't busted, but according to Fish, it looked as if it might have been tampered with, opened with a pick."

"Or a key?"

"Or a key," Sal conceded.

Rod continued to dance around the truth, a surefire, completely plausible scenario suddenly coming together in his mind.

"Then someone with a key, or a lock pick, stole them between the time all of you left, and when I came to work at midnight. That's seven hours, Sal. Seven hours during which the site is completely unsupervised. That's a long period of time, easily enough time for one of your employees to make off with your property," he insisted convincingly...or so he hoped, anyway. "Who but an employee would have a key to the shed, as well as to the gate? By the way, how many of your people have keys to both the shed and the gates?"

"Hmm, maybe ten, but as for the gates, anyone could just climb over them," he said, pausing to relight the stogie, which stunk to high heaven. "But then, as you said, who need keys, though, if they can expertly wield a lock pick?"

"So, if it's like you suggest, then it's happening early in the evening, and the thief is probably one of my own employees," he continued on, talking more to himself, than to Rod. "Someone with keys, or lock picks."

Rod sensed the old man was buying it. *Why the hell not?* He thought to himself. *It may actually be the truth!*

"All right, here's what we're going to do," Sal declared, holding up his hand, ticking off points on his gnarled, nicotine stained fingers. "*One*, I'll have one of my nephews, the least stupid of the three, which isn't saying much, patrol the grounds from five til midnight, when you get here. *Two*, unlike most people who bring their lunch to work with them, he'll bring a baseball bat instead and if the thief shows up, he'll be sipping his meals through a straw, at minimum. *Three*, if, as you say, it's an employee that's stealing from me, I can tell you right now that he won't be offered a blindfold, a last meal, or a cigarette," this last said with icy conviction.

Rod involuntarily grimaced.

"Oh, and last but not least, there's number *four* and listen to it carefully, because this one deals with you, kid."

Rod felt his stomach tighten as he waited.

"In the event it turns out that *you* are somehow involved in these thefts, I will be sadly disappointed, to say the least."

It was hot in the trailer, yet the temperature in the room suddenly seemed to plunge downward. Rod's mouth opened and closed a few times, but no words came out. His mouth had gone dry, his throat seeming to have filled with cotton.

Sal held up a hand, palm out.

"Now don't go wetting your Fruit-of-the-looms, Hot Rod, my boy," Sal cautioned, a fatherly look creeping across his heavily lined face. "I don't think for a minute that you're involved, but I had to let you know that if you *were*, there would be serious consequences," he threatened, pausing before continuing on. "Okay, enough said. Here, take your pay and scram now. Go see your girlfriend or something."

Rod was only too happy to leave.

Thinking about the conversation as he drove off, a highly unwelcome thought occurred to him. *What if he ever finds out that I've been taking off to the barn every night, not to mention ignoring the patrolling stuff, using the time to dig up Jumbo's remains instead?* Rod sincerely hoped that wouldn't ever happen. Yeah, he could hope. He could—and he did.

His thoughts returned to the present. Butch had just set him up with a cold one and was now talking a mile a minute.

"So, you pieced most of it together?" he inquired breathlessly. "I'll bet you did. Tell me that you did!"

Rod raised his hand like a traffic cop, signaling Butch to slow it down.

"Most of it," he said in a near whisper.

The noise level was near deafening at the bar, so there was little chance of them being overheard. Nevertheless, Rod wasn't keen on taking any chances, so he spoke softly.

"We'll work on it some more tomorrow," he said.

"Work on what?" came a raspy voice from behind, a voice of whiskey and smoke.

Rod watched Butch gulp, his Adam's apple bobbing up and down like a yoyo. Rod slowly swiveled his stool.

It was Fish, but then Rod already knew that. Staring at him now, Rod was struck by how Fish's slicked, short, dark hair came to a narrow widow's peak, just like Dracula's did. *How fitting.*

"This is a private conversation, Fish," he said with cool deliberation.

Fish laughed.

"Like confession, you mean? You know, back when I was about ten, I went to see Father Robitaille over at St. Joe's. I went in the confessional booth and told him I was wondering if I could get some absolution in advance, because I was going to be pretty busy for the rest of my life—*sinning as often as possible.*"

"How utterly fascinating. Would you mind getting lost now?" Rod replied, his voice laden with sarcasm.

Fish's face went taut, his cheeks flaming, his eyes like hard green marbles. Then suddenly he smiled, a smile as cold and uninviting as the icy Mohawk River in February.

"Anything else about me you don't like?" he asked, his fury growing. Rod sensed that the man was like a tightly wound spring at the moment, begging to be released, just waiting for the slightest of external triggers to set him off.

"I'll have to think about it. I'll get back to you, though. I promise," Rod said, casually sipping his beer.

"You know, it might be a bit too early to say that our relationship is heading for a deep ditch, but I can tell you that the wheels have definitely wandered onto the shoulder of the road," Fish snarled.

Rod studied him across a gap of incomprehension as wide as the separation between Cohoes and Hawaii, one of our newest states. Nothing Fish said should have surprised him, though. He was always spewing off-the-wall garbage. Bottom line, the jerk had a big mouth, especially when he was drinking, which by the way, was most of the time.

"Relationship?" Rod cried, incredulous. "What, you going queer now, Fish? Swinging both ways, are you?"

And then the wheels came flying off.

Fish's contrived smile faded like a cheap shirt, the first time it met bleach. He was so mad, you could have strummed "Oh, Susannah" on the veins popping from his neck...and as it turned out, Rod had been absolutely correct. Fish did indeed swing both ways, with a left and a follow-up right, but thanks to his ring training, Rod saw them coming and successfully ducked both. Unfortunately, because Butch had been leaning forward over the bar at the time, he ended up being the unlucky recipient of a bone-jarring straight right hand.

He swayed and wobbled, almost as if he needed a moment to decide which way he should fall. Gravity ultimately made the decision for him as he toppled sideways, face-first onto the floor. He'd gone down like a bag of bricks...and stayed there, out cold.

Later, when he had time to think about it, Rod recalled that everything seemed to have slowed down after Butch kissed the floor. From the moment Rod lunged at Fish, to the moment the fight was broken up, it all seemed to have happened in slow motion.

The fight was all one-way traffic, and Rod was doing the driving.

Upon seeing his best friend go down, he shot off the stool and delivered a devastating elbow to the big man's nose, following it up with a teeth-rattling right uppercut. His face a crimson mask, Fish staggered backward on wobbly legs. Rod grabbed him by the shirtfront and then hooked his foot behind his opponent's boot and pushed. Fish went down hard, Rod on him like red on blood, pinning his water buffalo shoulders to the floor, ignoring the goalie-mitt sized hands that encircled his throat, applying massive pressure to his larynx. He needed to finish Fish off quickly or risk being choked to death.

Rod nailed him with a series of vicious rights and explosive lefts, the kind of blows that rattle eyeballs in their sockets. Fish's face was a bloody pulp, his oft-broken nose once again severely out of alignment. As his strength waned, so did the pressure on Rod's throat. The sheen of desperation in Fish's eye seemed to say *'But I never lose a fight!'*

Rod got in three more crushing blows before feeling a pair of gorilla arms encircle him, rendering him powerless. Some guy named Van Zandt. It was just as well, and he knew it. *I could've killed him, right here and now,* he thought to himself. He shuddered, bile rising in his throat. Although he despised Fish, now more than ever, the fact that he knew he was capable of killing a man wasn't something that sat well with him. Truth be told, it scared the living hell out of him. He went in the men's room and tossed his cookies.

By the time they'd roused Butch back into consciousness, and had gotten Fish more or less up on his feet, the atmosphere in Bourkie's joint had pretty much returned to normal. Well, normal for Bourkie's, that is. The excitement now over, the patrons immediately refocused their attention on more mundane entertainment. People began watching *77 Sunset Strip* on the TV while the Wurlitzer cranked out the Kingston Trio's "Tijuana Jail," accompanied by the soft thump of darts hitting home.

Meanwhile, Bourkie was reading Fish the riot act. From this day forward, he was barred from entering the place. How much of Bourkie's words sunk in was anyone's guess. Fish may have been standing more or less erect, but it was a crapshoot whether or not he remained that way. He looked about ready to topple over again, which was the only reason Bourkie hadn't already booted him out the door. Little by little, however, he regained what few wits he had to begin with. As he was marched to the door, he stopped and turned around, his swollen eyes fixed on Rod.

"One of these days, you're going get yours," he growled through broken teeth, threatening Rod, the burn of humiliation coloring his face. "I'll scramble your eggs permanently," he vowed. "You're going to end up in the hospital, maybe even the morgue, and that's a promise, Hobbs!"

Rod held his glare, neither of them giving an inch. Impatient, wanting to get back to his poker game, Bourkie shoved Fish toward the door.

Rod's heart was still pounding like a blown engine with a bad cam, and his mouth was drier than the Sahara desert. Bourkie poured him a cold one, setting it before him as he sighed heavily.

"I saw what happened, so you can't be blamed for going after him, but in the future, you might want to watch your back a bit more than usual. That animal would think nothing of parking one in your ear and then delivering you to the landfill, burying you under a couple tons of garbage, or sending you over the falls in a permanently sealed concrete barrel."

This was vintage Bourkie, direct and to the point. Squat and chunky with thick, bushy eyebrows, like twin awnings over his eyes, he was built along the lines of a fire hydrant, and had a wreath of gray hair circling his shiny dome of open scalp. His ruddy drinker's complexion, replete with a fire engine-red nose, and jowls that were flecked with tiny red and blue veins, bespoke of a life that revolved around booze. Selling it, as well as generously sampling it.

Rod half-heartedly nodded in appreciation of the advice.

Bourkie gave him a long hard stare before continuing on.

"Have I gotten through to you?"

Rod drained his glass and asked for a refill.

As Bourkie poured it, a Camel hanging from the corner of his mouth, a questioning look lingered upon his weathered face.

"You think I'm kidding about this, Rod?"

Rod assured him that he wasn't thinking that at all. Jimmy Bourke was a great guy, someone he respected mightily. Although most of his advice was going in one ear and out the other, he wouldn't want Bourkie to know that. Besides, it was hard to concentrate when his throat was sore as all hell. *Say what you will about fish, but he's strong as an ox.*

"You don't mess around with monsters like him, beating the crap out of the guy without running up a tab. That's all I'm trying to tell you. So watch your back," he warned, adding "That scuzz-bucket ought to be in movies—playing Frankenstein. The only thing missing are the neck bolts."

Rod thanked him for the advice. It appeared that Bourkie had more to say, but then Butch walked out of the back room and all the attention shifted to him.

"You okay, Buddy?" Rod asked, clearly concerned.

Butch blinked, then blinked again. He was having a hard time focusing on Rod's face. No surprise there. He'd taken the shot right between his headlights. Both were as red as a bottle of *Jic-Jac*, puffy and half closed, not to mention that the inevitable purple bruising below his eyes was already beginning to blossom. Come morning it would be in full bloom, a painfully mottled rainbow of red, black, blue, yellow and purple...twin shiners, too. Then there was the nose. He could've applied for the Clarabelle the clown job. It wasn't broken, but it sure was swollen big-time. Poor Butch.

Rod gingerly put an arm over his shoulder.

"Are you okay?" he asked again.

Butch started to nod but caught himself, the pain in his head more than he could tolerate.

"That's all right, Butch. You don't have to answer," Rod said soothingly.

He felt a cold wave of guilt wash over him. The shot that had sent Butch to la-la-land had been intended for him. *If only I hadn't antagonized Fish!* Rod chastised himself. *Why didn't I just let it go?*

Butch moaned, effectively snapping Rod out of his self-flagellation.

"Come on," he said, taking Butch by the arm. "We're going to go down to Lincoln Avenue. I'm bringing you to the emergency room to get checked over."

"I'll be okay. I don't need to go to no hospital," Butch insisted.

"Yes, you do," Bourkie interjected. "Fish hits harder than a Hudson Hornet. You might have a conclusion or something."

"Yeah, he's right, Butch. You might have suffered a *concussion*. That's what he meant."

Bourkie was only mildly offended by the unsolicited correction.

With a sigh of resignation and a towel filled with ice against his forehead, Butch reluctantly agreed to go.

Two hours later, they walked out of the hospital. According to the doctor, Butch didn't show any symptoms of a concussion and so he was cleared to leave. The doc told him to continue with the ice and to take aspirin for the headache. That was about it. The swelling, the black eyes and assorted bruises would disappear in about ten days or so. Meanwhile, Butch looked like a red-headed Panda, what with the bandaged nose and double shiners.

Butch's girlfriend, Linda, had rushed down to the hospital just moments after receiving a call from Bourkie. Bourkie was good like that.

Naturally, she was very upset when she walked into the hospital. Rod saw her right off and waved her over to a chair beside him. He explained precisely what had happened...and *why* it had happened. He didn't pull any punches or sugarcoat it in any way. He openly admitted that, in his opinion, all of it was his fault, and that he felt absolutely terrible about it.

If he'd expected Linda to be understanding and go easy on him, he'd been dead wrong. It wasn't necessarily anything she said, but rather the ice in her eyes that told him all he needed to know. The only thing they were in agreement over was that...indeed, it had *definitely* been his fault. He felt lower than low.

As they eased Butch into her car, Rod sensed that it would be a while, if ever, before Linda would forgive him. He was quite certain that he'd be getting an earful from Dee Dee, as well. Linda was her best friend. Enough said.

Rod still had about an hour and a half to kill before heading down to the site. Dee Dee would be home by now, and he'd promised to drop by and see her for a few minutes. All things considered, he thought a short, immediate phone call might be wiser. Linda would be burning up Dee Dee's line as soon as she got a free moment. Rod decided to head her off at the pass. He had already suffered enough grief for one evening. He didn't need to listen to more of it. Oh, he'd definitely hear it from his girl. Of this he was sure, but it could wait a day...thank God.

CHAPTER 22

Surprise-surprise. Yes, Rod had indeed endured an earful from Dee Dee, but it certainly hadn't gone the way he'd anticipated it would.

"Why would it be *your* fault? She's got her nerve blaming you! You couldn't have known that that sicko-psycho was about to take a swing at you. You reacted the way any smart guy would—you ducked. Poor Butch just happened to be standing in the wrong place at the wrong time."

Go figure. You think you know how your girl is going to react toward just about anything, and the next thing you know, you're proven dead wrong.

It was a sunny Saturday afternoon and they were sipping chocolate malts in one of Charette's booths, a pleasant little luncheonette on Remsen Street. As she related her feelings about Linda's phone call, Dee Dee's eyes went from a warm, incandescent hazel to blizzard cold in a heartbeat, like the sun slipping behind a snow cloud. She and Rod may have had their ups and downs but she wasn't about to stand for anyone else downing him. She'd go to the wall for him and he knew it.

Dee Dee had a face that belonged on the cover of *Photoplay magazine* and a heart that belonged only to him. As he stared at her he felt himself melting, dissolving like an Alka Seltzer tablet in water.

She picked right up on it, too, milking it for all she could.

"Why are you looking at me like that?" she asked coyly, twirling a few strands of her lustrous hair around her finger. An impish smile hovered at the corners of her mouth, like a kid on the verge of pulling a prank.

Rod sometimes couldn't believe his luck. She could have had any guy she wanted and yet she picked him. Sometimes, when he thought about it, it left him choked up with emotion. This was one of those times.

Fittingly enough, the sound of Frankie Avalon's "Venus" began playing overhead. Frankie may have had to implore Venus to fulfill his wish for a beautiful girl in his life, but Rod would never be in that boat. He already had his beautiful dream girl.

"Are you all right?" she asked, effectively snapping him out of his reverie.

He attempted to put on a neutral face, trying hard not to give his thoughts away. He wasn't succeeding, however, so he gave up on it. Grinning broadly now, he reached across the table and squeezed her hand.

"I couldn't be better."

She looked into his eyes, glimpsing more than he could ever know. *Some women have a particular gaze from the day they're born*, he thought to himself. *They look at you as though they know exactly what you're thinking, and will always know. Unfortunately for me, Dee Dee is one of them. Keeping a secret from her is a hopeless possibility.*

She reached over and pushed a stray strand of hair away from his eye.

"You're thinking about how fortunate you are to have snagged little ol' me, aren't you?" she teased, deftly picking a thought from his mind, as a cunning thief might pick a wallet from a pocket.

He grinned, shrugging his broad shoulders.

"What can I say? You get a gold star for being a mind reader."

She ate it up.

"And don't you forget it," she kidded. "I also see something else going on up there behind those big blue eyes of yours," she added, growing serious now. "This thing with Dumbo is eating you up...as it should be."

Rod sighed.

"*Jumbo*, not Dumbo," he corrected.

"Well, it might be Jumbo, but you're personally trying awfully hard to earn the name of *Dumbo* for yourself, if you ask me," she said a bit heatedly. "Sometimes I think you're a few quills short of a full porcupine, *Mister* Hot Rod!"

The temperature in the little café seemed to have abruptly dropped a few degrees, the romantic flame of a moment ago suddenly blown out, like a match in the wind.

Stalling, looking to talk about anything *but* Jumbo, he noticed she'd only consumed about half of her malt.

"You going to finish that?" he asked, eyes downcast.

"No. I just lost my appetite."

"Can I have it then?"

"Knock yourself out," she said, sliding it across the table.

"Why are you so angry?"

"I'm not angry!" she spat angrily. "I'm just upset."

The ensuing frosty silence seemed to drag on forever. Then she finally broke the ice, her tone one of resigned weariness.

"Look, the way I see it, you have two choices. Either you can take those old bones, put them in the truck, then find a good spot with soft dirt and rebury them, or go through with this harebrained scheme of yours, a scheme that's guaranteed to jeopardize our future together."

Talk about being blunt. Her last words tore holes in him.

He shook his head.

"Rebury them? Never going to happen! The Genie is out of the bottle now and there's no stuffing him back in it now, Dee Dee," he retorted sharply. "How many times do I have to tell you that this is going to be a gold mine for us?"

She grabbed her purse off the table and stood up, her finger in his face.

"Sometimes I think some of the dots in your brain aren't connecting. However, seeing as how you're bound and determined to go through with this...this crazy idea of yours, then get a move on! Get it over with as quickly as possible, so life can go back to normal—whatever the hell that is."

Rod was taken aback by her outburst. He opened his mouth to say something, but then changed his mind. Some conversations don't need a final word.

The following day was Sunday, and they, along with Butch and Linda, had been invited to a wedding. The ceremony took place at St. Michael's down on the island. From there, it was a short walk to the reception being held at the parish pavilion, a place that was always booked solid, a good year in advance.

Rod had attended many a wedding reception there. It was a very popular place, so much so that by the time the reception was winding down, it always seemed as if about half of the remaining partiers had crashed the wedding. It was the Cohoes thing to do, or so it seemed anyway.

Today was no exception. Many a participant in the festivities wasn't on the invitation list, but as usual, no one made a big issue of it. After all, there was more than enough beer to go around.

Rod wasn't sure if Butch would make it, all things considered. Between his sporting a severely battered face, one that looked as if it belonged to a hockey goalie and Linda's simmering animosity towards Rod, it wouldn't have come as a surprise if they didn't show...but they did.

Evidently, Butch had convinced Linda that it wasn't Rod's fault, after all. If anything, he only had himself to blame, he insisted. Butch claimed he'd been bartending long enough, so that he should've known better than to stand within range of anyone's punches. He admitted that he'd sensed that all hell was about to break loose, and yet he'd never backed away from the bar, the way he should have.

Having made his case, Linda had no choice but to reconsider things and she did. All was well now, the four of them sitting together at a table, genially chatting away.

It was a typical Cohoes Polish wedding, which was just fine with Rod. In his opinion, Polish folks threw the absolute best parties and today's reception promised to be a real humdinger. A guy named

Busta married a girl named Burnet, both names pared down from their original, considerably longer polish names. But they were still Polish, through and through, and that's all you needed to know. It was absolutely guaranteed to be a good time. Let the party begin!

And begin it did, starting off with the *"Zeetones,"* a Polish-American band whose raucous rendition of "Roll out the barrel," was sung as only they could sing it—earache loud.

The band featured a bunch of well intentioned middle-aged guys on the accordion, sax, drums and organ, along with a lead singer named Lenny Zee; his last name a good bet *not* to be the one he was born with.

In between sets, trumpet-playing John Busta, a close relative of the bride, as well as a member of the popular local band, the *"Aristocrats,"* also entertained the crowd. Early on, he was joined by yet another member of his band, Frank Siudy, a top notch clarinet player if there ever was one. Between the two of them, they brought down the house, no doubt leaving the *"Zeetones"* feeling more than a bit insecure. Be that though it was, however, both sets of performers did their best to entertain the crowd and they certainly succeeded, as everyone had a thoroughly great time.

There had to be about three hundred people on hand for the festivities, most them actual invitees, including one of Rod's close friends, Gil Downs, who stopped by the table to say hello. Gil was one helluva of an eighteen year-old pitcher and was currently being scouted by a handful of major league teams, the White Sox among them. Sooner or later, he'd be signed to a contract. There was absolutely no doubt about that. He was just too good to be overlooked for long.

Rod chatted with Gil for a while and then got up and headed over to the men's room. On the way out he bumped into some other old friends—Jimmy Lacy, along with Squeaky and Porky Stanton. A shrewd gambler, Jimmy Lacy had been cleaning out run-of-the-mill gamblers for years now, be it at poker games in West End Park, or at nine-ball on the well worn tables at Ralph's Candyland pool room. Word on the street was, as a kid, he'd even rigged a soapbox derby, once or twice.

Cohoes was full of colorful characters like Jimmy and that was good, at least in Rod's opinion. Stuff a city with boring people and you end up with a boring city. Populate it with characters like Jimmy Lacy and the Stanton brothers, who certainly were a pair to be reckoned with in their own right, and you had yourself a city that was anything but boring. Small maybe, but hardly boring.

As Rod headed back to his table, a most welcome thought suddenly came into his mind. Lacy knew a lot of shady characters, some of whom no doubt had the kind of connections that Rod would require, if indeed he was ever going to realize his dream of striking it rich. The problem was, he'd have to spill the beans to Lacy, fill him in on what he had in mind. The very thought of it, however, made Rod squirm. It wasn't that he didn't trust Lacy, because he did. He just didn't think he could risk telling him, because there was no guarantee that Jimmy wouldn't inadvertently let it slip out some night when he was drinking heavily. It wasn't a knock on the guy. It just wasn't a risk that Rod was willing to take.

By now over half of the guests were up and dancing, having a grand old time. It was *twisting time* and the Zeetones were doing their best to show Chubby Checker's "Twist Again" some respect. He'd heard worse. They got an A for effort, anyway.

Dee Dee saw him coming and caught his eye, pointing a finger in the direction of the dance floor. They found a spot on the edge of the crowd; just enough room for the two of them to dance without getting accidently jostled and jabbed a lot by others.

As usual, she immediately garnered the attention of many a guest, the men, in particular. She looked absolutely ravishing, her shiny, glowing hair piled high atop her head, the sculptured, graceful curve of her neck adorned with a single strand of pearls. Her dress was a muted pink number and it was tight on her...real tight.

Looking at her now, near mesmerized by her overall beauty, the gold flecks in her gorgeous hazel eyes sparkling away, it was hard to even remember that she was still upset with him.

They'd barely exchanged a word in the car and when they did, it didn't go well. Every time she said something that required a reply, he simply grunted or offered a grudging yes or no reply. She told him that she really looked forward to the day that he'd outgrow monosyllables.

"You sound like my Mom," he complained.

"Well, she's not here, so I'm filling in for her. What do you think of that?"

"Why do women always want to know what a guy is thinking?" he whined.

"We just want to be sure that you actually *can* think. That's why."

Shifting around on the seat awkwardly under the weight of the conversation and her penetrating stare, Rod insisted that she wanted to argue and he didn't. Dee Dee begged to differ, claiming that she wasn't arguing with him. She was simply explaining how she was right and he was wrong. *Go figure.*

He'd been unable to mount a suitable comeback, but that was no surprise. Although he'd never admit it to anyone, especially her, he knew in his heart that she was considerably smarter than him. It bugged him.

Meanwhile, back at the reception, many an eye was fixed on Rod, as well, and they all belonged to women. It was that Fabian thing of his.

Rod looked good and he knew it. Sporting a new navy blue blazer and a white oxford shirt, set off by a silk maroon and gray paisley tie, he was feeling pretty slick. It had all cost him a pretty penny at Mc Martin & White's in Troy. He first thought about shopping at Seymour's, but he was still sore about getting shanghaied into buying those faggy Perry Como sweaters. That aside, Rod did indeed look the part of one cool cat, as the Beatniks would say. The charcoal gray pegged pants didn't hurt either. Add in the highly buffed Low Ducks and yeah, he could definitely give Fabian a run for the money.

It didn't hurt that the two of them looked like professional dancers in a sea of amateurs, either. All eyes were on them and they were critical eyes. The guys, regardless of age, were transfixed by the image of this beautiful young woman who seemed perfectly suited for the big screen. If not for the presence of their wives and girlfriends, they'd be panting after her...but then, they were probably panting a bit, anyway. As for some of the ladies, they'd already unsheathed their cat claws and were trying their damndest to find a flaw; *any* flaw would do, in the ravishing beauty that was dancing with the Fabian look-alike. They'd be looking for a long time, for the words—*'physical flaw'* and *'Dee Dee'* were never uttered in the same sentence by anyone.

Naturally, the balance of the women in attendance, particularly the younger ones, had their eyes set on one target and one only. As always, Rod could sense the admiring eyes and as usual, it produced mixed feelings. He enjoyed being stared at by women, but only up to a certain point. Invariably, he would begin to feel uneasy about it, and today was no exception.

He was glad when the song ended. He was happier still when the attention shifted to a most unlikely pairing of guests. Cohoes-raised and Hollywood-bred Mike Mazurki had just joined the party. Strolling in alongside of him was none other than Patrick "Pops" Shea, the city's foremost barstool philosopher and semi-retired rabble rouser.

A big cheer went up for the surprise guest as the Zeetones began playing "Hooray for Hollywood." Everybody loved Mike Mazurki, the Cohoes boy who'd made it big in the movies. The 6'5" brawny man, who regularly played the part of a thug in a ton of films, was actually nothing at all like the bruisers he portrayed. European born and reared in Cohoes, he was highly intelligent and a witty, charming conversationalist. A graduate of Manhattan College, Mike was quite the accomplished gentleman and everyone here admired him.

He was real good friends with the bride's father and had promised to show up for the wedding, come hell or high water, and so here he was. Deluged by adoring fans and longtime friends, he was swept away and steered directly to the bride's appreciative parents.

For just a moment, Rod thought that poor Pops was in danger of getting trampled by the crush of people. He worried for nothing. Resourceful as ever, the elderly gentlemen somehow managed to wriggle free of the mass of humanity that threatened to engulf him.

Nothing Pops did ever surprised Rod...including his showing up at the reception. He was dressed to the nines, too. Well, that is if you consider a double breasted suit and a pair of Florsheim's from the 1930's to still be in vogue. It didn't matter. It was clean and pressed. Pops was clean and pressed as well. He'd even gotten a haircut for the big occasion, one of those haircuts that are carefully arranged to hide bald spots. Unfortunately, the battle lines were widening and he was losing the battle.

"Hey, God himself couldn't have done a better job of it," someone said rather huffily.

It was Pops. He was standing in front of Rod.

"God? What are you talking about?" Rod asked, thoroughly confused.

"My hair. I saw you looking at it and I know what you were thinking."

He was talking to Rod but looking at Dee Dee. She winked at him. He winked back, as if they just exchanged some telepathic info. *Damn, am I that transparent?* He asked himself. *Bad enough she can read my mind, but now Pops can, too?*

"Let me find you a chair," Butch volunteered as he started to get up.

Pops threw up his hands, signaling Butch to stay put.

"No can do. I'm sitting with big Mike. I'm his date, in a manner of speaking," he said with a raucous laugh. "I ran into him last night at the Harmony and he said the invite was for two, and his wife was back in California, so why don't I join him? I'll tell you, it's a good thing Ed Cepiel down on Willow St. is an old buddy of mine. It ain't just any barber that'll open up on an early Sunday morning to give an ol' pal a much needed shearing. Of course, the fact that I'm a regular at his back room card game didn't hurt, either."

"That's a nice haircut he gave you," Linda lied.

"Well, taint exactly a blizzard up there, but so long as there's still a little snow on my roof, I'm content with what I got," he replied, shooting Rod a dirty look. "You, I'll talk to later," he promised...or threatened.

"I better get over there now, before I forget what I want to ask Mike," he added hastily.

"What's that?" Butch inquired.

"Mike just wrapped up the filming of *Some like it Hot* with Marilyn Monroe."

"Yeah? So?"

"Well, seeing as how he knows her so well, I want to see if he can maybe get me a date with her," he said with a straight face. "Hot Diggity Dog, wouldn't that be something?"

"Uh-huh. I see," said Butch, although clearly he didn't. "Isn't she, uh...married to Arthur Miller, the playwright?"

Pops leaned in close to Butch's mangled face.

"Sonny boy, I don't care if she's married to *King* Arthur," he said in a near whisper. "And about that face—you need to learn how to duck, boy. You look like you were on the wrong end of target practice, or have you been blocking punts with your face? Speaking of which, Fish was outside when we came in. He was about to try and crash the wedding, but was quickly turned away at the door. It kind of brought to mind the image of a dead atheist in a funeral parlor—all decked out in a suit and nowhere to go," Pops quipped. "He seemed rather disappointed, but then it was kind of hard to accurately read his puss, seeing as how someone named Hot Rod Hobbs had recently done a number on it. It looked as if his head had been run over by a forklift. On the other hand, it's probably an improvement over the mug he usually wears, the one that'd scare the shell off a snapping turtle."

Word got around Cohoes fast.

Pops laughed all the way to his table. He loved putting one over on his friends. *Me with Marilyn?* He mused. *Yeah, right. That's a laugh. When pigs fly, or a Catholic gets elected president, maybe.*

The reception turned out to be a blast. Everyone had a great time. Dee Dee even loosened up enough to momentarily forget about Jumbo and all of the dangers that accompanied him.

When the Zeetones gave Lloyd Price's "I'm going to get married," a shot, it served to lighten her mood even further.

"These guys are pretty good," she remarked as they swayed to the music.

He was about to agree with her when a thought suddenly occurred to him. A pretty good thought. *The one guy I know that can definitely keep a secret, drunk or sober, and is also very familiar with the local underworld, just happens to be here today. Patrick "Pops" Shea just might be the man to steer me in the right direction. Hey, it's worth a shot,* he told himself.

Once the song ended everyone headed back to their tables. The pastor, Father Zigmund Olszewski, was about to bless the new marriage and all eyes were on him...all but Rod's, that is. He was busy tracking down the whereabouts of Pops. He found him easily enough. The old fella was chatting with a woman. No surprise there.

As soon as the good father finished the blessing everyone applauded and then went back to what they did best—having a good time.

Rod excused himself from the table and headed over to talk with Pops.

The old boy was doing his best to charm some fifty year old woman. Say what you will about him, but his penchant for chasing skirts still hadn't diminished a bit. This particular lady, however, didn't seem to be in the mood to have her skirt chased, at least not by Pops, who was already half blitzed.

"What's your number, Doll?" he asked, pen in hand.

She looked as if she'd rather have her wisdom teeth yanked out by an intoxicated veterinarian, without the benefit of Novocain, than give him her number. Naturally, he overlooked her reluctance and kept hammering away at her, hoping to get lucky.

The poor woman sighed, determined to rid herself of this deluded pick-up artist.

"Okay, it's BE5...oh, darn. I seemed to have forgotten the rest of it," she lied. "Call information. They'll have it," the lady assured him as she rushed off.

"But wait! How can I call information when I don't even know your name?" he whined. It was too late. She was out of earshot by now...and no doubt, happily so.

"What happened? You're slipping, Pops." Rod kidded. "Your batting average gets any lower, and we're going to have to ship you off to the minor leagues—Green Island."

Pops failed to see the humor in the remark.

"Not funny. Come on over to the bar. I need some high-proof tension relief," he growled in a voice raspy from too many unfiltered Raleigh's.

The bar featured a large, Schlitz-themed mirror on the back wall, the words *"Niema Sclitza Niema Piwa"* emblazoned across the front of it, Polish for *"When you're out Schlitz, you're out of beer."*

He ordered a Screwdriver for himself. Rod settled for a beer. Pops quickly drained his glass and then turned to the bartender, asking for a Bloody Mary. The bartender didn't blink. He knew Pops. Hell, everyone knew Pops.

Rod couldn't help but say something.

"Don't you think you ought to slow down a bit? This shindig is going to go on for quite a while, you know."

"Yeah, but *I* might not go on for quite a while, so keep that in mind. I sure do. A man never knows when it might be his last drink," he insisted as he lit a Raleigh and laughed.

"What's so funny?"

"I probably have more preservative in me right now than one of Dufresne's freshly embalmed corpses have."

"I guess. What's with these drinks, though? You never drink these things."

Pops gave him a wry grin.

"Just making sure I get my minimum daily requirement of vodka, that's all. The juice doesn't hurt either. They say it's actually healthy for you. What do *you* think I should be having, *Quevic Vichy* with a cherry on top?"

Rod gave him a reproachful look.

"I hope that you at least ate breakfast this morning."

"Yep, eggs, bacon and more bacon, lots of it, all washed down with a shot of Four Roses and a Fitzie's back. A balanced breakfast is what I call it."

Rod sighed, exasperated.

"You know how dumb that sounds? Booze, along with a ton of greasy bacon for breakfast?"

"You know how dumb you sound? If I want booze with my breakfast, that's my business. Besides, greasy food is good for a man. It keeps his joints well oiled, which is why no men in my family ever got arthritis."

Rod lit a Lucky, shaking his head in bewilderment.

"That's probably because they didn't live long enough to get it."

Evidently, that last comment hit home.

"Maybe so, but what the hell—I've already lived plenty long and now I'm just an old man," Pops said wearily. "Truth is, I got a lot more yesterdays than tomorrows. Getting old sucks. Nothing to look forward to except getting dead."

Rod stared straight ahead, studying his friend's reflection in the bar mirror. Haggard, shoulders slumped; Pops suddenly looked like a man who was having an introspective and highly unpleasant conversation with himself. Rod began to feel badly for him.

"Come on. Don't go getting all bluesy on me. You're not old," he said, trying to lift Pops' spirits. "Just vastly experienced, that's all."

"Tell that to my liver. I drink too much. I smoke too much, too, but at a certain point in my life I accepted the consequences of my choices, and as long as I catch the bus to hell with a Fitzie's in one hand and a Raleigh in the other, well...a man could do worse."

"Tell me the truth—have you ever entertained the thought that just *maybe* you're an alcoholic?"

"Nope. Alcoholics go to meetings. I don't go to meetings, so I'm not an alkie. I'm just worn out. Not much tread left on the Uniroyals of this man's life and there's only two ways to handle one's impending demise—forget it's coming, or act as if it isn't. Only thing is, I can't seem to do either. That's why I drink a lot."

Rod threw his arm around Pop's shoulders.

"Come on. You're tough as nails and you know what they say—
when the tough get going..."

"The tough gets plastered?"

Rod couldn't help but laugh.

"You just need a challenge, Pops. You're bored, bored to death."

"Yeah, bored and old...and about as useful as feathers on a moose."

"Cut it out. You're not that old. Besides wasn't it Mark Twain that said, 'Age is just a matter of mind and if you don't mind, it don't matter?'"

"What'd he know? He's dead, ain't he?"

Pops ordered another drink.

"Humph. Maybe you're right. Maybe I am just bored," he admitted. "What's there to do, though, for an old codger like me, except to keep a barstool warm?"

"I've got something for you to do, and it'll be a big, big help to me. They'll be some real money in it for you, too. "

Pops turned, cocking a rheumy eye at his young pal.

"Is that right?" he asked, firing up another cigarette, forgetting that he already had one cooking.

"Yep."

Suddenly Pops seemed more than interested in what Rod had to say.

A moment later Rod noticed the servers carrying their heavily laden trays past him.

"Time to eat, but I'll catch up with you a bit later, okay? Do me a favor, though, would you? Take it easy on the booze. You're going to want a clear head when you hear what I have to say."

"You betcha," Pops replied merrily, back to being himself once again. "Hey, bartender, how's about a refill...or two?

About an hour later, Rod was able to free himself long enough to corner Pops and spill the beans. It went over about how Rod expected it to. Like a lead balloon. Pops stared at him in utter bewilderment, as if his friend had just spoken to him in a foreign language.

"Sure you haven't been dipping overtime into a vat of *Richard's Wild Irish Rose* rotgut wine? Seeing pink elephants now, are you?

Rod assured him that wasn't the case at all.

"Okay, so let me make sure I got this straight. You're telling me that you two, *Tweedledum* and *Tweedledumber*, dug up a complete mastodon skeleton and now you want to hustle it to some bone collector, expecting a big haul in return? How am I doing so far? Have I got it all about right?"

Grinning like the cat that ate the canary, Rod enthusiastically nodded in the affirmative, raising a finger to his lips as he did so, indicating that Pops needed to lower his voice. They were standing in the parking lot and no one was around, yet Rod still worried about someone overhearing them.

"Furthermore, you took it from Sal's construction site, close by the river bank, from land that just happens to be owned by the state of New York," he went on, scratching his head as he did. "I imagine that if this gets out, the city might end up wanting a piece of your hide, too. Boy, you sure do know how to open up a can of worms that it'd be better left sealed!"

Pop's normally placid face had gone hard, the skin so taut you could strike a match against it.

"And another thing," he continued. "You did all this while you were on Sal's time clock, shirking your duties, even leaving the site for a couple of hours each night so as to dump these bones in some old barn. Is that about right?"

"Yeah, yeah, I know, but so what? All that matters is that I got the goods and they're safely tucked away. So what do you think? Can you help me? Hook me up with somebody that'll find me a buyer?" Rod asked anxiously.

"I'd rather pass a kidney stone," the old man said dryly, yet Rod knew he was mulling it over in his mind. "You know what Sal will do to you, if he finds out that you dug up valuable stuff from *his* construction site, all the while he was paying you to do a job that you weren't even doing? You think you're lucky, stumbling onto a chunk of good fortune, but the fact is, you're not lucky at all, Hot Rod. If anything, you just stepped into a pile of you-know-what, but you just haven't realized it yet," he warned. "At best, Sal's nephews, Huey, Dewey, and Louie, drop the hammer on you and you just get your bone structure remodeled. On the other hand, you could very well end up as the center of attention in Looby's Funeral parlor, and I ain't just speculating here, kid."

"You'll think you're becoming the emerging star of Cohoes, while in actuality you'll be *submerging*, as in *submerging right out of sight,*" he warned. "You've been sucked in, thinking only about a big payday, paying no attention to the dangers that come with it. A goldfish swimming with sharks, that's all you'll be!"

Pops had had his say, the effort seeming to have sapped his energy. Sighing as he removed his glasses, he slowly wiped them clean with a handkerchief, stopping for a moment to rub the red indentations at the sides of his nose.

"*Can I help you*, you ask? Yeah, that's the $64,000.00 question, isn't it?"

He was thinking now, thinking hard, a half-smoked Raleigh hanging from the corner of his mouth. Another moment or so passed before he seemed to have arrived at a decision, a reluctant decision.

Blowing his breath out in agitated surrender, he asked, "Don't suppose I can talk you out of this, can I?"

"Nope."

"You know, they say wisdom comes with age. If that's true, then I've obviously been shortchanged," Pops said ruefully, shaking his head in defeat.

"Yeah, I can probably try to help you out, but I'll tell you right now that it'd be easier to find John the Baptist's head, than it'll be to find a fence, *and* a willing buyer for a damned mastodon skeleton! You'd be better off asking that Zoo guy on TV, Marlin Perkins, to find a home for those old bones. Sweet Jesus! The things you get yourself into!"

Rod blew out a breath of relief as he patted Pops' back.

"You won't regret it. I promise."

Pops dropped his cigarette on the sidewalk and stepped on it, snuffing it out with his heel.

"I already do."

CHAPTER 23

The following morning Rod and Butch picked up Pops for the ride to the barn. He lived on Division Street, next door to Joe's Bar & Restaurant. Leave it him to live right next door to a bar.

Rod was about to ring the doorbell when he noticed it was busted, the wires trailing down, disconnected. He knocked on the door.

"It's open," a raspy voice called out. "C'mon in."

Rod turned the knob and in they went.

The place was reasonably neat and tidy, considering that a single man lived there. Pop's cat, a scruffy-looking Maine Coon named *Pork Chop*, glowered at them. Somehow he didn't look as if he had any interest in being anybody's pet.

"I'm in the kitchen."

They walked through the narrow hallway, past the dining room, and there he sat, the Troy Record spread out before him on the table, the smell of booze leaking from his pores like an oil spill.

To his right sat a bottle of Four Roses and a shot glass. A bowl of Wheaties and milk was in front of him, along with an empty bottle of Fitzie's. He was about finished with the cereal. Hopefully, he was also about finished with the booze.

Rod Serling, take notice: If Martians from the twilight zone ever want to take over the planet and wipe out the human race, they simply need to convince the rest of us to regularly indulge in the same breakfast that Pops did.

Rod gave him a look of disapproval.

Pops noticed and wasn't happy about it.

"Hey, I said I'd cut back a bit on my daily intake, and I will, but that don't mean I'm going to hang up my drinking shoes and become a freaking Mormon! An old man needs a morning pick-me-up, just to get the ol' juices flowing, sonny boy. Besides, this just happens to be the *Breakfast of Champions*, as they say on TV—*Wheaties and Whiskey*."

"I don't recall Bob Mathias or Johnny Weissmuller ever mentioning whiskey in the commercials, Pops."

"Then you're not paying close enough attention to them. Want some coffee?"

They both politely declined.

"I'd offer you some Freihofer baked goods except the driver never stopped. What's the point of putting their '*Please Stop Here*' sign in your window if he doesn't bother to look for it? I swear, it's like having a blind jackass steering a horse and wagon down the street!"

Rod was getting antsy now, anxious to get moving.

"Yeah, well, what are you going to do? Nobody's perfect. Anyway, are you about ready to go or what? I don't want to rush you, but—"

"Then why are you?" he interrupted as he stood, bowl in hand, and walked over to the sink, depositing it in the soapy water. "You've been fidgeting like you got a bumble bee in your drawers," he added with a grin. "I'm only kidding. Actually, I'm looking forward to seeing your elephant."

"Mastodon. It's a mastodon, not an elephant," Butch corrected. "Code name—*Jumbo,* by the way."

Pops turned and stared at Butch, the same kind of stare Sister Anne Zita used to give him in third grade, after he'd said something incredibly stupid.

"I think we ought to take up a collection for you at the Blunder Bar."

Butch appeared mystified.

"Huh? For what?"

"Half of it for some plastic surgery on that face. Take it from me, kid, that mug of yours ain't ever going to be right again. Fish really messed you up."

"I don't care about that. What's the other half for?"

"Tuition to the school of the real world, that's what. Giving a name to a pile of bones! Surprised you didn't name him Fido or something. Come on, let's get out of here. I can hardly wait to get introduced to *Dumbo*."

Butch almost corrected him again, but then thought better of it as he headed for the driver's door on his old, beat-up Buick.

Pops called out to him.

"I'm not going anywhere in that dilapidated jalopy. Damn, you must be the best customer the makers of *Bondo* will ever have. Kee-rist! It looks like the golf ball retrieval vehicle they use at Hoffman's driving range."

The week before, Butch was driving through Maplewood and got caught in a ferocious hailstorm. His car had been hammered, liberally blanketed with hundreds of little dents and dimples. He'd attempted to fill them in with *Bondo*, not one of his better ideas. Add in the fact that it had the look of a Menands demolition Derby loser to begin with, and you get the picture.

Not surprisingly, Butch was offended by the comment.

"Hey, don't knock *Bondo*. It's the best invention since Moonpies! And for crying out loud, don't worry about my car's reliability, either. It'll get us there."

"Yeah, well, Hot Rod's car will get us there and *back*!"

"So will mine," Butch argued.

"Sure, chances of that are about the same as the Russkies have of colonizing the moon."

Butch struggled to get in the final word, but just couldn't seem to find it. In the end he had to settle for *okay*.

As Rod drove toward their destination, he turned on the radio. WABY. The sound of Sandy Nelson's drums filled the car with his latest hit, "Teen Beat."

Pops snorted his disapproval.

"The world's going to hell in a hand basket, you ask me. You call that music? I call it Excedrin headache # one," he fumed. "You just watch. This Rock & roll crap is going to be the ruination of your generation. Damn, whatever happened to *real* music—Rudy Valle, Glen Miller, Al Jolson and guys like that?"

"Well, for one thing, they're all dead. Secondly, this is a new age, Pops. You either get hip to the cool cat sounds of our music or everybody will be calling you a drip," Rod explained, trying hard not to smile.

"Humph. Well, I won't be lying awake worrying about that, I can tell you! A *drip*! Where do you kids come up with this slang of yours, anyway?"

"The Beatniks, I suppose," Butch replied. "Of course, that's just my opinion."

Pops ignored the comment. Although deep down inside he really liked Butch, the lad's opinion, was to Pops, like a chipmunk on the tracks to a locomotive engineer—not important enough to even notice.

Pops shook his head, waves of disbelief flooding his mind.

Sure, he had known what to expect to see, but simply *knowing* about it opposed to actually *seeing* it, were two completely different ballgames. Upon laying eyes on the gigantic, laid-out skeleton, he drew a deep breath, slowly exhaling. He was absolutely in awe of what lay before his eyes.

"*Goodgodallmightydamnwillyoulookatthat!*" he exclaimed, as if words had just been invented, and he didn't quite know where they stopped and started. "Jumping Jesus, this is incredible! You really did it, didn't you?"

Rod and Butch beamed with pride.

"We sure did...but then, you already knew about it. I told you yesterday, so why do you seem so surprised? What were you expecting, a Tupperware party?"

Pops didn't reply right off, his eyes still transfixed upon the skeleton. His gaze traveled down the length of it before settling on the long, curved tusks.

"Rod, the Jewel Tea Company guy could tell me that the *special of the week* is Jayne Mansfield herself. Doesn't mean I'd believe him, but then, if he opened the back door of the step van, and there sat voluptuous Jayne in all her hot-diggety-dog glory...well, that'd be whole different kettle of fish, now wouldn't it?"

"Huh?" The analogy was lost on Rod. He decided not to press for clarification, however. Lord only knows where that would lead.

"So what do you think, Pops? Ain't it something?" Butch gushed enthusiastically. "Think we're going to hit the big time with this? I mean, now that you've seen it, what's your gut feeling telling you?"

Pops exhaled noisily, the reality of what he was getting himself into, hitting him pretty hard.

"I don't have any gut feeling, but I do have an inner coward inside me and right now it's telling me to get the hell out of Tombstone before I end with my name carved *into* one, up there on Boot Hill."

"*Boot Hill*? *Tombstone*?" Butch echoed, clueless. "You mean like Wyatt Earp and Doc Holiday?"

"It's just an expression, Butch," Rod explained.

"Yeah, and here's another one—*I ought to have my head examined!*" Pops groused.

"Aw, come on. Quit worrying so much. We can do this. I know we can," Rod confidently insisted, confidence that in reality, he didn't actually have. Truth be told, he didn't have a clue as to whether or not his scheme had a chance in hell of working.

Pops nodded wearily.

"Yeah, right. We probably got a better chance of everybody down on the dyke getting flattened by an A-Bomb, Rod."

"The next time I agree to help you, do me a favor, will you?" he went on. "Lend me your hunting rifle so I can stick it in my mouth."

"Pops!" Butch cried.

Their reluctant partner sighed a weary old man's sigh.

"Oh well, in for a penny, in for a pound, as the old saying goes. With that said, let's get down to the planning, but not in here. This decrepit old barn has got bad breath."

Rod pulled over in front of the Golden Crust Bakery. Right off, he spotted an open table over by the window. They made a beeline for it.

There was no one sitting within twenty feet of them. Perfect. As long as they kept their voices down, no one would be the wiser.

After they'd been served hot coffee and Jelly donuts, they got right down to business.

"Our best bet is with a character that goes by the name of Bonesy," Pops announced with a smirk. "Kind of ironic, ain't it? Guy's got the most appropriate name, which, by the way, is one of the reasons why he popped into my mind."

Rod took a bite from his jelly donut. Golden Crust made the tastiest ones around, hands down.

"Mind if ask what the other reasons are?" he asked, using a napkin to wipe away the powdered sugar from his lips.

"Boneparte Francois Marceau, a.k.a *Bonesy*, just happens to be the foremost *go-to guy* when it comes to anything illegal around these parts. Still has the first dollar he ever stole. A very enterprising individual, there isn't much he won't do for money, short of murder, that is. He draws the line at that. Of course, from time to time he's paid the price for his indiscretions. Actually, he's got a rap sheet longer than Remsen Street. Most recently, he'd been a non-paying guest of the Dannemora hotel. He served a three spot for trafficking in stolen goods. I'm told that he convinced his *sometimes* faithful wife, Peggy Sue, that his criminal inclinations ended the same day his prison sentence did. *So much for that*. She probably still believes in Santa Claus, too. Word on the street is she left him a few months back. Went out for a loaf of bread and never came back. Somebody asked him if he missed her. He replied: '*Yeah, but my aim is improving.*'"

Rod was getting impatient. He really wasn't interested in this crook's complete biography.

"So what are you saying? This character ought to be able to fence our, uh...merchandise?"

"He's got the right connections, and all of them are of the criminal variety. Now I'm not claiming that he himself is some kind of master criminal, because he isn't. If he was, he wouldn't have been stacking time in a penitentiary. His expertise lies in hooking people up with other people. As a middleman, Bonesy is the best that I know of. I'll grant you that most of what he hustles are things like rare art, valuable antique jewelry, collectible cars like Duesenbergs and lord know what else, but it's all hot...as in *stolen* hot."

Rod was impressed by what he was hearing. The guy sounded as if he certainly had the right kind of connections.

"So how are we going to proceed with this? Just track him down and give him the info on what we're looking to have fenced?"

"That's about the size of it."

"You know where to find him?"

"Of course I do. His office is in the South End Tavern in Troy. That's where he conducts the bulk of his business."

"Where?" Butch asked. "You mean like upstairs over the bar?"

"No, downstairs, right at a corner table in the bar area. He's there every day but Sunday. On Sunday he goes to church. St. Augustine's up in the Burgh, I'm told."

"Hmm, now there's a surprise," Rod commented drolly. Religious, huh?"

Pops cackled.

"Not exactly. He goes to pray for two things—that he doesn't get put back in the slammer, and that his wife doesn't come back."

"Why doesn't he just quit the life? It's simple. If he doesn't commit any more crimes, he won't go back to the can."

"Because it's all he knows. The man would rather be strung up and dunked head-first into a vat of Sinclair gasoline then work for an honest living."

"Do you trust him?" Rod asked.

"About as much as I'd trust a cobra in my Sears-Roebuck drawers, but compared to most in his field of endeavors, Bonesy comes off looking like an altar boy," Pops replied. "In his defense, however, I do know of a number of instances where the cops squeezed him hard, trying to get him to name names, roll on the crooks he did business with. He never caved, ever. Bonesy wouldn't talk even if they held his mother hostage."

"Sounds like a real loyal guy, for a criminal, that is," Butch chimed in. "I'm impressed."

"Don't be. How long do you think he'd stay alive if he talked?"

Butch nodded, clearly getting it now.

"Didn't think of that," he admitted sheepishly. "But, hey, I did think of this—What if the guy doesn't want any part of it? What then?"

"We'll resort to plan B," Pops replied matter-of-factly.

"We actually got a plan B, Pops?" Butch asked, surprised

"No."

Rod was getting antsy again. He wanted to get the ball rolling and said as much.

"Okay, so my biggest question is this: How do we establish what the price should be for Jumbo?"

Pops shook his head from side to side.

"*We* don't. Bonesy does."

A wary look came into Rod's eyes.

"What if he doesn't ask enough?"

Pops was getting exasperated.

"Listen up, kid. First off, between the three of us at this table, we couldn't come up with an appropriate asking price if we had all year to do it. Who the hell knows what this kind of stuff sells for? Nobody, that's who! You know, it ain't like there's a Kelly Blue Book that lists the going rate for high-mileage used mastodons!"

Pop's voice was getting louder by the second. Rod glanced around nervously as he lit a cigarette, blowing a stream of smoke into the air.

"You want to keep it down, please?"

Pops immediately dialed it down.

"Sorry about that," he said. "Anyway, where was I?"

Rod thought it best to cut right to the chase.

"You were about to tell us when's the best time to meet with this guy," he lied.

"I was?"

"Yep."

"Okay, then let's go see him today. Get this show on the road."

"Great. What time does he usually hit the South end?"

Pops glanced at his old Elgin wristwatch.

"In about an hour, when they open for the lunch crowd."

"Sounds good. We'll finish up here and then head over. I got to stop for gas along the way."

Pops chuckled.

"Stop at an Atlantic station. They're giving away free glasses this week. Oh, and speaking of gas, as long as we're going to be at the South End, we may as well have lunch. The corned beef and cabbage is guaranteed to give you all the gas you never wanted."

As usual, the South End Tavern was doing a brisk lunch business. The place was nothing fancy. As a matter of fact, it pretty much looked the same as it did fifty years earlier. There were two entrances. One emptied right into the bar area. The other led directly into the dining room. That particular entranceway featured a neon sign over the door. One that read: *Ladies Entrance.* What was the draw, you ask? Food. Generous servings of tasty stick-to-your-ribs fare, meals that drew folks from far and wide. It may indeed have been nothing more than a glorified saloon, but nobody ever walked out of there hungry.

The bar on the other side of the building could also be accessed through a narrow archway. Waiters, young guys in Banlons and Dungarees, darted through it regularly to pick up their orders from the open kitchen located near the end of the bar.

Although it was but only noontime, the bar itself was jamb-packed with blue collar guys on their lunch hour. The ambiance consisted of a tired old *Rock-Ola* jukebox, a wall mounted Zenith, which at the moment, was on the fritz, and a Toohey dart board that'd seen plenty of action in its day, all of it wrapped in a thick haze of dense cigarette smoke.

Down at the end, some old tables were scattered around rather haphazardly. One in particular was set up in a corner, close by the door. A solitary man dressed in a shiny black suit sat there, his back to the wall. He was hunched forward over a newspaper, his elbows splayed out on the table. His face was round and hard, creased with deep, weathered lines. The guy had an Errol Flynn moustache, and a head of thick, curly black hair with matching winged eyebrows, to boot. Rod knew this to be their man. On the drive over Pops mentioned that some people referred to Bonesy as *Skunk head* due to the white streak in his hair, one that ran down the center of his head. It was a wholly unwanted nickname, one that no one ever dared call him to his face. Bonesy was sensitive that way. According to Pops, the last guy that called him *Skunk head* to his face had an unfortunate encounter with a lead pipe, ending up as an extended stay occupant of a Samaritan hospital bed. Bonesy simply wasn't familiar with subtlety.

Rod didn't doubt it for a moment. The guy looked as if he could bench press a Buick. His hairy forearms were the size of bowling pins, and he had a neck that seemed to go directly from the jaws to the collarbones without the slightest taper.

As they approached his table, he spoke, without as much as a glance up at them.

"What's up, Shea? I haven't seen you around in quite a while. What brings you in today?" he asked in a voice colder than a Cohoes winter, deep and gruff.

"A business opportunity," Pops replied.

The big palooka raised his eyes, taking in the three men who stood before him, studying them, as if they were nothing more than fresh road kill. His cobalt blue eyes were piercing in their intensity. They were also pretty tired looking. He looked like a man who'd recently fought the world and lost.

"Pull up a chair."

Once seated, Bonesy gave them each the once over, his machine-gunner eyes sizing them up, going from one to the other and then back again, like two pin balls trapped between rebound cushions.

Pops started to speak but Bonesy cut off him, making a tut-tut sound with his tongue.

"What's with Mutt and Jeff here? I don't know that I want to discuss business in front of two punks. You ought to know better than that, *Shea*." he growled, somehow stuffing a world of warning into one syllable; a mere four letters of sound. "What's the story?"

Pops got right to it, his voice pitched unnecessarily low, thanks to a hardhat dropping a quarter in the jukebox, selecting "Mule Skinner Blues," along with two other equally raucous tunes. The possibility of anyone overhearing their conversation ranked right up there with the odds of finding a trustworthy guy in the Kremlin—slim and none.

Bonesy gave Pops his full attention, his face never once registering even the slightest surprise at what he was hearing. Only after the old-timer had finished pitching his story, did Bonesy indicate what was going through his mind as he'd listened.

"Are you crazy?"

Pops shrugged his shoulders.

"Probably, but then I never claimed to be normal."

"Well, I'll say this for you. You got a lot of chutzpah coming to me with this, Shea."

"Thank you, Bonesy. Good of you to say that."

"It wasn't intended to be a compliment," he rasped. "Now then, I've handled my share of oddball merchandise, but this? What makes you think I can retail it for you?"

"Because you make things happen, that's why."

Bonesy, never one given to humility, readily nodded his agreement.

"Ok, so supposing I'm able to uh...give you some informal economic assistance with this, just how much are you hoping to get?" he inquired with the air of a man granting a great favor.

"I don't have a clue," Pops admitted. "That's your area of expertise, not mine."

Bonesy liked Pops' answer.

"Yeah, it's important that a man know his limitations," he declared resolutely.

"Uh...can I ask you a question?" Butch interrupted.

Bonesy looked across the table at Butch, much the way a hawk eyeballs a baby squirrel. *Easy pickings.*

"Depends on the question. But before you ask it, I'd recommend that you don't," he warned softly, his tone of voice cold but smooth, like Vaseline on ice. "Any questions put to me should only come from Shea. You got that, kid?" he asked with a menacing scowl. *So much for smoothness.*

Butch gulped as he nodded, his Adam's apple bulging as if he'd just swallowed one whole. Gruffly put in his place, he looked like a kicked puppy.

"You know, with that red hair, you remind me of Woody Woodpecker, kid."

"No need to insult the man, sir," Rod interjected.

Bonesy's hard eyes swiveled toward Rod. He just stared at him, saying nothing, seemingly content to drum his fingers against the tabletop.

Pops cleared his throat before stepping in.

"He didn't mean anything by that, Bonesy."

Bonesy shot Pops a withering glare.

"Hmm, is that right? Well, they say that to err is only human and to forgive is divine. Nice, but I don't buy into it. Never have and never will."

Funny thing was, the man didn't really seem to be all that upset by Rod's butting in. If anything, his mind appeared to be elsewhere as he stared ever harder at the young man, appraising his face and trying to put a name to it, as if accessing a mental rolodex. A moment later it came to him.

"You look like that kid that I saw sing on the whatchmacallit...the Ed Sullivan Show. What's his name? Avalon? No...Wait a minute. Fabian! Yeah, that's it."

As usual, Rod's face flushed.

"Yeah, so I'm told,"

"Humph. You could do worse. Me, I got a face like one of the bulls that run the streets of Pamplona. I should be so lucky to have your kind of looks, kid."

Rod shrugged, his blush deepening.

"Okay, enough with the teen idol crap. Time to get down to business," he announced quietly, crooking a finger in Pop's direction. "Yeah, I may be able to give you some informal economic assistance with this. Write down your phone number for me. Then gimme a week or two to see what interest is out there. I'll get back to you with whatever I come up with...if anything. Take some pictures of this thing, too. I'll need them."

With that said, Bonesy directed his attention back to the newspaper. He'd had his say and now they'd been summarily dismissed.

"Are we going to eat?" Rod inquired of his pals.

"No, I lost my appetite," Butch replied sourly, still smarting from Bonesy's biting wisecracks.

Once outside and heading for the car, Pops smiled broadly, rubbing his hands together in delight.

"Hoo-Hah! That went even better than I'd hoped for!" he crowed merrily, like a kid who'd just stumbled across a twenty dollar bill on the ground.

Rod looked at him curiously.

"What do you mean?"

"What do I mean?" the old man echoed. "What I *mean*, is this worked out great for us, that's what! Hell, truth be told, I half figured Bonesy would tell us to take a long walk off a short pier."

"But I thought—"

"Yeah, I know. You thought it was a sure thing, but let me tell you, there's no such thing when it comes to him. For all I knew, he could have just blown us off...but he didn't, so be happy, boys."

"Oh, make no mistake about it, I'm happy, all right," Rod replied. "I just wish we didn't have to deal with Bonesy. Talk about rude!" he complained, kicking at a fallen chestnut and missing.

Pops dismissed the comment with a wave of his hand.

"Don't take it personal. He never has cared much for people in general, but then, he don't like himself much either, so at least the man's consistent."

CHAPTER 24

A couple weeks later, around noontime on a sunny Tuesday, Pops called Rod at home. Rod's Mom answered the phone. She told him Rod was still sleeping. Pops politely asked her to wake him. He needed to talk to her son right away, if at all possible. It had to do with something important, he explained. When she went and rapped on his bedroom door, saying, "rise and shine," Rod jumped right up and out of bed. He'd been in the midst of a bad dream and was grateful for having been awakened by his mother. Her voice had cut through the dream like a knife through paper. For a moment, against his better judgment, he strove to recall some of it, but the connecting ribbon to it had been forever severed. *Just as well*, he thought to himself.

His mom opened the door a crack.

"Sorry."

"I'm not," he replied, yawning.

She told him that Pops was on the phone. As he hurriedly threw on his raggedy old plaid robe, a series of jumbled thoughts raced through his mind. *Pops never calls here. It's got to be about Jumbo. Maybe Bonesy found a buyer. Maybe Bonesy couldn't find a buyer! Maybe this-maybe that.*

Cinching the robe tight around his waist, he rushed out into the hall and breathlessly picked up the receiver.

Pops told him that he'd just received some good news from Bonesy. Rod felt raw excitement course through his body. *Hot dam,* he thought to himself. Then he caught his mother giving him a curious look, the kind of look that always preceded a battery of wholly unwanted questions. He forced himself to calm down. It wasn't easy.

"Bonesy says he found a guy who knows a guy who could be a conduit for funneling the bones through to yet another guy, one that's big into this sort of thing. Filthy rich he is, or so Bonesy claims. Anyway, I got a lot to tell you, starting with—"

Rod cut him off, saying, "Uh, this isn't exactly a good time to talk," hoping that Pops would catch his drift.

He did.

"Let me guess. Your mother's listening and giving you the evil eye at the same. Is that about right?"

"Yep, you nailed it," he replied. Rod could hear a jukebox playing in the background. It was one of those Johnny Ray cry-in-your-beer tunes. "So where are you, anyway?"

"Right up the street. I'm on the payphone in the Garner St. Grill."

"Okay," Rod said in a hushed tone. His mother was doing her ironing in the kitchen, no more than twelve feet away. "Give me about forty minutes to get cleaned up and then I'll meet you, but not there. Not enough privacy. Why don't you go home and I'll meet you there?"

"Home? Hell, no. My sister, Aggie, is there cleaning the place up. Once a month she insists on coming over and turning the joint upside down with her Hoover, mop and a can of *Babo*. A man can't hear himself think while she's there. The cat hides under the bed. Come to think of it, so does the dog. That old Hoover's louder than the Battle of the Bulge, so forget that idea. Just come up here. I'll grab the empty table in the corner. Nobody will be able to hear us talk, so don't worry about it," he assured him. "You can buy me lunch. Spaghetti and meatballs would be good, or maybe a pizza. Bring money. I'm not a cheap date, you know."

Rod quickly brushed his teeth, washed up and shaved. After throwing on a pair of dungarees and a black Ban-Lon, he was ready to motor. Fortunately, and rather surprisingly as well, his Mom didn't attempt to squeeze him for information concerning the phone call. She was slipping. Usually, a thorough interrogation followed any questionable calls that he received. If a stranger ever heard her conduct one of her typical investigations, they would no doubt assume that *she'd* been the cop in the family, rather than her husband.

The Garner St. Grill was a typical blue collar neighborhood joint, one that rarely saw trouble, mainly because the proprietor, Mario Constantini, was always right on top of things. Start trouble in there and you were tossed out the door before you even knew what happened, but then, that's the way the cookie crumbled when you messed with Mario.

He served basic, but tasty Italian food, and a pretty damned good pizza, to boot. The décor was about what you'd expect—Neon beer signs, a jukebox, cigarette machine, dart board, a few tables and of course, the bar itself. It was clean, the prices were reasonable and Mario wasn't above hosting a poker game or two. Pretty good card player himself, aided no doubt, by the fact that he had one lazy eyelid that regularly drooped, as if one side of his face was taking a snooze. It made for one helluva great poker face.

The Seeburg jukebox was playing when Rod walked in—Kay Starr's "Wheel of Fortune." There were two guys talking at the bar. Three more were eating lunch at a table toward the back.

Pops was doing a *Bonesy*—a corner table by the front window, his back to the wall. He motioned Rod over. Pops had his usual in front of him. A shot of Four Roses and a Fitzie's back.

"Did you get those pictures developed yet?"

Rod tossed a Kodak packet on the table.

"Is the Pope Catholic?" he replied, pulling out a chair.

Pops opened the packet, thumbing through the photos without removing them from the envelope.

"Not bad, not bad at all. What'd you use, your mother's Brownie?" Pops asked as he fired up a Raleigh with his battered, old Ronson. "Would've have been better to have had them even sooner, though."

"Like when?"

"Like yesterday," he replied, picking a stray strand of tobacco from his lip.

Rod shrugged. He'd dropped the film off at Liggett's Drug store in Troy four days ago, and then picked up the developed photos just yesterday. In his opinion, that was about as quick a turnaround as he could have reasonably expected. Sure, there was an abundance of places in Cohoes that he could have gone to, but he feared someone in a local store might get nosey and decide to eyeball the film, or worse yet, the developed photos, and then put two and two together, which would be disastrous. Talk about throwing a wrench in the works! Yeah, Troy had been the way to go, no doubt about it. Better safe than sorry.

"I took care of it as quickly and as *safely* as I could, Pops," he insisted.

"Okay, don't get your Woolworth briefs in a knot. This is fine. I was just saying," he replied. "So what do you want to do, eat first or talk first?"

"Are you kidding?" Rod exclaimed in a near whisper. "My stomach's doing somersaults in anticipation of what you've got to say. So talk now—we'll eat later."

The old fella grinned from ear to ear, his high-mileage face crinkling with hundreds of tiny lines.

"Get yourself a drink first, and while you're at it, you may as well get me another little pick-me-up, too."

Rod was back within moments, a fresh set up for Pops and a ginger ale for himself.

"Thanks, but what's with the Cott's ginger ale? That stuff will kill you."

"Too early for beer," he said, quickly adding, "At least for some people, anyway."

"Humph! Now is that nice?" Pops spat, rather indignantly.

Rod laughed.

"Not trying to be nice."

"Well, you're certainly succeeding. Good thing for you that I'm rather fond of you, or else I'd drop a dime on you with Sal," he said, a mischievous twinkle in his eyes. "You'd join his other dead enemies in a graveyard, or in the Mohawk, wearing a pair of cement Keds."

Rod Zippoed a Lucky.

"Not funny."

"Neither are the wisenheimer remarks about my drinking habits."

"Okay, you got me there," Rod admitted sheepishly. "Sorry."

Pops waved off the apology as if it was totally unnecessary...and it was. These two had been playfully exchanging barbs since Rod was knee-high to a dachshund.

"Down to business now," Pops announced in a low voice. "Here's the deal. Bonesy's guy tells him that there's a potential customer up in Montreal, a society muckety-muck who's got more money than Henry Ford. Furthermore, he's got a hobby, a very expensive hobby, one that revolves around the collection of rare items, the older the item, the better. Turns out that he owns his own personal museum and it's filled with everything from some of Shakespeare's writings to Roman statues to Egyptian pharaoh mummies and uh...dinosaur bones, all of it obtained illegally, I might add. Hell, it wouldn't surprise me to hear that the guy even owns St. Patrick's favorite pair of green drawers."

Pops watched as his words slowly sunk in. He enjoyed seeing Rod's eyes grow wide in anticipation of the biggest payday of his life. He couldn't resist the tease, dragging it out, prolonging the details, playing it out little by little, like pulling at a thread on a sweater, unraveling it slowly, inch by agonizing inch.

Rod leaned across the table, his nose almost touching Pops'.

"You said *dinosaur bones*! C'mon, will you? So, what else? Was a price mentioned?" he whispered, his heart beating ever faster.

Pops continued to milk the moment, casually lighting another Raleigh, leisurely sipping his beer. Watching Rod fidget sort of tickled Pops. Once he felt the lad had suffered enough, however, the old boy relented, spitting out the rest of the story.

"Based on the scuttlebutt that Bonesy gleaned from his guy, this rich Canadian recently dropped a big bundle for a few dinosaur bones. A hundred grand, to be precise."

Rod gripped the edge of the table, his knuckles turning white. Truth be told, the lad felt as if he might faint at any moment.

"A hundred grand," he echoed softly. "Oh, my God!"

"Yep, and ain't that a fine kettle of fish?" Pops remarked with a grin. "But before you start mentally cashing checks, keep in mind that the dinosaurs were around long before Dumbo and family walked this earth. That means anything from Fred Flintstone's era is going to be considerably more valuable than what we're trying to shop around."

"*Jumbo.*"

"Whatever. *Bimbo-Dumbo-Jumbo-Mc Mumbo!* What's the difference what we call him...or *her*, for all that you know? It's still just a glorified elephant in a fur coat, and a longtime dead one at that, so stow the sensitivity, will you?" he groused. "Now then, you want to hear the rest or not?"

Rod calmed right down.

"Hell, yeah."

"Bonesy figures while the man paid that much for just a few dinosaur bones, he doesn't have anywhere near a complete skeleton. That said, the fact that our big boy comes fully intact, ought to make him *at least* as valuable as a couple of dinosaur bones. Sure, the dino bits and pieces are rarer, but that's all they are, just bits and pieces. We can offer him the whole mastodon enchilada in its entirety. That ought to count for something, according to Bonesy, and I agree with him."

Rod's mind was running on overload, fuses popping left and right. To say he was merely excited was like saying Ted's Fish Fries were merely *okay*, and would do in a pinch. No, Rod's wheels were churning and burning like never before, leaving behind a weave of deep skid marks on the pavement of his imagination, each and every one of them in the form of a dollar sign.

"So, what you're saying is that Bonesy is going to ask for a hundred grand?" he asked tremulously.

The song changed on the jukebox. Presley's "My Wish Came True."

Pops drained his shot glass before replying.

"Nope. He's going to ask for twice that amount."

"Holy Toledo! No kidding?"

"No kidding."

"You think the guy will go for it?"

"How the hell would I know? I'm just telling you what Bonesy told me, although I do know this—if a kid wants a puppy, the surest way to get it, is to start out asking for a horse."

CHAPTER 25

Later that evening, about six miles south of Cohoes, Fish sat at a bar in Troy, stewing. Ironically enough, the name of the joint was *The Volcano,* a name that also fit this particular customer like a custom made suit.

Still seething from the humiliation he'd suffered at the hands of Rod Hobbs, Fish was indeed a volcanic eruption just waiting to happen, the magnitude of which was too scary to even contemplate. His face, battered and bruised though it still was, looked beautiful in comparison to the beating his psyche had taken. The physical pain was still significant, but bearable, for hate was a stronger pain killer than anything a doctor could ever prescribe for Fish.

He'd been in plenty of scrapes over the years, and he had won all but the most recent one. The fact that he'd been not just beaten, but soundly so at that, gnawed at him like cancer eating away at his soul, if indeed he even possessed a soul.

Dishonorably discharged from the army after almost beating his Fort Dix drill sergeant to death, Fish had first spent a few months in the stockade before it was deemed that in fairness to the soldier, he was probably more a fit for the shrinks than he was for the MP's, so off to the shrink ward he went.

When it was all said and done, Major Harry Hurditall the III, the army headhunter that ended up doing the evaluations, probably wished he'd listened to his father, Harold the II, and chosen the field of proctology instead. Not a very fulfilling profession, but it paid the bills.

The official findings indicated that Fish, in the good doctor's opinion, was borderline psychotic and only a few distorted brain cells short of becoming an out and out sociopath. The records of what Fish had talked about with the doctor made for entertaining reading, if say for example, you're the kind of person whose definition of a fun day is watching a double feature of *Psycho,* feeling an urge to play the Anthony Perkins part for real, and *Murder Inc,* over and over and over again, wishing that the theater would never close down for the evening.

The report went on to say that while the man was indeed borderline psychotic, he was better characterized as being borderline *charismatically* psychotic. What this meant, in a nutshell, was that Fish, despite his rough looks, had the uncanny ability to charm virtually anyone he chose to cast his net of manipulation over. Most of the time it was women, of course, but he was also more than capable of getting men to like him, trust him, and worst of all, at least for them, turn their backs on him.

Naturally, Drill Sergeant Max McGurk hadn't fallen for any of it. Like men of his ilk the world over, drill sergeants weren't given to being friendly with recruits. If anything, they preferred their men to hate them, that hate serving to fuel the men's desire to prove their sergeant wrong, that they could indeed accomplish everything he claimed they couldn't. It was a time-tested, well proven method and it never failed to produce good soldiers. Well, most of the time, anyway. There were always exceptions, and Fish was a glaring example.

Born lazy and manipulative from the get-go, Fish couldn't understand why his sergeant failed to develop a liking for him. After all, he thought of himself as fungus. Give it time and he'd grow on you.

He didn't take rejection well, not even from a grizzled, hard case drill sergeant. Whenever Fish didn't get his way with somebody, he became frustrated and reacted the way he always did under those circumstances. He went berserk.

Six weeks into basic training, the burly sergeant ordered Fish to do something and *make it snappy!* Fish made it anything but snappy, opting instead to tell the stunned sergeant to go to hell. As you would expect, once he got over the initial shock, the sergeant got right up in his face, screaming at Fish for a good four minutes, referring to him as *a hemorrhoid with ears*, among other niceties, such as *"It's too bad there isn't such a thing as retroactive birth control!"* As things turned out, he may as well have been talking to the wall, for all the good it did him.

Fish moved his head from side to side while tapping his feet rhythmically against the ground, as though listening to a tune, one that only he could hear. To the sergeant's mind, there was strange behavior and then was *Twilight Zone* Behavior. This definitely qualified as an example of the latter.

They eyed each other in perfect mutual loathing.

"Did anyone ever tell you that you're out of your tree, Fishowski?" McGurk spat.

"Not if they planned on going on living," Fish shot back, the less than subtle challenge hitting the mark.

Ever more furious now, his nerves frayed and sparking, the sergeant back-handed him hard across the face, an act that supposedly, anyway, was strictly forbidden according to army doctrine. Yeah, right. *So much for supposition.* Not that it happened all that frequently, but it nevertheless had been going on since the American Revolution, and wasn't in danger of being curtailed any time soon.

Fish was rocked by the blow but instead of displaying any anger, he simply smiled and asked, "Did I ever tell you how good your wife is in bed? Man, that whore just wears me out."

The words hit Sergeant McGurk with the force of a sledgehammer, his chiseled features going taut, his rage soaring off the charts. As he drew back his fist, he hesitated for just a split second, debating with himself over the wisdom of beating the crap out of this guy in front of sixty other recruits.

I demolish this jerk, right here and now, and I'll get cashiered right out of this man's army, he warned himself. *I'll be screwed eight ways to Sunday. Later—I'll get him alone later. No witnesses. Then I'll make the scumbag wish he was never born!*

That's how it should have of gone, but it didn't. He'd have been better off heeding his initial primal instincts and worrying about his career later. That miniscule moment of hesitation cost him big time.

Fish's cold smile suddenly vanished, his eyes turning into pinpoints of sheer hatred, his body tensing, like barbed wire ready to snap and tear into flesh...and he did just that.

He kicked his tormentor in the groin. Hard. The man's face went beet-red, then eggplant, eventually settling into a deep shade of purple as he went down on his knees, both hands clenched to his privates, his mouth locking open with pain so intense that no sound came forth from his throat.

Fish then knelt down on the ground, his face scant inches from the suffering sergeant's contorted features. Taking his time about it, basking in the glow of the agony he'd thus far visited upon McGurk, Fish launched a straight jab right from the shoulder, landing it flush on the unfortunate sergeant's chin, the sound of it, like ice cracking underfoot. The man keeled over, his eyelids fluttering like two dying butterflies. Then the fluttering stopped. He was out cold.

Usually, the sergeant had at least one other noncom at his side, but not today. He was all alone and truth be told, the other draftees weren't about to step into the fray. Half of them really enjoyed the show, as the sergeant most certainly wasn't on their Christmas card lists. Actually, just as the sergeant hoped they would, a lot of them flat-out hated him. As for the rest of them, one of the southern boots, a good ol' boy from Tennessee, put it best when he said *'Trying to break up a dog fight is a sure-fire way to get bit.'*

Fish finished the job with a violent flourish. It'd didn't matter a whit to him that his victim was already unconscious. Fish continued to hammer the man, until mercifully, a bunch of the guys pulled him off the sergeant. Even the ones that detested McGurk had decided that enough was enough. As for a description of how Fish further damaged the target of his fury, I'll spare you the details, just in case, you, the reader, tend to be a bit squeamish about such things. Suffice to say that by the time Fish was dragged away, the sergeant was still out cold, a few of his bloody teeth sitting on the ground, about three feet away from his prostrate form. Off to the right sat his crushed hat, kept company by yet another tooth. Sarge hadn't had a good day at all.

An hour later, a handcuffed and shackled Fish was escorted to the Stockade, the army term for jail. Arrested by three huge MP's, he'd offered no resistance, effectively exercising uncharacteristically good judgment for a change...or he was just so tuckered out from beating on the sergeant, that he had nothing left in the tank.

The MP Captain who interrogated him quickly came to the conclusion that Fish wasn't simply a violent man. He was well beyond that label. *"Homicidal Maniac,"* was how the officer described him on the report.

They locked him up in the stockade until the shrink could determine the most appropriate choice of action—Leavenworth Prison, an army mental facility, or simply a dishonorable discharge.

To his credit, Doctor Hurditall didn't drag his feet when it came to his recommendation. Fish, in his professional opinion, was a walking, rechargeable hand grenade, one that most certainly could be counted on to detonate yet again. Consequently, the doctor ruled out conventional prison time. In fairness to the brute, he didn't belong there. He was a sick puppy, a man whose mind had been incorrectly wired, not one of your typical, run-of-the-mill criminals. If anything, Fish required some serious psychiatric care, which meant placing him in one of Uncle Sam's Funny Farms where quite possibly, shock treatments or maybe even a frontal lobotomy would be called for, should conventional therapy fail, and Hurditall was fairly certain that it would. You could attach jumper cables to the man's ears and then turn on the juice, and it probably wouldn't solve the problem. Besides, these would prove to be costly options for the army, especially considering that as a raw draftee, they'd only invested six weeks into him. On balance, that hardly seemed fair to the army, so the doctor concluded that a discharge was the way to go, one based on mental instability, of course.

The post's commanding officer, Major General Timothy Belanger, roared his disapproval of Hurditall's recommendation. He wanted Fish locked up in Leavenworth for years, lots of them. Locked up and the key thrown away, as a matter of fact. The sergeant had suffered, among other injuries, a broken jaw, a busted nose, the loss of six teeth, and worst of all, in the general's opinion, irreversible damage to his, uh...most cherished equipment, that being his severely messed-up privates.

They went around and around for a good hour or so, the doctor arguing that the man required psychiatric help, not prison time. The general wasn't buying it, the doctor's advice carrying about as much clout as the corny message in a fortune cookie. In Belanger's book, Fish needed to be tried, convicted of attempted murder, and then sent up the river, period!

What ultimately saved Fish's bacon, was the fact that the general had a date with a golf course that afternoon. Tee-off was but an hour away and so he wanted this thing wrapped up soon, but the damned shrink refused to sign off on what the general wanted. He exhaled with annoyance. Aggravated and frustrated by the fact that, unlike regular officers under his command, he couldn't just order the doctor to do what he was told. No, the shrink had a professional responsibility to report and recommend only what he thought was in the best interests of the soldier...and the army. The general kept glancing at the clock on his desk. Still fuming, he nevertheless finally caved in. He didn't want to be late for his golf date, but he'd be damned if this psycho boot named Fish got off with only a Section Eight discharge, one that was based on Psychological instability and or, character traits that the army, in its infinite wisdom, deemed undesirable. No, it'd be a cold day in hell before he'd ever agree to granting Fish a discharge based on that psycho-mumble-jumble. He would, however, agree to go along with discharging Fish, provided it was a standard dishonorable discharge, one that would mark Fish a bad apple for the rest of his life.

Doctor Hurditall sighed, his shoulders slumping in defeat. He knew when he'd been beaten. He could bug the old man until he was blue in the face, and it still wouldn't help. Besides, becoming a barb in the side of a general was a risky undertaking, one that could negatively impact the doctor's quest for a promotion to Lieutenant

Colonel. Like it or not, Hurditall's choices were slim and none...and slim had left the building.

Fish took the news of the dishonorable discharge all in stride. What the hell—he never wanted to be drafted in the first place. As for the supposed stigma that came with being dishonorably discharged, he couldn't have cared less. The sort of people he planned on working for weren't ever mentioned in the same sentence with the words—*Honest and upstanding citizens.*

Once comfortably settled back into Cohoes, Fish quickly returned to his old ways. Poker games, running a few numbers, booking horses, drinking a lot, sampling the wares of a handful of ladies who unfortunately fell under his spell, taking a foreman's job with Sal and, oh yeah—stealing from Sal, too. *Are you surprised by this? I doubt it.*

Yep, the thief that Rod had been hired to hopefully deter, or catch in the act, was none other than Fish himself, a guy who viewed honesty as being a character defect. He'd been swiping stuff off the site for months. Some of it, like the four portable generators he'd stolen, along with the two surveyor's transits, had brought a good buck. As for the smaller items, consisting of about a dozen or so large power tools, he didn't turn his nose up at them, either. Money was money. If it wasn't nailed down, Fish would steal it. That was his mantra.

He'd sold everything to a guy in Albany. He probably could have unloaded it all right here in Cohoes, but that was looking for trouble. Too risky.

It had been easy pickings, like found money, until Hobbs came along. Fish had the keys to the gate, the trailer and the tool shed. It'd had been like taking candy from a baby, and Sal had never once suspected that Fish may have been the thief. Sure, Sal was as con-wise as they came, but he dropped his guard when it came to Fish. He'd managed to convince Sal that he was the best employee the man had ever hired. It was the classic Fish scenario, charismatically pulling the wool over yet another sucker's eyes. Full of himself as always, it never occurred to him that Sal might one day discover the thief's identity. No, Fish never once bothered to give it a moment's thought. Ultimately, that would prove to be a critical mistake on his part, but that's a matter for a future chapter.

At the moment, Fish was busy boiling, his festering outrage at having been bested by that punk, Hobbs, driving him nuts. Like a throbbing abscessed tooth, one that should have been yanked long ago, he'd have no peace until the source of his torment was removed—Permanently removed.

Difficult though it was, he forced himself to put all that out of mind for the moment. It wouldn't hurt any, he told himself, to let his bristling anger, along with his red-hot burning desire for revenge, marinate off to the side for a bit. Besides, as Sal was fond of saying, *revenge is a dish best served cold.* Fish bought into that one hundred percent.

He also bought into the notion that there was more than one way to skin a cat. He could force himself, if he had to, to hold off on the physical aspect of revenge, long enough to deliver a different kind of blow, one that would bring about the loss of Hobb's job at minimum, and a helluva lot worse at maximum.

Fish chuckled inwardly. *Yeah, I'm liking this. I'm liking it a lot.*

While driving by the site the following evening, after a few drinks at Del's Tavern, a tantalizing thought suddenly occurred to Fish. *Wouldn't it be cool to steal something tonight, right out from under this quiff's nose? Yeah, try explaining that to Sal the next day, Hot Rod!*

Fish, however, never did get around to swiping anything, thanks to the distraction that Rod and Butch had unknowingly provided.

He'd watched the two of them haul stuff up and out of the pit, then load it all onto an old truck. His curiosity piqued, he observed them for five straight nights. Getting up for work in the morning after spending way too many hours peering out from behind a tree, had been a real chore. Fish had lost a lot of sleep, but he was convinced at the time, and even more so now, that it was well worth it.

He wished that he could've snuck up closer, so that he'd have been able to determine just exactly what the bundled things were, that the two of them loaded into the old pickup, night after night. More than once, they had Fish scratching his head, trying to figure out what the hell this stuff was. Some of the wrapped bundles were small, while others were pretty good sized. Add in a bunch of huge ones, and Fish was left completely perplexed. One, in particular, was so large that they used a winch to load it. That was the night Fish came close to being discovered. His curiosity getting the better of him, he'd decided to inch a bit nearer, so as to get a better view. He'd no sooner taken a few cautious steps when *Craaaack!* He hadn't noticed the big, dry branch and had stepped right on it, snapping it in two. From where he stood, to his ears, it sounded like a rifle had just been fired. As quietly as he could, he made a beeline out of there, but not before Hobbs almost caught up with him. As luck would have it, Fish had had just enough time to secret himself away under one of Sal's dump trucks. On his knees and scrunched down behind a rear wheel, he went undetected as Rod walked past the truck, casting the beam of his flashlight in every direction, except for the only one that counted, that being downward.

Fish watched Rod and Butch amble back toward the pit. Once they'd descended back into it, he pulled himself out from under the truck and headed for the fence, climbing over it with relative ease.

He'd parked his car about a block away. As he turned the engine over, he glanced in his rearview mirror. The construction site gates swung open. Turning off the engine, along with the lights, he decided to wait there a bit longer, curious now.

His patience paid off. Three minutes later the pickup pulled out and then stopped just outside the gates. Hobbs got out and closed them, snapping the padlock into place. Once back in the passenger side, the truck moved off in the direction of Mohawk St.

Fish would have given his eye teeth to have known where they were going with those bundles, but he had to get some sleep. Otherwise, he'd be useless come time for work. Besides, he didn't have any eye teeth left to give. Hobbs had knocked them out of his mouth.

Maybe it doesn't really matter what's in the truck, or where they're going with it, he thought to himself. *I could drop a dime on Hobbs just by mentioning to Sal that I'd been passing by and happened to observe his pet, "Fabian," taking off with a truckload of stuff, leaving the site totally unprotected, to boot.*

The more he thought about it, the more excited he grew. The idea of throwing Hobbs to the wolves, or rather, one particularly vicious wolf, really appealed to him. *Still, maybe the smarter thing to do would be to wait. I can always come back tomorrow night and follow them, if and when they take off again. Yeah, that's the way to go. I'll just wait. I don't really want to, but I will. Besides, if whatever they drove off with has any real value, and it must, then I'll snatch it for myself.*

He'd felt pretty damned good as he fired up his 58'Pontiac, a car he'd won by cheating in a mob guy's Schenectady poker game, a guy who had a rap sheet longer than Congress St.

Yeah, Fish definitely enjoyed living on the edge.

He turned on the radio as he drove off. WTRY—Brook Benton's "It's just a matter of time," came through loud and clear. Fish hummed along with it, smiling for the first time in weeks. *It's just a matter of time. Yeah, ain't that the truth?*

CHAPTER 26

"I don't feel like going skating at Guptill's," Rod complained. "Let's go to the movies instead. *Anatomy of a Murder is playing.* Oh, and *The Beat Generation,* starring Ray Danton, is the second feature and you know how much you like that guy."

Dee Dee smirked.

"And I also happen to know just how much you enjoy watching his costar, Mamie Van Doren strut her stuff, or should I say *bounce her stuff?*"

Rod would have liked to have denied it, but he couldn't, because it was true. Mamie really did rev up his engine. Why not? What red-blooded Cohoes boy *didn't* get all stoked up at the sight of her onscreen?

"You just don't want to go because of what your Uncle Harry said."

"That's not true!" Rod insisted, but it was true. His ultra masculine uncle, a hard-edged cop if there ever was one, once had told him that in his opinion, roller skating was strictly for girls. He then went on to say that if a guy went roller skating, well, then, he must be a little light in his loafers. Rod knew better, but still, his uncle's words had stayed with him.

"How about the Troy Theater? They're playing *The Diary of Anne Frank* along with *The Gene Krupa Story,*" he suggested, giving it one last try.

She scrunched up her pretty face in distaste.

"Forget it. The Anne Frank thing is too depressing and I already know all about Krupa. He plays the drums and gets paid a lot to do it. End of story. Ho-hum," she said with a phony yawn. "No, let's go see '*Dee Dee and Hot Rod go skating*,' instead. It's going to win an Academy Award this year. I guarantee it."

Rod sighed. He knew when he'd been whipped, and he had definitely just been whipped.

It was Saturday, about four in the afternoon. They'd just pulled over, top down, in front of Howard's delicatessen on the corner of Main and Columbia, and man, oh man, was it ever humid out there!

"Tell you what, let's run over to Stewart's and talk about it in there. I'm broiling out here," Rod complained.

"Good idea, but no more talk about the movies. We're going skating, *period*!" Dee Dee declared in a tone that would clearly brook no further argument.

"Yeah, I got that impression," he replied sourly.

They were inside the frosty-cool ice cream shop on Remsen St. within three minutes. It was as though—*Presto*, and they'd gone from the Sahara, directly to the Arctic. It felt great in there.

"Just don't go overboard with the ice cream. My Mom will be serving dinner in about two hours and we don't want a repeat of the last time, now do we?" she reminded him.

Rod recalled it all too well. He'd begged off after no more than a few mouthfuls of her mother's cooking, blaming his lack of appetite on the late lunch he'd had. It was a lie, of course. He simply hated Mrs. LeBarron's cooking. Too damned much garlic in everything she prepared. She would have slipped some into her husband Benny's bowl of Quaker Oats, if she thought she could get away with it. Rod had long suspected that Benny, being the super nice guy that he was, had no more liking for his wife's cooking than Rod did, but in the interest of maintaining marital peace, he suffered in silence.

"I'm just going to have an orange sherbet cone," he told her. "What are you going to have?"

"Mmm, sounds good. I'll have the same."

He walked up to the clerk and put in his order.

A minute or so later he returned to the table armed with two cones, one a single scoop number, the other a towering three scoop job.

Dee Dee's mouth dropped open.

"What are you doing?"

"Having a cone...obviously. Here, take the other one."

She snatched it out of his hand, clearly exasperated.

"You said you were only going to have a small cone!"

"No, I didn't. I said I was just going to have *a cone*, and that's exactly what I got. I never once mentioned the word *small*."

"Well, all I know is, you better save room for dinner, because I'm not in the mood for listening to my mother's complaints about how you always disrespect her cooking."

The top scoop on Rod's cone began to lean perilously in the direction of the floor. He carefully pushed it back into position with his little finger.

"I don't know. Is disrespecting her cooking necessarily the same as just not liking it?"

"Well, *duh*, of course it is!"

"Well, in that case, yeah, I suppose I really do disrespect her cooking. Probably always will, too."

She made a face.

"Well, as you would say, *in that case*, I suggest you begin making an effort to reverse your feelings on that subject, *if*, you know what's good for you, Mr. Hot Rod Hobbs," she warned, clearly implying that their love life could, and probably *would,* take a steep nosedive should he continue to be less than appreciative of her mom's culinary offerings.

He abruptly stopped licking his cone, his shoulders slumping in defeat.

"Are you catching my drift? It would certainly seem that you are," she said sweetly. "Your body language always gives you away."

"Yeah, I'm catching it, and okay, you win."

What a night this is going to be! Her mother's cooking followed by roller skating. Some days it just doesn't pay to get out of bed, he silently moaned to himself.

As it turned out, dinner wasn't half bad. Who'd have guessed it? Maybe Dee Dee had finally gotten through to her old lady, convincing her to cut back on the garlic, at least for one night. Whatever the reason had been, it was more than okay with Rod. The pork and rice dish, something with a French name, actually tasted pretty doggone good. So good in fact, that he asked for a second helping. Mrs. LeBarron's eyes lit up upon hearing the rare request. She even tossed Rod an appreciative smile. Now there was a first!

As Dee Dee and her cute little sister, Anna, helped their Mom with the clean-up, Rod settled into a comfy, overstuffed chair that sat alongside the floral sofa that Dee Dee's dad, Benny, had just plopped down upon. Comfortably clad in jeans and a tee shirt, Benny kicked off his penny loafers and stretched out.

The TV was on. Howard Tupper had just finished up the channel six weather report and was about to be followed by the Earl Pudney Show, a quartet comprised of local guys who played a lot of 1940's stuff. Definitely not Rod's preferred brand of music. Evidently, it wasn't Dee Dee's brother John's kind of thing either, for he suddenly appeared with his acoustic guitar in hand, pleading with his dad to turn off the TV for a couple of minutes and listen to him play "Johnny B Goode."

Benny loved Pudney's music, almost as much as he enjoyed western style cowboy songs, but being the good-natured guy that he was, he agreed to go along with his son's request.

The fifteen year old kid was good, *real* good. Rod really enjoyed listening and watching him play, the boy's blond hair flopping down around his eyes as he made that guitar talk.

He'd be playing in someone's band soon. Of that, Rod had no doubt. The kid was that good, playing like he was in control, yet out of control at the same time.

Heck, even his mother and the girls threw down their dishtowels and wandered into to the living room to *ooh* and *ah* over the boy's skills.

Unfortunately, the people in the flat below them failed to appreciate the genius of Johnny's music, making their feelings known pronto, by way of a few loud raps with a broom handle against their ceiling. Benny got the message, promptly signaling his son to shut it down. Disappointed, the lad reluctantly complied.

Once the family began applauding, however, his smile quickly reappeared.

"Next year, I'm going to build us a house, up around Baker Avenue," Benny declared. "Nobody below us and nobody above us. Then you can make all the music you want, son."

He'd bought land up there about year ago and was working his behind off now, putting in forty hours as a machinist at the local Bendix factory, also earning extra money by doing body work, and painting cars on the weekends. Built like the guy on the Charles Atlas matchbook cover, Benny always managed to find time for weight lifting and his other passions as well, that being fishing with the kids and roaring around town on his shiny, black, *Indian* Motorcycle. He was quite the guy and Rod truly admired him. He couldn't say the same about Benny's wife, Delores, but maybe tonight signaled a breakthrough of sorts. After all, she'd even smiled at him, sort of, but you take what you can get.

The roller skating actually turned out to be a lot of fun, once he'd put aside his uncle's dumb thoughts on men in skates. Rod felt a tad self conscious at first, but once he'd slipped into the skates and sped onto the rink, he was fine.

They were there for about three hours, every minute of which, Dee Dee thoroughly enjoyed. Gratefully, they'd finally come to an understanding on the subject of Rod's rare find and subsequent, grandiose plans to make a ton of money from it. Granted, the ceasefire agreement between them was on pretty shaky ground, but it was better than nothing. Simply put, Dee Dee promised to stay off his back, provided Rod made every effort to get *this thing*, as she called it, over and done with. *As if he needed encouragement to do just that!*

With their fragile truce in place, they were able to get back to what they did best—have fun together.

While making his way out of Guptill's parking lot, Rod declared that he was famished, suggesting that they head over to the Palace Diner in Troy for a nice, thick, juicy cheeseburger. Dee Dee said she was game, fumbling with the radio tuning dial as she spoke.

Settling on WPTR, she sat back and began singing along with Andy William's "Hawaiian Wedding Song," nudging and winking at Rod as she *tried* to sing along. *Hint-hint.*

As always, her so-called singing left much to be desired. He tried his best to tune her out, but to no avail. As for the hints about getting married, he was more than fine with that. Truth be told, he was chomping at the bit and couldn't hardly wait for that day to arrive. Last year he'd purchased a nice, modestly priced engagement ring from Timpane's jewelry store, proudly slipping it onto her finger that very same evening.

She hadn't pushed him to set a date and for that, he'd been more than grateful. At the time Rod felt as though he needed to put away a good chunk of cash before he could comfortably set a date. Thankfully, she hadn't bugged him to set a date either, seemingly content to settle for the ring, at least for the moment.

Since then, only once had she broached the subject, and that had taken place about a week earlier when she remarked that she'd changed her mind about wanted to getting hitched at St. Agnes'. Now she wanted to have Father Riley marry them at St. Rita's, provided he didn't die of old age first, her favorite line. Considering that just like Father Ashline, the priest was far from elderly, Rod clearly got the message. That said, come next week, she'd probably change her mind yet again and opt for tying the knot at St. Marie's.

He'd promised her then and there that within the year, they'd set a date to get married *somewhere*. Mollified, at least temporarily, she said no more about it. Until tonight, that is.

Convinced that he'd soon be flush with a ton of money, Rod decided to go for it.

"I've been thinking. What do you say to our doing the deed a year from tomorrow? Get married on Sunday, July 8th, 1960?"

No sooner had she taken a drag on her Salem when he'd popped the question. Clearly, the surprise of it all had taken her aback, causing her to cough and choke on the smoke she'd just inhaled.

"You okay?" he asked, concerned now.

"It just went down the wrong pipe, that's all," she replied, the coughing beginning to taper off.

She patted her hand against her chest.

"You really know how to startle a girl. I'll give you that, Hot Rod, my dear."

Rod chuckled.

"What?"

"*What,* he asks? Jeez, right out of the blue, you tell me we ought to get married a year from tomorrow, mentioning it as casually as you might tell me that the Red Chinese Army just invaded Cohoes."

Another chuckle, louder this time.

"Well, it's just that with the money I'll soon be raking in, why wait any longer? I'm figuring we'll even be able to have a house built up on Baker Avenue, near the one your Dad's going to build. Hell, then we got the honeymoon to consider, too. Where would you like to spend it?"

"Whew!" she exhaled noisily. "Give me a minute here, will you? This is a lot to digest all at one time," she confessed, lighting a fresh Salem. "Honeymoon? I don't know. The Poconos, maybe?"

"The Poconos? Nah, I'm thinking more along the lines of Paris."

She peered over at him, confused.

"Paris? You mean up around Utica? Excuse me, but that rinky-dink little village doesn't really strike me as being a Mecca for honeymooners."

Rod leaned across the seat, squeezing her hand, a big grin on his face.

"No, Paris, *France*, is what I meant."

She stared at him, her mouth agape.

"You know—the place that's got the Eiffel Tower and all that good cooking, the city where Brigitte Bardot makes all those sexy movies?"

Dee Dee didn't reply. She just kept staring at him.

"No good, huh? Well, how about Hawaii, our new state? You know, where they film *Hawaiian Eye*, that TV show you like, the one with Connie Stevens?"

She shook her head from side to side, flipping her cigarette into the wind. She only smoked a cigarette about halfway down before discarding it. Rod wondered why she bothered to smoke at all.

"Before you start spending money that you don't have, and may very well *never* have, you need to understand that I'll be perfectly happy spending our honeymoon in the Poconos. I don't need Paris or Hawaii. All I need is you—in one piece."

A new song came on the radio, the Flamingo's "I only have eyes for you." Rod choked back the lump that had suddenly formed in his throat.

CHAPTER 27

Bonesy phoned Pops early Sunday morning, skipping the chit-chat, cutting to the chase.

"My guy put the feeler out to Mr. Canadian deep pockets. Bottom line, he expressed a great deal of interest in the goods. So much so that he's sending somebody down next Saturday to check things out, evaluate the condition of our wares, determine that all the parts are there, and then report back to the money man."

Pops listened carefully, trapping a Raleigh between his dentures, lighting it as Bonesy went on.

"I'll bring the guy to you. Keep in mind, however, that I don't know where you got the stuff stashed, so plan on meeting me and the guy somewhere in Cohoes. Noontime would be good. From there, we'll follow you."

Bonesy delivered the details in his usual, brusque, matter-of-fact manner, like a man who'd been down this road many times before, and indeed, he had been.

"Sounds good. Thanks, Bonesy."

The man grunted, as close as he ever got to saying *you're welcome*. If anything was for certain, it was that Bonesy would never croak from over-excitement.

"You can bring Fabian with you, but I don't want to see Red Skelton Junior in the mix. That kid is too jumpy. He reminds me of that skinny drip, Don Knotts, on Steve Allen's *Tonight Show*. I've seen hoods in the electric chair look more relaxed. We don't want him distracting our guy, so pay attention to what I'm telling you and park him somewhere. Got that?"

"I hear you loud and clear. Butch stays home."

"Good. Now as for the financial aspects of this venture, let's just say that I floated a number through to the man, a number that begins with a *two*. Based on what I heard back, that number seems wholly acceptable to Mr. Big Bucks."

Holy Toledo! Two hundred grand, Pops excitedly thought to himself, reveling in what he'd just heard. *Wait until Hot Rod hears about this!*

"You still there, Shea?"

"What? Oh, yeah, I'm here. Sorry."

Another grunt.

"Already thinking about how you're going to spend it, eh?"

"No, I was just wrapped up in listening to you talk, that's all," he lied.

"Yeah, sure. Okay, that's it for now. Give me a call Friday at the South End. You can tell me then about where to meet."

Pops was about to reply, but Bonesy had already hung up.

He poured himself a celebratory shot of Four Roses as he listened to the bells of nearby St. Marie's clanging away, reminding parishioners that mass was about to get underway. *I probably ought to go to church more often...and I would, if only they'd let me smoke in there. Aah, forget it. The stained glass windows would probably shatter the minute I stepped foot in there.*

Quickly downing the shot, he picked up the phone, dialing Rod's house.

The phone rang and rang. He was about give up when Rod answered.

"Hullo," he said sleepily.

"It's Pops."

"Huh? Oh...uh, how are you?"

"Just peachy. Can you talk?"

Still Drowsy, Rod took a gander around the hallway, poking his head into the kitchen and parlor.

"Yeah, it's safe. My parents are in church. So, what's going on?"

Pops wasted no time in giving Rod the news.

Rod was, in a word, *ecstatic.*

"When is this going to happen?" he asked excitedly.

Pops sighed.

"I just told you *when* ten seconds ago. What'd you do, take a bottle of *Tango* to bed with you?"

"Oh, yeah, that's right, you did. Noontime on Saturday. Sorry about that. I'm just all—"

Pops chuckled.

"Wound up?" he accurately guessed, finishing Rod's sentence for him.

"Yeah, that'd be about right," he admitted, his voice brimming with excitement. "I can hardly believe it, to tell you the truth."

"Well, don't get too excited yet. We got to hope that Dumbo really is one hundred percent intact. Otherwise, it could put a real damper on things, maybe even cause us to lose the sale," he warned.

"Jumbo."

"Huh?"

"It's *Jumbo*, not Dumbo. We've been through this before, Pops."

"Humph! Jaysus, you act like the damned thing is still alive. Who cares what we call it? It kicked the Cohoes bucket thousands of years ago, you damn idjit. A bunch of moldy old bones is all it is now!" he ranted. "You want to give it a name? Good, but give it a name that fits! Call it the *Pachyderm Payday*, why don't you?" he yelled, hanging up as he did.

Rod knew he shouldn't have corrected the old man. After all, he'd been right, Rod admitted to himself. Bestowing a name on a collection of bones was kind of dumb, now that he thought about it.

Maybe, but then again, maybe not, he reconsidered. He hadn't told a soul about the nightmares, not even Dee Dee. They began the night he'd first stumbled across his find, and since then, the freakish dreams only intensified, night after night. He couldn't remember the last time he'd gotten a good night's sleep.

The dream rarely varied in content. It was always pitch black and he would invariably be standing in the same place, on the banks of the Mohawk, watching something huge, yet unidentifiable, lumber along the edge of the falls. Then, suddenly this massive prehistoric creature would stop and swing its wooly head in Rod's direction, staring at him with coal black eyes before snorting, with what sounded like indignation. Then, as the image of the beast began to fade into the dark of night, he heard the most unearthly scream. It was at this point, every single night, that he would awaken, startled, his mind doing flip-flops. He would struggle to recapture the images and the sounds, but he never could bring them back, at least not completely. The fact that he was unable to retrieve the dream in total, produced a feeling of melancholy that was almost overwhelming, a puzzling sense of sadness over... *over what? Something he couldn't he couldn't even put a name to? Ridiculous!*

He knew of course that the dream was, in essence, all about the mastodon, yet...why did it haunt him so, night after night?

Well, the answer to that question was beyond him, so he pushed it out of his mind and went into the bathroom to shower and shave. Hopefully, he'd be gone before his parents returned. His Dad still wasn't talking to him which made things awkward, to say the least.

He picked up Dee Dee in plenty of time for mass at St. Marie's. He liked to get there early, so as to have time to scan the weekly list of Vatican-condemned films that all Catholic churches posted in their vestibules. It was an invaluable source of information for Rod, his thinking being that if it's condemned—it must be one *helluva* good movie, one that he'd be sure to catch.

Dee Dee was a parishioner of St. Rita's, yet she enjoyed spreading it around, attending mass at a variety of different churches. She claimed that it made her a better, all around Catholic. Rod never quite knew what to make of that, so he just kept his mouth shut and went along for the liturgical ride.

Father Touchette was saying mass today and Dee Dee was very fond of him, claiming that when the priest spoke in French, he sounded just like the actor, Yves Montand, that lucky dog who, according to the National Enquirer, anyway, had been known to sample the favors and flavors of a few shapely costars, namely

Marilyn Monroe and Brigette Bardot. *Mmm*, he mused. *A guy could do worse.*

He reminded himself that he was about to step in church. It wouldn't do to have Marilyn and Brigette on his mind, so he attempted to push them from his thoughts. It didn't take, but then, after all, he was only human.

Later that evening he rapped on his friend's door.

A yawning, disheveled-looking Pops swung the door open, rubbing his eyes as he did.

"What are you doing here?"

"I just wanted to stop by and apologize for being such a jerk on the phone, making a big deal about a name given to a pile of bones," he said sheepishly.

Pops sighed heavily, adjusting his pants, hiking them up until they were just below his chest.

"No big deal. Come on in," he said, his blind, three-legged dog, *Lucky*, alongside him, struggling to slip through the door. "Now cut that out, you. You're not going anyplace."

The poor dog had been far from being lucky, until the day Pops took him in, that is. A *Heinz 57* mutt, if there ever was one, the forty pound, long-haired canine had a painter's palette of a coat, ranging from white and black to gray, yellow and brown. He was a good dog, though, and as friendly as the day is long. Had Pops not opted to adopt him from the pound, four years ago, the dog most certainly would've been given the gas. Three-legged blind mongrels weren't exactly in high demand. So yeah, all things considered, he'd turned out to be pretty darn lucky at that.

Rod followed Pops and the whimpering mongrel through the parlor and into the kitchen. Pop's nasty, ill-tempered cat, *Pork Chop*, glared at Rod from atop the old Kelvinator.

"Have a seat. Want something to eat? I was just about to throw one of these Swanson, new-fangled TV dinners in the oven. I got another one I could toss in there if you're interested," he offered.

"No thanks. I'll pass. I'm not hungry right now."

Pops snickered as he turned the dial on his old Crosley Bakelite radio to WROW. Sarah Vaughn's "Broken-hearted melody."

"Now that's what I call music," he declared. "As for the Swanson stuff, you're not missing much. They're convenient, but nobody will ever confuse these things with Betty Crocker's cooking."

"True enough," Rod agreed. "Nevertheless, thanks for the offer. I will take a glass of water, though, if you don't mind."

Pops drained his shot glass.

"Water? Never touch the stuff. Sure as I'm sitting here, the chlorine in it will eventually kill you. You can bank on it," he said with absolute certainty. "You want chlorine in your water; you ought to go take a dip in Lansing's or Carlson's pool."

"But, if you're sure that's what you want to drink, then that's what you'll get," he went on, walking over to the tap in the sink. "Sure you don't want a glass of Fitzie's instead? It tastes better and it won't kill you...at least not right away."

"No, I'll stick with the water, thank you."

"Okay, have it your way," he relented, filling the Welch's Davy Crockett-emblazoned jelly glass and placing it in front of Rod. "So what *really* brings you here this evening? It's Sunday and you should be out with your girl tonight, not chewing the fat with an old reprobate like me."

"I just dropped her off at her house. I'll see her later, but meanwhile, I need to talk to you about our, uh...merchandise."

Pops poured himself another shot of Four Roses.

"So talk. I'm all ears."

"Well, you said this guy is coming on Saturday and that's great, but there's something bugging me about the whole thing."

Pops blew his nose; getting his money's worth, too, sounding like a freight train approaching the intersection of Remsen and Newark, or a horny goose in heat.

"And what would that be?"

"I was thinking that once the guy sees the bones, we're going to have to move them. The location will no longer be a secret, so what's to stop him from coming back, breaking the lock and making off with the whole kit and caboodle?"

Suddenly a warning light began to glow on the instrument panel in Pop's mind. He rubbed his mouth and chin with his hand, then ran it up his face and over his balding pate. Of all the things he expected Rod might say, this eye-opening revelation hadn't made the list.

"Good point, damned good point. I'm slipping. I should have of thought of that, but I didn't," he admitted, clearly embarrassed. "It's good to know somebody's on the ball."

Rod waved off the old fella's apology.

"Hey, you can't be expected to think of everything, so don't be so hard on yourself. Besides, we're a team, a team that's coached by you, but at some point, Butch and I have to use our noggins for something other than a place to put a hat."

Pop's pride had taken a hit, yet rod's words seemed to have had the desired effect.

A slow grin began to form on the elderly man's cracked lips. Then he laughed, a genuine head-thrown-back laugh.

"You say Butch has to use his noggin, too? Hmm, now there's something to contemplate," he said, smirking. "Now, I'm not saying he's out and out stupid, but I do believe the screw-up fairy paid him a visit and then decided to stay forever. One thing is for sure—he'll certainly never develop any brain calluses from over-thinking."

"Now, is that nice?"

"Not trying to be nice, just accurate, that's all."

"Butch is a lot smarter than you think," Rod countered defensively.

"Uh-huh, right, and hockey's played by dainty guys with full sets of teeth."

"Stop that, Pops. He's my best—"

Pops lifted his palm, a traffic-halting gesture, bringing Rod up short.

"Take it easy. Don't get your Monkey Ward's drawers in a knot. I'm just kidding around, pulling your leg, that's all. He's a good kid with a big heart and I know that," he said placatingly, lighting a fresh Raleigh with the butt end of the one he was about to ground out in the ashtray.

"Anyway, back to the bones. It's good that you thought of this, Rod. We'll have to move them right after the guy leaves. Any suggestions as to where we can safely stash them?"

"I was thinking we ought to rent a garage, somewhere off the beaten path. We don't want to draw any attention, if we can help it."

Pops sucked on his cigarette as he chewed over Rod's suggestion.

"My sister, Aggie, has an empty garage. We can use it rent-free. She won't care. I doubt if she's even stepped foot into it since her boyfriend, Alf, a.k.a '*Lash*' Leroux, up and croaked, and that was ten years ago."

Rod's face brightened right up.

"That's great!"

"What's great? *That Alf croaked*?" Pops kidded. "He probably thought so. Anything to avoid getting married would have appealed to him. They got engaged to be engaged back when Calvin Coolidge was president, and after forty years of shacking up together, Aggie finally gave Alf a marital ultimatum. He reluctantly caved, telling her okay, he'd do the deed, but then he got cold feet, looking for a way out, and his wish was granted, buying the farm before Aggie could finally drag him to the altar, kicking and screaming."

"Come on. You know what I meant," Rod said. "Anyhow, where exactly is this garage?"

"The house is on Broadway, and the garage is set back a good hundred feet from the road. It's also off to the side a bit, not at all visible from the street, which makes it all the better."

"Won't your sister want to know what we're stuffing her garage with?"

Pops smiled a confidant smile.

"No. She knows better than to question me about anything, so relax. She won't cause any problems. Maybe I'll even soften her up with a brotherly bouquet of flowers...or better yet, a new pair of combat boots. They'd make a more fitting gift, that's for sure."

CHAPTER 28

Fish had tailed Rod all weekend long and had nothing to show for it, other than a strong suspicion that Pops Shea was somehow involved with whatever Hobbs was up to. Seething with frustration and exhausted from a lack of real sleep, Fish was an explosion just waiting to happen.

Taking it out on the foam dice and mortarboard tassel that hung from his rearview mirror, he batted them back and forth until he grew bored. Pushing the dice aside, he angrily snapped the string that secured the graduation tassel, tossing the fringed doohickey out the window. What the hell. It wasn't his, anyway. He'd only made it halfway through his sophomore year before getting the boot from Miss Hickey. Something about bringing a bottle of *Thunderbird* wine to school every day, passing it around in the boy's room.

He strove to remind himself that he needed to be patient, although truth be told, the next time he displayed patience, would also be the first time.

The man hadn't shaved or showered in God knows how long, looking like something the cat dragged in, but that the dog would be reluctant to drag back out. He reeked of dried sweat, his clothes smelling as if he'd worn them for a week—and indeed, he had.

Although it only served to frustrate him all the more, Fish had to admit to himself that he couldn't keep this up. Sleep deprivation was catching up with him.

Well, if I can't find out where they took the stuff that they lifted from the site, then I'll just have to settle for ratting them out to Sal, he thought to himself. *Soon, too. Real soon. Maybe Sal will fit*

Hobbs for a pair of concrete flippers and take him for a midnight swim, or better yet, just cut his throat and be done with it.

The mere idea of it tended to relax him ever so slightly. He turned over the Pontiac Bonneville's engine, the throaty rumble from the dual Hollywood mufflers reverberating off the blacktop. He then pulled out from his Division St. parking spot and sped off, the black car's exhaust pipes snarling and roaring like two angry tigers, leaving behind a cloud of acrid blue smoke.

Yeah, he was feeling considerably better now. He turned on the radio. WTRY—Darin's "Mack the knife."

It was one of Fish's favorite songs, no doubt because the title included mention of his favorite tool, that being a nice, sharp knife.

A wicked smile bloomed across his ugly face as he drove off, contentedly humming along with the song.

When Rod reported for work early Monday evening, he found a note taped to the trailer door. It was from Sal. He wanted Rod to stop by the office ASAP.

Rod felt more than a bit uneasy, his mind racing as he considered the possibilities as to why the boss would want to see him right away. None of them were good.

Doing his best to shrug it off, he locked the gate and walked the two blocks to Sal's gloomy, so-called headquarters.

Approaching the porch of the building, he began to wonder which sagged more—the dilapidated porch or Sal's sister's face.

He fervently hoped that she'd already left for the day. Normally, he avoided her like a ninety-eight mile an hour fastball under the chin.

No such luck.

As usual, he struggled with the weather-warped door until it grudgingly, and rather noisily, swung open.

Sal's feisty sister, Angie, was sitting in her usual spot, behind a cluttered desk, a permanent, clenched fist combativeness stamped on her round, pudgy face. Over the top of her rhinestone-encrusted cat eye glasses, she sent Rod the usual withering glare, her knifelike gaze pining him to the spot.

Some people had a talent for glaring. Angie? She had a divine gift for it.

"Your mother must have dropped you on your head when you were a baby and jumbled up your brains, buster!" she hissed, her signature beehive hairdo beginning to list to port. Her head brought to mind the image of a bowling ball with a leaning tree atop it. She either needed to give up the ghost and hack it off, or slap another coat of lacquer on it.

They stared at each other in mutual loathing, a haughty glitter in her mean pig eyes. Rod did his best to match it.

"I'll thank you to keep my mother out of this," he spat, returning her glare with his own, clearly indicating that he was more than willing to give as good as he got. She may have been the boss's sister, but he'd be damned if he was going to put up with any more of her nasty attitude.

She began to fire back with one of her patented, venomous retorts, when he cut her off in mid-sentence.

"How about putting a cork in your nickel and dime act? Just cut the crap and tell Sal that I'm here. He's expecting me and I haven't got all day. I got to get back to the site," he growled, leaving no doubt as to his being fed up with her baloney.

The woman suddenly gripped the edge of her desk, leaning forward as if to get a better view of him, the scrawny tendons in her neck extending, so much so that she reminded Rod of a turtle deprived of its shell.

Clearly rattled by his totally unexpected and completely out of character demands, Angie became noticeably flustered, the blood draining from her face like a victim in one of those vampire movies. It was obvious that she didn't know how to react. None of the usual sarcastic crap would fly, of this she appeared certain, and so she simply caved, picking up the phone to let Sal know that Rod was here.

"You can go in now," she said meekly.

Will wonders ever cease? He mused, while at the same time summoning forth some counterfeit courage as he walked past her and into Sal's office.

The scent of her cloying perfume, *Eau de floozy*, just about gagged him. It wasn't much better in Sal's office, either.

It was hotter than hell in there, the greasy old Westinghouse fan in way over its head, clearly not up to the job.

The stifling heat didn't seem to bother Sal a bit. Decked out in one of his customary charcoal gray suits, he looked as cool as a cucumber. But then, Sal was nothing, if not an icy cold character at heart. *Not a comforting thought.*

A thick blanket of acrid cigar smoke hung over the room, like a storm cloud just biding its time.

Sal glanced up at him, his head wreathed in smoke, a look of studied indifference on his face. He was a hard man to read. *Yet another less than comforting thought.*

"Have a seat," he said gruffly, his tone clearly indicating that it was an order, rather than a polite offer.

Rod sat down on the hard wooden chair. Sal stared at him with those cold green eyes, saying nothing, his heavily lined face taut and his pronounced cheekbones as sharp as elbows.

Tensing up, Rod felt a slight tic develop under his left eye, as if a spider had just walked across the skin.

"You know why I called you over here today?"

"Uh, no, I don't."

Sal's eyes took on an ominous glint.

"I think you do."

Rod looked away as he reached into his rolled-up sleeve and shook loose a Lucky.

Sal slid his table lighter across the desk.

Rod fumbled with the Dunhill a bit before finally mastering it, the inhaled smoke a godsend to his frayed nerves.

An old *DuMont* TV was on, over in the corner, one of those mid 1940's jobs—big, dark, wooden cabinet with a tiny screen. Channel six, Arthur Godfrey crooning and strumming his ukulele to the tune of "Shine on Harvest Moon."

Rod moaned inwardly. *Like I'm not under enough torment as it is.*

Mercifully, Sal got up and walked over to the TV, turning it off.

A solitary drop of sweat rolled off the end of Rod's nose and onto the glowing tip of his Lucky Strike, the hiss from the cigarette, the only sound in the room.

Time seemed to stand still, the only other sound that of Sal's nicotine-yellowed fingertips drumming against the top of his scarred, old oak desk, keeping rhythm with Godfrey's God awful warbling.

"So you really don't know why I had you come here, eh?"

"No, sir, I honestly don't," Rod replied truthfully.

Something that might have passed for a distant cousin of an actual, warm smile suddenly settled across Sal's craggy face, his thin lips curling upward, revealing an uneven row of tobacco-browned teeth.

Rod felt himself relax ever so slightly. He could have done without Sal's ghoulish smile, yet it was a helluva lot better than the usual grimace he associated with his boss. *Maybe I'm worrying for nothing.*

And that's precisely how it turned out.

"I called you in to give you a verbal pat on the back. Nothing else has been stolen since we had our little talk a few weeks back, so your presence there has obviously been enough to keep any would-be thieves away from the site."

Rod felt the tension melt away. To say that he was relieved would be a major understatement.

Sal leaned back in his chair, throwing his feet up on the desk. He puffed on his stogie, a plume of smoke rising into the air.

"Another thing. You suggested that the thefts were probably an inside job, an employee or employees making off with my equipment," he recalled, his cigar paused halfway to his mouth, the smoke curling upward. "I have to admit that until you mentioned that possibility, I'd never once considered it, and for good reason."

A loud silence filled the room. Sal liked to take his time.

"Want to know what that good reason is?" he asked, grinning, a grin as wide and ugly as the grille of an old Buick.

"Uh...sure," Rod replied uneasily.

"The only men I put on my payroll are people that I trust. I also take pride in my ability to sort out the trustworthy types from the ones who are less so. It's all in the eyes, son, and *yours truly*, can read eyes the way gypsies can read palms."

Rod attempted to keep his eyes as neutral-looking as possible. He hoped he been successful.

"But when you hired me, you said it was because you didn't trust *any* of your employees, not a one them," he reminded Sal. *How do you un-ring that bell, Boss?*

Sal snorted contemptuously.

"There ain't a snowball's chance in hell that I *ever* said that to you."

"But—"

"But nothing!" Sal brought him up short.

Rod took a deep breath and exhaled noisily, but said nothing.

"Now then, where was I?"

"You were, uh, talking about how you only hire trustworthy people," Rod said.

Sal smiled...or maybe it was a smirk. It was hard to tell with him.

"That's right, and I've rarely been proven wrong. Only once did I make an error in hiring. It was a guy who eventually worked his way up to foreman," he explained, his creepy smile suddenly disappearing, like a roach after the kitchen light is turned on.

"Just like Fish did, eh?"

"Yeah, just like Fish did, except this guy was smarter. Smart as a whip, he was, and strong as a bull to boot. Hell, he could probably bench-press a cow, and then turn around and eat it."

"It sounds as if he was quite the man."

"Yeah, he was, but no more," he said ominously, the cigar clamped ever more tightly between his rotting teeth. "He had a strong back, but a weak mind."

"But I thought you said he was real smart?"

"He was, until the day he proved just how weak his mind really was," he said dryly. "By the way, I see you busted up Fish pretty good, a few weeks back. Came to work looking like he was the jackass who played *pin the punch on the donkey* and lost...badly. He still doesn't look so hot, either. You really did a number on him. Beat him up pretty good, didn't you?"

"Yeah, I guess I did."

"Unusual."

"What's unusual?"

"Fish getting his butt kicked. Fish getting his teeth handed to him. I don't doubt but that he instigated the fight, but you want to be on the lookout for a payback. It may come soon, or it may come later, but as sure as the south end of a north-bound skunk stinks, Fish will be coming for you, mark my words. "

Rod chewed that over for a few moments, not that it was anything he hadn't already considered, but coming from Sal, the warning carried extra weight.

"I was hoping he'd learn from his mistake and stay away from me in the future. Guess not, huh?"

Sal snickered.

"I'll put it like this—if you polled both his handful of friends, as well as his numerous enemies, asking them to use one word to describe Fish, the word *'forgiving'* definitely wouldn't make the cut. Of course, that same scenario could, and probably would, apply to me, too. Like Fish, I never have subscribed to the notion of turning the other cheek, either. Only sissies do that."

Rod scratched his nose and looked down at the floor, hoping that Sal didn't see the swallow in his throat. Dearly looking to change the subject, he directed Sal's attention back to the story of the foreman.

"You were telling me about that foreman of yours, the strong back—weak mind guy?"

Sal dropped his feet to the floor and leaned over the desk, his face now mere inches from Rod's. He gave him a wintry smile, the breath emanating from his mouth vile enough to knock the shoes off a horse.

Rod tried hard not to flinch and pull back. It took every bit of resolve to bring it off, but he did indeed manage to do just that. *Will wonders ever cease?*

"He was an inveterate gambler."

"Like Fish?" Rod asked.

Sal's eyes hardened.

"Yeah, like Fish. He was also a risk-taker. Tell me...are *you* a risk-taker, Rod?"

"Not really," he replied, successfully suppressing a serious gulp.

"Good, because sometimes, certain risk-takers have a death wish."

The door to his office suddenly swung open. It was Angie and she was carrying two hot cups of coffee. She gingerly placed the steaming cups in front of the two men and then turned and walked back to her desk, quietly closing the door behind her.

"You know, I heard you giving her a piece of your mind when you came in earlier. You must have made quite the impression on her," Sal remarked. "Standing up to her, you seemed to have earned her grudging respect, the only kind of respect she ever gives, by the way."

Rod shrugged as he peered suspiciously at the cup of coffee in front of him.

"You think maybe she spit in mine?" he asked, dead serious, not believing for a minute that Sal's sister, the leopard lady, could ever change her spots.

"Probably."

Rod pushed the cup off to the side of the desk. No way was he drinking it.

"Anyway," Sal went on with the story. "Unlike Fish, the guy was a lousy gambler, somebody who should've stayed away from the tables and the races, but he didn't. Eventually it all caught up with him. He was close to losing his house, his car and his wife, so he came to me and spilled the beans, as if I didn't already know all about it. The banks wouldn't front him a penny, so I agreed to float him a pretty considerable loan. Naturally, the *vig* on the loan was pretty high as well, but that's the price you pay for coming with your hand out to someone like me."

"Loan Sharking?"

Sal snickered, staring at Rod as if reading his thoughts.

"You say that as though they're two curse words. That's the thing about money. It's like sausage. Everybody loves it, but nobody's interested in thinking about how a lot of it's made."

"But I didn't mean—"

Sal cut him off, going on for a bit longer about money, blah-blah-blah, before returning to his story. And it was a good one.

Rod was intrigued by it, his worries temporarily relegated to the back burner in his mind.

"So the guy paid you back?" he asked.

"Some of it, but he was having trouble covering the weekly v*ig*, which ultimately led him to make some very poor choices.

Rod was lapping it up now, eager to hear about those choices.

"What'd he do?"

"You know your Apostles?" Sal asked casually, a question right out of left field.

"*My Apostles*? You mean, like the guys in the bible?"

"Exactly."

"Well, sure, of course I do," Rod assured him, wondering how in hell the Apostles fit into a conversation about a loan-sharking operation.

"Good, then you'll have no trouble following me. It started when the man looked in the mirror one morning and said to himself *Hello rock—meet hard place*. He was running two months behind on the *vig* and he sensed, and rightfully so, that I was about to come down on him like a ton of bricks. Consequently, the man panicked, which led to the poor choices that I mentioned a few moments ago. In a nutshell, he opted to approach yet another, shall we say, alternate loan organization, a well-known crew out of Schenectady. They make him a loan, which he immediately uses to pay me the overdue V*ig* on the first loan."

"This is where the apostle analogy comes into play," he continued. "What he was doing, in effect, was taking from Peter to pay Paul. Then, quite naturally, he couldn't come up with the Vig to satisfy Peter, so he borrowed even more money from James, a shylock from Troy, and used the fresh infusion of cash to cover the vig that he owed Peter," he explained. "You with me so far?"

Rod nodded in the affirmative, although he really wasn't all that certain. *Apostles and loan sharks?*

"So now, a week later, he comes up short with the vig for James *and* Paul. What's he do? Why he takes the bull by the horns and goes and hits up yet another apostle, of course," Sal snorts, his mouth twisting into a cruel sneer. "We'll call this one Luke, an Albany-based apostle, just to keep the theme moving along. Well, wouldn't you know it, but that he takes Luke's cash and pays James and Paul the vig that he owes them? Next thing he knows, another week passes, and now he's running out of fresh apostles to hit up, so what's he do? The fool decides to visit one of my Troy construction sites on a Sunday morning, unlock the gates, and then proceed to load one of my brand-new Caterpillar front end loaders onto a long flatbed that a buddy of his so thoughtfully provided."

"From there, they head to Green Island where this same pal of his happens to know of a long vacant warehouse, one with a tall, garage door entrance. They jimmy the lock and bingo—they're in."

Rod could hardly believe his ears. *What an incredible story!*

Despite the sweltering temperature in the room, he was in no hurry to leave. He thought to himself—*I can hardly wait to hear how it all turned out!*

Shortly thereafter, however, he wished that that particular thought had never occurred to him. *What's that old saying? The less you know—the better off you are?*

"Word on the street was they had a guy lined up to make the buy, a guy from Jersey. He was supposed to drive up here with a big, flatbed rig, load the goods, and then head back home. My guy, my *Judas*, if you will, would then have enough money to keep all of the apostles, myself included, at bay for quite a while, even pay off a couple of us in full. Hell of a plan—if only it had worked," Sal concluded scornfully.

"What happened?"

His eyelids suddenly drooped, his face hardening into a mask of thinly disguised, smug satisfaction.

"I got my equipment back, but I did take a hit on the original loan."

"So he never paid you back...but then how could he, from prison?"

"Prison! That Judas never made it to prison. The way I heard it, one of the apostles snatched him off the street that very same evening, intending to remodel one or two of his limbs, or so the story goes anyway. He attempted to pay them the long overdue vig, and they certainly accepted the payment, but they felt as though he still needed to be taught a rather harsh lesson. Opposed to just taking the lesson in stride, Judas chose instead to offer resistance, a real bad decision on his part, I might add."

"So they busted an arm or leg?"

"Worse. He fought them hard, ultimately putting both men in the hospital."

"Whoa! So what happened after that?"

Sal stifled a yawn before fixing Rod with a look as cold as a Mohawk River ice floe.

"What you hear in this room stays in this room. You understand? *Capiche*?"

"Huh?"

"*Huh* isn't the answer I was looking for."

"Oh, yeah, of course! Abso-frigging-lutely, Sal," he hurriedly replied, his palms clammy, a thin line of perspiration popping out along his forehead.

"Good. As for your question, let me put it this way—it was rumored that Judas is now part of the concrete reinforcement in some building's foundation. But then...that's just a rumor."

Rod knew Sal well enough to know when the conversation paused, lingered or ended, and this one had just ended.

Sal got up, walked over to the TV and turned it on. *American Bandstand*—Fabian singing his hit tune—"Tiger".

Sal glanced at the screen, doing a double-take, glancing at Rod once or twice, then back at the screen again.

"This kid really does look a lot like you."

As usual, Rod's face turned red as an apple.

Sal changed the channel. Evidently, *Queen for a Day* was more his cup of tea.

Rod couldn't wait to get out of there. His nerves were shot. *Concrete reinforcement!*

Upon finally leaving, Sal let him know that he was keeping an eye on each and every construction site employee, while at the same time doing a bit of *digging* around their personal lives as well.

"If indeed there's a fox in my henhouse, it's going to get skinned alive," he vowed.

Back at the site now, Rod walked over to the lip of the huge pit and peered into it. The footings had been put in about a week ago. Today they poured the pad, ensuring that Jumbo's former gravesite would remain forever undisturbed...well, maybe not quite forever, but at least until the next time the site was excavated, probably within the next hundred years or so, when the auxiliary power plant would no doubt be demolished and replaced by yet another building. Nothing lasted forever.

That thought brought him some unexpected comfort. Exactly why it had that effect on him, he didn't have a clue. It just did, that's all. It just did.

Man, oh, man, what a day this turned out to be.

Putting that thought aside for a moment, he fired up a Lucky and reached into his lunchbox, pulling out his transistor radio. He switched it on, looking to get his mind off his worries.

WPTR. The Impalas—"I ran all the way home."

Given his present state of mind, the song was anything but relaxing. *One of these days soon, I might be doing just that—running all the way home.* It wasn't a comforting thought.

He switched over to WTRY. The Fleetwoods—"I'm Mr. Blue."

Better, but not by much.

CHAPTER 29

"You sure they'll show up?" Rod asked anxiously.

Pops sighed heavily, his patience with his young friend worn to the nub.

"Is Eisenhower the president? Is Father Guillaume Catholic? Is Finn's Tavern a bar? Does *Jean's Beans* sell baked beans? Kee-rist, but you're driving me nuts! For Pete's sakes, stop it, will you? Bite your fingernails or something! Holy mackerel, what a worrywart you are!"

They were parked on the corner of Columbia St. and Broadway, alongside a *Commodore* dry cleaning establishment. The Canadian's agent was due to meet them there at noontime. It was now eleven-fifty and they'd been parked there for twenty minutes, just in case the guy showed up early.

As witnessed by Pop's outburst, Rod was a nervous wreck, but then, that was to be expected. He'd never before came within sniffing distance of the kind of money that was at stake here.

He rubbed the back of hand over his forehead, pinching the bridge of his nose with his thumb and forefinger, in a futile attempt to calm down. *Lots of luck with that.*

"Sorry, Pops. I'm just jumpy, frayed around the edges a little."

The elderly man's taut features softened a bit, the beginning of a smile blossoming at the corner of his mouth. He reached into his shirt pocket, extracting, of all things, a grape flavored Tootsie Pop.

"Here, suck on this. It'll give your yap something to do, other than send me to the loony bin in Poughkeepsie."

Rod laughed as he tossed his cigarette out the window and went to work on the lollipop, a lopsided grin on his face. If the candy on a stick had been intended to loosen him up, it most certainly had done the trick.

"Never would have figured you for a Tootsie Pop guy."

"Well, Rod, you would've figured right then. I bought it for you at Mayo's yesterday, figuring it'd come in handy today and it certainly has." he explained, lighting a Raleigh as he spoke. "Of course, should some enterprising company ever market a Liquor laden lollipop, well then, I might just develop a fond taste for them."

"Don't think that'll ever happen, but—"

"But *what?*"

Rod hooked his thumb in the direction of the high school.

"I think our guy just flew past us."

"Black Chrysler Imperial with Canadian plates? Was there a black 59' Lincoln Continental in front of it?"

"Not sure about the plates or the Lincoln, but yeah, the Chrysler was black, and it was definitely an Imperial."

"Go!"

"Bonesy isn't going to be happy about this," Pops muttered under his breath.

"Why?" Rod asked as he turned onto Columbia. "What's the big deal? We'll catch right up with them."

Pops ignored the questions.

"Just drive!"

They spotted the two black behemoths straight away. They'd pulled over in front of Boyer's Bar.

Rod eased the Chevy into a spot behind them and started to get out.

Pops placed a cautioning hand on Rod's arm.

"I better do it. Just stay put."

He was back inside in the car within a minute.

"No problem. Just a case of being in the right church, but the wrong pew. Let's go."

The caravan of cars headed for Western Avenue.

Ten minutes later they pulled up in front of the old ramshackle barn. Everyone got out of their cars, everyone but the Canadian, that is.

Despite Pop's words to the contrary, Bonesy looked kind of pissed, but then, maybe that was his standard, everyday expression. Rod bet that it was.

It wasn't.

"Shea, you know, what with my being a Troy boy and all, I don't know this part of town all that well. That corner where youse was parked might as well've been a gangway, for all the visibility it's got," he fumed, trying to keep his voice level so as to not be overheard by the Canadian. "When and *if* we ever do this kind of thing again, try harder to pick an easier spot to meet, will ya?"

It may have been framed as a question, but there was no mistaking it as anything other than the demand, or rather, *Command*, that it truly was. Bonesy didn't screw around mincing words.

Pops nodded in the affirmative.

"Okay, then," Bonesy said. "Go unlock the door and then I'll escort our guest over to the goods."

Within three minutes all four of them were inside the gloomy old barn. The Canadian, his face as smooth as an ice sculpture... and just as cold, was an impeccably well dressed man of about forty, one who looked over his surroundings with an air of distinct distaste, his nose wrinkling, his mouth turned down at the corners, like a man who'd just tasted something gone bad.

Tall, slim and fit, he wore an expensive, hand-tailored, navy blue suit, his shoes buffed to a mirror shine, similar to the luster emanating from the diamond ring on his finger, the stone the size of a clove of garlic. *Talk about looking out of place.*

He introduced himself as Guy St. Pierre, no doubt a phony name.

"Nice to meet you, Guy," Rod said cordially.

The man appeared a bit miffed.

"It's pronounced *Gee*, but I'd prefer that you address me as Mr. St. Pierre," the blue eyed Canadian said haughtily. "And your name is?"

Rod was starting to get ticked off.

"Rod Hobbs. It's pronounced *Rod*, but you can just call me Mr. Hobbs." *Touché!*

Pops gave him an elbow in the side, wordlessly reminding him to behave himself.

The Canadian didn't seem to have noticed. He was busy with a comb, his sparse brown hair on the fast track to thin and gray.

The man had smooth, well defined facial features, yet his ultra-pale complexion brought to mind the pallor of a night watchman's, someone who obviously didn't gravitate toward sunshine. It was those blue eyes, however, that captured Rod's interest. Ice cold blue eyes. *I'll bet this character hasn't smiled since he was in diapers.*

"Okay, let's get down to business, shall we?" Bonesy asked, his raspy voice getting everyone's attention. "Rod, you want to show the goods to our guest?"

Rod hurried over to the rear wall of the barn and quickly began removing a thick layer of moldy hay from atop the skeleton. After about five minutes or so, the job was finished. There before them were the remains of a full grown, six ton mastodon, the age of it somewhere between four and thirteen thousand years old. Rod and Butch had been careful to lay it out perfectly, or at least, they'd tried to, anyway.

St. Pierre's cold eyes scanned the merchandise, taking his sweet time looking it all over, but never once deigning to lay a finger on any of it. Moments later he produced a packet of photos from the inside pocket of his silk suit jacket. They were the photos that Rod had taken.

"It would appear that the skeleton is fully intact, just as you stated it was, Mr. Marceau. Admittedly, I'd been concerned that perhaps some of the smaller bones, in particular, might be missing, but obviously, my fears were unjustified."

Bonesy grunted.

Rubbing his hands together in anticipation of the deal being closed, Bonesy then got right down to business.

"So, if I'm hearing you right, this deal is a go. That about right?" he inquired bluntly of the man from Montreal.

The man offered no reply, each of them now focusing on reading the ensuing silence, picking up on what *wasn't* being said, but *was* being thought.

Eventually, St. Pierre raised a manicured nailed to his lip, a clear indication to Bonesy that the negotiations were about to begin.

"Well, I can tell you that my employer has given me free rein to do as I see fit," the snob replied teasingly. "Consequently, any or all decisions are mine, and *only* mine to make."

Anticipating that the man expected him to play the fool and fawn all over him now, Bonesy purposely didn't take the bait. He'd been down this road many times before, and as a result, had long ago learned that a man's silence is a statement in itself and thus, Bonesy remained silent.

Meanwhile, off to the side, Rod was getting antsier by the moment. He fumbled with the pack of Luckies tucked into his shirt sleeve until he finally shook one loose from the pack. Pops nudged him, giving him a look, reminding him that smoking in this tinder-dry old barn was taboo. Rod sheepishly tucked the cigarette away behind his ear. Smoking would have to wait, so he settled for a stick of Beeman's gum.

About thirty seconds had passed by now, and neither of the two negotiators seemed willing to start the ball rolling. The Canadian was clearly enjoying himself as he waited for Bonesy to initiate the wheeling and dealing.

A moment later he got his wish. Realizing that this pompous stuffed shirt would probably remain mute until the cows came home, Bonesy dove in, making the first move.

"Two hundred Thou," he said, just as casually as if he'd been talking about the weather. "No more-no less."

St. Pierre, seemingly content to buff the surface of his gold cufflinks with a handkerchief, didn't give the slightest indication that he'd even heard Bonesy speak.

That didn't sit well with the burly fence, as evidenced by the black cloud of anger that was beginning to settle across his face. *Not good.*

As if to drive home that very point, Bonesy inhaled deeply, causing the massive muscles throughout his rock-hard body to swell and bulge all the more prominently, his Sansabelt pants and Munsingwear shirt now stretched to the point of tearing.

Rod didn't know whether or not the Canadian was now sufficiently intimidated, but he knew that *he* certainly was!

At any rate, it was a moot point because shortly thereafter, the Canadian quit playing the cool cat role and got down to business.

"I'm prepared to offer you one hundred thousand dollars for the merchandise," he said smugly. "Nothing more."

Rod fought the impulse to yell *"We'll take it!"* but only because Pops took hold of his wrist, squeezing it hard.

Bonesy rubbed his chin as he considered the offer.

"I got two other parties seriously interested in the goods, and both have indicated to me that they'd be willing to pay the asking price, provided that it's all intact, and as you yourself earlier noted, it is indeed all here. That said, we appreciate your coming down today from Montreal, but if that's all you're willing to offer, then I guess it's time you were heading back to Canada. Have a safe trip home, *Gee,*" he concluded curtly, his tone, heavy with sarcasm.

Rod cast an incredulous look at Pops who was just standing there, calm as could be.

Bonesy then swung the barn door open, his arm extended out to the side in a gesture of—*after you.*

It took every ounce of Rod's self control to keep his mouth shut. *What in the hell are you doing, Bonesy?* He fumed silently, his insides beginning to churn like chestnuts in a blender. He'd be damned if he was going to let this guy walk! Fully primed now to pounce on the Canadian's offer before the man could get out the door, Rod was spared the consequences of such a rash action by none other than St. Pierre himself.

"Perhaps I could see my way clear to offering an additional fifty thousand, but that would absolutely be my final offer," he said firmly. "As you people are so fond of saying—*take it or leave it,*" he added, his manner resolute.

Rod's eyes now brought to mind the image of a spectator watching a ping-pong match, his orbs furiously flitting from Bonesy to St. Pierre and then back again and so forth, his neck swiveling to and fro.

During the ensuing fifteen minutes of accelerated give and take, Rod became absolutely certain that he was going to keel over at any minute, dead as a doornail as a result of a massive heart attack.

A splitting headache was doing a jitterbug with his churning stomach. *If I survive this nerve-wracking day it'll be a miracle!*

Then he glanced across the barn at Pops. As calm as road kill, the old boy was sitting atop a mound of hay, listening intently to the stubborn give and take that was going on, the expression on his face that of someone taking in an engrossing movie at the Cohoes theater.

Then it all came to an abrupt end, the two sides finally coming to terms, Bonesy having his way. Two hundred thousand dollars, payable in cash. American cash—not Canadian.

At first, St. Pierre insisted on paying with a cashier's check, but Bonesy quickly nixed that idea. It'd be drawn on a Canadian bank which meant it would end up being discounted here, the exchange rate netting them only eighty American cents on each Canadian dollar. Forget it. Besides, where the hell would they deposit the check? Talk about raising a red flag!

No, cash was the only way to go. As to where he'd stash his share, Rod would worry about that later. Right now he was too busy flying high, his mind swirling with ideas on how to spend the money.

By the time St. Pierre had driven off, even Bonesy appeared to be drained of energy.

"That Canadian is so tight with his boss's bucks, he squeaks when he walks," he declared dryly. "Hey that joint I noticed down at the bottom of the hill, *Falato's,* or something like that, ought to be open by now. What do you say we go have a celebratory drink and talk about wrapping this all up?"

It sounded good to Rod and Pops certainly didn't need to be asked twice.

"Are you kidding? I'm so dry, I'm a walking fire hazard! Lead the way, Bonesy."

Driving off, little did the unsuspecting trio know that from the moment they'd arrived at the barn, they'd been keenly observed from the relative safety of a nearby copse of Elm trees. True, Fish had absolutely no idea as to what had transpired behind the closed doors of the barn, but he definitely sensed that something was going on and it involved money, more than likely, a lot of it, too. Guys with new Cadillacs and Imperials didn't routinely visit decrepit old barns. It just didn't add up.

He was glad now that he'd decided to give it one more shot, tailing Hobbs one last time in the hopes of discovering what he and his cronies were up to. It had finally paid off.

Five minutes after they'd driven off, Fish walked over to the barn. At the door now, he glanced around the surrounding area. No one in sight. Reaching into his back pocket, he pulled out a packet of lock picks. Within a minute he was inside. The old Yale padlock had been a piece of cake.

He shut the door behind him. The sunlight that filtered through the loose fitting old boards was more than sufficient. Walking over to the skeleton, he stopped and started to say something aloud, but no words came out. He just stood there, gasping like a beached bass, disbelief flooding his mind. *Jumping Jesus! It's a mastodon!*

He thumped his forehead with the heel of his hand hard. *I should've known! They took these bones from the site!* He stewed, chastising himself for not figuring it out sooner. *What else could it have been? Nothing else, that's what!* He castigated himself, thumping his forehead with the heel of his hand, feeling like eighteen different kinds of idiot.

His mind raced as he ran his rough hands over the equally rough-textured bones, his warped, but shrewd mind processing what he was seeing, calculating what it could possibly be worth. It was a waste of time, though, as he didn't have a clue as to its relative value. He did, however, know that it had to be worth plenty.

Hell, that expensive Imperial had Quebec plates and the guy who was driving it looked as if he'd just stepped off the cover of *Esquire* magazine. Then factor in the presence of Bonesy, a well known fence, and it all added up to one thing and one thing only, that being money, lots of money, as a matter of fact.

I got to think about this, he told himself, taking a number of different avenues of possibility into consideration. On the one hand, he could come back tonight with a big truck and haul it all away, except that, incredibly strong though he was, there was no way that he alone could lift some of those huge pieces. He'd require help, not a good thing.

What's that old saying? *Two people can keep a secret if one of them is dead?* Yeah, he'd always liked that one. No, there was no way he'd cut anyone else in on this...but then, the more he thought about it, it was a moot point, anyway. Where would he stash the stuff? Where would he get a big truck to use?

Yeah, he supposed procuring a truck wouldn't be a big problem, but as far as trying to hustle the bones went, he knew he'd require the assistance of a fence, somebody like Bonesy. Lots of luck with that, for obvious reasons. Sure, there were other fences around, but those guys had sort of an informal network, exchanging occasional info with each other as they saw fit, so that's out. Bonesy would know about the heist in no time flat, and if there was one guy that Fish didn't want to mess with, it was Bonesy Marceau. Although he didn't care to dwell on it, the truth was, he was afraid of Bonesy, and for good reason. Five years earlier, Fish was in a card game in Watervliet. Bonesy was playing in it, as well. He caught Fish double dealing. Suffice it to say, it didn't go at all well for Fish and he'd avoided card games in Watervliet ever since.

He put all that out of his mind as he considered the remaining options. He could toss Hobbs to the wolves right now. Sal would peel him like an onion, layer by layer, the only tears coming from Hobbs. *Yeah, and it won't be any skin off my back, but it be will off of Hobb's.*

Walking back to his car which was parked quite a distance away, another thought occurred to him. *I wonder if the state, city, or even* the museum people in Albany, might want to claim dibs on this pile of bones?

Now wouldn't that be nice, throwing Hobbs to those wolves, too? Sal might have the sharpest teeth, but hey, the more wolves the merrier. Yeah, I'm definitely going to look into that.

CHAPTER 30

That very same afternoon, it took the three of them four hours, and seven round trips to move Jumbo's carefully wrapped remains from the barn to Aggie's garage. Gramp's old truck may have seen better days, better years, even better decades, and it certainly groaned and wheezed a lot, but it nevertheless still managed to do the job.

Butch had been a bit miffed over being excluded from the negotiations but quickly got over it, his jubilation at being informed of the results of the negotiations, more than offsetting the injury to his pride. A forty thousand dollar windfall usually did have that kind of an effect on a man.

After subtracting the usual third that a fence like Bonesy commanded, they'd be left with one hundred and thirty three thousand dollars. *Roughly Forty-Four grand apiece!* Not bad, not bad at all considering that Butch and Rod each earned about $5000.00 the previous year, give or take a few hundred.

If, however, Pops ultimately got his way, and no doubt he would, then their share of the loot would rise dramatically.

Thus far he'd been steadfast in his determination to accept no more than five thousand, which according to him, would keep him well-marinated in booze for the remainder of his life.

"Are you kidding me?" Rod cried. "You can take a trip around the world, buy a new house, or anything else that appeals to you!"

"Nope—not interested. As long as the booze bill is taken care of, that's enough for me. But don't worry, I'll spend every cent of it, because Lord knows, I can't take it with me when I go, and if anyone ever disputes that with you, just ask them—*When's the last time you saw a hearse with a luggage rack?*"

"Booze! You got a one track mind."

"At my age, it's the only track worth playing, my boy."

The guys kept harping at him, trying to convince him otherwise, but to no avail, so they put it on the back burner for now.

The three of them were in Rod's car now, the radio tuned to WPTR, Dinah Washington singing "What a difference a day makes." *Ain't that the truth?* Rod joyfully thought to himself.

"So, what's the next step here?" Butch asked as they headed for Pop's house. "When is this guy coming back with the money? When's the whadda-ya-callit? The rendezvous?"

Pops sighed and took his time answering. He was dog tired and he looked it. Despite Rod's protests, their elderly friend had insisted on giving them a hand loading and unloading the goods. Gratefully, the sticky, oppressive heat of the last few days had disappeared, replaced by fall-like temperatures. Nevertheless, all of the lifting involved had taken a toll on Pops.

"What'd you call it?" Pops asked Butch.

"A *rendezvous*. It's French for *getting together secretly*," he explained, yawning as he did.

Pops shook his head from side to side, closing his eyes, silently counting to ten for patience, but only got to about four when he opened them.

Bonesy is right. You *aren't* altogether normal."

"Huh?" Butch asked sleepily.

"Nothing, he was talking to me," Rod fibbed.

"Oh, okay. Boy, I don't know if I'll ever be able to get through a night of bartending," he groaned. "I'm ready to pass out right now." And he did.

"We wore him out this afternoon," Rod said guiltily. "And he's got to go to work in about an hour or so."

Pops chuckled.

"No different than any other day. That boy could fall asleep while dancing a Jitterbug with Tuesday Weld."

Later that evening Rod got together with the love of his life. All Dee Dee could talk about was the plans for the wedding. No surprise there.

"Although I'd prefer to have Father Touchette perform the ceremony at St. Marie's, we're going to have to get married by Father Riley at St. Rita's, because after all, it is my parish. Unless of course, you want to get married at your church, St. Agnes', the one you hardly ever go to," she said pointedly, unable to resist a little jab in her intended's direction.

Rod feigned outrage.

"What do mean? I go to church there," he insisted half-heartedly.

She laughed in his face.

"Yeah, right, and our next president will be a Catholic, too" she kidded. "If I didn't personally drag you there, you'd *never* go to mass. Who are you kidding? Furthermore, you haven't gotten your Lenten ashes, or your throat blessed, in I don't know how long."

"I was working all the time and couldn't get away to go. You know that," he replied defensively before switching gears and asking, "So you don't really think this Kennedy guy can get elected?"

"Nah, the country on the whole, will never elect a Catholic, at least not in our lifetimes. Maybe someday, but now. Southerners will never vote for him. Like it or not, Tricky Dick Nixon, that weenie with all the charisma of a gnat, will be our next president, God help us all."

"Hmm, I don't know," he mumbled, less then convinced that she was right.

"Enough of that," she said, switching the subject back to her favorite topic, that being the wedding plans. "Wait until you see the gorgeous gown that I'm buying!" she gushed enthusiastically.

"I'll see it the day we get married," he replied, smiling broadly.

"And not a day sooner!" she warned. "Oh, and by the way, my Dad wants to have the reception at the OCA Club. What do you think?" she said, all excited. "Won't that be great?"

"Well, yeah, of course, but uh...there's no need for him to shell out the money for the reception. Hell, with all the cash I'm going to be getting, we can easily afford to have it at Raphael's in Latham and it won't cost him a dime."

Dee Dee's smile vanished, replaced by a look that said that her husband-to-be needed to get his head examined.

"My dear *not so Hot* Rod, must I explain to you that it's not only customary, but also just about mandatory, that the father of the bride always foots the bill for his daughter's wedding reception," she lectured, her tone reminiscent of the one that nuns usually reserved for their dimmest students.

Rod didn't immediately reply, due to the fact that his mouth was full of pepperoni and mushroom pizza. They were sitting at a table in Danny's, and it being Saturday night, the place was packed— Loud as hell, too.

The jukebox was playing Jackie Wilson's "Lonely Teardrops," although it was barely audible over the din of the crowd. Lots of teenagers. *We should have gone to Caradori's,* he thought.

He washed down the pizza with some water and then replied, "I know all that, but just because that's the tradition doesn't mean that I can't make it easier on him. He's been saving to build that new house and the cost of a reception is going to put a serious dent in those savings," he said stubbornly. "Besides, wouldn't you rather have it in a swanky place like Raphael's?"

Dee Dee exhaled sharply, a clear indication that her patience was wearing thin.

She looked at him appraisingly.

"Dense."

"What's dense?" he asked, clueless.

She rolled her eyes in frustration.

"It's not *what*—it's *who!*"

Rod picked up another slice of pizza, pausing to brush some crumbs from his lips.

"I assume you're talking about me."

She cocked her head, looking at him askew.

"You want the truth?"

"No, I want you to lie to me," he replied sarcastically.

"Why would I bother to? No, you assumed right. You see, evidently, you just don't get it. It would be a major blow to my father's pride if you foot the bill for the reception and I just won't allow that to happen," she insisted rather heatedly.

Rod raised a surrendering hand, palm outward, in the manner of a man who knew he'd just been overruled. You would think that the mere idea of having a fortune in cash come their way, would've made Dee Dee ecstatic, but no, she couldn't have cared less. To her, the worry she'd been forced to endure over Rod's possibly getting himself in *way* over his head, just wasn't worth the potential windfall.

"Okay, okay. I get your point. Your Dad can pay for it," he relented, knowing it was futile to argue the point further.

Pacified, Dee Dee reached across the table and squeezed his hand.

"I knew you'd see it my way."

"Did I have a choice?"

"Of course you did," she lied sweetly. "After all, you're the man in this relationship and everyone knows that the man is always the boss," she purred, laying it on ever thicker.

The song on the jukebox changed. Ricky Nelson singing, "Just a little too much."

Rod pointed a finger in the direction of the jukebox.

"Hear that? That's you—piling it on *just a little too much*. Give me a break, will you?"

She rested her chin on the palm of her hand and smiled at him. As usual, her incredibly radiant smile just about paralyzed poor Rod.

Dee Dee loved the effect her smile had on him. She also enjoyed watching him squirm under her spell.

"What?" she asked with a feigned air of innocence. "Why are you staring at me like that?"

"As if you don't know," he replied drily.

As always, she looked absolutely beautiful. Dressed in a pink sleeveless blouse and a white, pleated skirt, Dee Dee looked stunning, her slender neck graced by her ever-present strand of pearls, each of them the color and shape of a full moon.

The half-eaten pizza now totally forgotten about, Rod felt himself edging ever closer to swooning territory.

Yet again, the song on the Jukebox changed. Annette Funicello's "Tall Paul."

"I have an idea," she said coyly. "Why don't we head over to the Crooked Lake Hotel? Tino and the Revlons are playing there. We'll dance a little and once we've had our fill of that, well...who knows what else we might find to do?" she asked with a suggestive wink.

Rod grinned from ear to ear.

"Let me get somebody to put the rest of this pizza in a box," he said, rising and walking over to the cash register counter.

He returned shortly, pizza box in hand. As he dropped a buck on the table to cover the tip, yet another jukebox selection began playing. Bobby Rydell—"Kissing time."

Oh yeah, he thought to himself. *Maybe I can convince her to skip dancing altogether and proceed directly to the 'Game of love.' What the hell, it sure beats playing Scrabble!*

CHAPTER 31

Fish had done quite a bit of research Saturday night, ultimately concluding that the land that the bones were removed from belonged to the state of New York. He was mildly surprised to learn this, assuming all along that because it was within the confines of the City of Cohoes, it therefore stood to reason that the site of the excavated pit, and anything in it, belonged to the City. Not so, according to a recently acquired lady friend of his, one who worked in the City Assessor's office.

Plying her with drinks in Jack Rapp's place on Columbia Street, it wasn't at all hard to get the needed information from her. As plain and unexceptional as the name she was born with, Mary Smith was a mousy little woman about five feet tall, slender and shapeless, one who was burdened with a sallow complexion, a pronounced overbite, and dull, lifeless brown eyes nestled between thick, dark eyebrows and sagging pouches of skin. Her drab brown hair hung loosely over her thin shoulders, her facial features as unremarkable as the rest of her.

Poor Mary was a good person and kind to a fault, but thus far in life, the cards she'd drawn in the game of love had all been jokers. On the far side of her thirties now, she would soon be staring her fortieth birthday in the face, the mere thought of it weighing heavily on her. She wanted...no, she *needed* a husband and at this point in her life, she felt that she couldn't afford to be fussy about candidates to fill the position. After all, she didn't exactly have any dents in her door from eligible bachelors pounding on it. Hence, here she was sitting in a local dive with none other than Lenny Fishowski, a brute of a man whose reputation for wanton violence, penny-ante crime and excessive gambling was well known throughout the city. Mary may have been something of a shrinking violet, but she certainly wasn't ignorant of the facts, and worse yet, the bone-chilling rumors that hovered over Lenny like a cloud of black flies.

Given all that, and despite the warning signals that her brain was frantically sending her, Mary's lonely heart ruled the day, winning out over common sense and hard earned wisdom. Whatever Fish wanted from her, short of doing the *horizontal hokey-pokey*, because after all, she was a good Catholic girl, she'd do her best to give him. If she couldn't hook *this fish*, Mary figured she may as well hang it up and join a convent.

As it turned out, he seemed more interested in what she *knew*, opposed to what she might *give him*. After an hour or so of sipping her third Singapore Sling and listening intently to his questions, Mary correctly surmised that Fish's interest in her was purely one of information-gathering.

Recognizing this, it only served to depress her, the familiar, customary gloom now beginning to descend upon her once again as she stared up at the ceiling, as if trying to extract answers from the plaster.

Struggling to maintain her composure, she decided then and there, that regardless of Lenny's motives for asking her out for a drink, she was going to make every effort to somehow snare him. Sure, he was dressed like a refugee from one of St. Rita's rummage sales and his hair, despite an overdose of *Vitalis,* was sticking out all over the place, but she was willing to overlook his imperfections. No doubt it wouldn't be easy to capture his heart, given her lackluster track record with men, but try she would! Granted, he was a no prize catch, but then, neither was she, or so she believed, anyway. She was wrong about the last part, but that's a story for another day.

So she gladly volunteered all of the information that Fish asked for. Mary knew her stuff, having worked in the Assessor's office ever since her graduation from Keveny Academy in 1938.

Fish certainly hadn't planned on sharing much info with her, but he really didn't have a choice. After all, she was bound to wonder why he was asking her questions about the land, and who owned it. And naturally, she did just that, interrupting him early on in the conversation to inquire as to why he was so curious about the subject.

Fish was nothing if not shrewd and clever, but convincingly evasive? Not so much...and he knew it. *Mary may not win any beauty contests, but if there's any flies on her, they're paying rent,* he thought to himself. Consequently, he correctly concluded that he had no choice but to spill the proverbial beans, and so he did.

Mary's mouth dropped open upon hearing the news. Held rapt by his story, she could hardly believe her ears, but then, the more details he provided, the more she came to believe it.

Having gotten through the worst of it now, that being having to share his scheme with her, Fish plowed on, revealing to her what he planned on doing and how she would be invaluable in helping him to accomplish it. Mary had the connections to the right people in Albany and thus, she would write the letter to those same people, outlining precisely what had been removed from the state-owned property and where it was currently hidden away. Writing letters wasn't one of Fish's strong points. Left to own devices, he'd have probably used a crayon to pen the letter.

She didn't need to be told that none of this was to be shared with anyone, including her co-workers...*especially* her co-workers. As for the possibility of her getting dragged into the subsequent investigation, Fish immediately put her mind at ease, instructing her to bring him the letter after she typed it up, whereby he would sign it, assuring her that for all intents and purposes, she'd had nothing to do with it.

His address and phone number would be in the letter, so he'd be the only person involved, he further explained. It had the desired effect. Mary calmed right down. Of course, her fourth Singapore Sling may have played a part in it, as well. Booze does that to people.

Now that the cat was out of the bag and Fish had clearly specified what he wished of her, they each became visibly more relaxed, exchanging a few banalities here and there, talking about this and that, enjoying themselves in general.

Yeah, Mary was definitely feeling it now, the effect of the drinks causing her to feel more than a little uninhibited. She suddenly began to wonder what it would be like to make love to Fish.

"It's funny, but here we are, two people without much in common, sitting across from each other in a bar. Crazy, isn't it?" she asked him.

Fish laughed a singularly mirthless laugh.

"Yeah, but sometimes crazy is a good thing. Look at me, for example. Everybody thinks I'm crazy, but do I let that stop me from having a good time?"

Mary let loose with a totally out of character shrill laugh, so high-pitched, it threatened to shatter every glass in the joint. Everyone at the bar turned and stared at her. Fish turned and stared back at them, like an attack dog on high alert. One piercing, malevolent glare and they all wisely went back to their own business.

Fish's eyes roved over her spare frame. Mary wasn't at all like his usual type of woman, stacked, swivel-hipped...and dumb, but he wouldn't throw her out of bed, either.

Somebody had just dropped some coins into the jukebox slot. The Everly Brothers began to warble in unison "Take a message to Mary."

Fish grinned, the gaps between his few remaining crooked teeth, courtesy of one Hot-Rod Hobbs, adding a distinctly ghoulish caste to his cratered face. It was a mug that only a mother could love... or just maybe, a woman named Mary. Stranger things had been known to happen.

"Hear that song? *Take a message to Mary?* I got a message for you, too. It says—*come on, let's dance, Mary Baby."*

Mary hadn't had a man ask her to dance since...well, since *never*, she realized. A bit unsteady on her feet, she willingly allowed Fish to help her from the chair, then take her by the hand and guide her over in the direction of the tired, old Rowe Jukebox. As they began to dance, he squeezed her tightly to his chest, not a totally unpleasant experience for her, all things considered. His body odor was on the border of being out and out rank, but Mary didn't mind. *Beggars can't be choosers*, she unfairly reminded herself. Mary deserved to be in the company of a better man than this one, but that was life for you. Some lucky folks were dealt aces while others were forced to settle for discards.

After the dance they headed back to the table. Once seated, Fish took her hand in his and gently kissed it.

Mary almost gasped, a warm glow settling upon her, one she'd never before experienced.

"Why don't we go over to my place on Saratoga Street? We'll have ourselves a little nite cap and then I'll take you home. Sound good?"

Mary suddenly found words hard to come by. Admittedly, she was thrilled at the prospect of being invited into a man's home, yet on the other hand, a little voice in her head kept telling her *No! After all, she was a good, upstanding Catholic girl, wasn't she?*

"I don't know if that's such a good idea," she sputtered, her nerves on edge now. "Besides, drinking isn't normally one of my vices and lord knows, I've already imbibed more tonight than I usually do in an entire year," she admitted, her words slightly slurred. "But then, I suppose there are worse vices to have."

Fish laughed, a laugh devoid of any humor.

"Yeah, there are, and I freely indulge in all of them," he boasted. "Every chance I get."

Had Mary been sober, she no doubt would have heeded her inner voice's warning and asked the bartender to call her a cab. That's what she could have done, and *should* have done, but that's just the way the cookie crumbles sometimes. It's hard to save some people from themselves. Tomorrow she could beat herself up, a litany of coulda-woulda-shouda's, but for tonight, she was going home with Fish. *Poor Mary.* By the time morning rolled around, she'd no doubt want to take a shower with peroxide and bleach, scrub her body with a wire brush. Yeah, Mary definitely deserved better.

CHAPTER 32

True to his word, St. Pierre returned the following Saturday at noontime, ready to put the deal to bed. He was driving the Imperial while the three swarthy looking characters who'd tagged along with him, were right behind him in a large truck.

Bonesy knew the goods had been moved to another location and fully agreed that indeed, it had been a good idea to do so.

He and Pops arranged to meet the Canadians in front of Boyer's bar, a spot that St. Pierre was already familiar with. From there, it was but a short drive to the garage on Broadway.

Rod and Butch were standing at the curb when they arrived. After exchanging a few brief words with Bonesy and Pops, Rod had the truck driver back into the driveway, taking care to avoid running over Aggie's flower garden.

He halted the vehicle just short of the old garage's double doors. The three Canadians exited the truck. The driver was about thirty, tall and strapping, his duck-tailed hair as glossy and black as patent leather, his unshaven face as expressionless as an unplugged TV set.

The second guy could never pass as his twin. Short, middle-aged, and with a gut that hung over his belt like a bag of cement, the man sported a dark brown Einstein hairdo, the kind you end up with after you stick your finger in a light socket. Judging by his equally wiry, dense beard, this was a man who'd never formed a serious relationship with a razor, either.

The third one was about forty, a burly, jug-eared man of medium height and wary eyes. He wore a baseball cap and an unpleasant scowl. Taking off the hat and running a red hanky over his torpedo shaped, perspiring head, Rod couldn't help but think that it reminded him of the ball atop a bottle of *Mum* roll-on deodorant.

Pops led Bonesy, St. Pierre and Butch over to the garage. Bonesy wasn't thrilled with the idea of having him here, but once Pops assured him that Butch would keep his mouth shut, Bonesy relented, albeit only reluctantly so.

Rod politely greeted the strutting, haughty money man, only to have his greeting ignored, the man glaring at him with distaste, the way someone might eyeball a spider in their soup. Rod's face involuntarily reddened and twitched, as though slapped, but he quickly put the insult aside, focusing instead on the money that was about to come his way. *The next time I care about his opinion of me, will be the first time. Screw it– after today I'll never be seeing this hoity toity drip again, anyway.*

St. Pierre was wearing a pair of tortoiseshell eyeglasses today, ones that matched his outfit which consisted of a black and brown silk paisley shirt—hand tailored, no doubt, along with a pair of expensive, black linen slacks.

Evidently, this was his idea of *work clothes*, but then, Rod seriously doubted that the snobby Canadian would actually handle anything, other than the money, that is.

Pops turned the key in the padlock, removing it from the hasp, swinging the door open. There, laid out as neatly as possible, were the wrapped remains of *Jumbo, Cohoes Mastodon number two*.

St. Pierre stared at them as he called out to one of his men in French. Within seconds, the three guys were carrying in thick rolls of insulation, heavy, quilted blankets, and about a dozen or so large crates.

St. Pierre then snapped off a number of commands to his men, this time in English.

"I'll want to inspect each piece, ensuring that they're all here," he explained to Bonesy, who merely grunted and shrugged. No problem.

That said, the Canadian then reached into his briefcase and pulled out a handful of masterfully executed drawings, drawings of mastodon skeletons, drawings that were ultra-precise in detail.

One by one, he then had his guys yank off the burlap and canvas that the bones were swaddled in. Methodically checking off each piece on the drawings as he matched them to what lay before his eyes, St. Pierre, over the course of an hour, concluded that despite it having been moved to a different location, the skeleton was indeed still fully intact.

Content now in knowing that he'd successfully ascertained that it was all there, St. Pierre offered Bonesy one of his patented, arrogantly smarmy smiles.

Bonesy nodded impatiently, anxious now to get a glimpse of the money.

"Why don't you get these guys to packing it up while we see about the cash?" he suggested, although it was far from being a suggestion...more like an order, actually. Rod liked that about Bonesy. He didn't screw around.

St. Pierre raised a finger, indicating that he'd be right back, and within two minutes, indeed he was, carrying what appeared to be a large, metal toolbox, one that had been carefully stowed away in his cavernous trunk.

Placing it on the dirt floor, he told his men to wait outside. Closing the doors behind them, he then hit the light switch, the bare bulb's harsh, bright light illuminating the dingy interior of the former carriage house.

The Canadian unlocked the red toolbox and lifted the cover. There before them sat bundle upon bundle of Ben Franklins.

Rod gasped. Butch just about swooned. Pops merely licked his lips. Bonesy? Well, he just went to work, his thick, sausage-like fingers surprisingly nimble as he counted the money with the dexterity of a bank teller. It was all there.

Bonesy nodded his approval as he closed up the toolbox.

It took two hours to carefully wrap, and then load the goods into the truck. Even the floor of the huge vehicle had been carefully padded with about sixteen inches of something soft and billowy. Some kind of insulation, Rod figured.

The Canadian didn't bother to wave goodbye as he drove off, the truck just behind him.

Just for the sake of making small talk, Bonesy had asked him about the possibility of the truck being stopped at the border, its contents getting checked over.

St. Pierre sneered.

"We won't be crossing at any of the conventional border stations, so there's no danger of our being stopped for an inspection," he replied haughtily. "Besides, even if we are stopped, there's no crime in transporting a truckload of bones into Canada, is there?"

Probably, but Bonesy just grunted, his standard reply. Truth was, he couldn't care less one way or the other, now that they had the cash...and did they ever!

"I'm proud of you, Butch," Pops said. "You actually kept your mouth shut."

"Once I saw that all money, I couldn't have talked if I wanted to! Geez, it's like a lifetime of Christmases all at once, Pops!"

"Okay, enough already with the *Father Knows Best* dialogue. Let's divvy the loot up, shall we?" Bonesy asked dryly.

It took about fifteen minutes to accomplish the exceptionally pleasant task. Once his cut was securely tucked away into an old Siena College duffle bag, Bonesy grunted and walked toward his car.

"You think he really went to Siena?" Butch asked, as he jubilantly stuffed his share into an Empire Market grocery bag.

Pops laughed.

"No, but he did go to Sing-Sing, down in Ossining. I'm sure he got quite the education there, too," the old fella wisecracked.

As Rod stuffed his share into the toolbox that St. Pierre had left behind, his mind was racing, thinking hard on a safe place to stow the cash, at least temporarily.

"Where you going to stash yours, Pops?" he asked.

"I'll stick a few C-Notes in my pocket, and then I'll hide the rest in Aggie's attic, or down in her cellar. How about you two? Where are you going to hide it? You can't exactly walk into the Cohoes Savings Bank and deposit it all. Too many questions, ones that would definitely lead to trouble for all of us," he predicted.

Butch looked perplexed.

"After I take out enough money to go and buy my new Corvair and new Edsel, I'll probably bury the rest in the yard, just like the pirates used to do. You know, Blackbeard, Captain Kidd, those pirates of old."

Pops scratched his chin, frown lines notching his forehead as he reached for a Raleigh with his other hand.

"That's probably not the best idea you've ever had, son."

"*Which* idea?" Butch asked, clueless as ever. "The Corvair, the Edsel, or the pirate thing?"

"Well, the Corvair you can explain away—a great aunt croaked and left you some money in her will, or some bull like that, but buying an Edsel, too? Don't be a fool. How old are you, anyway?"

"I'll be twenty two next month. Why?"

"*Why*, you ask? It ought to be as plain as the skin on your nose. A young bartender from Cohoes just doesn't go out and buy two new cars, that's why!" he fumed. "Use your head for once, will you? And as for burying the money in your yard, you need to come up with something a bit more secure than that! Build a bomb shelter in your yard and stick the cash in there, why don't you? Hell, they're all the rage today, folks worrying about the Russkies dropping an A-Bomb on Cohoes."

Butch scratched his head, deep in thought.

"Yeah, I see your point about the cars. I'll just get the Edsel for now, a nice Edsel Corsair convertible in turquoise and white," he said, his mind made up.

Pops was getting steamed now, so Rod wisely stepped into the conversation.

"A moment ago you said you'd settle for the Corvair," he reminded his pal.

"I know, but what's the difference if I get a Corsair or a Corvair?"

"About fifteen hundred dollars," Rod replied dryly.

Pops threw up his hands in defeat.

"Do whatever you want to do because you will anyway!" he barked in frustration. "Trying to reason with you is like trying to take a sharp turn with an aircraft carrier. It just ain't going to happen!

Me, I'm going in the house now and stuff this forty-eight hundred away up in Aggie's attic for now. She won't care."

With that, Pops headed for Aggie's house, his burlap sack of cash in hand, stopping only to remind Rod that he needed to drive him home.

"On the way, you can stop and buy me a drink at the *Clairmont*. After all this work, I'm dryer than an undertaker's wit. Of course, at my age, everything either dries up or leaks," he said a bit mournfully.

"Yeah, that's fine except I don't want to carry this around in my trunk any longer than I have to," Rod said, clearly nervous.

Pops guffawed.

"So we'll ditch it in my place until you're done paying for my daily lubrication. Don't worry. Everything's under control."

Somehow Rod didn't feel too certain of that.

Meanwhile, Butch took off, stuffing his grocery bag into the Old Buick's cluttered trunk, hurrying to get to work on time, smiling all the way, no doubt.

As Rod pulled away from the curb, Pops leaned over and switched on the radio. WPTR. Eddie Cochran—"Summertime Blues."

"Aw crap, I don't want to listen to that garbage," he complained, shutting the radio off. "Damned rock and roll!"

Neither do I, Rod thought to himself. *I'm feeling my own blues, worrying about a safe place to stash sixty-four thousand in cash, and as God as my witness, feeling bad, almost guilty, about seeing Jumbo, a pile of bones, heading off to Montreal! Go figure. I must need my head examined.*

CHAPTER 33

The first thing Monday morning, true to her word, Mary typed up the letter and then walked it across the street to the post office. The New York State Department of Antiquities in Albany would most likely receive it the following day. She'd also made two copies of the letter, one for Fish, the other for herself...just in case. Exactly what *just in case* might entail, she wasn't certain, but if life had taught her anything, it taught her to always play it safe. Well, with one exception, that is, that being her throwing all caution to the wind on Saturday night.

This morning, upon awakening in her own bed after spending the previous two nights in Fish's, Mary felt as if she'd been on a roller coaster ride all weekend long. The dizzying, climactic heights that Fish had brought her to, would have been beyond her comprehension, just days before. She had no complaints, though! *Finally*, she'd had the opportunity to experience a heretofore unknown level of pure bliss, heaven on earth, if you will.

The low end of the ride was something else, however, yet another experience that was completely foreign to her, one that left her feeling more than a bit uneasy. She'd assumed that Fish would probably be a little rough around the edges when it came to making love, but just how rough he turned out to be, was something she hadn't bargained for.

Conflicting emotions swept over her. On the one hand, she was thrilled to have left her virginity behind. That said, however, Mary had always hoped that when the day of her deflowering finally arrived, it would be accompanied by all the joyful bells and whistles that her girlfriends assured her were part and parcel of the big event.

Well, she had certainly heard the internal bells and whistles going off inside of her, yet something had been severely lacking when compared to her expectations. The lack of genuine, mutual love involved, perhaps? She didn't know if that was it, but whatever it was, she quickly put it out of her mind. Better to focus on the fact that she now had her very own man, albeit, one who wasn't at all familiar with the word *gentle*. Yeah, she was feeling a bit sore this morning, the red marks on her spare body threatening to turn black and blue any moment now. Nevertheless, Mary knew she could live with his roughness. *She'd have to*, she told herself, considering the dire lack of alternate suitors. *Besides, maybe over time I can smooth him out a bit,* she erroneously thought to herself.

They got together later that evening at her place, a second floor flat on Egbert Street. Fish read the letter over, his lips moving, mouthing each word he read, his eyes slowly scanning from left to right as he laboriously struggled to read each line. But for racing forms, Fish wasn't much on reading.

Now he leaned back in the chair, smug with sweet satisfaction. She'd written it perfectly, concise and to the point, with emphasis on when he could best be reached by phone.

Tickled pink at the mere anticipation of the immense trouble Hobbs and his pals were going to soon be in, Fish's imagination ran rampant as he envisioned state agents descending upon those guys like Elliot Ness and the Untouchables coming down hard on bootleggers. Then, of course, they'd also be in contact with Sal, wanting to see just exactly where the bones had been unearthed, and then asking him if he'd been aware of the find? *Oh yeah, those guys are going to be dead meat! And me? I'll be singing "Who's sorry now?"*

They were sitting together in her parlor, the spacious room furnished with two, red, overstuffed chairs and a long, red couch, the arms of which were all covered with white lace doilies. The mahogany end tables were home to a pair of tall, red and gold Japanese figurine lamps. The lamps, all the rage now, were a nice touch, although Fish hadn't even noticed them, as his thoughts were elsewhere.

Comfortably sprawled out on the couch, he rubbed his heavily callused hands together in glee. *Oh, this is going to be great! Sweet Revenge!* He thought, reveling in what was to come.

"Feeling pretty good, eh?" Mary asked, picking up on his thoughts.

"Hell, yeah. This letter ought to work perfectly!"

"Thanks to me," she reminded him.

"Yeah, thanks to you," he said absently, his reply devoid of sincerity. His mind was elsewhere.

"I'll take that as a pat on the back then?" she asked.

"*Pat-pat.*"

She eyed him curiously.

"What are you thinking about, anyway? You look like a contestant that just gave the correct answer to the $64,000.00 question."

Fish let loose with a raucous laugh.

"Now that's a good one! You're pretty funny, you know that, Mary? I didn't figure you for that."

Mary felt her face reddening. What Fish also didn't know about her, was the fact that she had a pretty quick temper.

"What's that supposed to mean?" she demanded indignantly.

Fish abruptly stopped laughing and stared at her, as if truly seeing her for the first time.

"Nothing. I was just saying that you surprised me. That's all."

She wasn't buying what he was selling.

"You don't think I have much of a sense of humor, is that it?"

Fish was beginning to get steamed.

"Hey, cool your jets. You're beginning to get on my nerves, woman! "

"*Woman?*" she echoed, outraged now. "How dare you address me in that fashion!"

Fish's patience, something he never had much of to begin with, now redlined.

"I'll talk to you any way I want to, you skaggy excuse for a broad!" he snapped, his face a mask of fury. If indeed looks alone could kill, at that moment, Mary would have been dead as a doornail.

If she recognized the threatening, lethal look on his face for what it truly represented, she chose to ignore it, an unwise decision on her part. Instead, she plunged headlong into a verbal battle with him, one she couldn't possibly hope to win. Not that Fish could ever win a war of words. No, he was hopelessly outclassed when it came to that. He settled arguments with his fists, period.

"Get out!" she screamed. "I may be a lonely woman, but I'd rather be dead than spend another moment with you!"

"Oh, yeah? Well, let me tell you, I wouldn't take you to a funeral, unless it was your own!"

"Get out, you filthy, stinking excuse for a man. You make me sick!"

He grabbed her by the throat, his strong fingers digging in.

"Let tell you something, you miserable skank. People that talk to me like that always end up getting hurt," he snarled, his face now mere inches from hers, his forehead bright with pinpoints of perspiration, his eyes cold as marble. "Up front and personal...or maybe, upfront and *impersonal*. Either way, I always get my point across," he added, his words spoken with a certainty that couldn't be denied—and an obvious, malicious pleasure in that certainty.

With that, he gave her a brutal shove, sending her headlong into an end table. The lamp shattered as it hit the hardwood floor.

Mary should have kept her mouth shut at that point, but she didn't, opting instead to lambast him with words that would make a sailor blush, an altogether unwise move on her part.

If Fish had been an implement, he would've been a knife, his temper as sharp and fierce as any blade ever made.

He reached down, roughly yanking her to her feet. He then backhanded her hard across the face, and then again, the sound of the blows sickening. Falling to the floor in a heap, her nose bleeding profusely, Mary could hear church bells ringing in her head, air-raid sirens going off.

"That'll teach you to keep mouth shut, you skinny slut, you!" he roared before heading for the door.

Mary slowly gathered herself together, stemming the flow of blood with a kitchen towel. Her head was exploding with pain, the mere act of gently touching the towel to her nose, enough to make her gasp in agony. Nevertheless, she soldiered on as she waited for the nosebleed to stop...if it stopped, that is. She knew she ought to go to the emergency room. After all, her nose may have been broken.

She went in the bathroom and peered into the mirror, carefully lowering the towel. The bleeding had slowed to a trickle. As she gingerly attempted to further staunch the flow with a few tissues, she noted that her nose was still straight as ever, thereby eliminating any worry of it being broken.

As for what *had* broken inside of her tonight, that was a different story. *This is what I get for settling for someone from the dregs of society*, she chastised herself. Unbeknownst to Fish, Mary had, through a contact in the police department, thoroughly checked out his background, discovering among other things, that he was the kind of low-level criminal that gave other low-level criminals a bad name. Then there was also the discharge from the army. She was well aware of all the details concerning that, as well.

One call to the police right now, and she could have him locked up for felony assault. She thought about it, but in the end, decided against it. Once he was released from jail, he'd no doubt try to beat her up yet again, maybe even kill her. Of this, she was absolutely certain. No, she'd think of another, safer way, to get back at him...but get back at him, she would! Already, the seed of a dark, vengeful plot was taking root in her mind, slowly germinating before eventually coming into full bloom, and once it did, the only crop to be harvested would be *Fish*.

To those who thought they knew her well, she was simply meek, mild, and lonely, little Mary. Well, she'd freely own up to the lonely label, but *meek and mild*? Better think again!

CHAPTER 34

It was a beautiful, sunny Monday afternoon when Rod walked out of Woolworth's with three white bags of candy clutched securely in his hands. Since the time he'd been a little snot-nosed kid, the candy counter in Woolworth's called out to him regularly. Of course, he was the only one that could hear it. Orange slices, big, cherry flavored gumdrops and his favorite of all—soft, orange candy squares coated with some kind of white glaze. Oh yeah!

His longtime buddy, Steve Koval, worked there, and personally filled the bags, a few extra candies tossed in for good measure. Hey, that's what friends are for, although Steve did give him a curious look when he paid for his purchase with a hundred dollar bill, asking if he had anything smaller. Rod replied that no, unfortunately, he didn't.

He'd been walking around on cloud nine lately, joyfully preoccupied with thoughts of his new found riches and how, in time, he would spend it all. Everyone should be so lucky.

After shooting the breeze with Steve for a bit, catching up on things, they shook hands and Rod headed out the door. Seymour, the garment guru of Remsen Street, was standing by the entrance to his clothing shop, just across the street. He called out to Rod: "Stop in when you get a chance. I just got some new belts in—silver ones and gold ones—those narrow numbers that are all the fashion now. Buy two and I'll even give you a third for half price!" he yelled, the consummate shill always on the hustle. "If you don't want to be called a square, you got to stay on top of what's hot in fashion, you know!"

Rod waved him off with a smile. The man could have successfully worked the carnivals as a top notch barker, but he had a good heart, often extending long term, no interest credit, to boys barely into their teens.

Rod's car was parked alongside the Cohoes theater, just a block or two away. Stowed away in the trunk, under the spare, was an envelope containing ten grand. His next stop would be the Cohoes Savings Bank, where he planned on renting a safe deposit box. Next week he'd put some more money in it. It was definitely the best way to go, a helluva lot better than hiding it here and there. Now, if he could just convince Butch to do the same thing.

Contentedly munching away as he sauntered down the street, a twelve year-old by the name of Pete DeCicco called out to him from behind. Rod turned around, waiting for the boy to catch up with him.

"Hey, Hot Rod, I know what's in those bags. How about a piece or two for me, your ol' buddy?" the kid asked, grinning. Pete had been hanging around Rod for years, sticking to him like a husk on corn, ever since he'd been about seven. He was a good kid, full of the devil, and always cracking corny jokes. Tall and gangly for his age, Pete also possessed an uncanny knack for always being up on the latest goings-on in the city, whatever they might be, a regular fountain of inside information.

After Pete stuck his hand into the bag of orange slices, extracting a handful, he asked Rod if he could help him out with something.

"Sure. What's up?"

Pete smiled sheepishly, trying hard to project a Beaver Cleaver look of innocence. He failed to pull it off, however. He was a street kid at heart, about as similar to the Beaver as James Dean was to Wally Cleaver.

"Cut the act, Pete. The Timmy from *Lassie* routine is beyond your reach. Just spit it out, whatever it is."

"Aw, okay. Can I bum thirty cents off you?"

"What do you need it for?"

"I got to buy something, something I need *badly*, but I don't have any coin."

"What is it?"

"Something in Kresge's."

"Wow, that tells me a lot," Rod said with a laugh. "Come on, fess up, Pete—what do you want to buy?"

"Pie Ala Mode, with ice cream on it."

Rod began laughing even harder.

"What, are you Yogi Berra's little brother or something? Ice cream is *part* of Pie Ala Mode! It automatically comes with the pie."

Pete shrugged his narrow shoulders.

"So shoot me. What do I know? Anyway, can you lend me the money, or what? Please!"

Rod reached into his tan Chino's front pockets, fishing for some coins. He handed Pete two quarters.

"Thanks, Hot Rod! You don't want the change back, do you?" he asked, already knowing what the answer would be.

"Nah but let me ask you a question. What's with this *lend me* stuff? We both know you'll never pay me back."

A playful smirk passed across Pete's face.

"Hey, you never know. One of these days I just might!"

Rod reached over and tousled the boy's hair. He was a good kid and Rod never minded a bit tossing him a few coins every now and then. He was about to say as much when a car began slowly cruising alongside them, the radio turned up high, the sound of Johnny and the Hurricane's "Red River Rock" blaring away.

"I hate those guys. Those jerks are nothing but bullies," Pete said, letting loose with a stream of spit in their direction.

Those guys, as Pete put it, were none other than Sal's three nephews, a trio of gorillas whose IQ's matched their waistlines, each of them short on teeth and long on stupidity.

"Hey, you little twerp! You just spit on my car!" the driver screamed, yanking the wheel toward the curb, pulling in alongside Rod and Pete.

They were at the corner of White and Remsen. Rod's car was parked there, thirty feet away, and all he wanted was to get in it with Pete and then drive away. He didn't need, or want, to get into it with Sal's nephews, the three stooges who spent eleven years in grade school. Nothing good could come from it and he knew it. Sal claimed to not have much use for them, insisting they couldn't take a proper whiz without first consulting a diagram, but family is family, not to mention that their mother was Sal's sister, Angie. *Enough said.*

Yeah, Rod would have liked nothing better than to just drive off, but it wasn't to be.

The car was a customized hot rod, lowered and frenched, the whole nine yards. A 1948 Hudson Hornet with a grille like chromed teeth, it was lacquered in deep purple and generously festooned with blue and orange flames. Oh, and seriously sagging springs, too.

The driver, who had to have been shoehorned into the front seat, struggled to hoist his huge body up and out of the car. Once out, he pointed a finger in Pete's direction and began yelling. Problem was, neither Rod nor Pete could make out the words. The radio volume was loud enough to break glass.

Rod shrugged, pointing to his ear.

Surprisingly enough, Dimwitted Dominic got the message, reaching back through the open window, turning the radio off.

He then strutted up to where Rod was standing, a distinct chill emanating from the big brute, his bare arms bulging like boulders from a cotton shirt with the sleeves ripped off and buttons long gone. Young Pete stood behind Rod's back, an impregnable shield of protection, or so Pete hoped anyway.

"That little punk just hawkered on my car, so get out the way, Hobbs," Dominic warned ominously. "He's overdue for a swift kick in the ass, one he'll never forget, the little crumb!"

Rod raised a hand, palm up in peacemaking mode, as Pete braced himself for a quick takeoff.

"Whoa, take it easy. Don't go ape over it! It was an accident. The kid just spit toward the road. He wasn't intentionally aiming for your car."

"Bull!" the big gorilla fired back, his sandpaper voice, rough and gravelly, a glint as sharp as an axe in his angry eyes. "Now get out of the way or I'll take you apart!" he spat, his threatening words oozing danger, the way air will crackle just before lightning strikes.

Angelo, one of the other bone crushers, had somehow managed to winch himself out of the car, and was now standing alongside his brother, his face just as ugly and threatening-looking as the other's. He muttered something unintelligible to Rod, his jaws working as if cracking walnuts with his teeth. Rod thought it probably wasn't a compliment.

He suddenly felt the side of his face twitch, as if a spider had just walked across it. These two schmucks were the kind that opened beer bottles with their teeth. Not a comforting thought, he mused, as he measured, and evaluated the potential of his adversaries. Then, for just a split second, Rod felt as if dark hands were weaving a web around him, and he was a fly about to be eaten alive. But then it passed, the trained fighter in him taking over, the hair on the back of his neck beginning to bristle.

He didn't have to be clairvoyant to figure out what was coming next and truth be told, it was okay with him. He actually loved a good fight when the odds were stacked against him. Two against one was good odds as far as he was concerned, particularly against hoods who probably didn't know the first thing about fighting proficiency...unless it involved lead pipes or Louisville Sluggers, that is. Still, although nothing in these two lumbering elephants' physical appearance suggested that they could move quickly, Rod figured it would be unwise to dismiss the possibility, so he'd keep that in mind once the fireworks commenced.

Of course there was also Tony, the third brother, to consider, but then, he was lounging in the back seat of the car reading, or more likely, just looking at the pictures in an *Archie* comic book. If he attempted to come to their aid, it would probably take five minutes before he could extricate himself from the car, if at all. No sweat. Rod would handle him with ease, too. He was certain of it.

Time to put-up or shut-up, he decided, pulling the pin from a verbal grenade and lobbing it in their direction.

"I'm curious. Aren't you guys supposed to be working down at the site today?"

The unexpected question threw them off balance, the cogs in their pea-brains momentarily jammed, just as Rod suspected it would.

"We went to see Doctor Mitchell for our annual physicals. Ma makes us do it every year," Dominic rasped, "Why, what's it you?" he asked suspiciously, rubbing a knuckle against the tip of his bulbous nose.

"A people doctor?" Rod asked, feigning surprise. "No kidding? Hell, I figured you guys had your physicals done by a veterinarian."

"What'd you say?" Dominic bellowed, his face contorted by rage.

"I said you ought to take that toothpick out of your mouth. I'd hate to see you choke on it after I knock it down it down your throat."

And then it began.

For a fleet second Rod wondered which of the two would come at him first. Tossing a mental coin, heads the driver, tails the other goon, it came up heads. And he was proven right.

The driver's ears, along with rest of his ugly mug had turned purple with rage, the tendons in his neck as taut as guitar strings. Lunging forward like a Rhino bent on destruction, the big galoot charged Rod, his outstretched hands the size of manhole covers, intent on choking the life out of his target. That was how it was supposed to go, but of course, it didn't.

Coiled like an over-torqued spring, Rod sprang forward, stepping inside the behemoth's outstretched arms, landing a vicious left hook to the solar plexus. Quickly stepping back as the man sank to the ground, a whoosh of air expelling from his lungs, his mouth wide open as he desperately fought for breath, Rod turned to face the other one. Enraged, Angelo, the sumo-sized ape, a simian throwback if there ever was one, wagged his index finger at Rod.

"You shouldta ought done that!"

Rod tossed him his most engaging smile.

"Too late now. I already did it," he taunted. "Who's next? You, or the bozo in the Batmobile?"

"You're all mine, valentine," Angelo growled, flexing his meaty mitts against his thighs.

"Wow, you really have a way with words, Angelo. I'll bet you majored in poetry while in reform school."

The hood smirked, his attitude suggesting that this was going to be easy pickings.

"Some people just beg to get their bee-hinds kicked."

"Yeah, I agree. Some people do need to get their bee-hinds kicked. People like you, you big drip. It wouldn't hurt to get your face remodeled, either. Angie must've beaten you with an ugly-stick when you were a kid."

The enraged quiff reached into his pocket, producing a set of brass knuckles that he clumsily slipped over the tops of his sausage-like fingers. Once settled snugly onto his hand, he made his move, launching a looping, overhand right, one that seemed to take forever to reach its intended target, in fact, never arriving at all.

Rod ducked, although as it turned out, he needn't have bothered. Still, it was always better to duck and not need to, than need to, and not duck.

He came up out of a crouch and landed a right, straight from the shoulder, with weight behind it. It landed square on the bridge of the nose, the impact, felt right down to the soles of Angelo's size 15's. The guy staggered back, legs wobbling as he tried to regain his balance. Shock and pain registered in the man's eyes, but he was still game.

Rod landed a ferocious right to the head, Angelo's nose imploding in a geyser of blood. Despite the methodical demolition of his face, he still wouldn't go down, however. Rod continued to jolt him with hard, brisk shots that landed efficiently, time after time. Bruised in body and ego, the starch was now rapidly coming out of Angelo's sails.

"Are we having fun yet?" Rod asked as he took a short breather for himself. He didn't have a scratch on him, but he was tired from hitting the guy. The man just wouldn't go down. He was a tough one. Rod would give him that. A loser who didn't realize the final bell had already rung.

The stubborn ape made his final push, a roundhouse swing that Rod easily sidestepped. Rather than hit him yet again, Rod gave him a shove. He went down like a wounded B-52 flying fortress, one that had just flown its last mission.

Rod glanced over at the other one, Dominic the donkey. He was sitting on the ground about five feet away from his battered brother, holding his stomach as his breathing appeared to be getting back to normal. Rod almost felt sorry for him. Almost.

His gaze wandered over to the back seat of the car. Tony, ape number three, had opened the door, no doubt intent upon coming to the aid of his brothers, but evidently, he'd somehow gotten wedged between the seat and the door, like a jumbo-sized block of Spam that's in Limbo, hanging half in and half out of the can, forever refusing to budge any further.

Rod walked over to the distraught man.

Tony, the trapped tiger, stared up at him, his face a volatile mix of anger and frustration.

"When I get out of here, you're dead meat," he roared. "I'll break your neck!"

Rod chuckled.

"Yeah, right. The only thing you could break is the bathroom scale," he taunted, walking away. "See ya later, alligator."

Pete suddenly materialized in front of him.

"Man, you really tore those jerks up!" he gushed. "Wait til I tell my brothers about this!"

"I'm glad you took off when you did, but where exactly did you disappear to?"

"I was across the street on Billy Neiles' corner—in the doorway of the White St. Newsroom. It was funny when Mr. Charette came out to sweep the sidewalk in front of his luncheonette."

"What was so funny about it?" he asked, as he unlocked the door to his car.

"Mr. Charette saw you pounding the pee out of those two and shook his head, complaining: 'Where's a cop when you need one?'"

Rod failed to see the humor in that, but the mere mention of a cop was enough to get him moving. He'd fought in self defense, yet if the cops suddenly showed up now, there'd still be a lot of explaining to do, something he'd prefer to avoid, particularly if his uncle Harry happened to be among them. Self defense or not, Harry would give him holy hell for getting into a fight on the street, and then of course, he'd pass that information along to Rod's Dad. More grief would then be forthcoming.

He got into the car and started it up, asking Pete if he needed a ride.

"Nah, Kresge's is just up the street. I'll walk to my pie ala mode, thank you."

"Okay, take it easy...and stay out of trouble," he cautioned, glancing at his watch to see if he could still make the bank in time to rent a safe deposit box. It was too late. It was closed now. It'd have to wait until another day.

Pete snorted a derisive laugh.

"Stay out of trouble, you say? Ha! Look who's talking!"

CHAPTER 35

Fish walked into his crummy flat right after work. Normally, he'd have stopped at some gin mill and got half a bag on before heading home, but not this week. He wanted that phone call, the one from the state, the one he'd been waiting for. They should have received the letter by now. It'd been mailed three days ago. *What if it got lost in the mail?* He worried. *What if that dumb broad never even mailed it? What if this?—What if that?* All this worry was giving him a headache.

He also hated the fact that having to wait at home for the call was interfering with his usual after-work routine, one that consisted of devouring a pizza or two, washing it down with about a gallon of Piel's.

He was hungry. Yanking on the handle of the filthy Westinghouse, he checked out the possibilities. There weren't many. Cursing to himself, he had to settle for a few sardine and pickle sandwiches made with stale *Lady Betty* bread. Desert consisted of some pig's knuckles and a quart of beer.

Now finished with the less than appetizing meal, he wiped off his mouth with his shirt sleeve, wincing as a jolt of pain hit him where some of his teeth used to be. *That damned Hobbs!* Every time he looked in the mirror and felt the pain while gingerly using his razor, thoughts of what he had planned for Hobbs ran rampant through his mind. If not for those comforting thoughts...*well, who knew what he would do? Lose my mind? Ha! Now there's a good one!*

The phone rang. He grinned, picking it up on the second ring. "Yeah?"

"Is this Mr. Fishowski speaking?" a man asked politely, his voice smooth and low.

"Yeah, it is. Who are you?"

"Well, sir, my name is Cecil Abercrombie and I'm the Director of the New York State Department of antiquities. I received your letter and to be frank, I would very much like to speak to you about the matter."

Fish's grin widened considerably.

"Uh-huh. Okay, shoot."

"This information you sent—you are absolutely certain that it's the remains of a mastodon?"

"Yeah, no doubt about it."

Mr. Abercrombie coughed.

"Excuse me," he said. "Now then, if you're truly certain of it, then by all means, I'll need to take a look at these remains and verify that they are indeed what you say they are. I'm sure you understand."

"Yeah, sure," Fish growled.

"Ahem. Well, all right then. I'll need to view them as soon as possible, tomorrow, actually."

"I work, so it'll have to be tomorrow night, after five."

"I work, too, as you know, but only during the day. Therefore, you'll have to arrange to meet me first thing in the morning, say around nine."

"I can't do that. I got to be at work at eight."

"You don't *really* have a choice in the matter," the man replied, the polite smoothness of his voice gone now, replaced by an icy tone, one that clearly implied that he'd brook no argument. Fish got the message.

"Okay, I'll call in sick. No problem."

That said, they agreed to meet at nine in front of the high school, one of the few Cohoes landmarks that the Albany man was familiar with.

Just as Abercrombie was saying goodbye, some lady got on the party line, squawking about how she needed to call her sister, Stasia, shrilly demanding that Fish get off the line immediately.

The state guy hung up. Now it was just Fish and the woman. Precisely what he said to the woman, well, let's just say it's not fit for print and leave it at that.

Fish called in at eight sharp, claiming to Sal that he had a fever, his stomach acting up, too. Sal groused a bit, but then said okay, he understood.

Abercrombie showed up at nine on the nose accompanied by a trooper in a gray, plain-Jane state police cruiser. Fish was momentarily thrown by this, never expecting to see the guy pull up in a cop car with a trooper as his chauffer.

He was leaning against the fender of his Pontiac when Abercrombie exited the cop car, garbed in a navy pinstriped suit, bulging at the seams, and a maroon paisley tie. A dead ringer for an aging Pillsbury Doughboy, he was puffy all over, short, rotund and bald. Well, under the wig, he was bald, anyway. It was a gray, lumpy thing, like a squirrel had up and died atop his head. Appearing to be just a few miles short of retirement age, it was obvious that the guy had yet to master the art of aging gracefully. Probably never would either.

"Mr. Fishowski, I presume?" he asked, his voice resonating with a hoity toity inflection, one designed to let Fish know that he was an upper-crust kind of guy, a man much, much smarter than the likes of a blue collar mutt like Fish.

"Yeah, that'd be me," Fish replied, extending a meaty mitt in anticipation of the customary handshake, one that never materialized.

Abercrombie blew him off, preferring instead to get right to the matter at hand.

Fish was po'd by the slight, but quickly brushed it aside. He had more important things on his mind.

So did Abercrombie.

"Shall we go? We'll follow you," he said, not waiting for a reply to the question.

Six minutes later, they pulled up in front of the old barn. Abercrombie exited the car and walked over to Fish.

Flashing an insincere smile, he extended his arm with a flourish, saying, "After you."

The three men walked up to the barn doors. Abercrombie noted with some consternation that the doors were padlocked.

"No problem," Fish remarked casually. "I can pop it open it in no time flat."

"Ahem! Are you saying that you have a key to the lock?"

Fish smirked.

"No, but I can still open it, easy as pie."

The tall, rugged-looking trooper shot Fish a suspicious look.

"Yeah, I'll bet you can. You strike me as the type who's had a lot of practice working on locks," he surmised correctly, his tone sarcastic. "You also strike me as the type of small time hood that gives real criminals a bad name. Tell me, how did you manage to get a peek at what's inside if the doors were locked?"

"Weren't any lock on the doors that day, *Marshall*."

The trooper's eyebrows shot up.

"Marshall? Don't you know a trooper when you see one, wiseguy?"

Fish snickered.

"Sure I do, but it's just that you remind me of that Marshall on *Gunsmoke*. Matt Dillon," he explained. "Suspicious by nature, and not all that friendly, either."

The trooper glared scornfully at him.

"All right, enough of this foolish banter," Abercrombie barked. "I assume that this barn probably belongs to whoever lives in that cottage down the road. Would you happen to know if I'm correct in that assumption, Mr. Fishowski?"

Fish shrugged his broad shoulders.

"Beats me."

Abercrombie blew out his breath in annoyance.

"Stay right here. Trooper McCarthy and I are going to walk over there and find out if indeed, the inhabitants of that house are also the owners of this barn."

That said, they headed off for the house.

A few moments later, Butch's grandfather, a kindly old fellow with wispy white hair, heard the doorbell ring and went to the door.

"Yes? What can I do for you?" he asked with a frown, his voice a bit shaky. It wasn't everyday that a trooper showed up at his door. "Is something wrong?"

Abercrombie introduced himself, assuring the man that indeed, nothing was wrong. They just needed for him to come across the road and unlock the doors.

"Why?" the wizened little man inquired, curious now. He'd taken an instant dislike to Abercrombie, who, in Gramps' eyes, looked more like a casket salesman than a state official. "It's just an old barn with nothing but hay in it."

"We're here on official business."

"What kind of official business?"

"The kind that's none of your business," Abercrombie snapped, making a dismissive motion, as if waving off a pesky fly. "Look, I have it on good authority that your grandson has been spending a great deal of time in there, along with his two friends. Why would they be doing that if the building is virtually empty, as you say it is?"

The elderly man scratched his head, bewildered. The fissures and crevices in his well worn face could be read like a map of distress, and distressed he was, becoming increasingly more so by the moment.

"I don't know. He said they needed to store a couple of old motors and transmissions in there, then work on rebuilding them little by little. I even lent Butch my old truck for a week or so, to transport the stuff. What's wrong with that?"

Abercrombie waved the question off dismissively.

"Have you personally been inside the barn within the last few weeks?"

"Well, no, I can't say that I have," Gramps admitted.

"Then you don't know if your grandson was telling you the truth, isn't that so?"

"I suppose, but why would he lie about it?" the elderly man shot back defensively, his dander up now.

Abercrombie raised a calming hand.

"I'll tell you what. Why don't you walk back over to the barn with us and unlock the doors? We'll have a look-see inside and then we'll be on our way. No fuss—no muss," he said reassuringly.

"Well, why should I?" the man groused, not falling for Abercrombie's act. "I watch *Dragnet* all the time, you know. You can't make me unlock those doors unless you have a warrant. You got a warrant?" he demanded to know.

Abercrombie's bushy eyebrows knitted together in annoyance.

"Because if you don't, that'll be a clear indication to me that you, and, or, your grandson, have something to hide. As for a warrant, I can arrange to have one in my hands within a few hours, but wouldn't it be simpler just to let me take a quick peek inside? Then we'll be out of your hair for good."

Gramps grumbled and mumbled for a bit, but then finally caved in, leading them back across the road, keys in hand.

"Who's that guy standing in front of my barn?"

"Don't worry. He's with us," Abercrombie replied, his impatience beginning to resurface.

Gramps fumbled with the keys a bit before finally finding the right one. The padlock snapped open. The doors were swung open, bright sunshine pouring in.

Abercrombie and Fish looked around, their eyes missing nothing...and nothing it was.

"Mr. Fishowski, would you mind stepping outside with me for a moment?" Abercrombie sputtered through clenched teeth, his face crimson with anger.

A good minute or so passed before Fish was able to muster a reply, his mind a stew of shock and disbelief. He just stood there, as if searching for words to describe his confusion, words that weren't in his vocabulary.

"Yeah, be right there," he replied absently, numbly striding past the trooper who was eyeing him with severe distaste.

Outside now, he attempted to plead his case, but to no avail. Abercrombie was fit to be tied.

"You have *wasted* my valuable time today, not to mention Trooper McCarthy's as well!" he fumed. "What do you have to say for yourself, for leading us on this cockamamie wild goose chase?"

"It was there! I saw it with my own eyes. I swear to God that I did!"

"God has nothing to do with this, you imbecile!"

Under normal circumstances, talking that way to Fish was a sure guarantee that someone was going to get seriously hurt, but it went right over his head. He was too busy grasping at straws, too distracted to feel offended. Then, suddenly, his thought process kicked into a higher gear

"Wait! We need to go back in there for a minute. Please!" he pleaded. "We never bothered to move any of that hay around. For all we know, those bones could still be hidden under there," he said unconvincingly, not even believing it himself.

Abercrombie muttered something to himself. Unconvinced though he was, he nevertheless strode huffily back into the barn, Fish close on his heels.

Gramps walked past them, shaking his head as he leaned up against one of the creaky old doors.

Abercrombie looked around some more, kicking at the old hay here and there, but uncovering nothing. Then, as if a light bulb had just kicked on inside his head, he stopped and rubbed his jaw, deep in thought now, his eyes riveted upon a few shallow depressions in the hay, along with a couple that were far from being shallow.

"Trooper McCarthy, I believe that you carry a tape measure in your car, isn't that correct?"

Surprise registered on the trooper's face.

"Sure, for measuring skid marks," he replied, wondering where this was going.

"I thought so. Would you mind fetching it for me?"

The trooper headed for the car, returning a couple moments later, tape measure in hand.

Abercrombie snatched it from his hand and headed for the depressions in the hay. He then methodically began taking measurements of the depressions, length, depth and width, stopping occasionally to jot down some numbers, and then comparing them to yet other numbers in his notebook. Then, last, but certainly not least, he approached the deepest depression of all, his fingers deftly working the tape measure. Once done with the task, a smug smile began to form upon his face.

He stood up and asked Gramps to come back inside and join him.

Sighing, the man reluctantly complied.

"See this impression in the hay? It definitely wasn't made by a motor or a transmission," Abercrombie insisted, cocksure.

Gramp's face scrunched up in confusion.

"So what? Who the hell cares?"

"I care. As a matter of fact, I care so much that I want you to call your grandson right now, and tell him to come over here immediately."

"But..." the old man stammered.

"Is he at work?"

"Well, no, he works nights."

"Perfect. Now get on the phone and call him."

"I don't know about this," Gramps said stubbornly. "But I know I don't like it."

"Would you rather I dispatch trooper McCarthy to his home? I do happen to know his address, by the way."

A look of severe consternation settled upon poor Gramp's face.

"No, that would upset his mother. I'll call him," he said resignedly.

Abercrombie's face fairly beamed with smug satisfaction.

"I thought you would. Oh, and tell him to bring his two friends with him, if that's at all possible." he continued, "If not, I can always have Trooper McCarthy go and fetch them. I also happen to know where *they* live, as well."

As Gramps headed for the house, Fish walked over to Abercrombie, his face flush with relief.

"What'd I tell you?" he crowed proudly. "That impression in the hay matches the skull of a mastodon, doesn't it?"

Abercrombie shot Fish a wintry glare.

"Thank you for leading us here, Mr. Fishowski. You're free to leave now."

Fish looked stunned.

"Leave? No, I want to see the look on their faces when they get here. It's going to be priceless," he replied, savoring what was soon to come—*Hobbs shaking in his shoes.*

"Fat chance of that happening."

"Huh?"

"Leave now, or I'll have Trooper McCarthy personally escort you to your car. It's your choice, Mr. Fishowski."

Fish's face turned brick red, the cords in his neck going taut. Enraged, he just barely bit back the question he so wanted to ask: *How would you like to be my first homicide victim?*

If not for that trooper being here, I'd snap this goniff in half with one hand and throw him in opposite directions, he raged to himself, his brain cells buzzing with fury, like wasps stirring to life inside their nest after someone poked it with a stick.

But in the end, he knew he had no choice but to leave, and so he did, his anger subsiding a bit as he drove off, content in the knowledge that the hammer was about to drop square onto the head of one Hot Rod Hobbs. *Yeah, it would've been nice to be there for the start of the show, but what the hell, I already know the ending.*

CHAPTER 36

Rod's mind was spinning its' wheels, mired in a bad dream, a *real* bad dream, the same nightmare he'd been having over and over for weeks now, a waterfall of images cascading through his mind, a kaleidoscope of disjointed, ghostly images relentlessly running rampant through his psyche. A huge, vague figure in the gray mist trying desperately to outrun, escape...*escape what?* Lightning flashes, unearthly screams of animal terror, mournful moans, all of it caroming around in his head like wrecking balls.

"Hey, wake up. You're turning into Rip Van Winkle, sleeping too much," his mother's voice rousing him, wrenching him out of his disturbing nightmare.

His eyes popped open, a look of bewilderment on his face, his forehead slick with sweat.

"I don't sleep that much," he protested weakly.

"Uh-huh, a regular rooster you are, up at the crack of noon."

Rod yawned as he stretched his arms above his head.

"What were you moaning about?" his mother asked, concerned.

He rubbed his eyes.

"What?"

"You were moaning and groaning in your sleep. Are you all right?"

"I wasn't moaning and groaning," he said with a yawn.

"Yes, you were."

"No, I don't think so. I was just sleeping, Ma."

"Trust me, you were moaning and groaning. I thought you might be sick," she said as she placed a motherly hand upon his forehead, checking for a fever.

"Well, but for a damp forehead, you seem to be okay. It's good thing, too, because you've got company."

Rod sat right up.

"Company? Who?"

"Butch. He says he needs to see you right away," she informed him, a hint of suspicion in her voice. "He came in here like his pants were on fire, looking bedraggled, baffled and bewildered. What are you two characters up to, anyway?"

"Aw, Ma, cut that out. You sound like Dad now. Just send Butch in here, will you?"

Her lips pursed in disapproval, she turned and walked out. Just exactly what it was that she felt she should be disapproving of, wasn't quite clear yet, but given enough time, she'd get to the bottom of it, certain that her son and his friend were somehow up to no good.

She showed Butch into the room and left, closing the door behind her.

"You believe in ghosts, Butch?" Rod asked, still preoccupied with the nightmares.

"Ghosts? You mean, like *Casper*, the friendly one?"

Rod sighed and shook his head.

"Never mind. What's up?"

"All hell is broke loose, that's what's up," he replied, his voice shaky as he explained what was going on out at his grandfather's house. "I'm screwed. You're screwed. We're all screwed!"

"Aw, crap!" Rod cried as he jumped out of bed, reaching for his pants, getting dressed in record time. "Did you call Pops?"

"Yeah, we're lucky he's home and not down at John's tavern drinking his breakfast. I told him we'd pick him in a few minutes. Man, I'm a nervous wreck over this. How much do you think they know?" he asked, his face taut with worry.

"How the hell would I know? Just keep cool, will you?"

Pops answered the door wearing his old, flea-bitten red robe, a Raleigh drooping from the corner of his mouth.

"Get dressed! Come on, we got to move it here, Pops." Rod griped. "You knew we were coming and here you are, not even dressed yet!"

Pops ignored the outburst and showed them in, the industrial—strength smell of boiled corned beef and cabbage strong enough to peel paint. Rod pinched his nose shut.

"You're cooking? Since when do you cook, especially this early in the morning?"

Pops shrugged.

"Just felt like it. It's going to be great, too. No water. I'm boiling the whole shebang in Four Roses. Nothing like a half gallon of good whiskey to bring out the flavor," he crowed.

Rod shuddered to think what else might be in it.

"No wonder it stinks. Hey, what are doing? We got to get going here!" Rod cried in alarm as he watched Pops sit down and begin scanning the Troy Record.

"Yeah, yeah, just as soon as I finish reading the Irish sports section."

Butch and Rod exchanged perplexed looks.

"The *what*?" Butch asked, scratching his head.

"The obituary sports page. You know—to see who lost lately. I like to check the daily scores to see who I outlived. I get a kick out of it. They'd be a helluva lot more informative, though, if they told you just *how* these folks croaked."

Rod yanked the newspaper from his hands.

"Get dressed."

Pops sighed, snuffing out his Raleigh in the ashtray.

"Okay, give me a couple of minutes," he said, rising and shuffling off to his bedroom. "If you want a drink, help yourself, boys."

Ten minutes later, they piled into Rod's Chevy and headed for Western Avenue. The radio was on. WTRY—Guy Mitchell crooning "Heartaches by the number."

Rod reached over and shut it off.

"More like *headaches* by the number," he mumbled to himself.

"Got any ideas on how we're going to handle their questions, Pops?" Butch asked, near frantic with worry.

Pops flipped his Raleigh out the window.

"Relax. First off, it's not as if we stuck up a bank, or kidnapped Gina Lollabrigida. Secondly, because the bones are long gone now, in another country as a matter of fact, there's no evidence of any wrongdoing on our part. As far as we're concerned, we don't know what they're talking about. *What bones?* The onus of proving anything is on them, and it can't be done. Jay-sus, don't you watch the *Perry Mason* show? If they can't find the body, then how can they charge someone with murder? They flat-out can't, and that's that," he said, cocksure of himself. "It's all shoes and no footprints."

"Then, thirdly, if there is such a word...uh..." he stumbled. "Well, I guess there is no thirdly, but if I think of one, I'll let you know."

"Okay, let's go over this once more," he continued. "Let *me* answer the questions, as much as possible, that is. Just like they do on 'M Squad,' they may choose to question us separately, see if we're all on the same page...or not. As long as you both remember that they can't prove a thing, there's nothing to worry about. Just play dumb, which ought to come pretty easy to you, Butch," he kidded. "Don't worry. We'll be there with you. We're all in the same boat."

"Yeah, I just hope it doesn't turn out to be the *Titanic*," Butch grumbled.

Pops turned and gave him a look, one that suggested he should shut up.

Everyone went silent for a few moments.

"Hey, what if they make us take a lie-detector test?" Butch asked plaintively.

Pops sighed as he lit a fresh Raleigh.

"There again, if you knew your *Perry Mason*, you'd know that first of all, they can't *make* you take a lie-detector test, and even if they could, the results would be inadmissible in court. Son, you really need to start watching more of Perry. You could learn a lot from him."

"What if they somehow get to Bonesy?" Rod asked. "If he ever talked, we'd be sunk."

"Bonesy?" Pops exclaimed with a laugh. "Never happen. There's nothing to lead them to him, and even if there were, there wouldn't be anything to worry about. Bonesy holds his cards so close to his chest, they're inside his shirt. They'd have about as much a chance of getting anything out of him, as I do of succeeding Eisenhower as president."

They were passing the high school now, everyone gone quiet, the only sound that of a Dzembo Dairy truck going by them, bottles of milk clinking together in the wire baskets.

"Uh, Pops, can I ask you a personal question?" Butch inquired softly, aware that he was treading on thin ice.

"Huh? Yeah, I suppose. May not answer it, though," he replied, the smell of booze emanating from his pores like an oil spill.

"Uh...are you drunk?"

"Probably, but then, asking me a dumb question like that is like asking Monsignor Kelly if he ever goes to church. But don't let my being a wee bit pickled worry you none. Booze makes most people slow and sleepy, but not me. If anything, it only serves to sharpen my senses. Now stop thinking so much or you're liable to get a brain hernia."

"Oh, great," Butch groaned. "You probably got enough in you to anesthetize a patient for a ten hour operation."

"Hey, sonny boy, let me tell you—I might have half a bag on now, but come this evening when I sit down for my corned beef and cabbage, I'll be sober...but you? You'll still be dumb."

Walking into the house, the first thing Rod noticed was a prissy-looking rotund guy in a dark suit, his body layered in rolls, sort of like *the Michelin Man* in those tire ads. The god awful wig didn't do a thing for him, either. *As a kid, he was probably the last one picked for a game of kickball*, Rod thought to himself.

Standing alongside him was a trooper, his posture as immobile as a statue, his *Smokey, the Bear* hat in his hands. He was a big one, looking as though he could bench press a school bus, tall and Irish looking: short red hair with a nose to match and a sprinkling of freckles over a pale complexion—the works.

Sitting in a rocker looking worried as all hell, sat Gramps, his face pale, a tremor in his hands.

The jamoke in the suit introduced himself to them, his tone of voice, that of a king talking down to his lackeys.

Rod took an instant dislike to the man for a number of reasons, none of them complimentary.

"Well, it's good to see that you exercised some good judgment—for a change," Abercrombie said snidely, his voice heavy with sarcasm, laying it on with a trowel.

"What's that supposed mean?" Rod snapped.

Abercrombie snickered.

"It means that you knew better than to make us come and pick you up. You're in enough trouble as it is without adding to your woes."

"Now just why would we be in trouble?" Pops interjected.

Abercrombie shot him a look of pure disdain.

"As if you didn't know."

Rod was getting hot under the collar, this pompous jerk really getting on his nerves now.

"I'm afraid we don't know what you're talking about, mister. Why don't you clue us in?"

"Oh, we're looking forward to doing just that, but not here," he assured them. "We're all going to take a little ride now, up to the Troop G State Police barracks. You'll be following us, unless of course you'd prefer to ride in the back seat of Trooper McCarthy's vehicle?"

Rod swallowed hard, hoping that it wasn't noticed. It was.

"Fine with us," he replied as nonchalantly as possible.

Abercrombie clapped his hands together, as if he were about to pray.

"Well, then, shall we go? I can hardly wait to bring forth all of the questions that I have waiting for you," said the twit, a bantam rooster cockiness to his step as he waddled toward the door,

The drive took about fifteen minutes, most of it devoted to Rod reminding Butch to keep his mouth shut whenever possible.

"Just remember that when they ask about Jumbo—you don't know what they're talking about. Just follow my lead. Better yet—play dumb. There is no proof, no evidence, no nothing, so if you just keep saying: '*I don't know what you're talking about,*' then it'll be no sweat. Can we *please* count on you to remember that, Butch?" Rod implored him, his knuckles turning white from gripping the steering wheel so tightly.

"No problem. They won't get anything out of me," Butch halfheartedly vowed.

"Good, I believe you," Rod lied.

"I wish I shared your optimism, but that's a slippery slope of faith that you're climbing," Pops chimed in. "One helluva leap of faith, actually, Rod. You might better stop at St. Patrick's and douse yourself with a quart of holy water, for all the good it'll do."

Rod knew in his heart that Pops was right, *but what are you going do? Hope for the best.* That's all he could do.

Offended, Butch shot back, "How do I know that *you two* won't crack under the pressure?"

"Because we won't, that's why," Rod replied matter-of-factly. "I'm sure of myself and as for Pops, they could pour a pint of sodium pentothal down his throat and he still wouldn't tell the truth."

Yeah, he was confident that no matter what they threw at them, he and Pops could handle it. *Butch, on the other hand?* Well, again, one could only *hope,* meaning that Rod could apply some blind faith to his misgivings about Butch, and *hope* that it takes.

Butch suddenly yanked a green rabbit's foot from his pocket, giving it a vigorous rubbing.

"What's that all about?" Pops inquired, curious.

Butch kissed it before replying.

"It's like praying. What've I got to lose?"

"Well, certainly not your mind," Pops responded glibly. "Obviously, that's already departed."

Rod parked on the side of the building, as per Abercrombie's instructions. Modern looking and sprawling, the state police barracks had only recently been constructed.

As they exited the car, rain began to come down in buckets, accompanied by slashing gusts of wind.

Trooper McCarthy guided them toward a side entrance. Once inside, he directed them down a hallway. Suddenly, Rod's mouth felt drier than the Sahara. With each step that he took, he felt the bravado within fading fast, replaced by the dread of a condemned man walking up the stairs to the gallows. Most of the time, Rod felt as if he had complete control over his life. This wasn't one of those times.

Abercrombie and the trooper ushered them into a large office, one that was furnished just about how you'd expect it to be—gray carpet, gray metal desks, gray walls, gray office chairs that looked as though they'd been intentionally designed to be as uncomfortable as possible, gray filing cabinets, and two graying BCI detectives. The only feature that wasn't gray was the overhead lighting, bright enough to produce sunburn.

Abercrombie, with a look on his face like a hungry cat ready to pounce on three juicy mice, was about to pull up a chair when one of the detectives told him he'd have to wait outside while *they* conducted the interrogation. His puffy face conveying considerable indignation, the doughboy insisted that he be present for the questioning.

He was politely, but firmly, told otherwise, the look on the cop's face indicating that the subject wasn't open to debate, either.

Steaming mad, Abercrombie waddled out the door. One of the detectives closed it behind him before turning to face the trio of would-be criminals. *A couple of standard issue detectives,* Rod thought to himself at first, not much different from the ones in Cohoes. After a closer look at this one in particular, however, Rod decided there wasn't anything *standard issue* about the man, other than his poker face.

Tall and muscular, about fifty-five years old, he had a head that was shaped like an upside down triangle—a wide forehead and a sharp, pointy chin, accented by a poker face that could break a casino. Suggesting perhaps an attempt by him to soften his hard looks, he was dressed in a well tailored charcoal gray suit, blue oxford shirt and a blue and gold regimental-striped silk tie, his black Endicott Johnsons buffed to a mirror shine. The cop looked smooth. Smooth, like a shark.

While he was polished, almost downright distinguished looking, his partner appeared to be *extinguished* and more than a bit tarnished. Looking more like a down on his luck mortuary plot salesman than a detective, the graying, red-faced Brillo pad-haired cop had an egg shaped head, a jutting jaw and the spider webbed nose of a career boozer. Garbed in a cheap black suit, a black clip-on bowtie, a Desormeau Brothers' plastic pocket protector, black suspenders, black shoulder holster, and sweat rings under his arms, the cop cut quite the figure—that of a boiled ham stuffed inside a black suit.

They did share one thing in common, however. They both had that *Cop look* on their faces –Hard, blank, and cold, much like the one that his father and uncle regularly displayed while on the job. Rod wondered if there was an entire police academy class devoted to developing and maintaining a poker face.

The well dressed one directed them to a long table situated in front of two desks. Rod and the others pulled out a chair and sat down. Although the building was fairly new, the table had clearly been around for a while, its gray Formica surface scarred and gouged by countless cigarette burns.

The two detectives propped themselves against the two desks, their arms folded, their eyes fixed on the three men sitting before them.

The red-faced one, a toothpick at a jaunty angle in the corner of his mouth, flipped open a leather wallet. The other did the same, the pair of shiny badges glinting like a set of freshly sharpened teeth.

"I'm Dick Denby," said the ham in the suit. "And this is Detective Joe Peerless, and trust me...he lives up to the name. When it comes to conducting an interrogation, he has no peer. He's the best. As for myself, let's just say my investigative talents aren't too shabby either. I get results."

Talking out of the side of his mouth, as if the other side had been stitched shut, he nonchalantly imparted this information with all the matter-of-factness of a conversation about the weather. If he said it was going to snow, you could damn well bet that it would snow.

"Ok, so now that that's out of the way, let's do a roll-call, figure out who's who here. Robert 'Butch' O'Brien? Let me guess," he said, pointing a finger in Butch's direction. "That'd probably be you, the Howdy Doody lookalike. Did I get that right?"

Butch shifted in his chair uncomfortably, droplets of sweat multiplying on his forehead, as if someone had turned on a sprinkler inside his skull.

"Yeah," he admitted shakily, a classic deer-in-the-headlights look in his eyes.

Denby nodded to himself, as if checking off a box in his mind.

"Patrick 'Pops' Shea. Hmm, no doubt that'd be you, old timer," he said, pointing a finger at Pops.

"I'm impressed. You figured that out all by yourself, detective?" Pops asked, feigning astonishment.

Denby flashed a humorless smile, drumming his fingers against the desk top, like a drum roll prior to an execution.

"A regular jack Benny, eh? Did you hear that, Joe? We've got a comedian on our hands."

Peerless, the well dressed one, glanced at Pops in a friendly sort of way.

"Yeah, they're so cute at that age, aren't they?" Peerless quipped, the friendly look now vanishing as quickly as it had appeared. "We'll deal with that soon enough, Dick," he promised. One look at him and Rod concluded that if indeed this cop had ever harbored doubts about his abilities, he'd had them surgically removed at an early age. Yeah, he was that intimidating.

Pops is always ragging on Butch about how he's always saying the wrong thing, but Pops himself ought to have a brake mechanism installed between his thoughts and his mouth, Rod thought to himself. *Why go out of your way to antagonize these guys?*

Peerless cocked his head to one side, staring at Rod, as if intrigued by something.

"That just leaves you, then. Rodney '*Hot Rod* 'Hobbs."

"*Hot Rod!*" Denby spat, his tone derisive. "I don't think—"

Peerless held up a hand, signaling Denby to hold off for a minute. He then stared at Rod, studying him, as if sorting out faces on a Rolodex wheel.

"Hobbs. You're the kid that was a boxer, the one that got his head handed to him a few years back, courtesy of Andy Vincent down in Albany. Isn't that right?" he asked.

"No."

"No?" Peerless echoed.

"No, actually, it happened in Troy, not Albany, sir." Rod replied politely, his tone intentionally deferential in an attempt to offset Pops' ill-advised wisecrack.

Peerless managed something that might have been a smile, but it was hard to tell for sure, what with him having a face all lumpy and hard-edged, as though it had been layered from putty that had dried unevenly. But for the pointy chin, his features were hard and harsh.

"Oh, yes, Troy. Now I recall it. I'm surprised that a young man with your looks would've ever considered entering a ring. Anyone ever tell you that you bear quite a resemblance to Fabian?"

"Yeah," he admitted, his face flushed.

"Well, attempts to move up in class in boxing, and, or, criminal endeavors, often result in dire consequences. Broken jaws and broken noses in the ring—long prison terms outside of the ring. Catching my drift here, Rodney?"

"Rod."

"Okay. You catching my drift, *Rod*?"

Rod gulped and hoped that it wasn't noticed...but it was.

"I understand, sir, about the boxing part, that is. As for the crime part, I wouldn't know."

Smirking, Denby raised a questioning eyebrow.

"Really? Well, we think otherwise, which leads to the question: Where did you stash this mastodon skeleton? We know you moved it from the barn. Where is it now?"

Pops guffawed loudly.

"A mastodon skeleton? Is that what all this rigmarole is about? For Pete's sake, that's why you dragged us in here?" he cried, seemingly shocked by the revelation. "Kee-rist! We wouldn't know a mastodon from Doris Day!"

Peerless raised his hand, a shut up gesture.

"We'll get to you, but for now, I want Rod to answer the questions, not you," he said softly. "Think of it as a little favor to me."

"But I don't owe you any favors," Pops replied evenly.

"Yeah, but you probably will," Peerless replied gently, playing the role of good cop, although his eyes were as hard as pale green marbles.

"Don't hold your breath waiting. It could kill you," Pops fired back, refusing to concede an inch.

"Shut up, old man!" Peerless snapped, the gentle tone replaced by one laden with ice.

"So, Rod, I'll ask you again: Where is the skeleton at the moment?"

A sudden chill crept down Rod's back. Ice cubes.

"I honestly don't know what you're talking about, sir. The only mastodon I know about is the one in the museum."

Peerless laced his fingers together, placing them behind his head, leaning back in his chair, his eyes never leaving Rod's as he searched the handsome face looking for *tells*—facial tics and body language, giveaways that clearly indicate a lie had been told.

Rod squirmed under the relentless stare, looking down at the floor, shaking his head each time the question was repeated, four times in all. *Cops*, he thought to himself during round four—*Always trying to trip you up.*

"Want something to drink, coffee or a coke?" Peerless asked, suddenly displaying a hospitable side.

Pops opted for coffee, the other two settling for cokes.

"Yeah, I'll bet you can use some java, seeing as how I think you got half a load on as we speak. Drink a lot, do you?" Peerless inquired.

Pops smiled a mirthless smile.

"Not as much as I probably should, all things considered. Like the way today is going, for example."

"Have any blackouts lately?"

"None that I can remember," Pops replied drolly.

Peerless smirked and stood up, heading for the door.

Once he'd closed it behind him, Denby slipped back into the bad cop routine. It fit him like a glove.

"You know, I've been a cop for years now, and nobody's fool for even longer," he bragged. "How much did you sell it for? Who bought it?" he pushed, his face mere inches from Rod's, his sour breath, potent enough to deck a moose. "You didn't move it to another location, did you? You sold it!" he insisted. "Well, let me tell you something. Once I get you guys alone, one by one, you'll be lining up to tell me the truth!"

Poor Butch. The impact of Denby's words hit him with the force of a sledgehammer. Naturally, the cop noticed the effect that his snarling threat had had on the young man, and so now his gaze was fixed directly on Butch.

"You're the one that'll give it up. I'll drop some coins in your slot and then you'll sing a song of truth. I just know it," he insisted, cocksure of himself. "Come to think of it, you remind me of the weakling in the Charles Atlas ad on the matchbook covers, getting sand kicked in his face," he said mockingly. "Yeah, I'll pull on the loose end of your thread and unravel the whole story little by little. Yep, I'll crack you easily, so why don't you save yourself beaucoup grief later on, and just spill the beans right now?"

Rod snuck a glance over at his pal, Butch. He looked like a man who'd just been dropped onto a bed of nails. His forehead glistened with a sheen of oily sweat, the type of adrenaline-based perspiration that only fear produces. His upper lip quivering, Butch somehow kept himself together, drawing in a deep breath and exhaling slowly.

"You can do anything you want to me," he vowed." But I can't tell you diddly-squat because there's nothing to tell!"

Rod felt a wave of pride surge through him, pride in his pal.

Denby smirked as he ran a hand through his unruly mop, flecks of dandruff floating to the floor.

He was about to toss some more threats in Butch's direction when Pops jumped in: "He's right, you know. You can ask us the same questions, six ways to Sunday, but the answers ain't ever going to change."

Denby snickered.

"Is that right?"

"Damn straight it is."

"So that's the song you're going to sing, eh?"

Pops shrugged his shoulders.

"It's the only song I know. It's entitled 'The Truth,' and you requested it, so now you'll have to listen to it."

The door swung open, Peerless returning, his hands full of beverages.

He set the drinks down and then lit a Belair, the menthol—infused smoke billowing overhead.

"Mind if we smoke, too?" Rod asked politely.

Peerless nodded his okay, reaching into a desk drawer, producing a pair of black plastic ashtrays that the cops lifted from the Crossroads restaurant. He placed them on the table. All three suspects fired up a smoke.

"Make any headway while I was gone, Dick?" he asked casually.

Denby shrugged.

"Can't say that I did, but then again, I can't say that I didn't, either. Why don't you have a go at them, Joe, while I enjoy my cup of java?" he suggested with a telling wink. Role reversal time. Peerless would now step back into the bad cop role.

"So, tell me, Pops—it is okay if I call you that, right?" Peerless asked.

"No, as a matter of fact, it isn't," Pops replied resentfully, placing his cup back on the table. "Only my friends call me that. *You* can call me Mr. Shea."

Peerless smiled an insincere smile.

"I understand."

"I doubt it."

Peerless' smile faded.

"I see."

"I doubt that, too."

A few seconds of silence ensued, which seemed more like an hour. Peerless leaned back, folding his arms across his chest.

"Hmm, you know, playing the hard case isn't going to get you anywhere. You're in enough trouble as it is, *Mr. Shea*. I strongly advise you to wise up and change your tune."

Pops snuffed out his cigarette in the ashtray.

"Some things never change," he said dryly.

"Yeah, I'm still asking questions and you're still stonewalling me."

Pops shrugged.

"Ask me if I give a tinker's damn about what you think."

"So how much did you get for the skeleton?" Denby asked.

"What skeleton? I don't know anything about no skeleton."

"I think you do," Peerless shot back, his voice, as hard and cold as a steel blade. "Tell me—how did you find a buyer? You must have used a fence to shop it around. Mastodon remains aren't an everyday consumer purchase. Who moved them for you?"

Pops yawned.

"Think maybe I could have another cup of Joe?"

Peerless ignored the request.

"You want to play hardball with us, it's no skin off my behind," he warned. Then, as if to verify this assertion, he gave the area in question a good scratching. "But it might be off of yours."

Pops sighed.

"How much longer is this mental arm-wrestling contest going to go on for? I got to take my heart medicine at six."

Denby and Peerless exchanged smirks.

"You're not going anywhere until we get the answers we want to hear," Peerless snapped, quickly dispensing with any guise of civility. "We'll lock you up for the night if we have to. Then we'll get right back at it tomorrow morning!" he vowed, the threat, as far as Pops was concerned, carrying about as much clout as the words inside a fortune cookie.

"Give me a minute, will you, Sherlock, while I record that under *B-s*?" Pops shot back, his irritation growing. "You can't lock somebody up unless you arrest them first, and you ain't about to arrest us because you ain't got no grounds for it," he spat. "And furthermore, I'd rather drink battery acid than own up to something I didn't do!"

Peerless glared at him.

"That's where you're wrong, old man," he said ominously, the disdain in his voice unmistakable. "And as for grounds, I'd arrest Santa Claus for home invasion if I thought it'd stick."

Denby stood up and unbuckled his straining belt, giving his big belly a breather.

"Why don't I take him in the other room, Joe?" he suggested with an air of impatience. "The old boy seems to have an inability to appreciate the impending consequences of his crime. He also seems to think he's got academy award potential for his acting, but I got news for him—he's not going to make the cut. I'll personally see to that."

Peerless nodded his agreement.

"Yeah, good idea. Take him, Dick. Meanwhile, I'll see what Heckle and Jeckle think about spending the night with us."

Denby buckled back up and then reached for Pop's arm.

"Is Broderick Crawford, here, going to get me my coffee or what?" Pops asked Peerless.

"We'll see. Depends on whether or not you play nice with me," Denby replied, marching Pops through the door of an adjoining interrogation room.

Peerless opened a desk drawer and fished through it, pulling out a rubber band, hooking it over the tops of his thumbs, stretching it back and forth.

"Okay, boys, *let-me-clarify-things-for-you*," he said, enunciating each word slowly and carefully, as if he were speaking to two four-year olds. "I know you thought you could get away with this, but you're not going to. I promise you that. So, having said that, it's now time that you both reconsider the enormity of your miscalculation and then do the right thing—own up to it. Tell me where the skeleton is, or if it has already been sold, who bought it?"

Outside, the rain had stopped and the sun was now blazing away. It was getting hot in the room. As calmly as he could, Rod fired up a Lucky, drawing the smoke deep into his lungs, feeling the heat from the sun-cooked room, as well as from Detective Peerless.

"I don't know what you're talking about," he replied evenly. "We don't know anything about any mastodon skeleton."

Peerless dropped the rubber band and reached back into the desk drawer, producing a blank sheet of paper. He began to fold it as he spoke.

"You guys thought you'd make a killing on those bones, using a fence as the host of *The Price is Right*. Trouble is, it's a game you can't win," he insisted as he continued to fold the paper in different directions. "Tell me, do you like quiz shows, Mr. Hobbs?"

Rod shrugged.

"What's that got to do with anything?"

"Plenty. Why don't you make believe that I'm Garry Moore, and you're a contestant on *I've Got a Secret*? Then, seeing as how nobody has guessed your secret, you now show your hand," he explained, sailing the paper airplane directly into Rod's face.

Rod grunted as the point of the paper projectile glanced off the side of his nose. Peerless grinned a malicious grin, gloating over his dead-eye aim.

"I think I want to call a lawyer now."

"Me too," Butch chimed in nervously, perspiration poorly freely from his forehead.

"Aha, gotcha!" Peerless exclaimed, pointing his finger at Butch, cocking an imaginary trigger with his thumb. "What do you need a lawyer for? We're just talking. You're not under arrest—yet. Of course, if you continue to stonewall me, I will arrest you. Make no mistake about that," he warned, shooting them both a scornful look. "Yeah, and if it gets to that, you can call Willie *Whiplash* Weinstein or one of the other lowlifes that defend guys like you, but for now..." he said, his words trailing off.

"Either of you want another coke?" he abruptly asked, throwing them a curve, taking the both of them by surprise.

They both nodded in the affirmative. Peerless left the room, closing the door behind him.

Rod sucked in a deep breath.

"That's what they do," he said.

"What do you mean?" Butch asked, fumbling around in his shirt pocket for his Zippo.

"Try to throw you off. One minute threatening—the next minute playing Mr. nice guy."

"What do you think—?"

Rod raised a cautioning finger to his lips, effectively cutting Butch off.

"Shh! Don't talk. For all we know, there could be a microphone hidden in here," he whispered.

Butch glanced nervously around the room, taking in the ceiling as well, searching for telltale signs of a microphone.

Peerless returned, cokes in hand.

"Here you go, gentlemen."

Once settled back behind his desk, Peerless turned his attention to Butch, viewing him as easy pickings.

"Mr. O'Brien. Can I call you Butch?" he asked, back into friendly mode.

"Sure. Everybody does," he replied warily, bringing to mind a scared rabbit in the shadow of a circling hawk.

"Okay, Butch, then keeping with the quiz show theme, let's play a little game of *Truth or Consequences*. I'll ask the questions and you'll provide the answers. Then, if you're truthful, I'll see what I can do to help you out of the hole you've dug for yourself. How's that prize sound to you? Think you're up to winning it?" he asked, smiling at Butch in a way that chilled him to the bone.

Butch fidgeted in the chair, his nerves frazzled, his Adam's apple bobbing up and down like a piston. He looked to Rod, as if for support, but his pal was staring straight ahead, oblivious to Butch's attempts at telepathic distress calls.

Then, just as fragment after fragment was being steadily chipped away from the stone wall he'd erected around his resolve, his heart beating like a runaway train, Butch suddenly reminded himself of Pop's instructions: *Just keep telling them that you don't know what they're talking about. The goods are long gone and nothing can be proven, anyway!*

Buoyed now by the memory of Pop's sage advice, he took on his determined interrogator head-on.

"Sure, ask me anything you'd like."

Rod held his breath, hoping for the best, but fearing the worst. Despite all the coaching, you could never be sure with Butch. Rod dropped a hand to his side, crossing his fingers as he did so.

"Have you sold the skeleton yet, Butch?"

"What skeleton?"

"How much did you get for it?"

"Get for what?"

"Who bought it?

"Who bought *what*?" Butch asked, feigning utter bewilderment, as if Peerless had suddenly spoken in a foreign language.

While Rod fought back a smile, Peerless fought back a growl.

"Might I remind you to answer the questions and not ask them?"

Butch gave him the phony altar-boy look. *Who? Me?*

Peerless ignored the act and pressed onward.

"Perhaps you don't realize it *yet*, but when you sold the skeleton, you committed a major felony, according to the New York State Antiquities Act of 1906.You familiar with that particular law?" he inquired, looking Butch square in the eye.

Butch shrugged.

"The Act provides for imprisonment of those who harm, destroy, *excavate and remove* any object of antiquity located on state-owned land. Then it goes on to say that should said object of antiquity be sold for profit, the prison sentence shall be considerably longer, probably doubled, in my estimation," he said, taking pleasure from watching their faces drop. "Yeah, I always have relished being the bearer of bad news. I get off on it."

Butch felt a metaphorical knife plunge into his gut.

"What's the matter? You look like a guy about to be pushed off a speeding train, Butch. Was it something I said?" the cop taunted, all the while regarding him with a bemused expression.

"Abercrombie measured the impressions in the hay, and one of them matched the dimensions of the Mastodon skull in the museum to a tee, so we know it was there," he continued on, twisting the knife in ever deeper. "So, the question is: Where is it now?"

It took Butch a few moments to regain his composure, but in the end, much to his credit, he did just that.

"Where is *what* now?" he asked, as nonchalantly as he possibly could.

"Remember, Butch, its *Truth or Consequences*. You don't tell me the truth, you're going to face the consequences...and you won't like them. I guarantee it," Peerless warned through clenched teeth.

"You told your grandfather that you guys worked on some old engines and transmissions in the barn. Where did they go? Abercrombie didn't see any sign of them in the barn," he pressed, switching tactics.

"Uh, we gave up on the project and ditched them."

"Where did you ditch them?"

Butch stumbled badly here, unable to come up with a feasible reply, the panic smell, sharp and acrid, emanating from him in waves.

"What's the matter, Butch?" Peerless asked, smirking. "All of a sudden, you look like a rodent searching for a hole to escape into."

"We tossed them in the canal," Rod interjected, a sheepish look on his face. "I know, we shouldn't have, but everybody throws stuff in there."

"In Cohoes? What part of the canal?" Peerless prodded, trying to catch Rod in a lie.

"Where it runs behind Saratoga St."

"What part of Saratoga Street?"

"Right down around the corner of Spring & Saratoga."

Peerless sneered, not believing a word of it.

"Forgive me if I'm a little slow to buy that," he said caustically, pausing to pop a stick of Black Jack gum into his mouth. "That's the thing about lies. They're easy to tell, but difficult to hide. Having said that, I can easily arrange to have divers check your bogus story out, you know," he threatened. "I'm just saying, you know? Wouldn't be at all hard to do."

Rod knew that he could indeed do that, but he didn't think it was anything to worry about. There were probably more than a few old engines and trannies in that filthy water, along with all kinds of other discarded rubbish.

Peerless leaned across his desk and steepled his hands, his thumbs under his chin, his sharp, cold eyes boring through Butch.

"You disappoint me, son. I thought we agreed that you would work on telling me the truth?"

A feeling of triumph coursing through him, Butch nonchalantly threw Peerless a Wally Cleaver *gee whiz expression. Who? Me?*

"But I did tell you the truth, sir," Butch lied. "I'm a good Catholic and like all good Catholics, I *never* lie. Shoot, if I did, I'd have to go to confession, and let me tell, from what I hear, confession with Father Flanagan sure ain't no day at the beach," he said with a dramatic flourish.

Butch was laying it on ever thicker now, Peerless raising his hand, a *stop the bull* signal, impatiently shutting him down. He'd heard enough. A sour look on his face, he picked up the phone and dialed Denby's extension. *Time to switch yet again.*

"You've been watching too many episodes of *Ozzie & Harriet*, son. You need to park the *Golly, gee whiz—isn't that keen* cornpone routine, because it isn't getting you anywhere."

A minute later Denby walked in, a look of frustration etched into his features. Everyone looked up at him, the way people in a hospital waiting room look up when a surgeon comes out to talk to them.

Peerless stood up, motioning for Denby to follow him out in the hall. Denby shut the door behind him, with just enough of a bang to convey his obvious irritation at having gotten nowhere with Pops.

Rod exhaled loudly as he gave Butch a vigorous thump on the shoulder. His pal beamed proudly and was about to say something but Rod quickly raised a finger to his lips, reminding him of the need to remain silent.

The detectives returned about five minutes later. Denby, a matchstick stuck in the corner of his mouth, resumed the hammering in earnest. Meanwhile, Peerless headed off for another go-around with Pops.

Pops was slouched over a table, a Raleigh hanging from his lip, a cup of tepid coffee in front of him.

"Oh-oh, bringing in the heavy artillery now. What happened to the other dick?" he wise-cracked, a mischievous twinkle in his rheumy eyes. "You pulling the ol' switcheroo routine again? Good cop—bad cop—worse cop?"

Peerless didn't reply, which was an answer in itself, Pops thought to himself.

The cop pulled out his chair and sat down, propping his feet atop the desk, his head tilted to one side in unmistakable inquiry.

"You know what I'm most curious about?"

Pops sighed deeply, like a tire deflating, as if this were all just a big waste of his time.

"No, I don't, but I just know you're going to tell me," he replied, smiling indulgently.

"Why, at your advanced age, would you want to risk spending however many years you have left, sitting in a prison cell?"

Pops glanced up at the ceiling, as if hoping to find some patience up there.

"You're preaching to the choir, Detective. For the tenth time, I'm telling you that I didn't do anything that could land me in a cell, so if that's the way this going to keep going, at least get me a deck of cards so I can play Solitaire while you talk to the wall."

Peerless waved aside Pops' wisecrack with a gesture of his hand.

"Let me give you some friendly advice," he offered, in a voice that wasn't at all friendly. "First of all—"

"Is a bell going to ring at the end of this lecture period?" Pops barked, cutting Peerless off in mid-sentence.

The cop gave him a tsk-tsk wave of his forefinger, chiding him for his cavalier attitude.

"A wiseguy, eh? Well, let me tell you—"

"You're a helluva good BS-er, I'll give you that, Peerless," Pops remarked, again interrupting the detective in mid-sentence. "The kind of BS-er that looks a man straight in the eye, unblinking, when he delivers his verbal load of manure."

By now, Peerless had to be wondering if he'd ever again get to finish a sentence.

"I don't think I like your attitude, old man," the cop hissed.

Pops put his coffee cup down, smiling indulgently.

"Nobody ever does," he retorted smoothly.

"I believe that."

Unperturbed, Pops reached for the cup of coffee, intent on bringing it to his lips until he noticed it was the ashtray, and not the cup. It was too much to hope for, that Peerless hadn't noticed his gaffe.

Peerless noticed, laughing heartily.

"You're losing it already, Shea. What are you going to do once you're locked up? You won't last a year before your mind goes south on you," he forecasted, a malevolent smile slowly forming across his face, like ice cracking on a pond.

Pops eyes flashed with indignation as Peerless sipped his coffee.

"Go ahead. Laugh at an old man. Knock yourself out, but at the end of the day, when I walk out of here, the laugh will be on you."

Suddenly, it was if Peerless' smile had gone on vacation and left behind a menacing look to house-sit.

He slammed his empty ceramic cup on the desk with such force, it was a wonder it didn't shatter.

"You don't start talking right now, the odds of you walking out of here today are about like this," Peerless threatened, using his thumb and forefinger to form a perfect 'O.'

Pops yawned and sighed, as if all of this chatter was a waste of his valuable time. Scoffing at the hollow threat, he lit a fresh Raleigh with the butt end of the one he'd yet to snuff out.

"You smoke too much," the cop noted.

"And just how much is the *correct* amount to smoke?"

Peerless raised himself up and out of the chair and began circling Pops, intent upon breaking him.

"You know, you really need to work on your poker face, Shea. As poker faces go, yours ain't much," he noted, his tone tinged with derision.

Pops took a casual drag on his Raleigh, exhaling perfectly shaped rings of smoke.

"Until today, I hadn't much needed one."

Peerless threw him a patented deadeye cop-stare, his, after so many years on the job, seasoned to concrete perfection.

"Not according to your record, back during the prohibition era. Running booze out of Canada until you got pulled in," he fired back, his face as cold as a Van Schaick Island winter. "You've been grilled before, so stow the innocent routine. I know all about you and your criminal past."

"What criminal past? The case was thrown out of court because of insufficient evidence."

"Doesn't matter. Once a crook—always a crook."

The detective was relentless, asking rapid fire questions in a non-sequential manner in the hopes of keeping Pops off balance. Unfortunately for Peerless, it was all for naught. He'd been fishing in a dry lake, looking to hook a liar. It was a waste of his time. Unflappable Pops wouldn't bite.

He and his pals had been there for six hours now. It was all he could do just to keep his eyes open. He needed a nap, a horizontal pause in his day.

"I'm going home now," he declared, rising as he spoke. "Unless of course, you're in the process of forming up a firing squad...and yes, if that's the case, I *would* like one last cigarette as you blindfold me, preferably a Raleigh."

Peerless gently pushed him back onto the chair.

"Good try, but sorry—no cigar. You're not going anywhere until you talk."

Pops sent a skeptical gaze the cop's way, like a card player trying to assess whether or not his opponent was bluffing, and indeed, he sensed that the detective was truly bluffing. Peerless had nothing. Pops knew it and Peerless knew that he knew it. Armed with that knowledge, Pops went all theatrical on him.

"I want to call my lawyer right now!" he demanded, his face flush with indignation.

Pops could see that Peerless was carefully weighing his response.

"I told you—we're just talking. You don't need a lawyer."

"And I told *you,* that if as you say, I don't need a lawyer, then that means I'm not under arrest, and if I'm not under arrest, then you *cannot* keep me here one minute longer!" he raged, his blood pressure climbing.

Peerless said nothing as he glared at the old man. Pops went equally silent, the look in his eyes sufficiently eloquent enough to make his point. Peerless pulled the chair away and fell into it heavily, his hands rubbing his temples. Pops heard a groan, uncertain if it came from the man or the chair.

The silence dragged on, as did the exchange of hard, unyielding, baleful stares, reminiscent of two boxers circling each other in the ring, each waiting for the other to make the first move.

Eventually, Pops forced Peerless to blink first.

"Are you going to arrest me today, and if so, on what charge?" Pops demanded to know.

Silence...but for the ticking clock on the wall.

Peerless sighed, rubbing his hands together as if washing them clean of the old fellow sitting before him.

The skin around his eyes tightened, a muscle twitching in his jaw. Suddenly, he wheeled about and strode out of the room. He was back within three minutes, no doubt after conferring with Denby. From the look on Peerless' face, Denby had struck out as well, their combined efforts failing to yield the desired results. A pained expression on his face, Peerless reluctantly uttered the words that were music to Pops' ears.

"No, you're not under arrest, but be warned: We're not about to let this go. We'll be checking around and I have no doubt that we'll uncover *something* that'll lead us back to you, so you can expect that we'll be asking you for a return trip to that chair. Excuse me, did I say *asking you*? My mistake. No, actually, we'll be picking you up. You can count on it."

Pops flashed him a Cheshire cat grin, a grin that said everything, yet nothing at the same time. "That'd be like asking a three-pack-a-day smoker to come back for a second chest x-ray, not to mention a waste of the taxpayer's money, you ask me."

A heartbeat later, he stood and headed for the door.

Peerless held up a hand, motioning for Pops to hold up.

"I didn't say you could go yet, did I?"

Pop's hand went to his unshaven face, rubbing a week's worth of grey stubble.

"Let me get this straight. I'm not under arrest, right?"

Pops watched as Peerless carefully weighed his response, before grudgingly nodding. "No, but hang onto that thought, because it may still very well come into play."

"Then you're not going to cuff me?"

The detective shook his head no.

"And you're not going to shoot me?"

Visibly startled by the absurd question, the cop again shook his head in the negative.

"Well, then, if you're not going to arrest me, cuff me, or shoot me, guess what? I'm out of here," he said, quickly shuffling past Peerless as though he were nothing more than a statue.

The door leading to the other interrogation room was wide open as Pops walked by. It was empty. Continuing on to the side entrance door, he could see Butch and Rod through the glass. They were standing in the parking lot, leaning against Rod's car, looking vastly relieved, smoking cigarettes, and trading stares with someone standing at an upstairs window. Abercrombie.

Pops pushed the door open. The rain had stopped, cooling things off considerably. He breathed in deeply. To his mind, that first breath of fresh air was like a long, cool drink after a week in the desert.

He took a few steps forward and then pivoted, looking up, finding Abercrombie glowering down at the trio, the skin on his face like damp dough lapped over on itself in multiple layers, the malice in his glare, enough to burn holes in the glass as he fumed over the cops' inability to pin anything on them.

Pops grinned at him, like the proverbial cat that just ate the canary...and got away with it. He then waved affably to Abercrombie, as if saying goodbye to an old friend, the gesture, intended to infuriate the man even further. And it did.

Once inside the car, Pops rolled down the window and stuck his head out, looking up to see if Abercrombie was still watching them through the window. Indeed he was, his pudgy face candy apple-red with frustration and anger. As Rod put the car in gear and began driving away, Pops raised his arm out the window, tossing Abercrombie the finger.

"You really think that was necessary, Pops?" Rod asked, his eyes rolling in exasperation. "I don't think pissing him off even further is really such a hot idea."

"Why not? He's like a gun with no bullets. Him and those two BCI jamokes can't hurt us," he crowed confidently. "They're all foam and no beer. The *Untouchables*, they ain't, that's for sure! Why, those two flunkies couldn't find their bee-hinds with a compass and a map!" he ranted on. "And Abercrombie? That doughboy couldn't find a book in a library. It's over now, boys, so relax. It's done, just like I told you it would be, provided we kept our traps shut, except to say that we didn't know what they were talking about."

Pulling out onto route nine, Rod visibly relaxed, Pops' encouraging words having had the desired effect.

"You did real well in there, Butch," Pops admitted, albeit only grudgingly, still finding it hard to believe. "Rod told me how well you handled yourself under the pressure after we were separated, and well, I never thought I'd ever hear myself say this, but the truth is, I'm real proud of you, son."

Butch beamed from jug ear to jug ear with pride.

"Well, you aren't the only one who thought he'd never hear you say that. Thanks, Pops!"

"You're welcome," Pops replied absently, his mind already on something else. "Only thing that I can think of that could cause us some trouble is if either of you deposited any of the money in the bank, or opened a safe deposit box account. *Please* tell me that you didn't do either of those things."

They both assured him that neither of them would have ever done such a foolish thing.

"Good, because I'm sure they're going to check with all the banks in the Tri-City area. While making a large deposit, in itself, isn't a crime, you'd nevertheless have to explain just *where* the cash came from and that *would* be a problem."

Rod involuntarily flinched, as if slapped, his car swerving, coming perilously close to sideswiping a Studebaker Hawk in the opposing lane. Straightening the car, he thought back on just how close he came to renting a safe deposit box, just a few days back. If not for the fracas with the three stooges on Remsen Street, he would've gotten to the bank in plenty of time to rent the box. Never before had he felt grateful to anyone for picking a fight with him, but this was a welcome exception.

"Jumping Jesus! What the hell was that all about?" Pops cried, his face ashen as a result of the close call. "I'm going to have to get you one of those magnetic Blessed Marys to mount on the dashboard!"

"Sorry about that. A big wasp landed on my face," Rod lied, his friends buying the bogus excuse.

"No harm done," Butch said. "Just as long as the wasp isn't still in the car, that is."

"Nope. Flew back out the window," he again lied.

"Another thing," Pops said, his mind now back on the subject at hand. "Tell me you haven't yet bought a new car," he inquired of Butch, fervently hoping he'd get the answer he wanted.

"Nope, but I was planning on going over to Bumstead Chevrolet on my next day off."

Both Rod and Pops breathed an audible sigh of relief.

"I'll tell you what, Butch," Pops began. "You wait a couple of months and then go over there if you want, but you're not going to buy a *new* car," he ordered, in a tone that would brook no argument. "Not yet, anyhow. I know you're itching to rid yourself of that jalopy that's ninety percent *Bondo* and ten percent tin foil, so go ahead, buy yourself a six or seven hundred dollar used car. Put down a hundred bucks and finance the rest. Then, maybe a year from now, trade it in, using it as a down payment on a new Corvair. You'll make payments on that, too, by the way, just to play it safe."

Butch started to protest, but one look from Pops and he thought better of it.

"Yeah, I suppose you're right. Buy what we want, but make payments, instead of paying in full with cash," he mused aloud, Pops' words of caution slowly sinking in. "At least for any big purchases, anyway," he added.

"Good. It's all settled then," Pops said as he fired up a Raleigh.

"What's settled?" Butch asked.

Pops took a deep drag, slowly expelling it through his nostrils. *Jaysus H. Kee-rist on a crutch! This kid could screw up a one car funeral procession,* he grumbled inwardly, shaking his head in wonderment.

"Rod?" he asked.

"What?"

"Do me a favor?"

"Sure."

"Punch Butch in the kisser. And get your money's worth."

Butch let loose with a raucous laugh.

"Remind me not to get on your bad side, Pops."

Pops glared at him, as if he'd just delivered the wrong pizza to the right house.

"Too late, Bozo."

"Aw, I was just kidding around. I knew what you meant. You know me—sometimes my mouth takes on a life of its own, all free-spirited and loose."

"Yeah, well, I hoped you enjoyed the compliment I gave you a few minutes ago, because it's the last one you'll ever get out of me, you nitwit!" Pops retorted, clearly peeved at Butch now, which was the norm.

Rod switched on the radio, hoping to drown out their squabbling, as he turned onto Columbia Street. WTRY—Ed Burns & Connie Stevens and "Kookie Kookie—Lend me your comb."

"Now, I suppose you call that music, a bunch of jazzzamarazz about a cockamamie comb?" Pops griped.

Rod fiddled with the dial. WABY—Dodie Stevens—"Pink Shoelaces."

"Like that's supposed to be better," Pops mumbled, an understatement that would do until a better one occurred to him.

Rod turned the dial once more. WROW—Sinatra belting out "That old black magic."

"Humph. Now that's more like it," Pops grudgingly conceded. "You know, now that I think of it, I don't believe either one of those cops really had their heart in the interrogation."

"What do you mean?" Butch asked.

"I could just tell. I mean, it wasn't like they were grilling real criminals, bank robbers and such. You ask me, they probably went into it halfheartedly to begin with, wanting to get it over with quickly, almost as much as we did. Enforcing the Antiquities Act, just to satisfy that freaking putz, Abercrombie, but knowing deep down inside that they were just acting out a charade. I mean, come on, will ya? Narcotics, murder, stuff like that; they'd have been on us like husks on corn...*but Dumbo's bones?* Gimme me a break!"

Rod nodded, Pops' words making a lot of sense.

"Yeah, but what if they got there before we moved the skeleton?" Butch chipped in, making a valid point.

Pops flipped his cigarette butt out the window.

"We'd have been screwed. But they didn't, and so all they had to go on was Abercrombie's suspicions, which isn't the same thing as having hard evidence. That's why I say their hearts weren't really in it."

"Yeah, but I got a question for you," Rod said as he reached for the radio switch, turning it off. "And it's a troubling question, one that only just occurred to me."

"Shoot."

"Who told Abercrombie where to look for the bones?" Rod asked softly, his words landing like a rock in a still pond.

Suddenly, all conversation ceased. Stone silence, like someone abruptly pulling the plug on a Hi-Fi.

"Good question," Pops mumbled after a few tense, introspective moments. "One that hadn't occurred to me, either," he sheepishly admitted, his euphoria at having outfoxed the cops faltering, then altogether disappearing, like smoke out of an open window.

"Well, don't feel bad. Like I said, it only now just occurred to me."

"Geez, I never gave it a thought, either," Butch admitted. "Anybody got any guesses?"

Pops heaved an old man's weary sigh.

"Not a clue."

"Me either," Rod replied. "But we're going to have to think on it, because whoever it was, if they knew where we stashed Jumbo, then who knows *what else* they know about?" Rod ventured, almost wishing that that particular question had never occurred to him.

"Well, whoever got to the blue ribbon blimp, knew what they were talking about, that's for sure," Pops said.

"Blue ribbon blimp?" Rod asked, mystified.

"Abercrombie. He reminds me of a *4-H club* hog I once saw at the Syracuse State fair, a blue ribbon winner."

All three laughed heartily, effectively breaking the tension...for the moment, anyway.

"We'll figure out," Pops assured them, brightening up a bit as he gave it some thought. "Even if we don't, what's the worst that can happen? I mean, suppose that whoever the hell it was that tipped Abercrombie off in the first place, now goes back to him and the cops, telling them that we did indeed sell Dumbo...to someone in Canada, no less. Well, let them try and prove it. Lots of luck with that, because it *can't* be proven, so now that I think about it, what the hell are we even worrying about it for?"

"You're right," Rod readily agreed, the tension within him beginning to melt away.

"Good point, Pops!" Butch cried. "Thanks for thinking of it, before I wet my pants with worry."

Pops' eyes wandered heavenward, as if searching for assistance from above.

"Lord, please spare me from the idjits of the world."

Rod laughed as he made the turn onto Broadway.

"Hey, do me a favor, Rod," Pops asked. "Stop at Don Lagasse's place, will you?"

"Yeah, sure."

"I told my sister, Aggie, that I'd settle her weekly grocery bill for her from now on."

"I'll bet she appreciated that," Rod remarked. "But did she ask you where the money is going to come from?"

"Nah. I trained her long ago. Ask me no questions and I'll tell you no lies."

Moments later, Rod pulled up in front of the small corner grocery, the guys asking Pops to grab a couple of *Jic-Jacs* for them. Nodding okay, he got out and strolled into the store.

Butch turned the radio back on, fiddling a bit with the tuning dial. WPTR—Freddie Cannon singing "Tallahassee Lassie."

Pops was back within mere minutes, two bottles of soda in hand. Rod wisely changed the station on the radio. No sense in riling him up again. WROW—Della Reese and "Don't you know?"

"All set?" Rod asked as he chugged down the black cherry flavored soda.

"Yep. He's even willing to let me pay the bill bi-weekly now, saving me extra trips. That's a rare exception for Don, but then I've known him since he was knee-high to a chipmunk, so no surprise there. Helluva of a nice guy he grew up to be. Nice family, too. Cute daughter, that Ruthie."

"Hey, didn't you get yourself a soda?" Butch asked.

"Nope, that stuff will kill you. I'll stick to my *Four Roses* and beer, thank you. And by the way, next time, grab your own sodas. That cooler filled with ice just about gave me frostbite!"

"How is Aggie, by the way?" Butch inquired, ignoring Pops' lament. "I always liked her. She's a real nice lady."

"Well, that's debatable, but to answer your question, she running low on cash and time. Most of the sand has already run through her hourglass. She'll be eighty-seven next month and getting frailer and poorer by the minute. That's why I'm helping her out."

"That's real good of you," Rod remarked.

Pops shrugged.

"What's a brother to do? She's my sister. That's why I agreed to take some money when you offered it. I got to help her out."

"Are you kidding me?" Rod cried. "You earned every cent of it. Without your help, we'd have been sunk! Hell, you should have taken a bigger cut, like we wanted you to. For that matter, you still can. Ain't that right, Butch?"

"Absolutely!"

Pops waved the offer away.

"Nope, I got plenty now, more than I can ever spend before I hit the dirt for keeps. But...in the unlikely event that I should live longer than I think I will, I promise that I'll hit you up for some more cash, okay?"

"Deal," Rod and Butch replied in unison.

Rod slipped the car into gear and headed for Pop's place.

While waiting at the Garner Street red light, Pops emitted a low sigh, shaking his head as he did.

"What?" Rod asked.

"Aw, I was just thinking about Aggie. The other day, she told me she wished she could afford to get her hair done down at the Hollywood Salon, so I gave her the money to cover it, along with cab fare for one of Ben Cook's taxies."

"So, that's a good thing, isn't it?" Rod asked.

"Not really. I have more hair than she does. She's just about bald, the poor old thing."

CHAPTER 37

A month had passed since Fish had led Abercrombie to the barn, and to date, he hadn't read anything in the paper, or heard anything on the news to indicate that Hobbs and his cronies had been arrested. Frustrated, he feigned a wicked toothache, left work early, and then placed a call to Abercrombie. His icy-toned secretary told Fish that Abercrombie wasn't interested in speaking with him, either at the moment, or at any other time in the future. Then she hung up.

Seething with anger, Fish slammed the receiver down hard, nearly cracking the base in two. After taking a long pull on a quart bottle of Piel's, he lit a Chesterfield, puffing hard, sucking the smoke in deeply. Lifting the bottle off the kitchen table, he drained it dry before violently throwing it against the wall.

He'd had a hard day at work, Sal riding him constantly, snapping at him, acting as if Fish was a new hire and didn't know what he was doing. It was tough to swallow, but unless he just flat-out walked off the job, something he wasn't yet prepared to do, there wasn't much he could do about Sal's disrespecting him.

If it had been anyone else, Fish would've punched him in the throat, but it was Sal, a guy even Fish wouldn't mess with...not if he wanted to go on breathing, that is. Sal was old and physically unimposing, but under his suit jacket he packed a pistol, seven days a week, and if that wasn't sufficient to deter someone, well, he had some bent-nosed muscle from Schenectady on his off-the-books payroll, pros that would make Fish look like a pure-as-the-driven-snow altar boy.

Not a comforting thought, so Fish willed his warped mind to wander elsewhere.

Well, if Hobbs is going to skate on the mastodon thing, and it seems that he will, then I'll have to handle my revenge the old fashioned way—sneak into the site after dark, hide, and then jump him while he's making his rounds. Yeah, that's what I'll do, he told himself.

Having come to a conclusion that provided him with immense satisfaction, Fish relaxed for the first time all day, popping the cap off another quart of beer and chugging it down. *After I get done messing up his face, nobody will ever again tell him that he looks like Fabian, that's for sure,* he chuckled to himself.

Bright and early the following morning, Sal received an unexpected visitor, someone he'd never met before.

The young woman had walked into his office after carefully noting that, indeed, his black Cadillac was parked in front of the ramshackle building, one that was sheathed in cracked, green asbestos shingles that had seen better days. She'd done her homework beforehand, finding out what kind of car he drove, and what the plate numbers were. Now, she could only hope that his foreman, Lenny Fishowski, was not on premise, as well. She didn't see his Pontiac around, but that didn't necessarily mean that he wasn't in there. *He's a foreman, so he'll be down at the construction site, not sitting here in an office,* she reminded herself. *Or so I hope, anyway.*

It took a number of attempts before she was finally able to push the stubborn door open. A short, stout woman wearing cat-eye glasses, with a pencil penetrating her beehive hairdo, like a stick pushed into a bird's nest, sat behind a desk. She cast a withering glare in the direction of the young woman.

"Can I help you with something?" she asked, her icy tone suggesting she would prefer to be of no help whatsoever.

"Yes, it's imperative that I speak with Mr. Coccalido, right away," the woman replied, her words laced with implied urgency.

The lady with the beehive hairdo gave her a quick onceover, her eyes taking in the plain looks, drab clothes, and resolute expression on her face.

"What's it about?" she demanded to know, icicles dripping from every word.

"It's personal."

"Yeah, well, I'm his sister, Angie, and me and him—we don't have any secrets between us, so you tell *me* first, then I'll decide if it's something he needs to hear directly from you. My brother is a very busy man, you know," Angie countered, all puffed up with self importance.

The young lady wasn't impressed.

"As I said, it's personal, and for his ears only," she replied coolly, her eyes locked onto those of the witch that sat before her.

Refusing to concede an inch, Angie dug in further.

"He prefers that people call and make an appointment—not just walk in and demand to see him," she snapped. "And *you* don't have an appointment!" she added, her shrill voice rising to a near screech, like fingernails across a chalkboard.

Wholly unimpressed and not in the least bit intimidated, the young woman smiled and crossed her legs, unwrapping a stick of Adam's clove gum as she did, nonchalantly popping it into her mouth.

"Let me put it like this—what I have to share with him involves the most important news that he'll hear all year. Furthermore, the longer he has to wait to hear it...well, sister or not, I for one, wouldn't want to be in *your* shoes when he discovers that you stonewalled me."

Angie's mouth flew open, her lips moving, but no words coming out. Her face turned crimson, her beehive quavered and teetered, threatening to take a nosedive, but then, just as she was about to lambast the plain-Jane sitting before her, verbally rip her to shreds, she suddenly reconsidered what the woman had said and thought better of it. *No sense in taking a chance on riling up my brother,* she reluctantly admitted to herself. *Not with retirement just around the corner, and him funding it, no less!*

Forced to swallow her pride, Angie, pressed down on the intercom button. Sal came on. She told him he had a visitor. He told her to send the visitor in.

With a look that could freeze a charging rhino in its tracks, Angie pointed toward Sal's office.

The young woman mustered as sweet and syrupy a smile as she possibly could, while deriving immeasurable delight from having won out over *Elsie the Cow*.

She turned the door knob and walked in. The office was dusty, shabby, smoke-laden and well...downright filthy, but she didn't care. She wouldn't be staying. Just long enough to drop a dime on Fish and then she'd be gone.

Much like his office, the man sitting behind the scarred, old oak desk wasn't much to look at. Garbed in an ill-fitting black suit, loudly accented by a garish purple and yellow tie knotted loosely around his turkey-wattled neck, he was rather scrawny looking and not at all an imposing figure—until he gazed directly at someone, his ice-blue poker player eyes boring into them, eyes that would cut holes in them, but revealed nothing in return.

Looking past the bad comb-over and hawk face covered in dark moles, as if someone had flicked a wet paintbrush in his direction, she saw a man who radiated power...and danger.

A chill coursed through her body as she spoke.

"Thank you for seeing me, Mr. Coccalido," she said softly. "My name is Mary Smith and I have some information that I'd like to share with you."

Sal relit his cigar and blew the smoke out at an upward angle, adding to the already dense cloud that hovered just below the ceiling.

Turning his eyes to her, he said nothing. He just stared at her, unblinking.

She found the silence and his steady gaze to be rather unnerving. Despite that, she sat there quietly, patiently, the silence accumulating, like snowflakes on a windowsill

Finally, he spoke.

"Well, it must be pretty important to you, whatever it is, considering the storm you just weathered out there," he said, pointing a finger toward the door that led to his irritating sister. "Yeah, I could hear her. Hell, the stiffs in Dufresne's mortuary could hear her. Stubborn, aren't you?"

Mary drew in a deep breath.

"Yes, when it's called for."

Sal smiled his trademark twisted smile.

"Okay, Mary Smith, what's this all about?"

"There's a man who works for you. Lenny Fishowski," she began, more than a bit nervously.

Sal nodded, but then stood, saying: "Excuse me for a moment," as he headed toward the door, swinging it open, nearly sending his sister flying.

"What'd I tell you about eavesdropping?" he snarled.

Her face red with embarrassment, *Elsie*...I mean, Angie, hoofed it back to her desk in record time.

Sal slammed the door shut behind him and sat back down at his desk.

"Okay, you were saying?"

Mary felt a tiny icicle of doubt slither down her back. She was beginning to regret having ever come here, her nerves now standing on end. She quickly weighed her options, spanning the gamut from zero to zilch. She couldn't just walk out now, not after having brought up Lenny's name. She'd already piqued Sal's curiosity, so there was no going back. *Besides, I want my revenge, don't I?* She reminded herself.

Sal continued to patiently wait for her response, each second that went by, further ratcheting up the tension.

"Well..." she began, stopping to clear her throat before going on. "I had the misfortune of spending some time with him a few weeks back and, uh, well he told me that..." Mary stumbled, her words trailing off.

"He told you *what*?" Sal prodded, his eyes suddenly flashing with interest.

Eager to get it over with, Mary decided to just blurt it out.

"He was drunk and he bragged to me about how he stole equipment from you, and then turned around and sold it all," she said, relieved now at having spit it out, a bad taste in her mouth now gone. "Furthermore, he claimed he'd been stealing from you for over six months. He also said you were too stupid to ever figure out just who the thief was. Then he went on to say that you would never suspect him, a guy you regarded almost like a son."

A facial muscle high on Sal's cheek began to twitch. He started to say something, but changed his mind, his jaws clamping shut.

He motioned for her to continue on, his eyes taking on the cold look of a hanging judge.

"Lenny also said that he had discovered the remains of a mastodon at the construction site, and that he had removed it from there, and then sold it for a large amount of money," she lied.

Sal blinked, only the slight flaring of his nostrils giving any hint of the fury he was suppressing.

"What else did he say?" he asked, barely able to contain his outrage, his anger increasing by degrees, rising so fast, it skipped a few degrees along the way.

Mary shook her head.

"That's it."

Sal leaned back in his chair and threw his feet up on the desk, his mind working, his gaze fixed upon Mary's face, studying her closely. He had an intuitive and uncanny accurate sense about people's underlying motivations, a sense that rarely failed him.

"You got an axe to grind with him?" he asked bluntly, his tone crisp and incisive, similar to the way a surgeon uses a scalpel to slice right through to the meat of an issue.

Mary didn't hesitate to answer.

"Absolutely."

"What'd he do to you?" he pressed, noting the fading traces of a bruise on her cheek. "To get you to drop a dime on him, that is."

"Let's just say I have my reasons."

"I'll bet you do." *Lie down with a dog and you'll get up with fleas,* he thought.

One of Sal's pet peeves involved men that beat up women, something Mary couldn't possibly have been aware of, but certainly worked in her favor.

Sal had personally iced more than a few men in his lifetime, and was indirectly behind the demise of even more, yet he never once lost a wink of sleep over any of them. Yeah, he'd been a cold blooded killer in his younger days, but having said that, the man nevertheless possessed, what he considered to be, anyway, a code of honor that he lived by, one that included a distinct aversion to visiting physical pain upon the fairer sex.

Fish, the poster boy for bad choices, was dead meat, just waiting to happen. The thefts were reason enough. Beating on a woman was icing on the cake.

"Did he mention who he sold my property to?"

"No."

"I'm also mildly curious about this mastodon thing," he admitted, rubbing his chin in thought. "Did he ever mention who he sold *that* to?"

Mary shook her head, trying hard to remain composed, but doing a lousy job of it.

"Well, I don't really care much about that, except...how the hell did he get it out of there in broad daylight, in front of fifty other workers, not to mention, in front of yours truly, as well? You know what I mean?" he asked, clearly puzzled.

Mary shrugged her narrow shoulders.

"I'm sorry, but I don't know. He didn't say."

Sal studied her face for a moment, looking for tells, sure signs that she was holding something back, or worse yet, lying. Other than the understandable nervousness she'd exhibited ever since she first walked in, he saw nothing to indicate that she'd been holding out on him, or lying. He was satisfied.

Suddenly, he reached across the desk and gently touched her shoulder, a surprising gesture, for Sal was anything but a touchy-feely guy.

"No need to apologize, uh...*Mary*, is it?" he asked, in the hushed tone that an undertaker uses when offering consolation.

"Yes...Mary."

"That's what I thought. Anyway, tell me, Mary, what sort of work do you do?"

She flinched a bit, the question out of left field, one that made her feel uneasy about answering, *but what the heck*, she reminded herself...this was Cohoes, a small city, and if she didn't volunteer the information, he'd quickly dig it up anyway.

She divulged it all; where she worked, where she lived, etc, etc.

Slowly but surely, a most appealing idea began to take shape in Sal's mind, and the more it grew, the more he approved of it.

"If you don't mind my being nosey, Mary, what's your weekly salary?" he asked in an amiable, *let's-make-a-deal voice*.

It was considered bad form to ask such a question, but at this point, it didn't much bother her.

"I take home $57.65 a week," she freely admitted.

Once again he relit his stogie, releasing yet another cloud of reeking smoke.

"And how long have you worked there?"

"Ever since I graduated from Keveny Academy."

"Hmm, not much more than just getting by then, eh?"

"Pretty much," she replied, a bit embarrassed.

"Well, my sister, the snoop, out there, is going to retire next month, and so, I'll need to replace her."

Mary nodded, as though she understood where this conversation was going, although in fact, she hadn't a clue.

"I'll need someone with office experience—typing, handling phone calls, filing, reminding me of my appointments, that kind of stuff, the same sort of work that you do now at your current job," he explained, the intent behind his words now beginning to sink in.

He's going to offer me a job!

"I'm offering you the job, Mary, because you strike me as someone who would handle the duties with ease and efficiency."

"But, I already have a job," she countered in a polite, yet firm tone.

Sal raised his hand, a stop sign.

"Just hear me out. Then, if you still don't want the job, fine," he assured her. "You say that you take home fifty-seven and change per week. Well, I'll triple that and offer you free, across the board benefits as well."

Mary's eyes just about popped out of her head!

She started to say something, but the words just wouldn't come out.

Sal smiled, content in knowing that he'd successfully hooked her.

"You may wonder why I'm willing to pay you so much, and that would be understandable, so I'll tell you why: Half of your pay will be a result of the work that you do for me. The other half should be considered a reward for coming in here today and telling me what you just told me. I admire and value your willingness to do it, whether your motivation behind it, is fueled by the idea of simply doing the right thing, or something along the lines of, shall we say... *revenge*? Seeing to it, that a certain *fish* gets filleted and fried?"

Mary felt herself involuntarily flinch as Sal nailed it right on the head.

"Whatever your reason, or reasons are, it doesn't matter, Mary. I place a high premium on people who look out for my interests, and by coming here today, you've demonstrated that you're one of them. So, what do you say? You'll take the job?"

Mary knew she might live to regret it, but how could she possibly turn her nose up at such an incredible offer?

"Yes, Mr. Coccalido, I most certainly will."

Sal clapped his hands together.

"Great! Now, as for the training, you'll need to familiarize yourself with the workings of the office, so I suggest that you start next Monday...and don't worry about my sister, for I'll see to it that she treats you with the utmost respect," he promised, a vow that Mary felt certain he would enforce.

"All right, I'll give my notice today, that I'll be leaving next week," Mary replied, giddy with the thought of making so much money. "There is one thing on my mind, however, that I'd like to talk to you about, that being..."

"*Fish!*" he spat, finishing her sentence for her. "Don't worry, you won't be seeing him around here," he assured her. *Or anywhere else, for that matter,* he promised himself.

He then offered her his hand. They shook.

"Thank you, sir. It's been...interesting, to say the least," a statement that had only a distant relationship to the truth. *Interesting? More like mindboggling!*

A few more niceties and assurances later, and Mary strolled out the door, happy as a lark as she walked toward her car. *Who would've guessed?* She thought to herself. *I'll be getting my revenge and a great new job, to boot!*

She put the key in the ignition of her gray Nash Rambler and turned the engine over, the radio coming to life as she did. WTRY—Connie Francis and "Who's sorry now?"

She wondered if she'd later experience even a smidgen of guilt over her part in what she presumed, would be the end for Lenny Fishowski. *Hmm, I doubt it.*

Alone now with his dark thoughts, Sal began to plan the impending demise of one Lenny Fishowski, a guy who was never overburdened with honesty or smarts to begin with. *Well, shame on me, as I should've seen it coming, but no, I just about considered him a son, blinding me to what should've been glaringly obvious.*

Sal was not a man for whom the world was a complicated place. He didn't see things as being black or white. No, he saw the world and the people in it, in primary colors, his favorite, the one he was about to paint Fish in—blood red. It was his civic duty, he believed, to help improve the city, by ensuring that Fish took permanent leave of it.

From part-time thief to full-time corpse, Fish had, thanks to his own loose lips, sunk his own ship.

That said, Sal nevertheless always prided himself on verifying, beyond any reasonable doubt, that someone had crossed him or done him wrong, prior to arranging a permanent under-the-dirt-nap, for the offending party.

He'd heard enough today to erase any lingering doubts about Fish's guilt.

Two days ago, while sitting at the bar in Smith's he'd run into a longtime friend, a salt-of-the-earth, local character who went by the name of *Louie the Horse*. After engaging in a bit of back and forth banter about the Yankee's chances for a another World Series ring, Sal did what he'd been doing all summer long, asking those who regularly had their ear to the ground, if they'd heard any scuttlebutt concerning his stolen equipment.

Louie the Horse was the kind of guy that liked to answer a question, in a most indirect way—by asking the questioner, questions of his own. Today was no exception.

"I've heard talk, but nothing conclusive, mind you," the big man cautioned...sort of. You never knew with Louie, who loved to talk in riddles, just to see if you were truly listening.

"*Who*? Just give me a name, Louie."

"Well, I can't really do that," Louie replied, pausing before going any further, a little internal debate going on about just how much he should share with Sal. "But, let me ask you this, Sal—Have you ever heard the old saying that goes like this: *If a Fish never opened his mouth, it'd never get caught?* It's testimony to the fact that for some folk's problems, there are no solutions, none that they'd heed anyway."

Sal didn't reply right off, his mind absorbing what he'd just heard, focusing on the word *Fish* and ignoring the rest. He was still chewing it over, his fury building, when Louie nudged him.

"Hey, I was just saying, you know? Beyond that, I don't know what else to tell you, Sal."

"You're absolutely sure about that? That you're not holding out on me?" he asked, once his blood pressure settled enough to allow him to speak coherently.

"Would I lie to you, Sal? Hell, I'd sooner pour hot coffee down my pants," Louie exclaimed, his face splitting into a wide grin.

Sal thanked him for the info, knowing that it would be futile to try and get any more out of the man. All he'd get for his efforts would be a bunch of convoluted questions about some obscure, archaic subject. No, he'd already provided Sal with the information he needed, information that was sitting in his stomach like broken glass.

One of Sal's few redeeming traits was his loyalty to those deserving of it, yet the one thing he could never abide was betrayal by those same people, an act that was guaranteed to drastically reduce their life expectancy. There was no smoothing things over with him, either, no assuaging with anything other than blood. You were either loyal to him, or you were circling the drain, mere moments from meeting your maker, or a more likely scenario, in Fish's case, the horned troll in the red suit, replete with pitchfork in hand.

The very next day, down at the site, Sal rode Fish hard, making scathing comments about the quality of his work, picking at him, verbally jabbing him, and all of it, within earshot of his co-workers.

Sal was incensed to think that Fish, his most trusted employee, would steal from him, yet until he could find someone who could corroborate, give weight to Louie's thinly veiled accusation, he wouldn't act, not yet anyway, he had told himself. It was Sal's way, needing absolute confirmation before snuffing out a life. He was funny like that.

Now he had that corroboration, courtesy of one Mary Smith, someone he'd grossly overpay, in part, to reward her, but also to buy her allegiance, her loyalty...and most importantly, her silence.

CHAPTER 38

With the project down at the falls nearing completion, Sal was now in the midst of breaking ground for the new hospital on Upper Columbia Street. Heavy earthmoving equipment was strewn throughout the five acre site, all of it sitting silently, as most of the men who operated the equipment had left for the day.

Just before dusk, two of Sal's nephews started up a pair of backhoes. Working directly across from each other, within forty minutes, they'd managed to dig a hole eight feet wide, thirteen feet long and twelve feet deep, carefully piling the dirt in huge mounds along the edges of the pit. Then, one of them went to work on carving out an earthen ramp, one that led directly down into the pit.

The dark of night had fallen by the time Fish drove through the wire-mesh gates, the construction site now pitch black, but for the faint beams of light emanating from twin Caterpillar graders, each of them perched ominously on opposite side of the pit, their engines silent, their blades at rest.

No sooner had Fish cleared the gates when Dominic, the third nephew, stepped from the shadows and slipped the padlock into place, giving it a sharp tug, making certain that it had locked. Satisfied, he then blended seamlessly back into the shadows, all the while keeping an eye out for any unwanted visitors.

Earlier in the day Sal had paid Fish a visit, down at the falls site. Placing a fatherly hand on Fish's brawny shoulder, he apologized for having been so rough on him lately. While Fish certainly enjoyed hearing the apology, he was also somewhat taken aback by it.

Sal never apologized to *anyone* for *anything*, so he felt genuinely honored by this most unlikely gesture.

Sal then went on to say that he'd like Fish's opinion on something, something he was thinking about doing up at the hospital site. Fish was enthusiastic in his reply, telling Sal he'd be more than happy to give his opinion, on whatever it was that Sal had on his mind.

His boss told him that he'd prefer that Fish meet him up at the site, to first see what Sal had in mind, rather than talk about it now. Naturally, Fish agreed, asking Sal what time he should show up. Sal explained that he'd be busy up until about eight-thirty, so if Fish could come up there right around nine, that'd be perfect. Fish told Sal he could count it.

Tonight was also the night Fish planned on jumping Hobbs, doling out sweet retribution for the beating he'd taken earlier in the summer. There'd still be plenty of time left for that, he assured himself, after meeting with Sal.

Fish was feeling good now, real good. *Yeah, tonight's the night Hobbs gets introduced to a certain lead pipe of mine, up close and personal like.*

As the car bounced through and across the ruts in the dirt road, the Bonneville's headlights framed Sal and another guy...definitely not one of his employees, but rather someone who looked more the part of a professional knee-capper, somebody who bit roofing nails in half just for fun. *One of those Schenectady guys*, Fish guessed, a lump beginning to form in his throat.

The two men were standing in front of what appeared to be a dirt ramp that led down into a good sized pit, one that was located about six hundred feet in from Columbia Street.

Sal waved Fish forward, throwing up a hand once the car was but two feet from him. Fish started to get out of the car, but Sal motioned for him to sit tight as he walked up alongside the Bonneville, the goon close on his heels.

Suspicious now, Fish felt an icy tremor run down his spine.

"Thanks for coming, Fish. It means a lot to me," Sal said as he leaned down, his elbow resting on the door sill, a ghoulish smile playing on his lips.

The car radio was turned on. Roy Orbison singing, appropriately enough, "It's over."

Hot night that it was, Fish had rolled down all four windows, just as Sal assumed he would do.

After exchanging a few banalities about the heat and the progress on the new job site, Fish asked Sal just what it was that he wanted his opinion on.

Sal straightened up, pointing to the pit directly in front of them, and then, just like that, Fish felt an invisible noose slip over his head, settling around his neck. A moment later, the noose tightened, the stranger leaning into the car from behind, the silencer on the business end of the gun jammed tight against the back of Fish's skull.

Fish knows what's coming, but rather than beg for his life, something he'd never do, he sighs heavily, a long and deep, defeated exhalation, like a boxer who'd been knocked down one time too many, and could do nothing but wait for the final eight-count to end.

"You stole from me!" Sal cried, a look of genuine disappointment flickering across his craggy features. "*Me*, who treated you almost like a son! Why? Why did you do it?"

A faint flicker of a smile lived and died across Fish's face, like a lightning bolt on its last legs, expiring now, fresh out of juice.

"Because I could," he replied, his voice cracking now, like ice in a hot cup of coffee.

"Well, that isn't necessarily the wrong answer, but it isn't the right one, either," Sal snapped, pausing before going on. "Oh, and before you leave us, why don't you tell me about this mastodon business that I—"

"Why the hell should I?" Fish spat, the last words he'd ever speak.

Desperate, with nothing to lose, he made his move, twisting away from the barrel of the gun, his outstretched arm blindly reaching behind for the hand that held it...too late.

The shooter relieved the fresh corpse of its wallet. Fish wasn't going to need it anymore, and Fifty-five bucks was fifty-five bucks. Then he put the car in neutral. He and Angelo pushed it down the ramp. After bouncing up and down on its springs a few times, the Pontiac settled nicely into its final resting place.

Within thirty minutes, the pit was filled, tamped down, and then graded to perfection.

As Sal drove home he thought about what had just transpired, and almost felt a little bad about it. Almost.

CHAPTER 39

A week later, Rod showed up for work at five pm, just as the construction workers were leaving for the day. As he walked through the gates, one of the guys told him that Sal was in the trailer and wanted to speak with him.

Rod thanked him for the heads-up and made his way over to the field office, mildly curious as to what was on Sal's mind.

As he grasped the door knob, a large man suddenly pushed the door open, nearly bowling Rod over. He mumbled a few words of apology as he made his way past Rod. Once inside, Sal eyed Rod with suspicion, like a watchdog preparing to snarl at a stranger at the door.

"Have a seat," he barked, his dead eyes, empty tunnels, hollow tunnels of distrust.

Rod gulped, a lump of ice forming where his heart was supposed to be. He had a bad feeling about this.

"What's the matter? You look like you just swallowed a dose of castor oil."

"Nothing's the matter. I'm fine," Rod replied, smiling as he lied. "Who was that guy?" he asked, looking to change the subject.

"That's my new foreman. His name is Zandri. A good man—lots of experience," Sal answered, a stinking stogie clamped between his teeth.

"What happened to Fish? He's not working for you anymore?" Rod asked, hoping that, indeed, that was the case.

"No, he isn't, but then that's what happens when a man goes a week without showing up for work. He loses his job. Hell, he didn't even bother to call in, either."

Rod tried his best to suppress a smile at hearing the news. Tried but failed. Truth was, it was the best bit of news he'd heard in quite a while.

"Yeah, no love lost between the two of you, eh? Especially after you beat the crap out of him?"

"Nope," Rod admitted. "I mean, I'm not exactly all broke up over the news."

"Oh, and by the way, I understand you also had a run-in with my nephews, one of them, Angelo, ending up in the emergency room."

"They didn't leave me much choice, coming at me the way they did," Rod explained carefully, like a man attempting to defuse a bomb. "If there'd been a way to avoid it, Sal, believe me, I would've used it, but there just wasn't anything I could do. It was either me or them," he insisted, maybe a little too defensively.

"And just when, Angie, their mother, was starting to respect you," Sal remarked dryly.

Rod squirmed, reaching for the cigarettes tucked into his rolled-up sleeve.

"Lucky for you, the day after the fight, Charette told me what he observed from across the street, them provoking the fight."

Relieved, Rod got his cigarette going, snapped the lid of his Zippo shut, and said, "Well, like I told you—"

"That's ancient history now," Sal interrupted, cutting Rod off in midsentence. "Let's get back to Fish."

"Sure. What about him?"

Sal drew on his cigar, releasing yet another putrid cloud of smoke into the air. Four or five flies swarmed around his head, but he paid no attention to them, as if they were just some old pals dropping by.

"Just the other day I heard a rumor about Fish, a most unsettling one, I might add," Sal said.

"What exactly did the rumor concern, if you don't mind my asking?"

"I heard that he discovered the remains of a mastodon, right here on this site. What do you think of that?" he asked, his eyes fixed upon Rod's face, gauging his reaction to the news, looking for tells.

Someone could've have fired a cannon through the trailer and it wouldn't have surprised Rod as much the broadside Sal had just leveled him with.

Equally shocked and confused by Sal's revelation, he fought to get a hold of himself, trying hard to maintain his composure. It wasn't easy.

"Really? *A mastodon*? No kidding? Like the one in the museum?" he asked, feigning astonishment.

"No, believe me, I'm not kidding," Sal replied, his face hard, his voice cold. "I never kid."

At a loss for words and totally befuddled by what he'd just heard, Rod ran it all through his survival meter. *So it's rumored that Fish took mastodon remains out of here. Well, he's got it half right. How anyone knew about the bones, Lord only knows, but as long as Fish is the suspected subject of the rumor, well, what I am worrying for?*

Rod began to relax, just a bit.

"So, are you going to track this rumor? See if there's anything to it? It's pretty farfetched, you ask me," Rod said rather nonchalantly, or, at least he tried to come across that way.

"Good question. But before I answer it, I have an even better question."

"What's that?"

"If indeed he did manage to discover the remains in question, how the hell did he get them out of here?"

So much for relaxing.

Rod shrugged his shoulders.

"Now, there's a real good question."

"Isn't it, though? You see, to my way of thinking, he sure as hell wouldn't have been able to spirit the remains out of here in his lunchbox," Sal said, pausing to relight his stogie. "And he certainly couldn't have walked out carrying huge bones over his shoulders, or dragging a rope behind him, tied to a mastodon skull, at least not without anyone noticing, and we would've. No doubt about that. So..."

"So?" Rod echoed, a growing sense of dread introducing itself to his stomach, the spicy foods he had for lunch beginning to make war with each other.

"So, that means *if* the rumor is true, then he couldn't possibly have gotten the bones out of here doing working hours," Sal claimed, cocksure.

Air-raid sirens went off in Rod's head. Where this conversation was heading was a mystery to him, but the road it was currently on, was a bit too close to home...*way too close.*

Rod spread his arms wide, palms out.

"Beats me. But then, you don't really believe this cock and bull rumor, do you?" he asked. "I sure don't. Too farfetched, you ask me. I'd gloss right over it, if I were you. A freaking mastodon? Yeah, right. When Pigs fly."

Rod sincerely hoped Sal would buy his song and dance. He didn't.

"Oh, I don't know, I've heard stranger things, but those are tales for another day. Getting back to the story at hand, if he did actually do what the rumor purports him to have done, Fish would've had to remove the bones during the evening, when no one was here, no one but *you*, that is."

It may have been hot outside, but the atmosphere in the trailer had suddenly reverted to winter.

Sal sent him a hard stare, arching an eyebrow questioningly as he did.

This is getting weirder by the minute, Rod fretted. *As Pops would say—the man's in the right church, but the wrong pew.*

"So, for the sake of argument, let's just say that the rumor's true," Sal continued, his eyes never leaving Rod's face. "Which, as I said, would have to mean that the bones could only have been removed during the dark of night, while *you're* supposedly guarding the site."

He paused before going on, snuffing out the stogie and lighting up a fresh one, taking his time about it, the silence growing heavy.

You could cut it with a knife, a reference that Rod now wished hadn't occurred to him.

"Which could only mean that *you* were in on it with him...if the rumor proves valid, that is," he went on, shaking Rod's tree, looking to see what might fall out.

"Are you serious?"

"Dead Serious—I don't get any more serious."

Rod fought back a gulp.

"Do you know how ridiculous that sounds?" He asked, opting to play the role of a seriously offended man. "First off, I absolutely hate the guy and he absolutely detests me, so how could you believe that we'd ever do *anything* together, other than trade punches?" Rod blustered, gathering dramatic steam as he went on. "Secondly, this whole rumor thing has got to be a joke. Mastodon bones! Give me a break!"

Sal removed his metal-rimmed glasses, rubbing his nose.

"You'll be glad to know that your first thought also occurred to me—the two of you working a deal together? Not very likely, so I'll give you that. Still...where's there's smoke, there's usually a certain amount of fire."

"Meaning what?"

"Meaning that a rumor as seemingly preposterous as this one, doesn't just surface out of nowhere. There's probably something to it, maybe just a kernel of truth, but *something*."

Rod wondered where Sal was going with this, now that he seemed to have let off Rod off the hook. Yeah, he wondered, but odds were, he was better off not knowing.

"Maybe so, Sal, but that kernel doesn't have my name on it."

"Cross your heart and hope to die?" Sal asked with a brief smile which might have indicated humor, but you never would've convinced Rod of it.

"Cross my heart and hope to die," Rod lied solemnly.

"Well, consider yourself lucky then," Sal told him. "Because if I thought for a minute that you were in cahoots with him, I'd start a fire under you, feed it and stoke it until you felt as though you were parked in a furnace," he snarled, the threat rolling out of his mouth like a grenade, him reminding Rod of his good fortune, him deciding not to pull the pin.

Rod didn't offer a reply. He just sat there, a surprising calmness coming over him. He'd had enough. Confused and angry, the fear-induced adrenaline seesaw had taken a toll on him. *No more*, he decided then and there. *The hell with Sal and the hell with his threats!*

"All that aside, for the moment anyway, this job is almost finished and so I'll no longer require the services of a certain someone," Sal declared breezily.

"And that would be me?"

"And that would be you."

"Hey, at least the stealing stopped while I was here."

"Hmm...Maybe. But then again, maybe not. If there were indeed mastodon remains found on this site, they belonged to me!" he snapped. "Which would mean that someone stole them from me!"

Rod shrugged.

"Like I said, you're beating a dead horse, if you ask me...or dead mastodon," he added, the irony lost on Sal.

"Nobody asked you, but as long as we're laying our cards on the table, there's something you ought to know."

"What's that?" Rod asked, mildly curious.

"When I gave you this job, it was partly because I genuinely liked you."

"And what was the other part?"

Sal snickered, a smirk forming at his mouth.

"Your old man, the retired cop, that son-of-a-bitching father of yours. I knew he'd blow a gasket over your working for me."

Rod felt his neck turning red with heat, his hackles rising, his fists clenching.

"And that's why you hired me?" he asked, incredulous.

"Yep, that's why I hired you. Because I hate your old man."

"He gave me nothing but grief, all the time he was on the force, going out of his way to pin something on me, constantly feeding crap leads, bogus information, to the detectives!" Sal raged on. "A real pain in my backside for twenty years, he was. So, like I said—I hate his guts, period!"

Rod was ready to walk out. It was either that, or beat the living crap out of Sal, right then and there.

"You shouldn't told me all that. He's my father and your words offend me, to put it mildly."

Sal's smirk widened.

"I wouldn't have it any other way."

Funny how things can turn on a dime, Rod thought to himself. *Five minutes ago, I was scared to death of this guy, but now? Now I'm thinking—screw it, maybe I'll just punch him out, then drag his sorry-ass carcass outside and run him over with my car.*

Sal seemed to divine his thoughts.

"Tsk-tsk," he said, waving a naughty-naughty finger in Rod's direction. "You'd be fish food by midnight," he warned.

Rod stood and headed for the door.

"Wait—Don't you want your final paycheck?" Sal asked, flipping the envelope in Rod's direction. It fell short, landing on the filthy floor. Rod reached down and grabbed it, shoving it in his back pocket.

"Didn't you ever wonder why I paid you four times the going rate for a menial job like yours, that of a flunky, a two-bit security guard?"

"No, actually, I didn't," he lied, again making for the door, anxious to get out of there. "I don't wonder about it now, either, seeing as how I'm fresh out of give-a-damns."

"I offered you a paycheck that I knew you couldn't possibly turn down, just so as to aggravate your old man," he cackled, the sound of it grating on Rod's nerves. "I'll bet he lost a ton of sleep over it, and *that* makes me happier than you could ever imagine."

Rod strode out the door, banging it shut as hard as he could, the glass panel in the upper half of the door shattering into tiny pieces. Rarely, had slamming a door felt quite so satisfying.

Heading for Dee Dee's house, still fuming, he turned on the radio, hoping to hear a calming tune. Music spilled forth from the speakers. WTRY—The Bell Notes singing "I've had it." Not exactly what he had in mind, but it would do. *Fairly appropriate anyway*, he decided, relieved to be free of Sal.

CHAPTER 40

The following afternoon Butch invited Rod and Pops to go for a ride in the 55' DeSoto Firedome he'd purchased from Newell's just yesterday, a clear upgrade over the geriatric *Bondo-mobile* he'd been clanging around in. A red and white coupe, the DeSoto had 65,000 miles on it, not a bad buy for $580.00.

"Look, it's even got a Powerflite automatic Transmission. No more shifting!" he gushed proudly. Ain't she a beauty?"

"Absolutely," Rod readily agreed.

"You could've done worse," Pops chimed in from the back seat. "And you didn't spend much, which is even more important. Oh, and by the way, what'd they give for the *jalopy from hell* for a trade-in?"

"The finger."

"About what you've should expected, in other words," Pops wisecracked.

"Actually, they promised to take it out back and shoot it, before hauling it away to Sam Cohen's junkyard."

"Pretty generous of them, if you ask me."

"How much did you put down?" Rod inquired.

"I put down $100.00 and financed the rest, just like Pops told me to do."

Pops chuckled.

"I guess there's hope for you after all," he quipped.

"Wow! Was that a compliment that I just heard, the second one you've given me within a week?" Butch asked, impressed.

"I suppose it was," Pops grumbled, slipping back into his customary persona, that of a good-natured grouch. "But then, they say there's a first time for everything. Just don't hold your breath waiting for the next one, though. It could kill you."

Rod and Butch both laughed.

"You got a radio in this future clunker?" Pops asked.

"Of course," Butch replied, turning it on as he spoke. WPTR— David Seville and "The Chipmunk Song."

Pops clapped a hand to his forehead.

"What in the hell is that?"

"The Chipmunk Song," Rod explained, stifling a giggle as he did. "What, you don't approve?"

"I'd approve of you changing the station. Chipmunks! Sheesh! Rats with racing stripes down their backs!"

WROW—Jerry Wallace and "Primrose Lane."

"Better?" Butch asked.

"It'll do. But then, after that ungodly Chipmunk chatter, anything is an improvement," he groused. "Hey, why don't you head over to Watervliet? I got a hankering for a Ted's Fish Fry, or maybe one of Gallagher's. Sound good to you guys?"

"Great idea," Rod enthusiastically agreed. "Besides, I've got something to tell you, and I prefer doing it outside of Cohoes. Too many ears."

"Got some news to share with you, too,"

Their words went right over Butch's head. His mind was elsewhere. On fish fries, to be precise.

"Which one of them, do you think, makes the best fish fry, Pops?" he asked.

"Asking me that, is like asking me who I'd rather do the Mattress Mambo with—Mamie Van Doren or Sophia Loren? A tough choice, that's for sure," he mused, a salacious smile playing on his lips.

Rod shook his head in bemusement.

"That's one helluva leap in conversation—from fish fries to the Mattress Mambo."

They settled on Gallagher's, grabbing a picnic table, munching on the second-best fish fries in Watervliet.

"Mmm...Just what the doctor ordered," pops gushed, happy as a pig in mud. "Okay, what do you have to share with us, Rod? Come on, spit it out."

"You first," Rod mumbled, his mouth jammed full with fish.

"What is this? The old *I'll show you mine if you show me yours*?" Pops teased.

Rod looked around as he swallowed the food. Nobody within earshot, so he launched into his story, hoping it wouldn't give his pals a serious case of indigestion.

Neither of his friends interrupted him, not even once, both rendered near speechless upon hearing the news.

Once he'd completed his tale, he asked Pops for his opinion on what he'd just heard.

Before the old fella could offer it, Butch jumped in, asking, "I wonder what Sal did about Fish?"

"Assume the worst," Pops replied matter-of-factly.

He then took a deep breath, blowing it out loudly as he reached into his back pocket, producing a wrinkled envelope, flipping it in Rod's direction.

"Read that. The answers to all of your questions are in it, the whole kit and caboodle."

"Huh? What do you mean?"

Pops put his hand up, stopping rod dead in his tracks.

"Just read it."

Rod gingerly removed the somewhat crumpled pages from the envelope.

"Damn, will you look at *this*!" he exclaimed, his eyes poring over the first page, Butch standing over his shoulder now, peering down at the letter.

Dear Mr. Shea,

Considering that you live alone, thereby minimizing the possibility of someone other than yourself opening the envelope, I decided to send this to you, rather than to either of your friends, or should I say—accomplices?

Relax. I have no desire to cause you any trouble. If indeed you and your friends were able to sell the mastodon remains for profit, well, all the more power to you. No, worry not, for you can rest assured that your secret is safe with me. My lips are sealed.

Now then, enclosed is a copy of the letter that Lenny Fishowski sent to Mr. Abercrombie at the NYS Department of Antiquities. Clearly, the intent of the letter was to land you and your friends in some seriously hot water. As we all know, things didn't quite pan out that way, much to the chagrin of Mr. Fishowski. Having said that, I now imagine that all three of you, that handsome hunk, Mr. Hobbs, in particular, are warily looking over your shoulder daily, expecting Mr. Fishowski to put in an unwanted appearance at any moment. Well, allow me to allay your fears. The chances of that happening range from zero to none. How do I know this, you ask? I just do, that's all. I just do.

Now, having done one good deed for the day, I suddenly find myself wanting to perform yet another. I guess it's just your lucky day, gentlemen.

I'm certain that Mr. Hobbs can clearly recall his last conversation with his former employer, the discussion that revolved around said employer's reference to a particular rumor, one that concerned the discovery and subsequent removal of a mastodon skeleton from his construction site... along with Mr. Hobb's possible involvement in that removal?

Well, yet again, allow me to quell your fears. After carefully taking into consideration the mutual animosity, or more to the point...sheer hatred that existed between Mr. Fishowski and Mr. Hobbs, their former employer, albeit only reluctantly so, came to the conclusion that there was no conceivable way that these two arch enemies could, or would, ever join forces in any venture, no matter how enticing the potential for significant financial gain. Now, that doesn't mean that he's completely forgotten about the whole thing, but I can assure you that he's put it on the back burner, in a manner of speaking, and you can expect the flame under said burner to die out fairly soon. How do I know all this, you ask? Well, that's a reasonable enough question, one that warrants an equally reasonable reply, so here it is: As luck would have it, Mr. Hobb's former employer recently discovered the identity of the culprit behind the theft of his property, the valuable equipment that was systematically stolen from him over the course of the past year. Supremely satisfied now, the thief having been sufficiently brought to task for his sins, the owner of said property is still quite busy savoring those results, and not at all inclined to dwell on other, shall we say...questionable matters. Lucky you!

Needless to say, I fully expect you to now take a match to both of these letters, for obvious reasons. Don't disappoint me.

The three of them read the letter over and over again, the import of the words contained within it, just about flooring them.

"Whew," Rod sighed. "This is an awful lot to absorb all at once."

Pops grinned wide, quite a feat when you consider he had a lit Raleigh dangling from his lips.

"Let me have those."

Rod leaned across the table, handing Pops the letters.

Pops glanced around the general area. They were the only ones sitting outside at the moment.

He flicked the wheel of his Ronson lighter, the flame mere inches away from the edges of the letters.

"Whoa," Butch said. "Maybe we ought to hold on to them, just in case."

"Just in case of *what*?" Rod asked.

Butch shrugged.

"I don't know. Just in case we need them, that's all."

"Too late now, Butch," Pops told him, the pages curling up in flames, turning to ashes below his feet. "She said burn them, and so I did."

"*She?*" Butch asked, puzzled. "How do you know it was a woman that wrote them?"

"Easy. Her choice of words, how she phrased things, and last, but not least—she referred to Rod as *that handsome hunk, Mr. Hobbs*. When was the last time a guy referred to you as being a *handsome hunk*, Hot Rod?"

Rod looked away, his face reddening a wee bit.

"Exactly. That's why I know a dame wrote it. Just who she is, I couldn't begin to hazard a guess, but it was definitely a dame. I'm sure of it," Pops insisted, kicking at the ashes, watching them scatter.

"Well, I wonder why she did it. Write the letter, I mean," Rod said, clearly grateful that she did, yet curious as to her motive for doing so.

"My guess is that she's someone who had it in for Fish, not at all an unlikely scenario, given his rotten ways," Pops suggested reasonably.

"You said *had*, using the past tense. Are you thinking what I've been thinking?" Rod asked.

"Bull's eye!" Pops exclaimed. "He went from being a part-time thief to a full-time corpse. Sal threw him a going away party, and that, you can absolutely take to the bank. He's either floating face down in the river, lounging under some freshly poured concrete, or taking a permanent nap under the grass somewhere. Take your pick, but any way you cut it, you can bet your life that he's a goner. What a tragedy, eh?" he asked with a broad smile. "Couldn't have happened to a nicer guy, either."

"Yeah, I'm all broke up over it," Rod agreed, his smile even wider than Pops'. "Well, at least now we know who made off with Sal's equipment, and we also know who blew the whistle on us, feeding our names to Abercrombie. Obviously, at some point, Fish followed us to the barn and then, after we left, he picked the lock and went in, saw what was in there, and then fed us to Abercrombie, the state of New York, the cops, the whole shebang. No doubt he saw it as a perfect way to get even with me for the beating I gave him."

Pops nodded his agreement.

"Come on. Let's get out of here," he said as he stood up. "Time to head home. I need a nap, a horizontal pause."

"Yeah, right," Butch kidded. "You need a drink, more likely."

"Well, let's just say it crossed my mind," he cheerfully admitted. "Yeah, I definitely need me a post-fish fry shot of Four Roses. About ten of them, actually. I'm way too sober. Sobriety makes me sleepy."

Once on the road, the conversation wandered back to the identity of the mystery woman who typed the letter.

"For her to know that Sal had Fish down as the thief, that means she must be close to Sal, or at least close enough to pick up on what's what," Rod surmised with more than a little conviction. "The only woman that works for him is his sister, Angie, and the odds of her being the writer, are about the same as my becoming chief of Police in Cohoes," he went on. "Zilch. Furthermore, Angie couldn't write that eloquent of a letter, and even if she could, she'd never feel inclined to do so, not after the number I did on her two sons, Blimpo and Bluto."

"How about a wife?" Butch wondered aloud. "Sal's married, isn't he?"

"He was," Pops replied. "She bought the farm a year or so ago. Heart attack, or something like that. Considering whom her husband was, she was probably looking forward to it, just dying to croak," he quipped.

"Well, you might have something there, Pops," Rod remarked, laughing as he did. "But that only leads us back to that same question again—who wrote the letter, and also, *how* did she get her hands on the copy of the one Fish sent to Abercrombie?"

"Easy. Fish didn't write that letter to the state. She wrote it. She wrote both letters."

"How do you know that for sure?" Butch asked.

"Well, first off, the only thing he ever wrote was his name on the back of paychecks. Fish couldn't spell *Beer* if you spotted him the *B,* so forget it. Nope, it was her who wrote it. Same sort of phrasing, same style. That's why she had a copy of the letter to the state. She's the one who typed it up in the first place."

"Hmm, a girlfriend then?" Butch pondered aloud.

Pops guffawed.

"You ever see one of his typical girlfriends?"

"Yeah, you got a point there," Rod chipped in. "IQ's of a steamed clam."

"So I guess her identity will remain a mystery?" Butch mused.

Pops fired up a Raleigh, the smoke drifting out the window.

"For now, anyway. In time, we might be able to figure it out, pin her name down, but to be honest with you? Better to leave it alone. The woman did us a huge favor, laying the whole mastodon thing off on Fish, shedding light on stuff, filling in some major blanks for us, not to mention whatever part she played in helping to rid the world of Fish. So her name is a mystery to us. Big deal. Besides, take it from me—some mysteries are better left unsolved."

CHAPTER 41

Fish's no-nonsense landlady, Renee Jacques, put a call through to Fish's father, Gustav "Gus" Fishowski, warning him that he had exactly two days to come and empty out the flat. He either did it, or everything would go to the curb, she promised, no two ways about it.

"Why would I do that?" the man rasped, a three-pack-a-day voice.

"Because he hasn't been around in quite a while now, and the rent's a week overdue. Obviously, he took off somewhere and ain't planning on coming back, from the looks of things...unless of course, you know otherwise. I mean, he *is* your son, after all. So, you know what's going on with Lenny, or what?"

"Lenny," the man echoed, the name dripping from his mouth like sour milk. "Some son he is."

"So is that a *no?* You *don't* know when, or if, he's ever coming back here?" she asked impatiently.

"How the hell would I know? I haven't seen him in four years, the ungrateful crud!"

"Well, has he got any other family around, people I could call, ask if they know what's going on with him?" she asked reasonably.

She could hear him snicker.

"No, nobody. His mother died years ago...*lucky her*, and he was an only child, thank God."

"Well, I called his employer and they said he hasn't shown up for work in weeks, so I got to believe he's gone for good, not coming back to this place, anyway."

"*Lucky you, too*, in that case."

"Yeah, well, maybe so, but I need a yes or no on his junk, his crappy furniture and clothes. Are you going to come over here to get his stuff, or does it go to the curb for the garbage man?"

"That depends. Is the furniture really a bunch of crap?"

"Worse."

He hung up on her.

Mary Smith had never felt happier. Her training was over with, and Angie, her reluctant trainer, was finally put out to pasture, destined to spend her golden years watching *The Secret Storm, The Edge of Night,* playing church bingo, and regularly yelling at her three sons—dumb, dumber, and dumbest.

Mary had easily mastered her duties at the new job in record time, the occasional cat fight with Angie notwithstanding. Sal only had to intervene on Mary's behalf but once, the threatening look he gave his sister, intimidating enough to stop an enraged grizzly in mid-charge.

Now with the front office all to herself, Mary found the job to be a piece of cake, and the more she thought about the size of her paycheck, well, it wouldn't be long before she'd trade in her old Rambler on a new Rambler, something a bit more flamboyant this time, a red convertible perhaps.

Sal had been treating her like gold, even going so far as to take her to dinner at Smith's restaurant, not just once, but *twice* within the last week. On more than one occasion she'd also caught him staring at her in a rather peculiar way, a gleam in his eye, and a smile on his face.

CHAPTER 42

Summer was drawing to a close, Labor Day just around the corner, and Rod and Dee Dee were doing their best to enjoy these final days of August, even if it included Saturday night dinner at her parent's home.

When Delores, Dee Dee's mom, was in a good mood, she was all smiles. Trouble was, she wasn't in a good mood very often. Like tonight, for example, she had the look of someone permanently constipated.

Maybe it was because the big pink curlers in her hair were screwed on too tight...or perhaps it was simply because like any mother of an impending bride-to-be, she took a dim view of her future son-in-law's current employment status, that being one of a big fat zero.

The food wasn't bad, but then it was hard to screw up spaghetti and meatballs.

"So, tell us, Rod—do you have any leads on a job?" Delores inquired in a chilly tone. "A *good* job, that is."

"I think I got a pretty fair shot at landing a job with Cott's Soda Company as a deliveryman."

"Humph. Well, I know you're not wild about accepting unsolicited advice," she noted, a casually cynical understatement, if there ever was one. "But here's some anyway—do us all a favor and sign up for night school. Earn a diploma, and maybe then you'll be able to land a *real good* job."

Rod smiled smugly.

"I already did. I'll be starting night school right after Labor Day, three nights a week."

Delores' mouth opened and closed a couple of times, but no sound emerged.

"But thanks for making the suggestion, Mrs. LeBarron. It's nice to know that you're concerned about my future," he answered, somehow managing to avoid coating his reply with a layer of sarcasm.

"Yours *and* my daughter's," Benny LeBarron interjected, his tone not at all threatening. "After all, she is our pride and joy. I'm sure you understand, Rod."

"I hear you loud and clear, sir. And just like you, I want only the best for Dee Dee, and I'll do all that I can to provide it," Rod assured him, his words laced with conviction.

"Good. Now pass the meatballs, would you? *Rawhide*, my favorite show, is coming on in a few minutes and I don't want to miss a bit of it. Ever watch it?"

Rod shrugged.

"Once in a while."

"Well, mark my words—the kid that plays the Rowdy Yates character? One of these days that boy, *what's-his-face*, is going to be a big star, another Gary Cooper. Just you watch and see!"

"Clint Eastwood," Dee Dee chipped in, supplying the actor's name.

"Well, good for him, if indeed that happens," Delores remarked dryly. "I like nothing better than to see a young man make it big, speaking of which, once you've earned your diploma, Rod, just what sort of a *better* job will you be pursuing?" she probed, a smirk forming at the corner of her mouth.

He felt like telling her "*I'm going to peddle Girl Scout cookies door to door,*" but he didn't. No, he hit her with the truth instead.

"Cop."

"I beg your pardon?" she asked, scarcely able to believe her ears.

"A cop," he repeated, hoping that she wouldn't come back with something sarcastic, just to tick him off. "From the time I was a little kid, it's all I've ever wanted to be," he explained. "A cop, just like my father was, and just like my uncle still is."

"That is *not* a job that pays very much!" Delores snapped, her eyes now targeting Rod like a sniper setting her sight. "You disappoint me, young man. I would've expected you to aspire to be more than merely a policeman."

The fragile web of hope that Rod had spun had just been ripped apart, her words cutting him to the quick, making him feel about two feet high.

Dee Dee dropped her hand under the table and gave his hand a firm squeeze, a gesture intended to urge him to just let it go, and not blow his top.

Fortunately for everyone involved, he heeded her unspoken plea, electing instead to take the high road, ignoring Delores' digs and barbs.

"Well, everyone is entitled to their opinion," he countered, struggling to keep his tone level. "But if I were you, Mrs. LeBarron, I'd remember today as being the day when I promised you that in time, your son-in-law would become the chief of police for the city of Cohoes."

Delores just stared at him, her mouth agape, at a loss to think of a suitable comeback.

Rod smiled at her, the widest smile he could possibly muster. *Touché!*

A bit gusty though it was, Dee Dee insisted on Rod's putting the top down before they drove toward their destination, that being *Gizmo's Harmony House*, an establishment that rarely lived up to its name. A fun place to dance and party? Absolutely...but harmonious? Not so much. If they were lucky, Rod and Dee Dee would be long gone before the Saturday night fights kicked in...And they would. They always did.

Brawls aside, it was a great place to dance and tonight one of Rod's best friends, Chuck Diotte, lead singer of the *Magnatones*, an immensely talented local band, was providing the entertainment, and Rod had promised him that they'd show up.

Stunning in a pale blue dress, her slender neck, as usual, graced by pearls the color and shape of a full moon, Dee Dee reached for the radio dial, turning it on. WPTR—Frankie Avalon crooning "From Bobby Sox to Stockings."

Rod glanced over at her, his feelings for her, like bubbles in a pond, came bursting to the surface. She caught his eye and placed her hand upon his, squeezing it tightly.

"You look gorgeous," he told her, his voice husky.

She flashed him a blinding smile, like sunshine on a window pane.

"You trying to sweet talk me, Ace?"

"You betcha," he replied, adding, "Must be something in your mother's meatballs. They always bring out the Romeo in me."

"Well, that's good to know, seeing as how *I'm* the one who actually made them...with only a hint of garlic, I might add."

The breeze blew some of her hair across her face. Hooking a little finger under the long strands, she pulled the hair away from her beautiful hazel eyes.

"Well, it's working," she remarked.

"What's working?"

She gave him a playful tap on the shoulder.

"Your charm, big boy," she teased, a beguiling hint of mischief to her words. "Keep it up and you might just get lucky tonight."

And so, keep it up he did, laying it on with a trowel, as a matter of fact.

Upon entering the Harmony House, they were met with the sounds of the Magnatone's take on Phil Phillip's "Sea of Love," and it wasn't a bit shabby, either. Truth be told, Chuck Diotte's version was so good, it put the original to shame. Chuck could flat-out sing with the best of them.

And sing he did. For three hours Rod and Dee Dee danced their hearts out, everything from the twist to the jitterbug and of course, the waltz, their mutually favorite dance.

It was while dancing to "I'm Mister Blue," that Rod brought up the money.

"I'm not comfortable with keeping it stashed in the house, hidden though it is. If my parents ever stumble across it, what'll I tell them?" he groaned, clearly worried. "I just wish that I could stick at least some of it in a safe deposit box."

"Personally, I agree with Pops' take on the whole situation," Dee Dee said. "Like he told you, the cops didn't seem all that enthusiastic about pursuing the case. They probably just checked with all the local banks and once they came up empty, after performing the perfunctory tasks expected of them, giving it a minimum of due diligence, they just chucked the whole case."

Rod grinned.

"Listen to you, Miss Perry Mason—*Perfunctory* and *due diligence*. What'd you do, swallow a dictionary for dessert?"

Waltzing as they were, as close as close could be, it wasn't at all difficult for her to raise her knee and gently nudge the family jewels.

"Whoa! Easy, girl. I was just kidding around, you know."

"Yeah, I know," she said sweetly. "And lucky for you, that I was too."

He raised his hands in mock surrender.

"Getting back to the money," she went on. "We'll wait a few months and then *I'll* open a safe deposit box account in my name only. I won't put any of your cash in it, until a year or so has passed— just my birth certificate and stuff like that. Then, when I do get around to sticking some of your money in it, it'll only be, say, a thousand or so. After that, we'll add to it, a little at a time," she explained, proud of her plan. "So what do you think?"

"Not bad. Not bad at all, but for one thing."

"What's that?"

"You referred to the cash as being *my* money, when in fact, it's *our* money."

"Ooooohhh, Hot Rod, I'm so proud of you," she teased. "Already thinking like a husband should!"

A few minutes later, the Magnatones took a much needed break. Rod's pal, Chuck, came over to their table where they shot the breeze for a bit, catching up on things. After he left, heading for the bar, Rod and Dee Dee overheard a nearby couple quarreling, using words that'd make Lenny Bruce and his protégé, that young beatnik, George Carlin, blush in embarrassment.

So much for Harmony. They got up to look for another table, away from the verbal strife.

"That's marital dynamics for you," Dee Dee quipped as they sat down at a table on the other side of the room.

"How do you know they're married?"

"Easy. I watched her remove her wedding band prior to her bouncing it off his face."

"Well, let's hope we never get like that," Rod replied, shaking his head in wonderment.

She sent him one of her patented, high-voltage smiles, her warm, dazzling eyes the color of brown sugar. Helpless in the face of such beauty, he felt himself melting...From a man into a puddle of goo.

"I don't think that'll ever become an issue, Hot Rod, my boy," she assured him, her hand moving to his thigh, lingering there as she awaited his reply, "Don't you agree?"

Try arguing with that.

"Absolutely," he freely admitted.

Dee Dee winked at him.

"I thought you might," she purred, her alluring smile in full bloom.

The band started up again, singing the Fleetwoods' "Come softly to me."

They got up to dance.

"About the money," Rod began, as they waltzed across the floor. "No way I can chance using it to build us a house, at least not right away, anyway. Maybe in five years or so, but for now, we'll have to settle for a flat after we get married."

Dee Dee shrugged, indicating that it was no big deal.

"I don't care. Living in a flat is fine with me. I've lived in one all of my life. Don't care about ditching the honeymoon in Paris idea, either. Besides, I'm not crazy about airplanes."

"You're afraid of flying?"

Her bright smile dimmed considerably.

"Nope, flying is okay. It's crashing that worries me."

He laughed as he squeezed her tightly.

"The Poconos will do just fine, thank you," she assured him.

The song ended, the two of them heading back to their table when Dee Dee pulled up short.

"Ladies room time," she informed him, sashaying off, turning around slightly as she did, giving him one of those sultry, Jayne Mansfield over-the-shoulder smiles, the kind that can reduce a man to mush. And it did.

"At least the crazy dreams have stopped haunting me," he told her as they danced to Chuck Diotte's masterful rendition of Ricky Nelson's "Never be anyone else but you."

"Well, amen to that. Now you can devote your dream time to something more important—me," she teased.

"Sounds good to me. Real good!"

He'd never made a more truthful statement in his life.

"The only thing that still bugs me—" she started to say, but then faltered in midsentence.

"What?"

"Oh, nothing."

He gave her a "*Come on, will ya?*" look.

"Just spit it out, Dee Dee," he told her.

She took a deep breath, expelling it in a loud whoosh.

"It's just that despite the money and all, was it worth putting yourself and *me* through this emotional wringer? I mean, yeah, the money's great and all, but for God's Sakes, it could have cost you your life! And if Sal ever figures out the truth, it might still!" she ranted.

He tried to calm her down, allay her fears, but his words fell on deaf ears. She wasn't buying any of it.

Around and around they went, getting nowhere, resolving nothing, just getting more and more ticked off at each other.

Then, as luck would have it, and completely unbeknownst to them, the Magnatones saved the day, calming things down considerably when Chuck began to croon Tommy Edwards's big hit—"It's all in the game," Dee Dee's favorite song.

Even a heated argument couldn't win out over her urge to get up and dance. And it didn't.

"Oh, well," she said, as they glided across the floor, cheek to cheek. "Maybe one of these days you'll get it through your thick head that what I've been trying to—"

"Trying to what?" he asked, cutting her off.

She shook her head, giving up, defeated.

"Never mind. Just shut up and kiss me, fool."

The girl sure did know how to end an argument.

EPILOGUE

August 1st, 2004

Four weeks ago, this newspaper reported that while excavation for a new activities center was underway on the grounds of a Columbia Street nursing home, the former site of the Cohoes Hospital, one of the contractor's employees discovered the rotted remains of a 1958 Pontiac Bonneville. The car had been buried approximately twelve feet below ground and considering its highly deteriorated condition, it had been there for a very long time.

Upon raising the decaying hulk to the surface, dirt poured forth from the open doors, exposing what appeared to be human remains in the front seat.

The police, along with the Coroner, Joseph Mosseau, were promptly notified of the discovery and arrived at the scene within minutes. Upon close inspection, it was duly noted that indeed, the remains were in fact those of a human being, a man, more than likely, given the size of the bones and skull.

The severely corroded, yet still discernible serial numbers of the car were run through Motor Vehicle's data base where it was quickly established that the last registered owner of the car had been one Leonard J. Fishowski, his last known address, on Saratoga St. in Cohoes.

Today, at a news conference in city hall, the coroner shared the details of his findings, explaining that the remains are indeed those of a man, a large man between the age of twenty-seven and thirty years old. He then went on to say that based on the fact that a flattened 38 caliber bullet was found imbedded in the car's dashboard, a bullet that perfectly matched the hole in the back of the man's skull, it was safe to say that the individual in question was murdered, shot in the back of the head at point-blank range. He further went on to explain that given the car's age and the shape it's in, along with the condition of the skeleton contained within, it's a fair assumption to say that both were buried at the time the Cohoes Hospital was built, a frame of time that spanned mid-1959 through November of 1960.

Elaborating further, the coroner stated that despite the police department's best efforts to locate any living relatives of Mr. Fishowski, none, at least as of yet, have been found, rendering the possibility of DNA matching a moot point. Unless a blood relative could be located, they were at a dead end.

Stepping away, the coroner deferred any further questions to the about-to-be retired police chief, Rodney Hobbs, the strikingly handsome, silver haired veteran of forty-three years on the force.

Chief Hobbs echoed the coroner's concerns regarding the need to first locate, and then perform DNA testing on a blood relative of Mr. Fishowski. Without that, there was no way they could say for certain that the remains of the murdered individual were indeed those of Leonard J. Fishowski. The chief further remarked that the possibility of locating such a relative appeared to be very slim indeed. Having exhausted all of the conventional avenues open to them in regard to locating a blood relative of the man, the chief admitted that frustrating though it was, the true identity of the deceased may never be confirmed.

At this point the chief was asked whether or not a search for Mr. Fishowski's dental records might prove fruitful. He deferred the question to the coroner.

Mr. Mosseau replied that a search had already been conducted on a local level, as well as within the surrounding cities, the search yielding no results, whatsoever. Furthermore, a search of the military's dental data base proved fruitless as well. All he could say with certainty was that seven of the victim's front teeth were missing, and that it wouldn't be a stretch to say that their absence could be attributed to their having been violently knocked out, courtesy of a blunt instrument, or perhaps someone's fist.

Chief Hobbs was then asked if he had personally known Mr. Fishowski, a former employee of the Coccalido Construction Company where, prior to becoming a police officer, the chief himself had been employed, albeit but for only a ten week period.

The chief responded by saying, yes, he had indeed known Mr. Fishowski, but only to say hello to, explaining that while he himself worked the graveyard shift as an on-site security guard, Mr. Fishowski was a day worker, hence, they'd rarely crossed paths. Beyond that, he knew nothing further about the man and thus, couldn't shed any light on the man's life, such as it was.

When asked whether or not anyone from the Coccalido Construction Company, the company that had built the hospital, had been contacted and questioned about Mr. Fishowski, their former employee, the chief responded in the affirmative.

"Yes, early on in the investigation, detectives interviewed Salvatore Coccalido's widow, Mary Smith Coccalido, the current CEO of the company. During the interview, Mrs. Coccalido voluntarily accessed employee records, verifying that indeed, Mr. Fishowski had been employed as a foreman by her deceased husband's company for a period of three and a half years. She then went on to claim that the records indicated he was twenty-eight years old at the time he ceased showing up for work, this verification of his age, by the way, matching up well with the coroner's estimate of the victim's age."

"Asked whether or not she could recall her own, as well as her husband's reaction to Mr. Fishowski's abrupt no-show, she replied in the negative, pointing out that she had been hired as a secretary by Mr. Coccalido, her future husband, two days after Mr. Fishowski 's final appearance at the job site. Consequently, she'd never had the pleasure of meeting the man. As for her husband's reaction to Mr. Fishowski's no-show, she claimed to have absolutely no recollection of it whatsoever, not at all an unreasonable reply considering it happened forty-five years ago," Chief Hobbs concluded.

When asked to provide some final thoughts on the case, Chief Hobbs threw up his hands, as if to indicate he'd already said everything that could be said.

Maureen Geracitano, a local TV news reporter and a genuinely nice person, but by far the most tenacious of all the reporters present, refused to let him off the hook that easily, pressing him hard for a good, juicy sound-bite.

The chief blew out his breath in agitated surrender, rubbing his forehead, as if hoping to coax forth some sort of tidbit relative to the case, something that would satisfy her. He wanted to go home.

"All I can tell you is that my successor, Jim Young, will continue to pursue everything and anything that might lead to a satisfactory conclusion to this investigation, but keep in mind that for every murder case solved, there's three more that'll go unsolved."

His reply was met with a groan of disappointment.

"That's it?" Maureen asked.

The chief smiled.

"Yep, that's it. Now, if you don't mind, the news conference is over. Thank you all for coming."

"One last question, chief? *Please*?" Maureen pleaded.

The chief sighed.

"As long as it's not about the investigation...and as long as you turn off the camera."

"Nope, it's not about the investigation," she assured him while signaling the cameraman to shut it down.

The chief flashed her an indulgent smile.

"Okay, in that case, fire away, Maureen."

"As of tonight you're officially retired, chief. So tell me—where do you plan on spending your retirement years? Florida?"

Chief Hobbs smiled broadly as he reflected upon the question, recalling his good fortune, having spent the better part of his life with a woman who despite the years, was still drop-dead gorgeous, although it'd had never really been her physical beauty alone that defined her, but rather her sparkling personality and her innate goodness, that in his opinion, had made her different from everyone else he'd ever known.

"Uh...Chief?" Maureen prodded, snapping him out of his reverie, bringing him back to the present.

"*What?* Oh, I'm sorry, Maureen. What was your question again?"

"I asked you where you plan on spending your retirement years."

He gave her a quizzical look, as if she'd asked a question that, obviously, could only have but one answer.

"Why, right here in Cohoes, in the company of my lovely wife, of course. Where else would I spend them?"

As he drove toward home, Rod turned on the radio, tuning in to a "Golden Oldies" station. Eddie Cochran and "Summertime Blues," the song taking him back, the floodgates opening wide, a river of faces and memories gushing forth...most of them good, a few of them not so good. Pops Shea, Rod's parents, Uncle Harry, Rena Trimm, John and Virginia Daubney, Bonesy, Sal, and of course, Fish, all of them now long gone, unlike the mystery woman, the one he'd long ago identified as being Mrs. Mary Smith Coccalido.

Over the years, the cash he'd earned through the sale of good ol' Jumbo's remains had come in handy, particularly during the early years of his marriage, when a buck bought a helluva lot more than it did today.

Pulling into his driveway on Baker Avenue, Rod decided then and there to stow those memories away for good, slam the door shut on them, bury them as deep as Jumbo had been buried for eons.

Well, at least I'll try my damndest to do it, anyway, he thought to himself. *But then, as Pops was always fond of saying—"Once you boil it all down, a life lived ain't nothing more than a bunch of memories, some good, some bad. The good ones? You need to mull them over as often as possible, squeezing out all the juicy satisfaction and happiness that you can from them. As for the bad memories, no sense a'tall in regularly dragging them out, moaning and groaning over them, for what's done is done. They're like yesterday's beer—flat and sour. Only place for them is down the drain."*

Rod had chuckled aloud as he parted the curtains of time, fondly looking back upon the sage advice that the dearly departed Pops Shea had generously offered him some forty-five years ago, concluding that the old barroom philosopher knew exactly what he was talking about.

Just as he was about to turn off the motor, Tommy Edwards' "It's all in the game," began to play. He sat there, just listening... listening and smiling. Then, three minutes later, Rod Hobbs got out of his car and headed up the walkway, the one that led to Dee Dee. Life was good.